RULE

ELLEN GOODLETT

LITTLE, BROWN AND COMPANY
New York Boston

Little, Brown and Company
Hachette Book Group
1290 Avenue of the Americas, New York, NY 10104
Visit us at LBYR.com

Little, Brown and Company is a division of Hachette Book Group, Inc.
The Little, Brown name and logo are trademarks of Hachette Book Group, Inc.

The publisher is not responsible for websites (or their content)
that are not owned by the publisher.

First Edition: September 2018

alloy**entertainment**

Produced by Alloy Entertainment
1325 Avenue of the Americas
New York, NY 10019

Library of Congress Cataloging-in-Publication Data

Names: Goodlett, Ellen, author.
Title: Rule / Ellen Goodlett.
Description: First edition. | New York ; Boston : Little, Brown and Company, 2018.
| Summary: "The three secret daughters of the king of Kolonya must compete for
their father's throne, all while evading a blackmailer who threatens to reveal their
darkest secrets"— Provided by publisher.
Identifiers: LCCN 2017059758| ISBN 9780316515283 (hardcover) | ISBN
9780316515276 (ebook) | ISBN 9780316563628 (library edition ebook)
Subjects: | CYAC: Inheritance and succession—Fiction. | Sisters—Fiction. | Kings,
queens, rulers—Fiction. | Secrets—Fiction. | Extortion—Fiction. | Fantasy.
Classification: LCC PZ7.1.G6538 Rul 2018 | DDC [Fic]—dc23
LC record available at https://lccn.loc.gov/2017059758

ISBNs: 978-0-316-51528-3 (hardcover), 978-0-316-51527-6 (ebook)

Printed in the United States of America

LSC-H

10 9 8 7 6 5 4 3 2 1

✻

To Meraki, my band of Travelers, who are always willing to offer a piggyback ride, liven up an airport lounge, or jump off a bridge with me

✻

❊ 1 ❊

Zofi

Zofi woke to the sound of her mother's voice, louder than usual. She squinted at the tent interior. She'd been sharing it with her mother for the last two months, unable to sleep on her own. She saw blood every time she shut her eyes.

"Can you tell me *why* you're looking for her?" Mother said.

Something rustled. Parchment? "All this says is we're to bring Deena's only daughter back with us to the capital," a man replied. He had an accent. Something almost…*Kolonyan*. "You're Deena. Can you tell us where she is?"

Zofi bolted upright, shredding any last cobwebs of sleep. *Sands.* That had to be a Talon.

Mother ignored the question. "This is highly unusual," she said, just outside the tent.

"It's the king's request." His voice grew quieter. Mother was leading him away. Buying time.

Zofi shouldered her rucksack, an escape bag Mother had packed two months ago. The night Zofi brought this death sentence down on her head. *Stall them*, Zofi prayed as she drew her longknife and cut a slit in the rear of the tent. The Talons would be watching the front.

Outside, the frigid night air of the Glass Desert stung her lungs. She breathed in deep anyway to clear her head. If she could make it over the dunes, she could hole up in the crags, scavenge lizards for food, and gouge cacti for water. The desert would keep her safe for a few days, so long as she could reach it.

For that, she needed speed.

Zofi pressed the longknife to her forearm. The moment the blade broke skin, Zofi's eyes closed, her senses turning inward. Every vein in her body lit up like a map in her mind's eye. She watched her heart contract to drive blood through those veins, carrying air and nutrients throughout her body.

Air, nutrients, and something else. An extra spark, drawn into her body via the cut she just made in her arm.

The Blood Arts.

Describing the Arts to someone who had never tithed was as impossible as explaining an extra sense. The Arts tasted green, smelled like adrenaline, sounded cold. They first appeared in the Reaches four centuries ago, and no one outside this continent could tap into them. But for natives of the Reaches like Zofi—and, unfortunately, the Talons hunting her—the Arts made superhuman feats possible.

Tonight Zofi harnessed that cold green adrenaline like threading a mental needle. It took concentration, willpower—some people whispered incantations as they did it, but that wasn't necessary, just a trick to assist your brain. All you really needed to know to tithe was the anatomy of your body and the lengths to which you could push it. What your blood, your heart, your lungs, and your veins looked like when you strained them to the max.

Zofi had done this often enough not to need any words. She held all the potential of the Arts in her mind and channeled it into one purpose, one command. Watched her blood vessels expand the way they had so many times before, absorbing more air, flooding more power to her limbs.

She opened her eyes. The world looked different. Sand hovered around her ankles. Mother's and the Talon's voices, still audible on the far side of the tent, sounded impossibly slow, as though they spoke through mouthfuls of molasses. A fly hung suspended at her elbow, wings moving a fraction of their normal speed.

Of course, it only looked that way to Zofi. Because in reality, the world hadn't slowed.

She'd gotten faster.

Zofi sprinted toward the dunes, feet barely grazing the sand. In seconds, she crossed a hundred yards of desert to reach the base of the first dune. She leaped onto it, hands and feet darting from one handhold to another while the sand melted away beneath her. Halfway up, she checked over her shoulder for signs of pursuit.

Three moons illuminated the landscape. Nox and Essex, the first two moons, hung overhead. Syx dangled at the horizon like a globe fruit. Glacie, the little oasis town they'd camped outside of, loomed in the background—a perfect circle of palm trees and thatch-roofed buildings. And in front of the town was the Travelers' camp—several dozen tents around twin bonfires. A few members of her band still huddled beside the glowing coals, even though dinner ended hours ago. Up late swapping stories, a favorite Traveler pastime.

For a moment, Zofi's heart ached. She grew up in this band, moving every few weeks, drifting around the outer Reaches. Her band was her family—more than family, they were *home*. The only home she'd ever known. She didn't want to leave.

Yet if she stayed, she risked bringing the Talons' wrath down on everyone, not just herself.

Focus.

She scanned the camp. Two Traveler watchmen pretended to doze alongside the road. Another was positioned to watch the oasis itself—because even here, in a town that told Mother they didn't mind Travelers, they still needed to be careful. It took only one superstitious idiot raving about how Travelers ate babies to turn a whole village hateful.

They'd learned that the hard way.

Next to the roadside watchmen, the Talons' wagon was parked. Two draft horses were yoked to the wagon, with three more grazing around its wheels. But only one Talon sprawled on top of it, smoking. Where were the others?

Her veins itched. She only had a minute or two before this tithe wore off. *Mother will handle the Talons.* Zofi's job now was to get as far from camp as possible. She spun around to continue climbing.

How did they find her?

More important, if they'd come for her, what happened to

Elex? He'd never give her up. Not willingly. They'd have to torture a confession from him.

Stop thinking. Emotions would slow her down.

Ten feet to the peak of the dune. Her fingertips tingled—the tithe was fading. The Arts could make a person stronger, faster, immune to harm, but only for a time. Once a tithe wore off, your blood needed time to rebuild before you could tithe again.

Unless you knew the Travelers' secret.

Zofi's fingertips grazed her rucksack. Five glass phials—*boosts* as she called them—were tucked inside. If necessary, she could keep this sprint going. Though she'd rather not if she could help it. Sands knew she might need those boosts later.

As she hauled herself onto the peak of the dune, the last of the tithe trickled out of her veins. Her muscles slowed back to normal speed. It left her limbs shaky, her body sore.

That's when a rope snagged her waist.

"You Travelers," a man said. "So predictable."

Zofi flung her arms wide to stop the rope from cinching tighter. The attacker tugged, and she skidded toward him across the dune's peak. He'd been crouched on the far side, waiting. She had sprinted right into the trap.

Stupid. She should've stayed on flat ground, run away from the road.

No time for regrets. She raised her arms and threw off the rope. The Talon stepped toward her, and she swung at his face.

He blocked the hit with his forearm, her hand crunching painfully against his bone. "Whoa, calm down." He lifted his palms in surrender.

Zofi punched him in the nose.

He clapped a hand to his face. "Bloody drifters—" He broke off as she kicked his knee. Only then did he shove her backward. She stumbled, teetered on the edge of the mountain of sand.

Then she eyed the drop, thoughtful. It wasn't *that* steep. If she caught the sand at a roll, it'd be no more painful than skidding down a snowy slope in the Dawn Mountains.

"I'm trying to help," he said.

Zofi jumped off the dune.

With a frustrated yell, the Talon dove after. They rolled in a blur of leather and limbs. Sand filled Zofi's mouth, her eyes, her ears.

At the bottom, the Talon landed hard on top of her, driving the air from her lungs. She reached for her boosts. *Sands.* The rucksack was gone. She glanced back and spotted it halfway up the dune.

"*Listen.*" The Talon climbed to his feet, palms extended. "King Andros sent me." In the triple moonlight, he looked Kolonyan through and through, from his rich brown skin to his broad, regal nose.

He also looked young. For a split second, she felt a pang of something like guilt. Could she do this again?

She must. He was in the way.

He smiled, mistaking her hesitance for surrender. "I don't bite."

Zofi drew her longknife and leaped to her feet in one fluid motion. "I do."

Then a pinprick bit into her chest, no more painful than a bug bite. An instant too late, she spotted a second, older Talon a few yards away, a blow tube to his lips.

Poison. She grasped at the dart.

Next, nothing.

❋

Zofi was on a ship. Zofi *was* a ship. She rolled with the waves, sailed through an empty black sky devoid of stars.

Sometimes the sky spoke. It sounded like Elex. Elex, who'd finally kissed her, his lips soft and perfect and everything she'd ever wanted. Right before he took the fall for her sins. She reached for him but the ocean tore them apart. The world swam. She was drowning, vomiting seawater, the sky black then twilight then black again.

Finally, after what felt like years, one particularly hard wave threw her body against solid wood. Then she heard the rattle of wheels, the trot of hooves, and it all came flooding back, too much too fast: the desert, the Talons, the chase across the dunes.

The poisoned dart.

She wasn't in a ship at all. She was in a carriage.

Zofi sat up so fast her forehead struck an armrest. She groaned and doubled over.

"Aim for this." Someone nudged a metal bucket under her chin.

A surge of nausea rocked through her. Zofi heaved, but her stomach felt wrung dry. Nothing came up.

"Motion sickness. At least you slept through the worst of it."

She cracked one eyelid, then recoiled. Sitting across from her was the Talon from the dunes. She grabbed her belt. Alas, her longknife was gone, the scabbard empty.

He sighed. "You were out for three days. I'm sorry. My superior only used the phantasm venom because he thought you were about to stab me."

I was, she thought. Aloud, she said, "Phantasm venom?" Her voice came out scratchy and thin. She licked her cracked lips. "How am I alive?"

The Talon's mouth quirked. "It's only lethal in large doses. The darts we carry merely render our opponents unconscious. No lasting damage, though again, I'm sorry we had to resort to it."

None of this made sense—a shot that wasn't meant to kill, a Talon apologizing to a Traveler. "Where are you taking me?"

"We're almost there." He drew aside the window curtain. Zofi's eyes widened, and she leaned forward to press her nose against the glass pane.

A child of the deserts and the ocean, Zofi had never seen a jungle.

Trees with trunks as fat as the carriage towered overhead. Vines twined through the branches, interspersed with flashes of color—fruit or birds, she couldn't tell. Thanks to the thick canopy, it was dark as twilight on the forest floor. Humans, birds, and monkeys all chattered so loudly that Zofi wondered how she'd ever slept at all.

This must be the merchants' road—the main artery of the Reaches. It ran from the Northern deserts down through the Ageless Jungle. Farmers trundled past, pulling handcarts laden with fruit and abraca beans. Passersby wore kaleidoscopes of color—red and pink tunics, green and blue pants. Even the occasional passing Northerners wearing full-body robes were sporting bright fabric rather than the traditional black dress you'd see in the oasis towns.

Most people looked like the Talon next to her. Tall, lean, muscular, with oval faces and smooth brown hair either drawn back in buns or cut sharp at their chins, making their high cheekbones stand out even more. Their skin was deep brown, almost the same shade as hers. Otherwise they looked nothing alike. Nobody here had her black tumbleweed hair, her narrow face or small features. And she was about a foot shorter than everyone.

She stood out.

A passing merchant caught her eye through the window and held up his fingers in a warding sign, teeth bared, as though she were a demon. Zofi bared her teeth right back and felt a tiny surge of pleasure when he jumped away, startled.

There was no doubt where they were headed. The Ageless Jungle sprawled across the Reaches, beginning at the Dawn Mountains in the east and petering out in the Western swamps. Right at its heart, where the jungle grew densest, stood Kolonya City, capital of Kolonya, the Central Reach.

The only Reach that mattered anymore.

Her stomach rolled again, not from motion sickness this time. "If I'm under arrest, you have to tell me why. That's the law."

The Talon actually laughed. Bastard. Then he rapped on the ceiling. "You aren't under arrest, Zofi. You needn't worry about some petty theft accusation."

Zofi frowned. *Petty theft?*

Mother. She must have invented a story to explain why Zofi had run from the Talons. If they didn't know about her actual crime, they would have wanted to know why she was acting so guilty.

But if the Talons didn't know what she'd really done, then why had she been summoned?

"Is she safe?" Zofi finally replied, after a careful hesitation. "My mother."

"Deena is fine. She said to remember her counseling, whatever that means."

Zofi knew. It had been all they'd talked about for the last two months. What to do if the consequences of her actions ever caught up with her. *Play their game.*

The carriage jolted to a halt and the door burst open, startling her. The older Talon, the one who'd poisoned her, rode outside, two stallions in tow.

"Now that you're awake, we can ride," said the young Talon. "I thought you might prefer that."

The older one offered a hand. Zofi ignored him and climbed into the larger stallion's saddle. Outside, the jungle noise doubled.

Even from horseback, she was drawing stares—some curious, others outright hostile. She lifted her chin, ignored the passing mutters of "drifter" and "curseworker." Zofi had heard every insult out there by now. They rolled off her skin like raindrops.

"Bat wings!" cried a shopkeep. Dried pieces of meat, half of which she'd never seen before, dangled from the eaves of his vine-woven store roof.

Zofi grimaced. "Do people really eat those?"

The younger Talon laughed. "You'd be surprised. Bat wing is pretty tasty."

Zofi was still contemplating how desperate someone had to have been to eat the first bat when they rounded a bend in the road.

Ahead, the jungle fell away. Suddenly, Zofi forgot about the Talons, why the king wanted her. She forgot about everything because, *sands alive*. All the ballads and poems in the world did not prepare her for this view.

In the center of a vast clearing stood Kolonya City. One thousand ancient trees, grown trunk to trunk, fused into a solid brown living wall around it. At its foot lapped the River Leath. Ten stories above, the trees' dark canopy masked the strongwall behind them, the city's true defense. Soldiers patrolled the strongwall in leather armor. Beyond the wall, the ten towers of Ilian Keep pierced the sky. Each one was carved from different colored stonewood, from beech-white to deep ebony. The colors glowed in the sun, resplendent.

Zofi had spent her whole life moving around. By now, she'd seen every other city in the Reaches. None compared.

Thousands of people flowed in and out of the city gate—more people than drops of water in the river, it seemed. It was the kind of place that could swallow a person whole. Yet despite the danger those walls held, Zofi could not help admitting: It was beautiful.

"First time?" the young Talon asked. "The view always surprises new visitors."

Zofi scowled. She hated letting him see anything, even inadvertently. Instead of replying, she spurred her horse.

He kept pace as the road wound through fields of wheatgrass, chatting away the whole while. "You know, after the Reaches won their independence from Genal four hundred years ago, King Ilian himself seeded this wall. The trees have stood all these centuries, proof our city hasn't been assailed since. 'A crown for our body's beating heart.'"

Zofi cast him a sideways glance. She'd read *The History*, for sands' sake. Mother made sure of that—educated her the same way any Kolonyan girl would have been. *So you know exactly what the world thinks about people like us.*

"Personally, I find it telling that King Ilian dubbed Kolonya 'the heart of the Reaches' just before he set about conquering the other four," she replied.

The young Talon blinked in surprise. "We didn't *conquer* the other Reaches. The kings and queens of the four outer Reaches elected King Ilian of Kolonya to serve—"

"After the Second War, as a provisional ruler should the need to fight Genal arise again," Zofi interrupted. "As you just said, it's been four hundred years since Ilian's reign. How provisional does that sound?"

"You're forgetting the part where we *have* spent all those years fighting Genal."

Zofi shrugged one shoulder. "On and off. Often with decades of peace between. Besides, Kolonya City and her unassailed walls aren't exactly the ones suffering." Zofi had seen the wreck the Seventh War made of the Eastern Reach just last year.

"The outer Reaches are our body, our front line of defense," the Talon replied.

Zofi scoffed. "Ever ask those body parts how they feel about being disposable limbs?"

"I don't know why you despise Kolonya—"

"I might be angry because the king sent anonymous minions to kidnap me, drug me, and drag me against my will to this sands-blasted city," she snapped. Then she winced. *Play their game,* Mother had warned. Arguing with a Talon was hardly playing smart.

"Vidal," he said.

Zofi frowned. "What?"

"My name is Vidal. Now I'm no longer an anonymous minion." He tried for a smile, which only deepened her frown. It was more irritating when he acted nice. "We didn't mean to drug you. You've got the wrong idea—the king intended to invite you here, not drag you."

"Whatever he intended, I *was* dragged. And you've yet to explain why."

"Ask them." Vidal nodded ahead.

Zofi realized with a start that they'd reached the city gate. The bridge under the portcullis was crammed with farmers, merchants, and visitors. But in the center, parting the crowd like a dagger, was another carriage, bright gold. The stormwing crest of King Andros glittered on its doors.

The carriage halted before them. An impeccably dressed serving lady opened the door from within. "Lady Zofi. I've come to escort you to Ilian Keep."

Lady?

That one word gave her more pause than anything else she'd yet heard.

·⊰ 2 ⊱·

Akeylah

Akeylah's knees throbbed as she leaned into the horsehair brush, but press as she might, the stain refused to budge from the slate tile. How in Mother Ocean's name did her siblings create such a mess in only one meal? She wondered if she'd need to resort to another dousing of lye, when stumbling footsteps broke her concentration. On instinct she froze, breath held. She recognized that gait.

Father.

Perhaps he was already deep enough in the bottle to pass by without noticing her. Akeylah shut her eyes. She wished she could be like the sea. Water, flooding away between the cracks, unnoticed and unremarkable.

No such luck.

"What's all this?" Father swayed in place above her.

"I've almost finished—"

"*Almost finished*," he sneered in a high-pitched tone. "Did I bloody ask what this *almost* is?" He kicked her bucket and sent dirty mop water splashing across the dining room. "It's midday, girl. I have guests coming shortly. Do you expect us to watch you crawl about the floor the whole meal? Or was that your plan, to sour our appetites with the sight of your face?"

Akeylah ducked her head. She knew better than to provoke him. Her left wrist throbbed with the memory of the last time she defended herself. The bone never set right, and now it served as a constant reminder of the depths to which her father was capable of sinking. "I apologize, Father. It is my mistake."

"Damn right it is." He stumbled, then leaned against the table to uncork a bottle with his teeth. "Incompetent. A waste of your mother's sacrifice."

Akeylah gritted her teeth and scrubbed harder. She was used to the insults. *Worthless. You're the one who should have died.* Who knew? He was probably right. Akeylah had never met her mother, who died giving birth to her, but by all accounts she was the perfect wife. The perfect mother. Perfect in a way Akeylah would never be.

You look just like her, her older sister, Polla, would murmur at night as they huddled on opposite ends of the bedroom they were forced to share. *It's not fair that you're here and she isn't.*

The town mender talked her mother through every known healing tithe. In the end, the tithes probably wore her out faster, the Arts burning through her blood along with the strain of childbirth. Now here Akeylah was following in her mother's footsteps— using the Arts in a desperate attempt to save herself—and seas only knew whether it would work.

Crash.

She flinched as the empty bottle shattered, coating her skirt in glass.

"Did you hear me?" Father leaned down, and Akeylah forced herself to meet his gaze, trembling. "I said you're a waste."

What's taking so long? There should be an effect by now, some noticeable change. But he looked as hale as ever, aside from the telltale ruddy alcohol bloom across his olive-brown cheeks.

"I heard you, Father," she whispered.

Perhaps she'd done it wrong. Or perhaps she'd been taken for a shell-headed fool.

She'd spent months searching. Attending every market and trade fair in town, even obscure ones like the Ananses Festival, a traditional celebration from the Southern Reach where women dressed like great cats sold bundles of ripening herbs to help in childbirth.

Finally, she stumbled across a hint. A rumor that led her to an even stranger fair, one that only opened once every three months, on the full triple moons, down a fishmonger's alley. From there, a whisper led her to a black-draped stall run by a surprisingly pretty curseworker. A curseworker with a scar that split her cheek, all the way from her dark eyes to her narrow lips.

Finally, Akeylah thought she'd paid her penance. She'd suffered enough. Mother Ocean had sent her a savior.

The curseworker could've been anyone. A poor drifter or a madwoman. There was no guarantee anything she taught Akeylah was real. But when that woman cupped Akeylah's cheek in her calloused hand and murmured, "He will kill you within the fortnight unless you act," Akeylah believed it.

Maybe the curseworker was wrong. Maybe the tithe didn't take. Maybe all this would be for naught.

"You killed your mother." Father's spittle flecked her cheeks. "And for what? So we could be stuck with a lazy, empty-headed idiot girl, looking like her, reminding us..." His voice cracked.

"I'm sorry," she said. Again. But it never mattered what she said. It only mattered what he heard, and that was entirely up to him.

"You aren't. You enjoy this. You thrive off our pain." He grasped her neck with meaty fingers. Squeezed. Stars glittered at the edges of her vision. Her tongue felt swollen in her mouth, and her eyes widened as if they would burst. "I'd be doing the world a favor. No one would miss you."

She was going to die. The same way she'd lived. Alone in a family of vultures on a cliff at the edge of the world. She shut her eyes. Blood roared in her ears, reminding her of the sea. Waves on the beach.

Mother Ocean, accept my spirit, she prayed. *Bear me from this world...*

She couldn't remember the rest. Her head hurt. Everything hurt.

And then, air.

Akeylah collapsed to her knees, gasping as her lungs swelled with fresh breath. Blood rushed to her brain. The world tilted and swam. Her throat pulsed and her knees stung. But she was alive. She was breathing again.

Words. Voices.

"—sure?"

"Quite sure, Father." She recognized her oldest brother Siraaj's voice. Not that it brought her any comfort. Siraaj hated her almost as much as Father did. So did Koren and Polla. He'd rallied them all against her. She was the youngest, the unwanted one. The child conceived accidentally, too late in life for her mother to survive the birth.

None of them would be upset if he killed me, Akeylah thought. *They'd only complain that they had to take on my chores.*

"In the parlor?" Father asked. Then his footsteps faded down the hallway.

Akeylah remained on all fours. Her breath rasped. She'd sound like a frog tomorrow, trying to speak. Assuming she lived to see the morrow at all.

"What did you do this time?" Siraaj toed the shattered bottle. "You know better than to sass him when he's had a few. Especially at a time like this."

Trade was still slow, had been ever since the Seventh War ended a year ago. What few ships the Eastern Reach possessed had been hard-pressed to find enough sailors to bring in the amount of fish the Reach needed to export to Kolonya, to trade for all its other survival needs.

Akeylah studied the broken glass, the way the light reflected off the cut pieces. She'd thought perhaps the war would teach Siraaj a little sympathy. That on the battlefront he'd learn sometimes, when someone beat you, you weren't to blame. Sometimes the person beating you was at fault.

But if anything, war only seemed to make her brothers harder. Siraaj and Koren went away brutes and came back gods. They joked about the other soldiers in their battalion who had died. "Weaklings," Siraaj called them.

Only Akeylah seemed to notice the twitch in his eyelid when

he said such things. The fear behind his boasts. It was a nice lie. *The dead deserved to die.* If you believed that, you could believe you'd never be the one on the wrong end of the knife.

When she didn't respond, Siraaj stormed out of the room, too. Akeylah waited until he was gone. Only then did she lift her skirts and trace the edges of the scar.

Akeylah had a lot of scars. Cuts and bruises as well as deeper ones, internal ones. But none of her scars were quite like the one that trailed up her outer thigh, long as her hand and as thick as her finger.

This scar glowed.

It pulsed bright blue, like a vein come to life. Right now, it was Akeylah's only consolation. Proof that she'd finally carved a way out of this mess. Even if her father killed her, he could not escape this.

Do your worst, Father. I've already done mine.

A commotion in the hallway tore her back to the present. She dropped her skirts, hurriedly concealing the wound.

Everyone in her family used the Arts: Father tithed for memory in business meetings to recall every conversation. Polla tithed for strength to carry her shopping home from the markets, and Siraaj and Koren knew all the military tithes.

But those were the Blood Arts, the Arts gifted by the gods to the people of the Reaches for a reason. The Blood Arts saved the Reaches, made its people strong enough to free themselves from Genal. The Blood Arts made you better, faster, more able to protect the one thing the Reaches valued above all: family.

But this kind of tithe, the kind that left scars? That was worse than forbidden. It was an abomination, a curse. The scar was the mark of the Vulgar Arts. Unlike the Blood Arts, the Vulgar Arts let you tithe into *other* people's blood instead of your own. Only those who shared your bloodline—relatives within a few generations. With the Vulgar Arts, Akeylah was able to tithe into her father's bloodstream and plant a curse that would eventually kill him.

Use of the Vulgar Arts was worse than any physical crime. Worse than theft or espionage or murder. It was a perversion of the gods' gift. Even back in Queen Idrylla's day, when a group of Genalese spies infiltrated court and tortured Idrylla's daughter into cursing her mother, there had been no forgiveness for either the spies or the daughter. No matter what drove you to them, the punishment for using the Vulgar Arts was death.

"Akeylah." Polla leaned in the doorway. "Father wants you in the parlor." Polla glanced at Akeylah's skirts, and for a moment, Akeylah's heart faltered.

Did Polla see the scar? Does she know?

Her sister only clicked her tongue and shook her head. "You look a mess," she added before she swept out of the room.

Akeylah rose, unsteady. Her throat still ached from the attack, and her knees throbbed where she'd fallen. But when Father called, she answered. She'd learned that much by now.

In the hall, she heard voices. Unfamiliar men, probably traders. Father was the magistrate hereabouts, and their house was a thoroughfare of merchants and trappers, fishmongers and masons. Lately that meant a steady stream of gossip flowing through the house—first about the Eastern rebellion's sabotage (or "defense," as some who resented Kolonya called it) in Burnt Bay. Then more recently about the Silver Prince, murdered by a Traveler assassin nearly on their very doorstep. Speculation abounded—was the assassin paid by the rebels? Or hired by Genal?

Lately, all those rumors meant for Akeylah was more guests passing through Father's house—guests she served while they leered at her, more oft than not. Guests made up of rebel sympathizers and Talons alike, the latter usually on the hunt for the former. She'd heard stories about what happened to anyone caught aiding or supporting the rebels. How sometimes the Talons who captured them couldn't be bothered transporting them back to Kolonya City for a fair trial. How it was easier if an "accident" befell their captives on the road home.

Hearing that, Akeylah couldn't entirely blame the rebels for their actions.

No, she did not condone the attacks like Burnt Bay, where the rebellion sank Kolonyan ships, their own allies. And she didn't believe in assassinating your own leaders, even if those leaders, like the Silver Prince, were rumored to be behind many of the recent, more brutal methods of dealing with rebels.

But she understood the rage. Understood the tattoos she'd seen some merchants flash recently—the sailfish symbol of Tarik. The country this land used to be, before the Second War with Genal. Before Tarik bowed to Kolonya and became known only as the Eastern Reach.

So when Akeylah pushed open the parlor door and found herself facing two Talons of the king in formal uniform, beaked stormwing insignias pinned on their chests, all she could think was, *Those poor rebels.* The Talons must be here to hunt them down.

Her heart hurt just to think of it. She could not stomach more battles, especially not Reach against Reach.

Akeylah sank into a curtsy. "What may I serve your guests, Father?"

Father didn't answer. The silver-haired Talon leaned forward, elbows on his knees. "We have not come for your father. We've come for you, Akeylah dam-Senzin."

All at once, her fears shifted. Intensified. The Talon's smile was friendly, but Akeylah knew better than to gauge a man by that. Her stomach sank like an anchor. Unconsciously, her fingertips twitched toward the scar on her leg.

"I'm sorry?"

"You'll be surprised to see us, I'm sure," the other Talon interrupted. "We apologize for the abrupt arrival. We would have written ahead, but there was no time."

"We are here on the king's business," the silver-haired one added. "He invites you to the turn-of-the-month celebration."

Her eyes widened, then shot from the Talons to her father. Judging by his ashen countenance, he was as confused as her.

Silence stretched thin, until she realized the men were awaiting her reply. Akeylah was not accustomed to being asked questions, much less given a chance to respond.

What choice did she have? When King Andros extended an invitation, you accepted it. Though she couldn't fathom why he would ask her of all people to attend an event. Her family came from noble stock, insofar as Easterners followed that sort of thing. But if the king simply intended to welcome their family at court, the invitation should have come to all her siblings at once, or just Siraaj as the oldest child.

Could this be a ploy? A way to lure Akeylah to Kolonya City

so the king could find evidence of her treason? The proof itched on her thigh. All it would take was one person to glimpse it, while she was undressing or bathing, and King Andros would have all the proof of her sins that he needed.

Didn't matter. If it got her away from here, even a death punishment would be a welcome respite. The king would have more mercy in his execution than her father.

"I would be honored to attend to my king. Thank you, sirs."

"Glad to hear it," Silver-Hair replied. "Since we'll need to leave within the hour." His gaze dropped to her clothing, and her face flushed.

Akeylah knew she was not an attractive Easterner. Her hair was muddy auburn, hanging in weak waves that were difficult to plait. Her eyes were overlarge and an unusual yellow-green, not blue like her siblings'. The color made her skin—a few shades darker than her family's, yet still not as dark as these Talons'—look wan.

But the ratty cleaning clothes she wore now, a torn skirt and wrinkled shirt, only made her appearance that much worse.

To his credit, the Talon merely smiled. "Please dress for court, my lady."

Lady.

In Kolonyan terms, that was technically true, but no one had ever addressed her that way before. Not even the other Talons and soldiers passing through. It had only ever been "girl" or "wench," or sometimes, when they were deep enough in their cups to get saucy, "sweet sea-maiden."

Akeylah curtsied again. "I will prepare my luggage at once."

She was most likely dressing for her own funeral. Nothing

good could come of this. Still, when she opened the door to leave and found all three of her siblings elbowing for the spot closest to the keyhole, she could not help but feel a surge of amusement.

"Are those Talons?" her brother Koren whispered.

"I wonder if they're hunting rebels." Siraaj mocked punching a rebel in the face, and Akeylah sidestepped to dodge the blow.

"Maybe they're recruiting," Polla pointed out. "You both served in the war."

"Easterners are only good for ship rats and cannon fodder, you know that," Koren scoffed. "The king would never trust us to be Talons."

"Not even after we bled for him," Siraaj muttered.

Akeylah swept past, leaving them squabbling. Let them wonder what this was all about. As for her, she just prayed she could find one dress, in all her tattered closet, that would suit a trip to meet a king.

❈ 3 ❈

Florencia

Despite the predawn stars peeking through the windows, Lord D'Vangeline Rueno's suite in Ilian Keep bustled with life. His daughter, Lexana, presided over the dance floor, her shrill laugh echoing against the elaborate gold-plated ceiling frescoes.

He'd gone all out for this party, Lexana's official coming-of-age ball. The chocolate fountain filled its own cups, and large glittering silver decorations drifted overhead, shaped like the symbols of the Five Reaches. The sailfish of the Eastern Reach danced along the ceiling, chased by the great cat of the Southern, the sand-stepper of the Northern, the heron of the Western, and, of course, larger than all the rest, Kolonya's stormwing. The bird's vast wings nearly touched both sides of the vaulted ceiling at once—and that was only a slight exaggeration of its size in real life.

Florencia watched from her place among the ladies' maids.

She stood in the shadows beneath the loft balcony, out of sight and out of mind until her charge required her aid. Then she'd be expected to appear at the noblewoman's elbow immediately, as if reading her mind.

Normally, Florencia was very good at this. Tonight, she had other concerns.

Last month, a serving girl was caught in a lesser nobleman's bed. Usually she'd be dismissed for impropriety, but she was a favorite of Lord Rueno's. He gave his blessing on the match. After a man like Rueno stated public approval, the nobleman's parents had little choice but to allow him to wed the commoner. The girl even dined at court now, albeit at the fringes of the Great Hall.

Ever since, Florencia had trained a sharp eye on Lord Rueno's family. She had no intentions of skulking through the servants' corridors forever. If she became Rueno's new favorite, perhaps one day he could improve her situation as well.

Ren watched Lady Lexana chat with Lord Gavin. *There* would be a good match for Lexana. Gavin's family could trace their lineage back to the kings of Oonkip, when the Western Reach was still known as such. Here in Kolonya, they'd done well for themselves in the timber trade. Wartime meant Kolonya purchased a lot of hardwood. Need to build ships somehow.

A stab of regret struck her. *Seven ships, 1,854 soldiers.*

She couldn't think about it. Not now. She'd learned her lesson and she would never repeat it. Now she must look forward. To the future she'd carve herself.

Lexana leaned on Gavin's arm, a sparkle in her eye. Gavin's stories, Ren knew from experience, were of the endless-and-rambling variety. For once, though, he had found a willing audience. Lexana's laughter made his whole countenance light up.

But her laughter drew more stares than just Ren's. Including the worst one possible.

Ren slid out from the servants' alcove as the most poisonous viper in this whole pit sidled up to Lexana and Gavin.

Ren's charge, Lady D'Garrida Sarella, had a reputation for leaving shattered hearts and ruined reputations in her wake. Judging by the edged smile she turned on Lord Gavin, she aimed for a little bit of both tonight.

As Ren approached, Sarella batted emerald-tinged lashes. Sarella was beautiful in an almost surreal way, her cheekbones knife-sharp, her nose broad and elegant, skin a perfect Sun-blessed brown. Every inch the ideal Kolonyan woman, Sarella wielded her beauty the way a soldier would a sword.

"Gavin." His name melted like cacao on her tongue. "I haven't seen you all evening. You haven't abandoned me to this dull a crowd, have you?" She offered a hand.

"I wouldn't dream of it." Gavin lifted her fingers to his lips, Lexana all but forgotten.

Sarella curled her fingers around his elbow, where Lexana's had been only a moment earlier. "Sun be thanked. Last time we met, you'd only just begun telling me about your part in the Seventh War, and I've been waiting on tenterhooks ever since...."

"My lady." Ren barred their path. She served as Sarella's lady's maid and would normally be forced to take her side in a situation like this. But to win Lord Rueno's favor, Ren's priorities would have to shift.

Besides, she had to admit, Sarella bothered her more than most of the other women at court. This could be fun.

Sarella's gaze narrowed. "I did not summon you."

"I know, my lady." Ren bowed her head in faux apology. "But Lord Jadin was asking for you." Lord Jadin, who Sarella had spent half of this Sun-forsaken party seducing away from Lady Halley already. "Something about an item you misplaced in his care earlier tonight."

It took every ounce of self-control Ren possessed not to smirk at the fury that flared in Sarella's eyes. Gavin glanced from Sarella to Ren, then over his shoulder at Lady Lexana. Poor fool.

"Shall I fetch it for you?" Ren continued, her voice light and innocent. "Or would you prefer to meet Lord Jadin in his suite to recover it? It is your favorite, my lady, with the lace embroidery, so I assume you don't want to lose it."

That did it. Gavin disentangled his arm from Sarella's, his smile polite yet cold. "It seems you have unattended business, Lady Sarella. I'll save my story for another time."

Gavin and Lexana slipped away toward the dance floor. For a moment, Ren enjoyed the fruits of her labor.

Only a moment.

Then Sarella scowled. "You'll pay for that, girl."

Girl. Never mind that Sarella and Florencia were the same age. Raised right here in the Keep, nursed on politics and spite in equal measure. They were the same but for the accident of their births—Sarella's to a lord and lady; Florencia's to a maid and an unknown father.

It wasn't fair. It wasn't right that girls like Sarella got a chance to rise in the world, when girls like Ren—girls who were smarter, savvier, *better* at this game—were forced to stand meekly in the shadows awaiting their orders.

Ren only hoped she'd gambled correctly. She cast a glance over her shoulder, tracked Lord Rueno. He was occupied elsewhere. But surely his daughter would mention, if prompted, the maid who helped her win a dance with an eligible suitor....

Doesn't matter. Sarella always made her life hell. Raised petty complaints and summoned Ren in the dead of night, or drunkenly berated Ren for misplacing items Sarella herself had lost or ruined. Ren had lost count of how many times Sarella had reported her to Madam Oruna, the head of staff. One more series of complaints wouldn't make a difference—Oruna couldn't fire Ren even if she wanted to. Not when Ren knew whose bed Oruna warmed every night.

So Ren merely grinned when Sarella stormed off. Whatever blowback this caused, it was worth it for the look on Sarella's face. Worth it to stand her ground as Sarella beelined toward the sidebar.

Even when Sarella decided to deal with her embarrassment by downing several flutes of amaranth nectar in quick succession, it was worth it. Worth it when Sarella drunkenly summoned Ren to carry her home.

"Wouldn't do for a lady's maid to leave her charge floundering, would it?" Sarella hissed, voice low, right before she stumbled so spectacularly that Ren caught her on reflex.

Sun above. Even drunk, Sarella was a formidable opponent. She knew Ren couldn't neglect her, not at an event like this. Lord Rueno was watching, intent on ensuring his guests departed safely. So she bobbed her head in Lord Rueno's direction, looped

Sarella's arm around her shoulders, and began the laborious task of carrying the girl to the D'Garrida suites. The halls of the rosewood tower had never felt so long as they did with Sarella sagging against Ren's hip, breath hot and reeking of flowers.

"Home sweet home," Ren muttered when they finally reached the massive stonewood door. It took all her remaining strength to shoulder it open. When it slid inward, they both staggered across the threshold.

The sun was already painting the gauzy curtains pink with first light. She'd have to warn the morning maid to delay breakfast.

"So why Gavin?" Sarella offered her back to Ren. Florencia began to unlace her complicated four-piece silk ensemble, which seemed to consist more of knots and strings than actual clothing. "Have you got your eye on him?" Her voice slurred, but Ren would not make the mistake of underestimating Sarella twice.

She bit her tongue and tugged at the dress stays harder than strictly necessary.

"You can have him." Sarella tossed her head, fashionably short razor-cut skimming her cheekbones. "Me, I've set my sights higher. My favorite rogue returns to court next week."

Ren's fingers stilled. Unable to resist, she glanced at the mirror. Found Sarella grinning at her own reflection like a great cat about to pounce on a macaw.

Surely she didn't mean . . .

But Ren already knew Sarella's tastes. She remembered the way Sarella chased him last time. "The Eastern ambassador is coming back to us?" Ren's voice did not even falter. She was getting good at this.

"Ambassador Danton wrote to me last week." Sarella fluttered those painted lashes again. "Positively dying to reunite, he said."

Of course. Ren should have seen this coming. First Burnt Bay, then Prince Nicolen's assassination two months ago...Clearly the Easterners wouldn't stop until Kolonya was dead.

Which meant Danton would need more intel soon.

Her veins ran cold.

The Reaches were no strangers to bloodshed. Ever since five different groups of Genalese settlers colonized the previously uninhabited Reaches, they'd suffered. First as five separate abused, embattled colonies that Genal exploited for as much money as they could wring from the settlers' backs. Then, four hundred years ago, when the Reaches declared independence and kicked off the first War for Recognition, they bled and died for freedom. Since that first war, six others had wrecked their shores, each bloodier than the last.

But the battle at Burnt Bay was different. Burnt Bay wasn't a Genalese attack.

Six months after the ink dried on the Seventh Peace Accords with Genal, Eastern rebels ambushed the Kolonyan fleet in retribution for Kolonya allegedly hogging too much of the Reaches' resources.

As if more death could possibly be the right solution. As if an internal war would salvage the wreckage of an external one.

Seven carrier ships sank in Burnt Bay, a large portion of Kolonya's remaining navy. And 1,854 Talons, sailors, and foot soldiers died on those ships. Only a few survived to describe the horror of the flames licking across oil slicks on the water, the screams of their compatriots as they drowned in the flaming waters of Davenforth Bay—better known as Burnt Bay now.

Why did they die?

Because Florencia was fool enough to trust a man who built his life on betrayal.

"Which reminds me," Sarella was saying, "I must speak to Madam Oruna. I shall need a more capable maid while Danton is in town. His taste is... exacting."

Ren's hands shook so hard she barely managed to pull Sarella's dress off. She fought to keep her face blank, emotionless.

Inside, the memories surged.

Danton in the cave, their secret spot, the only place in the Keep they could be alone. Danton folding his arms around her, his smile reckless. Danton's lips on hers, searing hot.

Danton whispering in her ear, confiding about the trouble in the Eastern Reach, the difficulties he faced as ambassador.

Danton treating her like an equal, at least in private.

Danton in public, his gaze skipping straight past Ren. Danton flirting with the courtiers. Dancing with Sarella, his charmer's grin on, a hand around her hip. Matching her wink for wink as they danced around the idea of doing more.

Danton flashing Ren a look between dances as he went to top up Sarella's drink.

"I imagine you won't mind being reassigned." Sarella lifted her arms the same way she did every night. Sun forbid a lady be asked to dress herself. This time, Sarella's nudity felt like a challenge. A dare. "You never enjoyed seeing me with him, did you?"

Ren picked up Sarella's nightgown and draped it around her shoulders, eyes locked on Sarella's in the mirror. Ren smiled, broadly enough that Sarella wouldn't be able to see how forced it was. "Whatever you believe, my lady."

✳

The moment Sarella snuffed the candles, Florencia made for the maids' quarters. She could have bypassed the common area and headed to her cubbyhole—a single cot and a two-by-two shelf, the only space in the world she could call her own. But sleep would be impossible now. No matter how exhausted her body felt, her mind raced.

Danton is returning.

With him came everything Ren had spent the last six months avoiding. The desperate hunger when they kissed. The way he opened up, shared his deepest fears. The way she reciprocated, in a way she'd never dared before. She told him everything, more than even Audrina, her best friend. They shared their dreams, their hopes, their ambition to make more of life than what they'd been handed at birth.

Then that very same ambition drove him to stab her in the back.

Now he was returning, and with him came more than just a bruised heart. If he ever told anyone what she'd done…

No. Danton was many things, but never loose-lipped.

She hoped.

So, rather than sleep, Ren sought her best friend. Found her, as usual, sequestered in a corner. Ren didn't know which came first—Audrina's preference for solitude or the other maids' opinion that Audrina was too stuck-up to socialize. Ren had tried to involve Audrina in their wider social circle, but Aud always found a way to slip off on her own.

It was a shame, because Audrina was the smartest girl down here, with the possible exception of Ren. But if she preferred solitude, so be it.

"Aud." Ren plopped onto the bench, eyeing the pile of cleaning products and dirty sheets Audrina was buried in. "Try the lavender oil; it's easier on silk than whitener."

"Already tried it. I think this one might be a loss." Audrina scrubbed at the dark brown stains on the pale fabric.

"What happened, someone misplace their bedpan?"

Audrina snorted. "Nothing that foul. Lady Halley got overzealous with her late-night chocolate in bed."

Ren heaved a sigh. "It's a wonder some of these women can spoon their own porridge."

"Don't be ridiculous. None of them would stoop to eating *porridge*." They both laughed. Then Audrina caught sight of Ren's expression, and her hands stilled. "What's happened?"

Ren frowned. "You know, you're the only one who can do that."

"What, read you?" Audrina raised her eyebrows. "Doubtful. You slump your shoulders when you're upset." She hunched over in an exaggerated imitation. "And when you're angry, you get this pout, like a duck—"

"Enough." Ren swatted her friend's shoulder. "I get it, I'm an easy mark." Silence stretched, comfortable at first, but veering toward pointed the longer it lasted. Finally, Ren cleared her throat. "He's coming back."

She didn't need to say who.

"Sun above," Audrina swore. She knew nothing of the secret Ren and Danton shared—the true danger in his return. But she knew about his and Ren's dalliance. Had covered for Ren on more than one occasion when she needed to adjust her schedule in order to slip away with him for an hour or two. "How do you know? He didn't *write*, did he? If that no-good rogue tries to start things up again, I swear…"

Ren laughed bitterly. "Nothing like that. Don't worry," she added, when the crease between Audrina's brows deepened. "I wouldn't fall for it."

Audrina started to reply when the chamber doors banged open. They glanced up, startled. Only a half dozen other maids dotted the common room at this hour, most still lacing up their uniforms. Squeals started up as maids recognized the intruder—Josen, one of the male squires. Belatedly, he covered his eyes. "Summons from upstairs," he called over the protests. "Florencia's needed in the Great Hall."

Ren's insides turned to ice.

Servants were never summoned by name. Especially not by squires, and definitely not to the Great Hall. If a lady required assistance, she rang her bellpull and any maid available answered.

Ren rose and nodded to Josen, who disappeared. Then she exchanged a nervous glance with Audrina.

"I'm sure it's nothing," Aud whispered. Neither looked convinced.

If Lady Sarella went over Oruna's head and made a formal complaint, Ren could kiss her comfortable life in the Keep goodbye. Not to mention any hope of rising above this station. Sun above, how could she have gambled so poorly? Did Rueno even notice her helping his daughter? Was it enough to buy a pardon?

Then again. The cold in her gut sharpened to icicles. This might not be about Sarella at all. Nobles wouldn't be involved in the dismissal of a lady's maid—they'd leave that to Madam Oruna.

But if Danton decided to ingratiate himself with the king by exposing a traitor within the Keep...

In Kolonya, the only mercy a traitor could hope for was an overdose of phantasm venom, rather than a crueler execution. Either way, death was certain.

Ren straightened her shoulders, then lifted her chin as she marched across the chambers. *You cannot control your destiny,* Mama always said. *Only the way you face it.*

Whatever shape the Sun's judgment took, Ren would look it square in the eyes.

·◄ 4 ►·

Akeylah

R ight, off with your gown."

Akeylah stiffened. The king's Talons had escorted her
through the dizzying, busy streets of Kolonya City, then handed
her off to a troop of ladies' maids who carried what little luggage
she possessed up the spiraling steps of the mahogany tower of
Ilian Keep. "This is you," one maid had said, as though all this
actually *belonged* to her. Now she stood inside the most sumptuous room she'd ever seen, its walls and floor all mahogany
stonewood, the furniture oak accented with rosy silk. She'd been
starting to think she was mistaken. That the king didn't summon
her here to uncover proof of her treason. That the invitation to
attend a celebration was genuine. But then the maid reached for
her skirts, and Akeylah's panic returned.

"Quick." The stern-faced Kolonyan woman grabbed her hem.

"The king wants to see you in the Great Hall immediately.... My lady, are you quite all right?"

Akeylah backed away from the woman's grasp so fast she tripped on a stool and stumbled into the chamber wall. "Yes, fine." She smoothed her dress. It was ancient, long-sleeved and high-collared. A dress that had been in fashion sixteen years ago—which made sense, since Akeylah had stolen it from an old trunk of her mother's clothing. It was the closest thing to court-appropriate attire she could find.

"If the king has summoned me, I do not wish to keep him waiting." Akeylah pasted on a smile she hoped was winning rather than nervous.

In truth, all she could think about was the scar pulsing on her thigh. If this woman lifted her dress, she would see the bright blue glow, recognizable to anyone who grew up listening to tales of evil curseworkers who practiced the Vulgar Arts. On the off chance that the king *hadn't* sent this maid to try to strip her down in search of evidence...well, Akeylah didn't exactly want to go around proclaiming her sins.

"But, my lady." The maid frowned. "You have been traveling for days. Surely you would like to bathe and don a fresh outfit."

"No. Thank you, but...this is the only court dress I own."

That, at least, was true.

A knock at the door saved her. The maid opened it to a messenger boy, who bowed so low his nose almost touched stonewood. "I have come to escort my lady to the Great Hall," he informed the floor.

"Sun-forsaken Easterners, don't even dress for a king..." the maid muttered as Akeylah practically fled the room.

38

Akeylah winced. She hated representing her people this way. Seas knew Kolonyans already thought Easterners a lowly, uneducated sort. But there was nothing she could do about that right now. She faced bigger problems.

How could she keep her scar hidden? Even if the king's invitation was innocent, she must be careful never to let evidence of her treason show. If King Andros learned what she'd done, she couldn't expect any mercy.

It wouldn't matter that her father nearly killed her first, at least a dozen times. It wouldn't matter that it was self-defense. Akeylah would be seen as the abomination, the one who perverted the Arts.

She would pay the price for it.

It did not take long to reach the Great Hall. Carvings of famous battles decorated its immense cherry stonewood doors: King Ilian defeating King Morfean of Genal, King Gellien hoisting the flag of the new Reaches. On a central panel, four interlocking circles surrounded a central circle emblazoned with a stormwing—the outer Reaches united around Kolonya.

One rap from the messenger and the doors swung inward to reveal a vast throne room. An empty aisle led up the middle toward a dais on which a walnut of a man perched. "Akeylah dam-Senzin," he said. "Welcome to Kolonya City."

King Andros's shoulders were stooped, hair more silver than brown. He looked far older than the youthful king carved on the doors, yet she could still see the faded strength in his face—his broad nose and sharp cheekbones under even sharper eyes. The crown on his head, too, was unmistakable. Two golden talons cupped his face, and a circle of feathers above mimicked the silver-gold pattern of a stormwing.

King Ilian adopted that massive bird of prey as the symbol of Kolonya after a stormwing famously flew to his aid in battle, clawing the face of a Genalese soldier long enough for Ilian to decapitate the enemy. Now Kolonyan troops trained stormwings to fly into battle with them. *As stormwings rule the natural world, so Kolonya rules the Reaches,* Ilian wrote.

All Akeylah could think was that ever since that first stormwing helped a king, the once-mighty birds had become little more than trained pets.

The doors groaned shut. Akeylah sank into a curtsy so low her knees skimmed the floor. "Your Majesty. Thank you for the kind invitation."

She wondered if her heartbeat was audible in this echoing hall.

"You may approach the throne," said a woman.

Akeylah took in the rest of the audience. Next to an empty chair where Akeylah supposed the young Genalese queen ought to be, half in shadows, stood a different woman. One the king's age. The years had done her more justice—silver hair skimmed her cheekbones in a practical bob, and the few wrinkles she bore only accentuated her shrewd features.

Countess Yasmin. King Andros's twin sister.

Aside from the twins, two girls about Akeylah's age stood near the dais. One was short, with wild black curls and narrow features. She caught Akeylah's eye and bared her teeth.

Akeylah quickly looked away.

The other girl was taller, her straight brown hair cut fashionably short. Combined with her oval face, wide nose, and high cheekbones, she looked like the king, every inch as perfectly Kolonyan. A cousin, perhaps?

That girl lifted a brow, studying Akeylah right back. Akeylah flushed and lowered her gaze.

"Now that you are all here, we can begin," Countess Yasmin said.

A lump solidified in Akeylah's throat. Begin what?

Her gaze drifted again to the black-haired girl. She was clearly a Traveler, or related to one. *Just like the curseworker.* Maybe she was at the fair, maybe she'd seen Akeylah meet with the older woman, and she'd come here as a witness to the crime.

The king rose. For a moment, he wavered, until Yasmin caught his elbow. "You three have waited long enough to hear this."

She braced herself.

"As you all know, Prince Nicolen, my only son and heir, is... gone."

Yasmin touched the king's shoulder.

Andros cleared his throat. "Without a clear successor, the future of the Reaches has been thrown into doubt. My ancestors have served as Kolonya's head for generations, and I am determined that we will continue to serve for many more to come. We are the Reaches' constant heart. Without us, they will falter, fall into chaos."

Akeylah waited, silent. What was this? A history lesson?

"Luckily for the sake of all the Reaches," King Andros said, "we have other options."

He fixed them with a long stare, one after the other. When his gaze fell on Akeylah, her mouth went dry.

His eyes were green. Not the usual Kolonyan emerald, but a paler peridot color, almost yellow. Unusual, even in Kolonya. Yet Akeylah had seen the color before. She saw it every morning.

In her mirror.

"I wish I could have explained this to you all years ago. I wish it never had to come to this. But it was safer to leave you where you were—ignorance can be a shield. Had anyone known your identities, it would have put us all in danger. Kolonya has many enemies—enemies who would stop at nothing to harm our country, even torturing people into using the Vulgar Arts against their kin."

Akeylah's head felt strange. Like a buoy bobbing on waves. She couldn't make sense of what the king was saying.

"Family is the bond that holds the Reaches together. But to be a part of my family is as much a curse as it is a blessing. We need only look to my fallen son for evidence of that." The king reached up to grip his sister's hand where it rested on his shoulder. "For that, I am sorry to summon you three."

The air felt muggy. Hard to breathe.

Andros gestured to the Kolonyan girl, who stepped forward. "D'Martina Florencia." A bastard's name—normally Kolonyans would take their father's forename.

Her heart raced.

Andros looked to Akeylah next. "Akeylah dam-Senzin."

She stepped forward and curtsied, mostly to avert her face. *Mother Ocean, let me be wrong. Please, please...*

"Zofi of the Travelers," King Andros said, and Akeylah felt more than saw the black-haired girl join them at the foot of the dais.

"Kolonya needs you three." Andros glanced at Yasmin. His twin leaned forward.

"Kolonya needs one of you in particular," Yasmin said. "The

best one. Time will tell who that proves to be. Tomorrow night, a Blood Ceremony will be held. At this ceremony, we will publicly confirm your birthrights—"

"I'm sorry, our birth *whats?*" interrupted Zofi.

"Try to keep up," muttered Florencia.

"I find that a bit hard to do when everyone keeps dancing around the point." Zofi gestured at the king.

Akeylah looked up to find King Andros staring directly at her. "I apologize." For an instant it seemed he spoke only to Akeylah. "I should have been more direct." His attention shifted to Zofi, thank the seas, because his next words nearly made Akeylah's knees buckle. "The three of you are my daughters."

He kept speaking. Something about the reason he kept it secret—spies, curseworkers, enemies. She wasn't listening anymore. Waves rushed in her ears.

Deep down, she knew it was true. *The gods have a vicious sense of humor*, the traders always said.

"After the ceremony, you will serve in court with me," Andros said. "In time, we will determine which of you shows the most aptitude for leadership. I will name that daughter my heir."

Mother Ocean, let me melt. Turn to water, disappear. If only it were that easy.

"It's been two months since the prince died." Zofi spoke up again. "Why wait to summon us? Why not begin teaching us as soon as possible?"

A faint smile tilted the corner of King Andros's mouth. "Ah, Zofi. You are so very like your mother."

That quieted the girl. It made Akeylah pause, too, in realization.

Her mother—her perfect, angelic, adored mother, the one her siblings and father never stopped talking about... She had been unfaithful. Lain with this man, a *king* no less. *Why?*

For the first time in her life, Akeylah found herself wondering whether there was more to her mother than the stories her father shared.

Not my father, she remembered, and sank back into panic all over again.

"But you are correct, Zofi. As devastating as it was to lose my only son, my lovely young bride and I hoped that we might produce a new heir and never need to call upon you."

His new wife, who he wed a decade after the first queen's death. The Genalese princess shipped here a year ago to wed a king she'd never met, to seal the Seventh War's peace treaty through marriage. Akeylah wondered briefly where the girl was. Whether the marriage pact was going well, or if she was absent today because King Andros did not yet trust his new bride with information about his secret bastard heirs.

Didn't matter. That mystery queen's worries paled in comparison to Akeylah's.

Yasmin brushed the king's shoulder once more. He tilted his head, and so did she. Akeylah couldn't quite put a finger on what made their interactions seem odd. They were twins, so of course they looked alike. But they moved alike, too, their mannerisms similar. Andros pressed his lips together at the exact same moment Yasmin did, standing behind him.

"There is another reason," Yasmin said at last.

"And word of it cannot leave this room," Andros continued. "I entrust you with this information as a gesture of faith. It is only fair after I kept so much from you, raised you in ignorance of your true heritage."

Akeylah's throat tightened. *Please,* she prayed, to all the gods now. *Mother Ocean, Father Sun, sands, anyone. Let me be wrong. Let me have failed.*

But she could already see it. The pallor of his skin, the way he sagged in his chair while Yasmin stood. How much more ragged he looked than her, his twin.

Akeylah braced herself. Tensed every muscle in her body in preparation for the blow she already saw coming.

It didn't help.

"I am dying," said the king.

Akeylah shut her eyes and remembered.

The curseworker waited just inside the tidal cave. Akeylah tiptoed through tide pools of brittle starfish to reach her. She recognized the woman's silvery facial scar and flyaway black curls. Yet it was not until the woman raised her shirt to reveal thick, deep, pulsating blue scars that Akeylah truly realized what she was doing.

"Cut deep." The woman offered Akeylah the blade handle-first. "It won't be like a normal tithe. You'll need to reach past your body, feel the others beyond. You'll sense your father, like I explained."

Bile rose in her throat, even as she rested the blade against her thigh. This was wrong. But so was the way Father treated her. She lived like a hunted animal in her own home. Subject to his temper, his to beat or even kill whenever he decided.

She didn't belong to him. Like the Reaches cutting loose from Genal, she deserved freedom.

"Be sure you want to do this," the curseworker said. "There is no turning back."

"I'm sure," she replied.

Mother Ocean save her.

Akeylah dug the knife into her thigh. Like any time she tithed, her vision melted away. She saw only her body, her veins, her pumping blood. She tasted the Arts around her, let them enter and fill her veins with possibility, promise.

Then she reached deeper, the way the curseworker had taught her. Forced her mind out of her own body. It took time. Minutes upon minutes ticked past, the Arts burning hotter in her blood while they waited unused.

Then her mind burst through the wall, and she gasped aloud.

Around her, beside her, close enough that it seemed she should be able to reach out and touch them, stood outlines of other bodies, little more than shadow figures, a collection of veins and hearts. Some were close—her father, her siblings—others further away, third- or fourth-degree relations.

She ignored them all. Focused on her father.

She couldn't see his face or his external features—only the internal ones. She felt him. The shape of his veins, the scent of his blood that echoed in her own.

"Don't pour in too much," the curseworker had warned. "A few drops will make him sicken slowly, remove any suspicion of his illness being caused by the Vulgar Arts."

So she forced one tiny drop of the Arts from her blood into his veins. It burned, worse than any cut or broken bone, like being set alight from the inside out.

But Akeylah knew how to handle pain.

She focused through the stabbing sensation. Harnessed the drop of Arts she'd sent into her father's body—took that delicious

46

bright-scented ounce of possibility—and turned it inside-out. *Flipped it in on itself until it went dark, colorless, an abscess in his veins.*

Akeylah opened her eyes again, the Great Hall swimming through tears she could not choke back. She was sick for days after that curse, unable to work even a basic tithe for weeks. But when the curseworker hugged her, reassured her that she'd done it right, that within a couple of months at most, her father would be dead, she relaxed. Finally, her nightmare would end. Even when days passed, and Jahen showed no signs of illness, she held fast to the belief that she'd done it right. After all, she had the scar, proof of what she'd done. Eventually it would work. Eventually he'd sicken, die.

Turned out the curseworker was right. She had killed her father that day. But not Jahen.

Akeylah had condemned an innocent man—her *king*—to die.

❊ 5 ❊

Zofi

I'm not going to serve a *drifter*, for Sun's sake."

Zofi stood in the entrance to her chambers and watched the two maids, presumably sent up on the king's orders, bicker.

"Well, I'm not doing it either. And I've got seniority."

"Good." Zofi lazily unstrapped her longknife, which the king had—perhaps foolishly—returned. "Get out."

The maids didn't need telling twice. Only after the doors slammed behind them did Zofi grab her rucksack and shoulder it.

Play their game, Mother advised. Zofi thought she meant play the game in order to keep her head out of a noose. This? This was another game entirely. One that both her mother and the king hid from her. She'd be damned if she was going to sit idly around the Keep waiting on the king's Blood Ceremony—whatever that entailed—tomorrow night.

Mother couldn't have told her own daughter the truth? Some notice would have been nice. Zofi knew her mother had lots of flings, enjoyed men of every flavor and position...And she had heard rumors that Andros was a looker in his youth, not to mention a notorious flirt. But sands' sake, *a king*? That was a lot, even for the infamous Deena.

She needed to talk to Mother. Hear the truth from someone she trusted. Sands could swallow Kolonya whole for all she cared, the dying king, too. Zofi was a Traveler, built for a life on the move. Not cooped up with these haughty nobles.

She missed her band. The comforting sound of Norren snoring a few tents away, Bette and the kids chattering as they cooked breakfast. *Elex.* Elex offering her the best cut of rabbit every night, Elex entertaining her with stories during long desert rides. Elex, who gave up everything for her freedom, not so she could be locked up in some gilded cage.

Finding the stables was easy. Once she got outside the obsidian tower, she just followed her nose. Two stablehands manned the entrance, but nobody watched the rear window. Zofi climbed a hay bale and slipped inside.

The moment she entered the barns, she relaxed. The familiar scent made her feel far more at home than anywhere else in Kolonya City. Zofi hadn't seen this many horses in one place since the Eastern reunion fair, when the Traveler bands came together to trade goods, services, and tips on which towns wouldn't throw them out on sight.

She took her time perusing the mazelike stables, admiring enormous eighteen-hand war steeds, sleek bays, and dappled gray ponies. But the horses that really drew her eye were the sand-steppers. Lean, long-legged, nicknamed "golden horses" for their shining metallic coats, sand-steppers were the mounts Zofi grew up riding. They were Northern, bred for desert-crossing and distance.

Exactly what she needed now.

She knew she should pick one of the mixed sand-steppers— one with a midnight-black or dull auburn coat. They would blend in. But the moment Zofi laid eyes on the alpha, she couldn't help herself. His pelt shone bright silver, his glossy mane shock-white. His gaze was steady, intelligent.

This horse would draw every eye for a mile around. Zofi didn't care.

She needed him.

As she led him from the stall, he positively danced with pent-up energy. How long had it been since someone had taken him out? She saddled him with the first thing she could find— a leather tack finer than any she'd ever handled—all the while shaking her head. The king had these gorgeous horses and what did he do? Cooped them up like a treasure hoard, not living creatures who needed attention, care, space to run.

She'd rescue two hostages today: this horse and herself.

She swung into the saddle just as one of the stablehands appeared in the hall. *Sands.*

"How did you get in here?" the boy shouted.

Zofi donned her best haughty royal impression. "I'm here on the king's business. Mind your own."

A second stablehand, a tall girl, joined the first. "The *king*?" She scoffed. "What would the king be doing talking to the likes of you?"

"I wasn't aware ladies of court needed to explain themselves to servants."

The boy laughed. "If you're a court lady, then I'm a jester."

"Your words." Zofi spurred the horse's flanks.

It gave her a fierce spark of pleasure when the two dove out of her path. The stallion was antsy, raring to go. It barely took a kick to get him racing. The boy made a halfhearted grab for the reins, but Zofi was moving too fast.

The front gate was locked, but only three feet high, plenty of space above it. She kicked the sand-stepper again and he surged forward, leaped the gate easily, and flew out of the stables at a canter.

Ahead, the streets of Kolonya City rose up, narrow and winding. Zofi didn't know the exact route, but she knew the merchants' road lay to the north. She picked the northernmost street she saw and kicked the stallion into a gallop.

They flew along the cobblestones. Pedestrians dove out of the way, shouting curses and insults. She caught the word *drifter* more than a few times, but it only made her grin, now that she was back in her element.

Sands, it felt good to ride. Like shedding a heavy weight. Sprinting away from the king, from his words. *Father. Daughter.*

Mother always said, "The gods make jokes of us all," but this was pushing it, even for them.

At an intersection, Zofi turned right, wove north. First step, find the gate. Second step, talk her way past the guards. How? Well, she'd cross the bridge when she galloped onto it.

Speaking of gallop. She tilted her head, frowned. There were new shouts behind her, different ones. Along with that, the sound of another set of hooves clattering on stone. Not the slow plod of a trader horse.

She dared a glance over her shoulder and cursed.

A Talon.

Not just any Talon either. The same smug young loyalist who dragged her here in the first place. Vidal. She spurred her sand-stepper again. But she chose this horse for distance, not sprints. A few blocks later, Vidal was close enough to shout a command.

"*Baqateze.*"

Zofi didn't recognize the word, but her horse did. He skidded to a halt, so fast she had to brace herself against the saddle to keep her seat. By the time she righted herself, the horse stood dead still, flanks heaving.

"Come on, don't do this to me." She swatted his rump. Dug her heels into his flanks.

Nothing.

"He won't move." Vidal reined in beside her. "Not until I give the counterorder." As usual, he sounded pleasant, almost amused. "We train all our mounts to obey a few verbal commands. Prevents thievery."

Zofi scowled. "Did the king order you to tail me, or do you just enjoy following young ladies around?"

He smirked. "Little bit of both, in this case. Most ladies aren't nearly so interesting to babysit." He extended a hand, palm up. An offer of peace.

She ignored it. "You told me I'm not a prisoner. If I'm free, let me go home."

52

"You're free to leave whenever you like, Lady Zofi." He nodded at the horse. "But I can't let you take him."

She leaned back in the saddle. "King Andros owns hundreds of horses. You're telling me he can't spare one measly stallion?"

"The king might be willing to gift you a steed. You'd have to take that up with him. But I doubt he'll let you have this one."

Zofi snorted. "Oh, yes, I'm sure he's very attached to this particular horse—"

"*I* don't want you to take this one," Vidal interrupted.

"Is he yours?" Zofi glanced from the elegant sand-stepper to the chestnut mare Vidal chose to chase her. Somehow, the bright silver horse didn't seem his style.

Then she reined herself in. *His style?* As if she knew anything about this boy, besides the fact that his only goal in life was to chain her here.

"He belonged to a friend of mine. A friend who recently passed away."

"I'm sorry to hear that," Zofi said, sincere. "But surely your friend wouldn't have wanted you to lock his horse up forever just because he died."

Vidal's pleasant expression soured. "Tell me, do Travelers value horses over all human lives, or only Kolonyan ones?"

"You don't know anything about us," Zofi snapped.

"Please. I've ridden through the oases. Heard stories of the children you kidnap, the property you steal—"

"Children we rescue from abusive homes," Zofi countered. "And property that more oft than not is sold to us honestly, until some merchant realizes he can take our money and keep his goods, too, if he reports us for thievery."

"If that were true, you'd file counter reports. Stay and argue your case. Running around all the time like you do suggests guilt."

"As if anyone would believe a Traveler over a local in a fair trial."

"Can you blame them?" Vidal shook his head, incredulous. "The way you all live, without ties or loyalty—"

"Travelers understand more about loyalty than any of you spoiled Kolonyans."

A few people stuck their heads out of windows above. Others clustered at the nearest intersection, drawn by the sight of a king's Talon confronting a drifter.

Curse them all.

Vidal scoffed, oblivious to the spectators. "Your king invites you to his Keep. Gives you a plush suite, maids to serve your every whim, and you repay him by stealing his horse? Is *that* your idea of loyalty?"

"Is your loyalty so easily bought?" she countered. "What keeps a Kolonyan loyal—money? Fancy presents?"

"Family," he replied angrily.

"Travelers put family first, too. But for us, family means the people who ride at your side, not just blood relatives who you can keep in line with threats." She drew a finger up her inner forearm, a crude reference to the Vulgar Arts.

On instinct, Vidal raised his hand in a warding gesture. "That's—I never..." He scowled. "I am as loyal to my fellow soldiers as I am to my family. We fight alongside one another, *die for one another.* I've lost friends when..." He faltered, glanced at her horse. Suddenly, the heat left his voice, replaced by sorrow. "When I should have been there for them," he murmured, almost to himself.

Zofi loosened her grip on the horse's reins. The dead man's mount.

Vidal cleared his throat. "Maybe you're right. Maybe if I were *more loyal*, I'd have been at my friend's side the night he was attacked. Maybe I could have stopped one of *your* people from killing him. It was a Traveler, you know."

Zofi stiffened again. *Sands.*

"The murderer confessed. Seemed proud of it, witnesses said. The least I can do now is stop another Traveler from stealing Nicolen's horse."

She reeled.

Nicolen.

Prince Nicolen.

The crowd had grown larger. So many witnesses to hear Vidal's words. Words she wanted to run from, the same way she'd been running for two months.

Act normal, Zofi.

"Keep the bloody horse." A silver horse, just like the Silver Prince. She should have guessed.

She threw the reins at Vidal and dismounted. Before he could say another word, she stormed off, forcing her way through the crowd. Her only concern was to get as far from Vidal as possible before her reaction gave her away.

Nicolen. The brave Silver Prince who defeated Genal in the Seventh War. The same prince who was riding into the Eastern Reach to deal with the rebels when some coward assassinated him.

That's what the stories said.

The stories were true, as far as stories went.

The stories left out a few details.

Zofi's band was in a backwater tavern along the foothills of the Dawn Mountains, riding west after a long season in the Eastern Reach. They traded rounds of the local brew, a strange bitter ale Elex loved. Zofi thought it tasted like piss.

The king's Talons burst in, unannounced. The whole tavern went dead silent, the calm before the sandstorm. Everyone in there had some reason or another to fear Talons—Travelers more than most.

Then one Talon cracked a joke. The tension broke. Elex joined the soldiers for a hand of cards. Zofi ordered another round. The tavern began to hum again, comfortable, chatty.

Until the end of the card game.

One Talon, who looked vaguely familiar in a way that nagged at her, accused Elex of cheating. Elex emptied his pockets, spread the cards to prove his innocence. The Talon sat back, apparently satisfied.

But Zofi noticed the way he watched Elex. Time and again, he refilled Elex's beer, while leaving his own untouched.

Zofi had learned long ago not to ignore her instincts. So no matter how hard the Talon laughed at Elex's increasingly drunken jokes, she did not take her eye from him.

A few rounds later, Elex stood to use the outhouse. So did the Talon.

So did Zofi.

She crept after, listened to the men chatting amiably the whole way out of the pub and up the hill toward the outhouses. Here on the edge of the Eastern Reach, everything was outdated, facilities included. Just a couple of wooden shacks with triple moons carved into the lady's door and a sun on the men's.

Elex was reaching for the latter when the Talon shoved him to the ground.

"You cheated," he snarled.

Zofi inched closer, longknife already in her hand.

"I only played the game, my lord. I showed you the cards."

"No drifter plays that well. Nobody in the Keep has beaten me in years."

"I'm sorry, my lord. I've always been skilled at cards—"

"You're a liar and a cheat, just like the rest of your filthy kind. My father should have killed you all years ago. He would've, if that bitch..."

Zofi didn't hear the rest. She was too busy dragging the knife across her skin. Plunging into the tithe, forcing the Arts into her blood.

"Please. You don't have to do this." Elex was drunk, but even drunk, his voice was steadier than the Talon's. It had to be. Travelers learned from day one how to placate those higher up the food chain. How to smile, thank them as they kicked you in the face, in the hopes that smile would stop them from doing anything worse...

"Oh, I know I don't have to. I want to." The Talon drew his sword. "One less Traveler will only better this world." He lifted the blade. Swung it.

Zofi drove her knife into his back.

He wore leather armor, like every Talon. Normally that would have deflected a simple knife attack. But not with Zofi's strength tithe granting her the power of ten men. The blade sliced through armor and ribs like butter, straight into his heart.

The Talon's sword clattered from his fingers. He collapsed at her feet.

She wrenched her knife free, an easy move with the Arts in

her bloodstream. Then she lifted Elex from the ground. Elex, her best friend. Elex, her heart, her soul. Elex, who almost died over a damned card game.

She expected relief. Thanks. Instead, he grabbed her shoulders, panic on his face. "Sands, Zofi, do you know what you've done?"

"Saved you," she whispered.

She didn't realize until afterward. Until Elex kicked the body over, faceup under the glow of the triple moons, then fished a coin out of his pocket. Held it up beside the face, so she could glance back and forth between.

Only then did she realize why the Talon had looked so familiar. She'd seen that face every day for years, ever since the king printed new silver pence coins in honor of his coronation.

She'd killed the Silver Prince.

While the tithe still lasted, Zofi picked up the body, carried him farther up the mountain. It wouldn't hide him for long, but it would buy them time.

"It will be okay," Elex murmured, after the tithe wore off, as he held her shaking hands under the freezing-cold glacial stream. Scrubbed at the blood. So much blood. More than she'd ever known a body could hold. "We'll figure this out."

She nodded. She didn't know what she was agreeing to. Didn't understand why he kissed her or whispered goodbye. She was too numb from shock, too concerned with the immediate panic of what do we do with this body to think about Elex leaving. Until she heard the shouts. Watched the remaining Talons chase a lone figure into the mountains, all of them tithing for speed. Only then did she realize that Elex had confessed to her crime. Drawn the Talons' attention so she could walk free.

She wanted to do the same now. Run like he did, flee to her band, and let the Kolonyans sort out their inheritance problems on their own. But now...

She glanced over her shoulder. People were still staring. She couldn't be sure whether it was for her Traveler looks or because they'd overheard her fight with Vidal.

Running suggests guilt, Vidal had said. He was right. Much as she wanted to, she couldn't run yet. Not without a horse, proper provisions, a plan of some kind. She glanced up at Ilian Keep, visible over the rooftops of the merchants' houses.

Who knew? Maybe the king was wrong. Maybe this Blood Ceremony tomorrow would prove they had no relation. Mother took many lovers. This could all be some terrible mistake.

If so, then she'd be free to walk out of here.

If not? *Play their game.*

Angry though she might be at Mother, that was the last piece of advice she'd given Zofi. Her one clue to surviving this mess. She doubted quitting the game entirely was what Mother was suggesting.

So, despite the crushing regret in her chest, she turned back toward the Keep. Back into the king's game. He might make the rules, but like Elex, Zofi had always been skilled at cards.

❈ 6 ❈

Florencia

"Why didn't you tell me?" Florencia leaned against the doorway of her mother's room—the upgraded version of the closet in which Florencia resided. These rooms were reserved for the older Keep staff, women who'd served their time as ladies' maids to the young and desperate court newcomers and had now settled in to caring for the older courtiers, who preferred their maids polite and just unattractive enough not to tempt any husbands.

Until this morning, it had been the life Ren looked forward to unless she managed to secure a marriage proposal. Every week for years, she'd visited this room and stared at its whitewashed walls, its lonely single bed and cheap plywood dresser. She'd sit in the single visitor's chair, sip tea from a cracked mug, and allow the panic to slowly drown her.

This was it. The best she could hope for.

Then came the king's summons. The announcement that turned her life upside down.

Mama, at least, did not pretend to misunderstand. "He told you the risks, surely."

Ren waved a dismissive hand. "Assassins, plots against him. Still doesn't explain why you couldn't warn me."

"And invoke the wrath of a king?" Mama raised her eyebrows.

"Who has your loyalty, the king or your own daughter?" Ren countered.

Mama laughed. "You see? This is exactly why I didn't tell you sooner." She patted the bed beside her. "You always see things in black-and-white. Them or me, with or against. There are a million shades of gray, Ren, especially when dealing with kings."

Ren hovered in the doorway a moment longer, intent on remaining angry, self-righteous. But she was exhausted. From the sleepless night with Sarella, to the news about Danton, and now this. It was too much.

She sank onto the bed next to Mama. "Explain it to me, then. How did you wind up in bed with a king?"

"I wasn't always this old and impossible to desire, you know," Mama replied, a laugh lingering on the corners of her mouth.

"You're still beautiful, Mama," Ren said. "That's not what I asked."

Mama's gaze drifted toward the window, and her expression turned wistful. "It took some doing, I'll tell you that. But the king was a handsome man in his day, and I was a determined young thing." Her eyes sharpened then, honed back in on Ren.

"I suppose it runs in the family. I imagine your pursuit of Ambassador Danton took similar effort."

Ren blinked, taken aback. Mama had never mentioned Danton before. Had never even hinted at having an inkling of their relationship. "How long have you known?"

Mama's smile turned indulgent. "From the start, I'd wager. Don't mistake me, I'm not displeased. The ambassador is a powerful ally. That connection will help you in the future."

Destroy me, more like. But she relaxed a little. Mama only knew about their liaisons, then. Not what those liaisons led to. Ren refused to involve her mother in that mess. It was too dangerous to share with anyone, even family.

"So you cared for the king. That's why you lied to me? For him?"

Mama sighed. "The king kept me employed. Normally an unwed mother would be dismissed from the Keep—he overrode that."

"Seems like the very least he could do," Ren mumbled.

"And yet, he could have done less. Could have thrown me out, could have let you fall to the wolves. He did not, because he cares for his family. For you. Keeping you here but ignorant of your past was his way of ensuring your safety, Ren."

"Keeping me in the servants' quarters, you mean."

"Have you met his other children?" Mama replied.

Ren blinked. Somehow, in her anger about this secret, she'd forgotten the other two. *My half sisters.* She dismissed that thought. "A slow-on-the-uptake Traveler girl and some quiet Easterner. What about them?"

"Think about their lives. Andros left the Traveler out in the wild, to spend years of her childhood on the run."

Andros. Of all the surreal experiences she'd suffered today, the greatest was hearing her mother casually drop the king's name.

"And the poor Eastern child." Mama shivered. "Living on a warfront. I hear her mother died young. Andros held a little service for her here in the Keep—pretended it was because of her position, some Eastern branch of nobility. But his mourning was real. He cared for all of us, in his own way. Now imagine that girl's life—childhood without a mother, war on your doorstep, that horrid sea air.... Imagine it, and then tell me you got the sorest lot."

"She didn't spend her youth scrubbing ladies' bare arses," Ren muttered, though her tone began to soften. What *was* that like for Akeylah? Or Zofi, for that matter, growing up on the move?

"No, and none of them learned a Sun-cursed thing about life in court either," Mama was saying. "They're strangers to Kolonya City, to the Keep, to this life. You've spent your whole life learning."

"I could have learned just as much being a *member* of the court instead of serving it."

Mama clicked her tongue, a habit she had whenever Ren missed something Mama considered obvious. "What do I always tell you? 'The sunbeam illuminates the room...'"

"'But it blinds you, too,'" Ren continued wearily. "Mama, I know Ledero."

"Yet you seem to have forgotten the whole point of his passage. 'If you keep your eyes shadowed, you can see everything—darkness and light alike.' He was talking about the relationship of the underling to the master. The reason that servants often know more about the nobility than nobles know about themselves."

"And Ledero was the most brilliant philosopher ever to cook chicken for King Ulley. But he still spent his life in the kitchens."

"His son didn't. He raised his son with the knowledge of what drives nobles and servants, how to manipulate both. That son rose to become advisor to the king. Now Ledero's great-grandchild is one of the most powerful men in the Reaches."

"I know, Mama."

"Then perhaps I'm the one who is confused. Because it sounded to me like you'd forgotten all about it a few moments ago when you were ranting about how I made you work for no reason."

Ren groaned. Mama always did this. Won arguments. "Still. You could have told me who I was and explained why you wanted me to continue working as a maid."

"Would you have worked just as hard? Does a soldier learn to fight in practice or in war?"

Ren quirked a smile. "So you say I shouldn't be angry, then you compare working as a maid to fighting a war?"

To her surprise, Mama caught Ren's hands in hers, expression dead serious. "It was the fire you needed to walk through in order to truly appreciate the inferno you face now."

"Mama..." Her voice softened. For all they might argue, her mother had taught her everything she knew. How to collect advantages, who to pit against who. She never would have made it this far without her.

Mama squeezed so tight Ren's fingers ached. "You think you understand court politics, Ren, but you've only just begun to learn. Once you see what these nobles are really like, once you understand the depths to which they will sink for power... then you'll understand why I raised you like this. Why Andros and I tried to protect you."

She swallowed around a sudden lump in her throat. However Ren had felt about her life up until now, she owed Mama so much more than she realized. Mama and the king alike.

"Thank you," Ren murmured. "For doing that. Protecting me, raising me."

Mama rolled her eyes and grinned. "Please." In that moment, Ren glimpsed another person. The young, beautiful serving girl whose smile caught the eye of a king. "The moment I had you, Ren, I stopped caring a whit about anything else. You are my world. I'd do anything for you."

Ren tightened her grip on her mother's hands. "You've done enough, Mama. You taught me everything I know. How to succeed." She thought about the king's words—*Kolonya needs you*—and Yasmin's—*Kolonya needs one of you in particular.* "It's my turn now."

She would be that one. She would earn this throne. For herself and for Mama.

The king sent a message inviting Ren to her new rooms in the ash tower. Josen caused another bevy of shrieks delivering that message in the maids' chambers.

Ren was still standing in her narrow cubby of a room, debating how best to consolidate her few possessions, when she heard the other maids squeal once more. She sighed and flung the door open.

"What does His Glorious Majesty request now, Josen?" Ren stepped into the common area, then froze.

"I hoped I might request an audience, Lady Florencia."

Danton cut as dashing a figure as ever, damn him. Knife-sharp cheekbones, icy Eastern blue eyes, dark auburn hair now long enough to skim the corners of his ever-present smirk.

Lady Florencia. He knew she'd moved up in the world. But did he know why?

The maids' eyes darted back and forth between them, full of interest. Ren hadn't explained Josen's summons—she'd answered the flood of questions that followed his announcement with nothing more than a demure smile. King Andros hadn't yet declared her. He'd asked her to wait until the Blood Ceremony tomorrow night confirmed their relation publicly before telling anyone in the Keep who she really was.

She wasn't about to let Danton ruin all her careful dodging.

"I'm afraid it's quite improper of you to be in these chambers." Ren cast a slow, pointed look around the room. Most of the maids were dressed at least, and none looked too eager to let Danton leave, to judge by the way they ogled him.

All but Audrina, who had risen from her chair, a darning needle clutched in her fist as though ready to stab the ambassador.

Relax, Ren mouthed to Aud.

"My apologies." Danton swept into an exaggerated bow. "You know me—I hate to cause trouble." His grin widened. If he did know the reason behind her rise in station, he wasn't letting on.

"Get out, Danton."

A couple of maids gasped. That was exceedingly improper for a lady's maid to say to a court nobleman, let alone one as important as the ambassador to the Eastern Reach. But Ren was no longer one of them. She stood on equal footing to Danton now—higher, by some measurements.

"I will attend you at a more opportune time, Lady Florencia." With that, Danton bowed and slipped out. All the air in the room seemed to follow.

"Ren." Audrina was at her side, a hand on her elbow. "What in Sun's name is going on? First the new chambers, now that rat of an Easterner chasing you ..."

Ren couldn't stomach her friend's questions or her defensive anger at Danton right now. "I'll explain later," Ren blurted as she whirled and tugged open the door to her tiny little maid's room— the room she'd spent years confined inside. The room she was about to leave behind for good.

Only when she'd shut the flimsy bamboo door behind her did she let her expression crumple into anger.

He must have returned this very afternoon. And this was the first place he'd come? Maybe he'd learned exactly how high she'd risen. Maybe he was having second thoughts about abandoning her so callously.

Damn him.

Unfortunately, the thin door couldn't shut out the flood of memories that struck her now, brought on by the sight of his face, the sound of his voice.

"I need a favor," he whispered in the midnight privacy of the hidden cave, buried deep beneath the foundation of the Keep. His chambers weren't a safe place to meet—the king posted eyes all over the Keep, but especially in the ambassadors' rooms. Kolonya called the other Reaches family, put on a great show of affection.

But behind closed doors, the royals still worried that someday, one of those Reaches might begin to remember a time, centuries ago, when they stood on their own.

King Andros was right to worry.

So Danton met Ren in the cave, a location she discovered by accident far beneath the towers, even lower than the dungeons. Built by some long-dead king, it consisted of a quiet rock pond and trickling waterfall, lit by algae that shone blue-green as it digested.

In between trysts, they'd lie on the shore of the pond, limbs entangled, and talk of change. Of a future when Ren would rise in station, when Danton would advance the Easterners' causes, when things would improve for them both.

When they might no longer need to hide, if only...

If, if, if.

So when he begged a favor there, in their secret spot, reserved for confessions they couldn't voice in the real world, she replied, "Anything."

Stupid girl.

She knew about the rebellion. Knew, too, that Danton was sympathetic to the rebels' cause, if not their methods. He told her about the villages he'd seen burned; the fields that lay barren because every able-bodied member of the family who owned it had died at sea.

And she'd heard enough horror stories elsewhere to imagine the atrocities the Genalese invaders wrought when they invaded the Eastern villages. Men torn limb from limb, women beheaded, babies bludgeoned. All in the name of conquest. All because Genal believed they still owned the Reaches, were still due a profit off everything the Reaches produced.

She sympathized, even though she hadn't been there to witness firsthand.

She sympathized, too, when Danton cast a dark eye on the frippery at court. The king's lavish wedding to a daughter of said Genalese invaders. The turn-of-the-month festivals, which used to be quiet religious affairs and had exploded into monthly revels. Kolonya spent more money on celebrations this year than ever before, in the name of "lifting spirits" after the war.

Never mind that the Easterners were struggling to put food on their tables. Never mind that all the feasts took place in Kolonya City, for Kolonyans, not the Easterners who died to protect them from Genal.

So yes, Ren sympathized.

Danton preyed on that.

He studied her for a long, fraught moment. "You're still friendly with Josen, yes?"

Her brows knit. The king's errand boy? "I am." She'd done more than a few favors for Josen as he established himself at the Keep. He owed her.

Danton brushed a hair from her forehead. "I need access to the king's study."

Ren stared.

They'd traded secrets before. Gossip, courtly advantages. This was different. He was asking for far more than rumors.

"It's life or death, Florencia." She'd always hated her full name, except when he said it. The way it rolled off his tongue, accented by his broad Eastern vowels, it sounded right. Regal. "I know you don't agree with some things the rebels have done—"

"They attacked a contingent of Talons," Ren hissed.

"In self-defense," Danton countered. "The Talons were dragging innocent people from their homes, beating anyone they suspected of being a rebel, no matter how little proof they had. You know what would have happened if the rebellion let the Talons bring the people they arrested back to Kolonya."

Ren grimaced. She'd heard about the two rebel leaders King Andros managed to capture. They'd been tried and condemned by the regional council. One was executed, the other imprisoned for life in the dungeons below the alder tower.

"I don't condone violence," she said.

"There won't be any," he swore. "Not if you help me. The king deployed a fleet to Davenforth, a south port town where most of the rebellion has holed up. His men have been ordered to burn the entire town for collaboration." Danton caught her shoulders, gripped so hard, Ren gasped. She'd never seen him this desperate.

"Danton..."

"Thousands will die, Florencia. Unless we act. I just need to know when the fleet plans to anchor and where. If I can get that information, we can smuggle everyone out of town before the attack. Nobody needs to get hurt."

He had tears in his eyes. Danton, her Danton, the strongest man she knew.

She couldn't bear watching him suffer. If those rebels were killed, she knew part of him would die alongside them.

So she took him. Sun help her. She asked Josen to help carry one of her charges to bed after a particularly rough evening, and nicked the keys from his belt while he was occupied with the lady. Then she stood watch outside the study while Danton slipped in. Returned the keys less than an hour later, pretending she'd found them on her charge's floor after Josen left. Josen thanked her, face white in shock at having misplaced the keys, and she remembered the first kernels of guilt taking root in her gut.

She made excuses. Danton was her ally, her lover, her best chance. She helped him in the hopes of securing a marriage proposal, an advancement in life. That was what she told herself by way of meager reassurance.

The truth was more humiliating.

The truth was, she trusted Danton.

Trusted an Eastern rebel. With more than just her heart—she trusted him with all of Kolonya.

The next morning, court buzzed with rumors of Danton's sudden departure. He'd summoned his servants at the crack of dawn, sent a hasty excuse to the king, and bolted. People assumed it was an affair gone wrong. In a way, it was.

He didn't even say goodbye.

Ren cried that morning. For herself, for her broken heart. Even then, she did not truly understand. She still assumed he was a good person, even if he did not care for her.

Until the news broke.

The Kolonyan fleet had docked at Davenforth in the Eastern Reach, just as he said. Ostensibly, they were there to keep the peace. In truth, they carried a full military contingent—thousands of sailors, foot soldiers, and Talons. 1,854 of those soldiers did not return.

Ren knew the exact number. Had memorized it since. Chanted it to herself every night for weeks as she tried and failed to sleep.

The fleet anchored at night. They had men standing watch, but if they expected to see any opposition at all, it was from ships their own size. They didn't spot the sleek little fishermen's vessels, hulls *painted black, sailing on dark waters after all three moons set. Not until those boats collided with the Kolonyan hulls, loaded with gunpowder. Not until the calm night erupted in flames and screams.*

Seven flagships sank, the majority of what remained of Kolonya's larger navy ships after the war.

In all, 1,854 Kolonyans drowned in what people had since named the Burnt Bay. Innocent men and women. Strong, loyal soldiers.

"They knew we were coming. They knew exactly how many we were, where we'd anchor, when we'd arrive." That's what everyone said in the days after. That was the puzzle nobody could work out. How did Eastern rebels living halfway across the continent learn the king's plans?

Nobody could guess.

Nobody but Ren. Ren learned the hard way exactly what sort of charming, handsome rogue could romance his way into such news.

Nobody needs to get hurt, he had said. Apparently "nobody" only referred to his people, not hers. He told her thousands would die unless she acted, but apparently the death of almost two thousand Kolonyans wasn't worth preventing.

This was her fault.

When she felt steady enough, she gathered everything she owned into one large armful. She shouldered her door open and marched into the common chamber. Dumped it all on the central bench, every last dress and undergarment and trinket.

"If you want something, take it," she told the startled maids. Then she climbed the stairs to the ash tower empty-handed.

The Sun had granted her a fresh start. This time, she would not make any mistakes.

·◦⫶ 7 ⫶◦·

Akeylah

Towering high above the streets of Kolonya City, the sky gardens reminded Akeylah of the stories about the Blessed Sunlands: the afterlife for those deemed worthy, the good and innocent people of the world.

Knowing her own sins, this was likely the closest Akeylah would ever get.

The gardens were filled with Syx flowers and Nox blooms, creeping vines and parrot lilies and every kind of night-bud imaginable. Above, the sky seemed close enough to touch, doused in starlight. Nox had already set, and eclipsed Essex was a huge black circle in the sky, Syx its bright-lit counterpart. The only moon tonight, as Syxmonth began. Tonight, just a day after her world collapsed, the king would hold the Blood Ceremony. The setting for her formal introduction to court.

Adults dressed as brightly as flowers chatted near the fountain ponds. Servers wove through the throng with platters of spicy peppers, rice balls cupped in banana leaves, and tall glasses of sparkling nectar liquor. Children in fabulously expensive clothes played among the carefully cultivated gardens.

She felt a fleeting pang of regret. Her maids had returned that morning and again that afternoon. Tried desperately to talk her into letting them dress her. She refused, again and again. Bathed herself alone in the dark, late last night when she could be certain nobody would disturb her. She wore her same dress, because she'd seen the gauzy fabric of these noble gowns, and she couldn't be certain it would conceal the scar that pulsed on her thigh.

But she stood out just as much now, if not more, dressed as she was. Her black long-sleeved gown with its high white collar drew stares and stifled laughter. Someone stumbled against her, apologized, then did a double take. Akeylah forced a smile in response.

She couldn't breathe. Not only here in this crush of people, but everywhere, ever since yesterday morning. Ever since she learned what she'd done.

She wondered if the royal menders suspected the king's sudden illness of being Arts-induced. Surely they must be on edge after the Silver Prince's murder, even though, as far as she knew, it had been almost a century since anyone had been arrested for dabbling in the Vulgar Arts. Knowledge of how to do it was difficult to come by in the first place—tithing into someone else's blood wasn't as simple or instinctual as a normal tithe. And very few people dared pursue the knowledge with such a swift and certain punishment attached. Immediate execution. No exceptions.

As for the rest of the court, Akeylah had overheard a few

rumors. So far people seemed only to think the king was tired, overworking himself. How long could Andros maintain that cover? How long before people realized it was something worse?

Akeylah seemed to be the only one who noticed Yasmin hovering at her brother's elbow like a concerned shadow. No one commented either on the menders in their drab brown uniforms, who lurked at the edge of the party, attention fixed on the king, should their assistance be required.

Instead, the room buzzed with talk of tonight's feast. The turn-of-the-month feast was always a grand celebration, but tonight, the nobles said, the king had outdone himself. They suspected an announcement, though their guesses ran the gamut from confirmation of the king's new Genalese wife's pregnancy to whispers that that same wife had been jailed for war crimes.

"You really believe King Andros would announce his wife's betrayal at a *feast*?" a woman at Akeylah's elbow scoffed.

"Well, nobody has seen her in a week," the other woman countered, defensive. "She's either pregnant or locked up, I'm telling you."

"If it was war again, we'd have heard before now. My husband is a captain—"

Akeylah walked past, distracted. Voices drifted in and out of range, blending together until they sounded like waves crashing on shore, indistinguishable.

All she could focus on was King Andros. She watched him accept a glass of nectar liquor. He passed it from hand to hand, chatting with a noble, before he set it on a passing server's tray without taking a sip.

He wasn't eating or drinking. Probably couldn't, given the side effects of the wasting sickness she'd cursed him with.

Her stomach churned.

She may not agree with the king throwing feasts here while her people sweated blood to rebuild their war-torn shores. But she would only wish this kind of pain upon her worst enemy—upon the father she thought she cursed in the first place.

King Andros did not deserve this.

"Rayeh!" A young nobleman elbowed Akeylah. Then he startled. "Oh. I apologize—you look like my Eastern friend. Rayeh dam-Roken. Do you know her?"

Akeylah forced her mind to the present. *Seas below, Akeylah, you must act normal.* She managed a smile. "I do not, I'm afraid."

He asked something else, but the rush in her ears was too much. She babbled a cursory farewell and bolted.

A winding trail caught her eye. It led through dangling fronds of veil trees, away from the central square. On the other side, she found ivory stonewood parapets lining the fringes of the gardens.

The sky gardens spanned the entire rooftop of Ilian Keep, the highest point in the city. A few couples leaned along the parapets, but they were too entranced with each other to notice the Eastern girl step up to a neighboring ledge.

The entirety of Kolonya City lay at her feet. In the moonlit night, it seemed a reflection of the sky itself—pinpricks of candlelit windows in a sea of darkness.

Akeylah scratched at her high, stiff collar. *This blasted dress.* Surely she could have asked her maids to bring a dark silk gown instead. Asked them to leave it on the bed, dressed herself later. Why hadn't she thought of that?

She was too distracted by worry. She pressed one hand over her scar. It didn't hurt. The wound healed surprisingly fast, considering how deep a cut it had been. But the color, the faint glow of it, that would last her lifetime. A constant reminder of her mistake.

How long until someone found it? How long before this caught up with her?

She tugged at the collar again, too roughly. The white lace split in her fingers. Curse it. Curse everything.

Akeylah ripped the collar free and let it drop over the edge. The stark white lace stood out against the dark cityscape as it fell, a wounded bird spiraling into the abyss.

"It *was* an unfortunate collar," someone murmured, "but I don't know that it deserved that level of abuse."

Akeylah jumped. The girl laughed as she stepped up to the parapet. The fabric of her loose chiffon dress brushed Akeylah's arm, she stood so close. "I'm sorry. I didn't mean to startle you."

The girl—barely older than Akeylah herself—had a beautiful deep bronze complexion and chestnut curls piled high atop her head, woven with gemstones. Not Kolonyan, not exactly. Her hair was too wavy, had too much texture. Not to mention her curvy body and her full, lush mouth. Southern, perhaps?

"That's all right," Akeylah replied. "You didn't."

"How refreshing. A bad liar. We don't see many of those here at court." Her eyes caught the distant lamplight, deep blue as the sky above.

"I didn't mean to be dishonest. I only meant that you didn't— you needn't..." She stuttered to a halt. "Yes, you startled me," she tried again. "But it's not a problem."

The girl smiled, so open and bright that Akeylah had to catch her breath.

Oh.

"Yes, I can see you have worse problems to contend with." The girl glanced at Akeylah's torn neckline. "I'm not sure that's reparable. But you know, if you tuck it…" She reached up to fold the fabric, the backs of her fingertips brushing Akeylah's collarbone.

"How does it look?" Her voice came out low and breathy.

"Not great." She flashed Akeylah a conspiratorial grin. "But I think it'll pass for the evening." She left her hand resting on the dress for an instant longer. Her touch radiated cool through the fabric, reassuring. "You should call down to the tailors tomorrow," she said. "Have a new dress made." Her gaze dropped. "Perhaps one without the collar that offended you so."

Akeylah's mouth twisted in a wry smile. "One that fits in better here, you mean?" She wondered if the girl felt her heartbeat, pounding like the surf. *Her lips look so soft…*

The girl's hand dropped. "Don't trouble yourself about what I think. Dress for yourself. That's important for people like us to remember."

"Like us?" Akeylah echoed.

"Anyone who looks, shall we say, not strictly Kolonyan." The girl's mouth turned up at the corners and Akeylah tried not to watch it too closely. "When you try to dress like them, act like them, speak like them, they notice. They mark your difference and decide it's a fault. But if you remain your own person, wear your difference with pride, their perception changes." She gestured at herself. Unlike most other noblewomen, she didn't wear an ostentatious gown. Just a simple blue sheath. It did not cling to her every curve, but hung loose, hinting at long legs yet revealing nothing. "Suddenly you are unique. Desirable, rather than flawed."

That dress certainly did make her stand out.

Well. The dress and her strong features and jawline, plump lips, unusual dark blue eyes. All considered negative characteristics in Kolonya, and yet, she was breathtaking.

Akeylah understood. "Thank you for the advice." She glanced at her torn gown once more. "Mother Ocean knows I could use all the help I can get."

The girl tilted a little closer, and Akeylah could have sworn the space between them electrified. Her fingertips itched to reach out, close that gap. Brush the girl's arm, just to feel the cool sensation of her skin once more.

"I don't know about that." The girl leaned back to assess her in a cool, sweeping glance. "Dress mishap aside, you look every inch as noble as anyone here."

Akeylah forced herself to turn away, face out over the parapet to avoid doing anything unwise. "I see we're both bad liars," Akeylah commented, though she smiled as she said it.

Beside her, the girl leaned against the wall and threw her head back. "That was a compliment, not a lie. You'd best learn the difference quickly here."

"My apologies. I'm not used to sincerity. You'll have to warn me next time."

The girl laughed just once, softly, yet Akeylah's heart stuttered in its cage. *Seas below*, that was a dangerous sound. Addictive. Already Akeylah longed to find a way to make her laugh again. "No one has ever accused me of being too sincere before." The girl's fingertips danced across the parapet in a restless jig.

Akeylah watched her from the corner of her eye. "Are you normally not?"

The girl's gaze flickered to her. Lingered for a moment on Akeylah's auburn hair, done up tonight in plaits wound around her head, the only way she'd known to do hair for an event like this. Turned out that, like so many other things she took for granted, this hairstyle was a purely Eastern one. Just another reason to garner stares.

"Not here," the girl finally admitted. "Not with someone I just met. You have to keep your guard up in this court." She shook her head. "But where are my manners? Here I am boring you with warnings and I haven't even introduced myself." She extended a hand, palm up. The traditional Kolonyan greeting. "Rozalind."

"Believe me, any warnings you'd care to bestow are more than welcome." Akeylah placed her palm on top of Rozalind's. Let her fingertips curl around the other girl's wrist, and marveled how cool Rozalind's skin was, even in this jungle heat. "Akeylah."

"Beautiful. Eastern, no?"

"It is. I mean...I am." *Stop stuttering.* "I've only just arrived."

Rozalind released her grip to lean one elbow against the parapet. Casual, careless. Flawless. "I must admit I guessed that." She smiled again, her lips a perfect seashell curve. "Well, Lady Akeylah. Now it's your turn."

Akeylah blinked. "Beg pardon?"

"I lectured you first. Now you go." She held Akeylah's gaze. "Teach me something."

Suddenly, Akeylah felt far too aware of her body. *How do I usually position my hands?* Flustered, she shifted to stare out over the city instead. "Oh, I don't know anything of worth."

"Tell me about the Eastern Reach. I've never been, but I hear it's beautiful."

She sighed. "It was, once."

A quick glance showed Rozalind studying the city now, too, her brow knit. "The war?"

"It touched all the Reaches, I'm sure," Akeylah murmured. "But it hit the Eastern hardest. The nearest village to my home, it's…" She pressed her lips together. "The buildings left standing are in dire need of repairs. And the harbor is worse, the boardwalk naught but kindling now."

"Was your home harmed?"

"Unfortunately not," she replied, thinking only of her father—or the man who raised her, anyway. It would have served Jahen right.

Then she winced. *Damn.* Why did Rozalind make her so relaxed? Their conversation felt so natural, she forgot where she was. In Kolonya City, surrounded by nobles who, as Rozalind herself had only just warned, were not the trustworthy sort. "I—I only meant that, my family, we…would have been better positioned than most in our village to rebuild, had the need arisen. If we could have taken some of the blows instead of them…"

Rozalind tilted her head forward, mouth a quirked comma of disbelief. "I understand. I've often wished my own family would shoulder more of the consequences of our actions."

Unable to resist, Akeylah looked at her again. Something about the hard glint in Rozalind's dark eyes made Akeylah think there was a longer story there than she was willing to tell just yet.

"I don't fit in here," Akeylah blurted.

"No, you don't." Rozalind's eyes bored into hers. *Seas.* That gaze tore at Akeylah like the tide, drew on something deep and irresistible within her. "But your mistake lies in thinking that's a bad thing."

A gong rang in the distance, followed by a loud, measured speech. They were too far away to hear the words, yet Rozalind was already walking backward away from the parapet. "That's the start of the king's announcement," she said. "We should go."

Akeylah gathered her skirts, made to join Rozalind, but the woman was curtsying deeply in farewell.

"It was a pleasure meeting you, Akeylah dam-Senzin."

Akeylah never told her her last name.

For a moment, she watched Rozalind weave through the trees toward the distant courtyard. *What did the girl know?* She must have overheard rumors of a new arrival at court and discovered her surname somehow. Surely she didn't know more than that, wasn't aware of Akeylah's position yet. King Andros hadn't announced it.

Still, as she trailed after Rozalind, joined by a few other stragglers—the lovers on the neighboring parapets—she could not help but feel a sense of foreboding. After an evening of being gawked at, the last thing she wanted to do just now was stand on display before a mob of courtiers.

But it was the least she could do for the king. She owed her true father a debt she could never repay. She reached the central square, pressed through the mob toward the dais. She spotted Florencia and Zofi already on the steps below the throne, and her heart began to speed up, panic setting in at the thought of standing up there before so many people.

Think of something else.

Rozalind. Just the memory of her voice soothed Akeylah's nerves, allowed her to lift her chin and smile.

A storm would follow this announcement. The king, his sister, his advisors, the whole kingdom would judge every move she made from now on. She wouldn't be able to blink without someone noticing. But if she had someone like Rozalind on her side, a courtier to advise her, someone experienced... perhaps she could handle this challenge.

Then she reached the platform, took her place beside her sisters, and glanced up at the top of the dais.

At that moment, every ounce of calm she'd managed to find fled.

King Andros had risen to address the crowd. But her eyes weren't on him. They drifted past him, past Yasmin hovering at his elbow, to the throne immediately next to the king's. Horror bloomed in Akeylah's chest. Spread through her limbs like slow poison. Because there sat Rozalind, in a seat of honor. In the place reserved for... Akeylah couldn't breathe.

"Thank you all for joining us tonight," Andros was saying. "Queen Rozalind and I are happy to welcome you all."

Rozalind caught her eye. For the briefest instant, the corner of her mouth lifted. A secret smile, just for Akeylah.

People like us.

Anyone not strictly Kolonyan.

Nothing in her life could be simple, could it? She had to choose the worst possible woman in the world to ignite her. The wayward daughter of Genal. A descendant of the country's worst enemy, sent to end this war once and for all.

The Queen of Kolonya.

Her dying father's new wife.

✢ 8 ✢

Zofi

It took every ounce of Zofi's patience not to scowl. How much longer would they need to stand on this damned stage? She felt like a showhorse on an auction block. Not to mention the getup her maids had forced her into. She'd refused a gown flat-out, but they'd still insisted upon silk trousers, a loose blouse that scratched at the collar, even a tie for her wild curls.

She drew the line at slippers. If she was going to stand before the whole world and admit to being the king's blood, she'd do it with her boots on, thank you very much.

The blouse itched.

The king was still babbling about the glories of Kolonya. Not only "the benefits they offered to all the Reaches"—which she assumed meant the right to die in battle for your king, then pay him extra taxes so he could celebrate victory on your dime—but also Kolonya's unparalleled strength.

"United, we are the strongest force in all the world," King Andros declared. "No foe can stand against us when the Reaches act in unison."

That, at least, made Zofi's ears perk. She must be wrong, though. Because it almost sounded as if Andros were admitting Kolonya was not all-powerful. That Kolonya actually *needed* the other Reaches.

Which was true, of course. But it generally wasn't the type of thing the king went around admitting in public.

Something has changed.

Then she scolded herself. Of course it had. A dozen *some-things* had changed. The Seventh War ended, and for the first time in history, Genal offered a princess from their own family to wed King Andros. A lot of people had whispered that this meant the first honest attempt at lasting peace, for good.

Then Burnt Bay happened, Kolonya's ships all sank, and *someone* murdered the Silver Prince. The latter set off a whole new set of rumors, since most people believed—erroneously, of course—that a Traveler would only kill a man like Prince Nicolen for money. People whispered that Genal had paid his assassin and sent Queen Rozalind to lure Kolonya into a false sense of peace.

And people didn't even know the king was sick yet. Or at least, not *how* sick.

Zofi almost felt bad for Andros.

Almost.

Not that she regretted killing Nicolen—she'd do it a hundred times over if it meant saving Elex. But she understood now how much uncertainty she'd cost the realm in doing so. People were antsy enough after Burnt Bay. When the prince died, she could only imagine the panic that must have swept Kolonya City's streets.

Internally, she kicked herself. Who cared? These were the people who exploited every other Reach out here just so they could host galas like this one. If she'd made their grip on the throne of this continent a little more tenuous, well, *good*.

Except that throne might be yours to handle now.

Zofi scowled. All the more reason to hate Andros. For putting her in this position in the first place. One of three potential heirs to a kingdom she'd rather see collapse.

Someone dug an elbow into her side. Florencia. She narrowed her eyes at Zofi and mouthed, *Smile.*

Zofi realized she'd been glowering. Now she continued doing it on principle.

Florencia rolled her eyes and faced front again. The Kolonyan native fit right in here. She posed on this pedestal like she'd been born upon it, her dress every inch as frilly, expensive, and impractical as the rest of the noblewomen's. How could anyone fight in those heels?

Then there was the Easterner. Her dress looked slightly more practical, loose enough that she could move in it at least. Though it didn't seem very sturdy—the top was frayed and torn. Unlike Florencia, Akeylah seemed nervous. She tried to disguise it, but her pupils were globe-fruit-wide and her hands trembled.

Perhaps she was stage-shy. There were quite a lot of people staring at them right now. Zofi stared back. Had any of these

soft-handed, delicate men and women ridden across the Northern deserts or scaled the Dawn Mountains in search of food?

Had any of them ever been without food for a minute in their
lives?

Finally, the king reached his point. "These young ladies may
be unfamiliar to you," he said, "but they are as familiar to me as
the blood in my veins. I am proud to present them to this court,
an event that has been long since overdue."

The entire rooftop paused, breaths held. Zofi prayed for a
sudden thunderstorm to drench them all. Perhaps a well-placed
bolt of lightning to spare her the misery that would follow this
announcement.

"I would like to introduce my daughters."

The whole court exhaled at once. Most of the more comically
startled expressions, she noticed, were pointed at either her or
Akeylah. Typical for Kolonyans.

"As is custom, each of my children will offer up a proof of
her lineage." The king beckoned. An acolyte of the Blood Arts
stepped up to the platform with a silver bowl, engraved almost as
elaborately as the doors in the Great Hall. The king rolled up his
sleeve, and with a single, practiced prick of a needle-thin blade,
added a droplet of blood to the bowl.

"Lady D'Andros Zofi, step forward and make your proof."

That would be her name now. With a polished title and her
father's forename tacked on Kolonyan-style. It grated almost as
badly as the courtiers' stares.

The whispers doubled as she strode forward. She caught more
than a few people making warding signs in the air, or outright

scowling. *I know the feeling,* she wanted to say. *I'd rather not be related to him either.*

And another thought, hard on its heels. *Mother, why didn't you tell me?*

When most Traveler women decided they wanted a child, they bedded a strong, handsome stranger. Normally they never even learned the father's name, let alone informed him of his new child. A relative who doesn't know you exist is an innocuous one. One who can never harm you.

Travelers were more superstitious than most about the Vulgar Arts, because, rare as those perversions of the Arts were now, the older Travelers were some of the few people in the Reaches who had seen them performed. Stay on the road long enough, and you'll see just about everything—including the darker half of human nature.

Besides, what did Zofi need a blood father for? She had a dozen fathers, the older men in her band, who taught her how to tithe, how to create the Travelers' secret glass phials to store tithes for later use, how to do a million and one useful things.

She never asked for this. This whole new family, these new responsibilities.

Maybe it's all some terrible mistake.

But even as Zofi climbed the last step to stand beside the king, she knew that was a false hope. She could see the resemblance— the sharp chin and knife-blade cheekbones they shared. More than that, she felt it in her veins.

Sands curse them both. Mother and Father alike, who conspired to trap her here.

Zofi held out her arm to the acolyte. He rolled up her sleeve in one deft move. The blade pierced the crook of her elbow. She watched the drop of blood fall in slow motion.

Her veins itched. The Arts sparkled in the air, tempting. One shift in her perception and she could tithe now, let the Arts spill into her bloodstream. Maybe tithe herself for speed and race off this dais.

Zofi resisted.

The silver bowl rang faintly, as if someone were running a damp finger along the edge. When she looked inside, her blood wriggled across the basin in looping, serpentine arcs. It joined with the drop of her father's, and the whole bowl lit up a brilliant, blinding white. The ringing grew louder, piercing.

"Blood calls to blood," the acolyte announced, and King Andros summoned Florencia next. Zofi stepped aside and waited beside the dais while the other girls gave their offerings. Each time, the bowl glowed and sang. After Florencia's, the crowd cheered. Only then did Zofi realize they'd been silent for hers.

When the bowl sang for Akeylah, only a few people clapped halfheartedly. *Guess Easterners are almost as bad as Travelers.*

Then that was it. The deed was done. Every noble on this rooftop knew her now. Knew that Andros's blood ran in her veins. Knew that, for better or worse, he claimed her as family.

She wondered distantly how much money her head would garner a Genalese assassin or an Eastern rebel. Their enemies didn't know Andros was sick yet. Maybe they'd take it into their heads to run off with his new daughter, torture her into cursing him. Zofi wondered how much pain it would take to make her use the Vulgar Arts against Andros.

At this rate, not much. But she doubted anyone willing to

bleed a girl dry to curse a king would have qualms about slitting that girl's throat after the deed was done.

Despite the open air of the sky gardens, Zofi felt claustrophobic, as though the walls of the Keep were pressing in on her. There were so many powerful nobles here to witness this ceremony. So many people who knew now she was a king's daughter.

If she ran, fled home to her band, she'd be at risk from any of the kingdom's enemies. They all would be.

"My daughters are here to complete their educations, to immerse themselves in studying the governance of Kolonya and our way of life," the king was saying. "I trust you will welcome them to the court as warmly as I have welcomed you to my home. After all, one of them will someday follow me onto the Sun Throne."

The courtiers cheered and whistled. A flock of macaws burst from the gardens, released to perform a choreographed dance in celebration, as sparks flared from torches planted along the edges of the dance floor.

All Zofi could think about was where her band must be now.

If she closed her eyes, she could picture them around the nightly campfire, swapping stories and an after-dinner jug of spiced tea. She could see herself seated there, elbow to elbow with Elex, teasing him about his latest hairdo disaster.

That was real. That was her life.

This was some twisted nightmare.

"Do try not to fall asleep on the podium," Florencia hissed in her ear.

"What's it to you?" Zofi scowled.

"We've only just discovered our happy family," she replied,

tone dry as the sands. "I'd rather not be embarrassed by it already. Though Sun knows you're doing a good enough job in that getup."

"At least I can move. You look like a lobster trussed up for the cooking pot."

Akeylah laughed, a sudden, startled sound that made both Zofi and Florencia stare. The Easterner's eyes widened even further, if possible, and her smile vanished.

"You're one to talk." Florencia gestured at Akeylah's gown. "The two of you had best learn to put on a better display. Sun forsake me if I let you drag our new name into the mud."

Zofi scoffed. "*Our* name? You can bloody well keep it. I never asked for it." From the corner of her eye, she noticed courtiers turning their way. She lowered her voice. "I never asked for any of this."

"None of us did," Florencia replied. "But when life hands you a gift on a golden platter, you'd be mad to reject it."

"You call this a gift? Being trapped here, forced to stay in one location, stuck living like..." She gestured wildly at the nobles eating and drinking themselves silly, spilling nectar on their expensive gowns and sneering at anyone who looked different. "This?"

"Life could be much worse," Akeylah spoke up suddenly. Her voice held an edge to it that Zofi hadn't heard from her before.

"A gilded cage is still a cage." Zofi's fingertips danced toward the space on her hip where her longknife would normally hang, a nervous habit.

Florencia shrugged. "If you think this is a cage, then you're even more unimaginative than I thought. But fine. Run away. Me, I plan to use this gift to make a real difference in the world."

Zofi snorted. "How will you make a difference, sitting on rooftops eating cake?"

"You aren't looking underneath the surface. I guarantee you a dozen deals are being made right now—trade agreements, alliances between Reaches that deter violence...." Florencia's voice caught for a moment. Zofi eyed her curiously, but she cleared her throat. "Events like this *look* frivolous. But this is where change happens. This is where the future of our kingdom is decided."

"No wonder the Reaches are such a mess."

"That's why they need us." Akeylah glanced at Zofi, then away, toward where King Andros stood with his arm looped through Queen Rozalind's. "Those of us who aren't strictly Kolonyan. We see all this with fresh eyes. We can change things for our people."

Zofi thought about Prince Nicolen's fury as he lashed out at Elex. *One less Traveler will only better this world.* It wasn't about a card game. It never was. The prince, like so many others, hated the Travelers simply for who they were.

She thought about the maids cringing at the idea of serving her. The Kolonyans who tried to ward her off on her way into the city like some demon. All the insults she'd grown up hearing—*drifter, liar, cheat.* The towns that treated her band like stray dogs.

Or worse.

Could she change any of that? Was it even possible?

"Don't bother," Florencia said to Akeylah. "She's a drifter. It's not in her nature to stay put, much less accept responsibility."

Zofi opened her mouth, but another voice cut through the muggy night.

"I'd be pleasantly surprised if any of you turn out to have the right nature for this, frankly." The three spun to find Countess

Yasmin beside them. The Syxlight caught her hard hazel eyes, made them look more stonewood than human.

"Countess." Florencia sank into a curtsy. *Ever the well-trained Kolonyan*, Zofi thought. Akeylah followed suit a moment later.

Zofi remained standing.

The countess stood almost a head taller than her, and far more muscular, even at her age. Yasmin didn't move like the other noblewomen at court. She had a loose-limbed gait, a strength in her shoulders that told Zofi she'd seen combat in younger years.

"Nieces," Yasmin said, the word anything but endearing. "I hate to interrupt your little spitting match, but it is customary after an introduction to attend to your guests." Yasmin glanced pointedly at the nobles thronging around the dais. "Not that we can expect uneducated bastards to know such things, I suppose." She sighed. "This will be an uphill battle the whole way, I fear."

Good. If it was battle Yasmin wanted, at least Zofi understood that.

We can change things for our people. Maybe Akeylah was right. Maybe that was what Mother meant when she advised Zofi. *Play their game.* This could be Zofi's chance to make a difference.

Imagine what life could be like for Travelers if she sat on the throne. She could raise her band's status—no puny oasis town would kick them out if they were the family of a queen. And the Talons would be on her side, obeying her commands. No more attacking innocents. No more baseless arrests.

Her heart twisted. *Imagine life for Elex.* She could pardon him.

Screw running. Florencia might be insufferable, but she was right about one thing. This was an opportunity.

Zofi would be the one to seize it.

✳

Hours. She spent hours greeting the endless sea of nobility. Each one had a longer, more complicated name than the last. She'd never remember them all, let alone their status at court.

Playing this game proved more difficult by the minute.

Somewhere around midnight, Zofi managed to slip away. Only Akeylah noticed her leave, and if Zofi judged the girl right, she doubted she'd say anything. Akeylah didn't seem the loose-lipped type.

Then again, what did Zofi truly know of her? Of any of these people?

She couldn't trust anyone. Least of all her new so-called family.

That was the foremost thought in her mind when she shouldered open the door to her chambers. That probably accounted for why she immediately noticed the chill in the room, the flutter of the curtains.

She'd latched that window when she left.

The hair on the back of her neck bristled. She tiptoed to the mantel, unsheathed her longknife from the spot where she'd hung it. Tiptoed across the room in a crouch. At the window, she ripped the curtain down in one smooth motion, then spun to face her attacker.

Dim light flooded the room—torchlight from the other towers' windows.

Empty.

Except...Her gaze snagged on the headboard above the bed. Like the rest of the furniture, it was pale, bleached-white driftwood. The letters did not stand out—she only spotted them because of the way the torchlight caught the shine, made the message seem to glow.

Blood-Killer.

Zofi crossed the room. Touched the silver paint. Dry. Whoever did this had come during the party. Or even earlier, perhaps— she'd been summoned to the rooftop long before the noble guests arrived.

Practicality overwhelmed her fear. She knelt on the bed and dug her knife into the driftwood. It took a long time to work through the shellac. Even longer to saw through the soft wood and separate the whole headboard from the bed. She broke it into pieces, piled it in the fireplace.

She'd tell the maids she was cold and didn't have any wood. They'd believe any behavior possible from a Traveler.

Carefully destroying the evidence gave her plenty of time to think about what this meant. The words, the color of the paint. Silver. Like his horse, his hair, his nickname.

Someone knew she had murdered the prince.

·⊰ **9** ⊱·

Akeylah

*B*rilliant, Akeylah. You had a whole party full of nobles to talk to, and you decided to flirt with the most inappropriate one of all.

She'd spent the last several hours kicking herself for the misstep. Kicking herself and lingering at the fringes of this impossible party, praying to any god who may be listening that this would end soon.

Yet now, even with Syx set, the nobles showed no signs of slowing. Zofi had managed to sneak out an hour or two earlier, and Akeylah had watched her leave with a pang of jealousy. But before she could hope to follow, Yasmin swooped in, her unsettlingly birdlike gaze fixed on Akeylah.

"Move about," Yasmin had scolded. "Or at least entertain some company. You look like a particularly depressed shrubbery, planted here pouting. You'll start rumors you're ill. Or worse, a prude."

The countess swept away without awaiting a response, and despite the throbbing ache in the balls of her feet, Akeylah accepted a dance from the next person to ask, a pretty woman a few years older with gems the size of oysters dangling from her earlobes.

Akeylah didn't know the dance—it was so different from the roundabouts she'd watched traders perform at home. She feared she did irreversible damage to the poor woman's shoes on more than one occasion. After that, the invitations to dance stopped coming, and the whispers seemed to double.

Then, of course, there was Rozalind. Despite her best efforts, part of Akeylah's attention strayed to the woman again and again. She was impossible to resist—like trying to avert your gaze from the brightest light in the room.

Or trying not to watch a shipwreck in progress, thought some deeper, more cynical part of her brain. Because that was what it felt like. Especially when Rozalind rose to dance with the king— *my father, the father I've already cursed, seas below, I'm an idiot.*

When they took to the dance floor, they earned a smattering of polite applause, followed quickly by a round of sideways glances and whispers, hidden behind upturned palms, similar to the ones Akeylah garnered.

Clearly not everyone approved of the foreign queen.

Akeylah couldn't entirely blame them. Genal colonized the Reaches, abused them for centuries, then spent the past four hundred years since trying to reclaim the territory they believed rightfully theirs. This most recent war was only the latest in a series of increasingly brutal fights.

Still. That was hardly Rozalind's fault. She didn't ask to be born Genalese any more than Akeylah asked to be born in the

Eastern Reach or raised by a monster. And she'd been sent here as a demonstration of peace, in the hopes that both countries might be able to forget their past atrocities and move forward into a better future.

Even if some people didn't approve of peace, they must understand that Rozalind was a pawn in this game. Same as Akeylah.

A pawn who might someday be queened.

She drove that thought from her mind. Impossible. Despite this feast, despite the Blood Ceremony and the endless train of courtiers who pressed her hand and offered congratulations—for what, for being born?—she still couldn't believe this was reality.

She was the daughter of a king?

Worse, she'd unknowingly cursed that king. Not only was her crime so much worse than she thought, she was practically being rewarded for it. King Andros said it himself. If he hadn't fallen sick, he would have waited and hoped to father a legitimate heir with his new bride.

Her stomach churned again, this time at the idea of Rozalind in her father's bed.

Against her will, Akeylah peeked across the room once more. This time she found Rozalind bringing a pair of nectar flutes to a beautiful Northern woman in gold-dusted desert-crossing robes. The pair bent their heads together, whispered, then toasted with a laugh Akeylah could hear even across the dance floor.

More stomach-churning.

But she could have handled that. She was used to sticking to the shadows. Accustomed to never getting what she longed for. Her whole life had prepared her for disappointment.

She was not, however, prepared for Rozalind to catch her eye.

Or for the queen to lift her flute, slowly, meeting Akeylah's gaze as she took a sip of the nectar. When she lowered the flute once more, Akeylah could have sworn the queen winked.

In that instant, the room between them sank away. They were back on the parapet, just the two of them, Rozalind's cool palm pressed to Akeylah's heart. Feeling her pulse. Claiming her. Leaning in closer, those soft lips mere inches from Akeylah's own, curved in a gentle slope that made Akeylah ache to touch them, trace the outline...

She dropped back into reality with a jolt when someone tapped her elbow.

"Daydreaming, Lady Akeylah?" asked a young noble. She'd been introduced to him, but damn it all, she'd forgotten his name already.

"Oh, no, just clearing my head for a moment... my lord." Akeylah cleared her throat. Racked her memory. Garick? No. Gavry?

"Gavin," he said with a knowing smirk. "Don't worry, I take no offense. Sun knows you must have been introduced to a hundred people tonight."

"Surely at least twice that," Akeylah replied, matching his smile.

"Well. People will grant you an excuse tonight." He bowed his head a little. "I'm sure it must be difficult. So many new customs to learn. So much is different here than out in the east."

Her smile faltered slightly. She didn't like the way he hung on those last words. *In the east.* Yet he maintained his polite, neutral smile.

"Have you been to the Eastern Reach, Lord Gavin?" she asked.

"Oh, yes. I was there for the war. And afterward. Hunting down the rebels." His eyes narrowed.

"Then I must thank you for your service." She smiled. Her voice did not waver.

"It was nothing. The least I could do for Kolonya."

Kolonya. Not *the Reaches.* Before she could conjure a response, he bowed.

"I expect I'll see you again, Lady Akeylah."

She watched him drift across the floor to join arms with a pretty young Kolonyan girl, who he drew into a dance.

Akeylah needed a break.

She skirted the edge of the dance floor, made for the garden path out to the parapet where she'd lingered with Rozalind earlier. Just as she ducked under the first veil tree, she felt a cool touch graze her upper arm.

Her heart danced double-time when she turned to find the queen beside her. "Leaving already?" Rozalind asked.

"I just need some air."

Rozalind's smile deepened with amusement. "One night in court and you're already tired of the crowds?"

Akeylah's ears burned. "I've never been one for large gatherings." Not that she'd ever been invited to any before, but still. "Your Majesty, I'm sorry if I misstepped earlier—"

"Please," the queen cut in. "It's Rozalind. And I should be the one apologizing for not introducing myself properly. I was enjoying the chance to speak as myself for a moment, rather than as a queen. I hope you don't feel I deceived you."

"Not at all." Akeylah tried not to think about the space between them or the way the air warmed around her. *She's so close.*

"Good." Her eyes flickered down to Akeylah's mouth quickly enough Akeylah couldn't be sure whether she imagined it. "Well, don't let me detain you from getting that breath of air." Rozalind bowed her head, and Akeylah sank into a curtsy. By the time she rose, Rozalind had already disappeared back toward the party, leaving Akeylah's chest painfully tight.

You cannot do this, Akeylah.

She could not develop feelings. Not for Rozalind. Not for her father's wife.

She pushed onward through the trees. Past a few knots of chatting courtiers, including her half sister Florencia and a young man in a sharp suit and Southern-style dress. Florencia flashed her a curious glance but otherwise didn't acknowledge her. Which was just as well. Akeylah had had enough awkward conversations for the evening.

At the end of the path, devoid of any other nobles, she pushed aside the last veil tree. Then she froze. Stared straight ahead at the very same balcony where she and Rozalind chatted earlier that evening, shocked.

Someone had painted across it, dark red letters that dripped along the pale ivory.

Bloody seeds beget bloody crops, ryesdottir.

Akeylah glanced around her. There was nobody in sight, though she could still hear voices behind her in the trees, people chatting and laughing. Her heart began to pound against her ribs.

She recognized the phrase. Any schoolchild would know the rhyme. Seas knew her siblings chased her through the house chanting it often enough.

Bloody seeds beget bloody crops
What you curse comes back to haunt
And if the family blood you taint

You seal your own bloody fate

Like most children's rhymes, it was darker than it sounded. A song about the Vulgar Arts, promising that if you used those forbidden tithes, they would come back to curse you, too.

Akeylah was starting to believe it.

And the last word, *ryesdottir*. Tarik dialect. A banned language, just like their name, though many Easterners still spoke it in secret. Father never bothered to teach Akeylah, but she'd picked up bits and pieces from the traders. Enough to understand that term.

Rye. King.

Dottir. Daughter.

Akeylah's body went cold. This message was for her. She was sure of it.

She knelt and touched the paint. Still wet. With one last glance over her shoulder, she turned up the hem of her dress and began to wipe the words away. It didn't matter. Even after she'd cleaned the entire balcony, and the wet paint on the dress stuck to her legs, the message remained burned in her mind.

Somebody knew she had cursed the king.

* 10 *

Florencia

Ren's turquoise heels clacked across the ivory stonewood dance floor as she scanned for her next target. The party was still going strong, and there were plenty of nobles left to meet before dawn colored the sky. Ambassador Perry waved, but she'd already taken a long turn through the gardens with him. Any more would be leading him on. So she smiled and walked past.

All the nobles seemed quite taken with her so far. Impressed by her memory for names, a few declared. Little did they know, she'd learned far more than their names over the years. She knew how much they enjoyed their strongwine, which maids warmed some of their beds. Which scullery boys warmed others.

Mama was right. Serving gave her an immense advantage over the other two girls.

She fought down a surge of annoyance. That was the only

frustrating thing about this turn of events. She'd finally ascended to the nobility—to a rank miles above anything she'd dreamed of attaining. But she had to share the pedestal with the two least likely candidates in the Reaches.

The Easterner might be all right, given a proper wardrobe, for Sun's sake. But the Traveler? All muscle and no dignity. She might make a good foot soldier, but she didn't have the subtlety or depth to rule a kingdom.

Do I?

Ren pushed the query to the back of her mind as she passed another eligible nobleman. "Lord Hane."

"Lady Florencia, what a pleasure." Hane was handsome, with his mother's dark Southern eyes accenting his father's broad Kolonyan nose. Below her station now, but Ren certainly wouldn't mind flirting a bit. "Do you need a top up?" He glanced at her empty nectar flute.

Truth be told, she'd barely touched her drinks. This wasn't the time or place to pull a Sarella—she could not afford to lower her guard. "I'm fine, thank you."

"Then perhaps you'd prefer a partner for this next set." His gaze raked along her body.

Ren ducked her head, pretended to blush. She'd spent hours to appear effortless tonight—tousled hair, light makeup, no jewelry, bright turquoise shoes her only accessory. But the coup de grâce, her real armor, was the fiery red dress. It hugged her slim waist, the side slit showing off the shoes and her miles-long legs. In front it was high-necked. In back, it plunged low to reveal the stormwing tattoo nestled along her spine.

It took careful balance to walk that line. Sexy yet demure. Alluring yet unattainable.

Luckily, Ren had a lot of practice at both ends.

"I would like that very much," she was saying when a warm hand came to rest on the small of her back, right over the tattoo.

"Unfortunately, I'm afraid the lady is already taken for this dance. Perhaps the next."

Chills ran through her at the sound of his voice. Not to mention that touch, so familiar. *Too* familiar. She ought to swat him away. But her traitor body rebelled, secretly enjoyed his scent, the sensation of him standing just inches behind her. *Old habits die hard.*

"Next time, then." Lord Hane bowed.

Ren waited until Hane was out of earshot. "Ambassador Danton." She hoped he'd notice the venom laced behind those words. "How ... unexpected."

She turned to face him. Mistake. Those storm-blue eyes bored *through* her.

"You could at least pretend you're glad to see me." He swept her onto the dance floor, far more graceful than any of the nobles she'd danced with tonight. The scent of pine trees clung to him, the way it always did. A remnant of the alpine forest in which he grew up, far to the east.

"Why, to preserve your pride? Or merely your public image?"

They fell into step together. She hated the way it felt. Natural. Her body knew his so well, whatever her mind thought of him now.

"Florencia, please. I'm trying to help. You don't want anyone asking too many questions. 'Why does Lady Florencia dislike the ambassador? What might they have between them?'"

"No love lost," she muttered.

Danton's warm, calloused fingers brushed the base of her spine once more. Tracing her tattoo. "You say that," he replied, "yet you still haven't painted over my souvenir."

The stormwing itched, seemed to pierce and claw at her vertebrae. She still remembered the night he inked it onto her. The pain of the needle, the pleasure of his touch as he gently wiped away excess ink and blood, spread balm across the fresh wound.

"I do not need to hide my past. Only reclaim it." She lifted her chin. Ignored the rolls of thunder his smile set off in her chest. "The stormwing is the symbol of my house, after all."

"A fortuitous accident."

He was right—she'd chosen the symbol on a whim, for its beauty. It was not until tonight, as she dressed for this feast, that she recognized the symmetry. The stormwing represented Kolonya, the ruler of the united Reaches...and King Andros's personal house.

"Perhaps some part of me already knew," she said.

"The subconscious can pick up on a great deal more than we realize," he agreed. "And you have always been more perceptive than most."

The music shifted, the tempo increasing. Danton guided her expertly across the floor, and their legs flashed in unison, so fast now that if either of them missed a step, they'd land square on each other's toes.

Neither faltered.

"It's what I admire most about you."

It was too much. The dance, his voice. This conversation, an echo of so many they'd had before. Back when they had to hide below the Keep in some mad old king's cavern. Back when she still trusted him.

"Why are you doing this?" She lowered her voice to a whisper. He bent closer to hear, and her lips nearly grazed his cheek. "You got what you wanted from me. I won't make the same mistake again, so if you're hoping I will—"

"You think *that's* why I'm talking to you?" She glimpsed genuine hurt in his face. "Florencia, you know what I feel for you."

"I know what you claimed. Your actions spoke louder."

"Just hear me out, please. Let me explain."

Her chest ached. Threatened to crack open. "You say I've always been perceptive." She willed herself hard as stonewood. "But I wasn't before. Not when it came to the viper slithering right underneath my nose."

"Florencia—"

"Nobody else ever got close enough to sink venom into my veins," she cut him off in a furious whisper. "But thank you for the lesson." The final strains of music died away, leaving them standing still in the middle of the dance floor. "My eyes are open now. Trust is a weakness I will never succumb to again."

With that, she broke his grip and strode away. It took the whole walk across the dance floor before she was able to breathe without his scent in her lungs, his body warming her skin.

Curse him.

She caught a flute of sparkling nectar from the tray of a passing server—a server she recognized, Iolen. Ren nodded to him with a grateful smile as she stepped through the trees, toward the outer walls of the garden. Hopefully there, at least, she could catch her breath.

✳

A serving boy delivered the letter. It bore no signature, but Florencia knew the sender by his handwriting alone.

The sheer audacity. The party had begun to dwindle, the last-standing revelers departing in twos and threes, bent together for support as they tipsily braved the stairs. She'd flirted with enough lords—and even a couple ladies—to push Danton well enough out of her mind. Now he had the nerve to do this?

How many times must she rebuke him in one day?

She reread the note, tempted to ignore it.

Meet me in our spot. We need to talk. You can guess what about. I'm afraid I must insist, Florencia.

That last line made her realize she could not skip the meeting. *I'm afraid I must insist.* She worried what he might do if she ignored the request.

Best to keep him as content as possible while holding him at arm's length. She bid farewell to Lord Hane, her final dance partner of the night. Waved to a couple of ladies as she wove between the final throngs of the crowd. In the corner near the stairs, she spotted Sarella hanging off Lord Byer, stroking his arm and smiling that cat-grin of hers.

Ren smirked. She was clawing up the wrong tree there—Lord Byer had been having an affair with Lord Ymir for the last two years, right under Ymir's wife's nose.

With a pang, she departed her first feast as Lady Florencia. Though, to judge by the predawn light streaking the sky, she'd done a pretty good job of enjoying it to the fullest. She wished she could stay longer, forget about Danton. But if she didn't meet him now, ensure his silence, this could very well be her *last* feast as Lady Florencia.

Halfway down the grand staircase, Ren ducked behind a column and slipped off her turquoise heels. They ached something fierce by now, and if she wanted to sneak unnoticed, she couldn't have these clattering against the servants' steps.

She ducked behind a stern-faced portrait of King Ilian, one of the many concealed entrances servers used. Behind it, she followed the warren of tunnels. The maids and serving boys used these passages to run errands without interfering with the nobility. Because Sun forbid anyone suffer through seeing a servant and realizing their morning fire did not stoke itself.

Our spot. She crumpled the letter in her fist. As if it were still theirs. As if they shared anything but guilt now.

Ren had not visited the cave since the day Danton vanished, but her feet remembered the way. Deep in the bowels of the Keep, down an amber passageway underneath the third tower, she found the telltale chink in the wall. Felt her way along that crack until her fingers met the seam. A faint breeze against her skin was the only indication there was more to this wall than met the eye. She pried the door open and shimmied through.

The cave was everything she remembered. A self-enclosed fantasy world, built for Sun knew who in some bygone era. Forgotten until the day she and Danton stumbled upon it.

It was indeed a cave, though what it was doing underneath the Keep, Ren couldn't say. True stone walls jutted out at odd angles, as if the rock formed there naturally. (It hadn't, Danton assured her, after he dug up a corner of the cave to find loamy jungle dirt beneath.) In the center of the room was a deep pool, its water stemming from the River Leath. One whole corner of the wall was occupied by a trickling waterfall quietly feeding the pool.

Stalactites jagged down from the ceiling, and stalagmites spiked up from the floor, straining to meet them. Here and there along the stone walls, crystals sparkled in the low light. Diamonds, perhaps, or some other common semiprecious stone.

The light was the most peculiar part of the cave, a pale greenish glow that emanated from algae along the edges of the water. It made Ren relax in spite of herself. That was probably why Danton chose this spot. He hoped to disarm her. To fling her so deep into nostalgic memories that she forgot their present dispute.

Luckily Ren was not an easy person to lead.

She strode into the room to take a seat on the edge of the pool. But as she reached it, her steps faltered.

There was a blanket draped across the rocks.

It was what she and Danton used to do. Throw themselves faux picnics down here. Spread blankets at the water's edge, lie back and study the light playing across the ceiling. Then study each other in that light.

Did Danton really think she'd fall for this? Play house with him as though nothing was wrong? *Curse him.* She grabbed the edge of the blanket and ripped it aside, ready to throw it in the lake.

Instead, she froze, stomach curling.

Someone had painted across the rocks beneath the blanket. Black ink. No, not ink. It smelled strange. Almost like . . . lamp oil? Something used for starting fires, at any rate.

Or blowing up ships.

It made sense, given the message. No words. Only four numbers, more damning than any letters.

1854.

She uncrumpled the note. Stared from the blocky numbers drawn in death ink to the letter in her hand. Back and forth. This was not Danton's style. The note, the subterfuge, the cryptic numeral. If Danton meant to expose her, he would be straightforward, threaten her to her face. He wouldn't dance with her in front of the whole court, beg her to let him explain. This felt like something different. Some*one* different. Which, if true, could mean only one thing.

Someone else knew about Burnt Bay.

·∘⟨ 11 ⟩∘·

Akeylah

S leep proved impossible. When Akeylah finally managed to forget the threatening note long enough to drop off, nightmares
haunted her dreams. *Bloody seeds beget bloody crops.* She heard
her siblings singing it, chasing her through the Keep. She ran
from them, straight into her new half siblings. Florencia laughed
and joined in the singing, her teeth huge, mouth even larger. Zofi
jeered and shoved her. The king snarled, *You did this to me.*

She spun away, found Rozalind instead. Reached for her. But
Rozalind backed away, face slack with fear. *Murderer,* she whispered, and from Rozalind, it hurt worse than any of the others.

Akeylah jolted upright. Her heart slammed. It took her a
moment to realize where she was. The oak bed, the gauzy rose
curtains. The words still burned in her mind, stuck like a bad
tune. *Bloody seeds beget bloody crops, ryesdottir.*

Something rapped at her window. Akeylah startled, whipped toward it. But all she could see through the shifting curtain was a brilliant red bird, feathers edged in blue and green. A scarlet— one of the king's messenger birds.

She untangled herself from the covers and reached for the window latch. The moment she undid it, the bird head-butted inside and dropped something on the dressing table. A scroll. Before she could react, the scarlet took flight again. Outside, it let out a shrill cry and sped toward the aerie in the ebony tower eaves.

She reached for the scroll with shaking fingers. Would this be another threat? What did the sender want?

She breathed a faint sigh of relief when she spotted the king's name at the bottom.

Join me in the training field after breakfast. This will be your first lesson.

That was all. No further instructions, no explanation as to what a training field even was. She was still puzzling over it when a knock sounded. The maids didn't wait more than a second before they shoved the door open and strode inside.

Akeylah clamped a hand over her thigh instinctively and checked the nightgown she wore. It covered the scar, just barely.

Life in the Keep might be luxurious, but it certainly wasn't private.

A bevy of people spilled into the room this time. More than just her usual pair of maids. One woman stepped forward, bowed. "The queen sent us, my lady. She insists we provide you with a wardrobe more suited to your station, in whatever style most sets you at ease." She gestured to the other tailors, each of whom lifted a gown for inspection.

Akeylah caught her breath.

Each dress was more beautiful than the last—some loose and gauzy like the queen's last night, others a tighter fit. There were high, feathered collars in scarlet red, long-sleeved gowns in macaw blue, with lace embroidered along the forearms.

She wanted every single one.

How did Rozalind know her taste so well after one evening? She shook her head. "It's too much."

"Queen Rozalind insists. Please, let us know which you'd like us to fit to you today."

The panic flooded back in, along with reality. Her thigh seemed to throb. "I...I don't have time, I need to break my fast, and the king summoned me—"

"Queen Rozalind mentioned you might be a bit shy." She snapped her fingers, and two of the tailors laid gowns on the bed, then went about unfolding a silk screen, which they propped against the corner. "If you prefer, you may change into an under-gown yourself before we begin the fitting." She offered a slim-fitting undergarment, one that reached to the knees. It was the same color as her skin, but the fabric looked thick enough to hide the worst of the scar, as long as she kept her hand carefully placed during the fitting....

"Yes. Thank you," Akeylah agreed. "And..." She cast an eye over the gowns again, now that she felt a little more relaxed. "I'll try the darkest one today." She nodded at a black ankle-length gown, tighter than most, inlaid with iridescent beadwork. If nothing else, it would certainly hide the glow of the scar.

Less than fifteen minutes later, Akeylah stared at her reflection in disbelief. The gown hugged her hips, and the beads along it made her flash in the morning light, like a sunfish darting through water.

Yet after a moment of admiration, her stomach sank. Fancy dresses were all well and good, but she could not allow herself to relax. Someone out there knew her secret. And when they came for her, no pretty attire would stay their hand.

✳

The practice fields, as it transpired, were the lawns behind the Keep, between the Talons' barracks and the stables. Akeylah joined Zofi and Florencia, the latter of whom looked tired, distracted. Beside her stood the king, Countess Yasmin, and several Talons beneath an awning on the lawn. Only the king was seated, in an elaborate wooden chair with wheels. Unlike Florencia, he seemed much improved today.

"Thank you for coming, Akeylah." King Andros smiled. "Let's begin."

At that, the Talons—four in total—stepped out of attention and marched a few paces away, where they squared off, two against two. Countess Yasmin, who to Akeylah's surprise was dressed not in her usual dull court ensemble but a lightweight leather tunic and trousers, went with them. All four Talons' gazes tracked her.

Akeylah watched, though she kept her sisters in the corner of her vision.

Did one of them paint that threat? She'd seen Florencia in the gardens, near the parapet. Did Florencia want to force her out of Kolonya so she'd be one step closer to the throne?

"Today, I want to demonstrate what keeps our country strong. The Talons are our best soldiers, the men and women who stand between us and our enemies."

But how could Florencia, who grew up here, hundreds of miles from the Eastern Reach, have learned about Akeylah's treason?

"Their strength and abilities in the Arts are what make the Kolonyan army unparalleled in the world."

Zofi scoffed under her breath.

King Andros looked over. "Something you would like to add, Zofi?"

"Last night at the feast, you said we needed the united strength of all the Reaches to defeat our enemies." She grinned, mostly teeth. "Now you say the Kolonyan army is our only real power."

Or could it be Zofi? She was a Traveler, just like the curse-worker. Maybe she knew the older woman. Or perhaps she'd been at that fair, witnessed Akeylah's rendezvous.

"The other Reaches offer necessary support," Andros replied. "The Northern cavalry, the Western archers, the Southern suppliers, the Eastern navy—these are limbs of our strength. But the real power lies in our heart."

A few paces away, Yasmin raised her fist.

The Talons moved in one fluid motion—raised one forearm and clapped their other hand to it. Akeylah noticed a flash of silver between their fingertips, and realized they'd drawn bloodletters—special tools designed to slice only the top layer of skin, to open your blood to the Arts with minimal injury. For most tithes, those were enough.

Except the one Akeylah worked. Her fingertips itched to touch her scar, reassure herself it remained hidden. She resisted the urge, since it would only draw attention.

"We train our Talons extensively in the Blood Arts," Andros went on. "More so than any other force in the Reaches. They have studied every battle tithe, every aspect in which the Arts can be applied at war. They know every application of the Arts we've discovered, every way in which they can push their bodies to be *more*."

Yasmin spread her fingers wide. The Talons unhooked flaps on the wrist of their leather armor sleeves, revealing just enough skin for a tithe.

"They drill every day in both Arts-enhanced and unenhanced battle. Talons train on land, at sea, and mounted. Any single Talon, once they've earned their wings, is equipped to lead their unit in any form of combat should the need arise."

Yasmin dropped her hand in a sharp, slashing motion. With that, each Talon drew the bloodletter across their exposed skin.

One Talon suddenly moved so fast that all Akeylah could make sense of were his strikes as he lashed out at his sparring partner.

His partner, a woman, used a different tithe. Pale white light streaked along her veins, like lightning pulsing through her skin. The lightning spread, filled in the gaps, connected like spiderwebs until she shone like a person-shaped silver Sun. It almost hurt to look at her.

As Akeylah watched, the speeding Talon's sword glanced harmlessly off his opponent's now-impervious skin.

King Andros cast Zofi a glance. "In addition to their drills, there is another benefit to our Talons' regular practice. Prolonged and steady tithing expands the capacity of blood to absorb and process the Arts."

The other two Talons both used strength tithes. One lifted her opponent and hurled him halfway across the field. He caught himself with one hand and pushed off the ground so hard he landed right in front of his opponent. Yasmin sidestepped as the two of them collided in front of her. Akeylah winced, the sound of their fists hitting skin almost deafening.

"The other Reaches are effective shields," Andros said, "but the Talons are the blade Kolonya wields to master our enemies."

The crash of swords and smack of blows rang across the field.

"Why not train all the soldiers in the Reaches like this, if it's so effective?" Zofi smirked. "Or don't you trust our allies?"

"We trust our allies, but we also need to be smart about what information we share and with whom. For example, can you imagine if the rebellion leaders had access to all our battle knowledge?"

"You don't think withholding knowledge might be the reason they wanted to rebel in the first place?" Zofi pointed out.

"Is that what you think?" the king asked, his voice neutral. He seemed to be genuinely interested in Zofi's response.

But the Traveler just shrugged one shoulder. "Probably."

"What about you girls?" Andros's gaze flicked to Florencia, then Akeylah.

"Burnt Bay was unforgivable," answered Florencia immediately. "There's no excuse for such violence."

After a beat, Akeylah nodded. "I agree, that violence was terrible. But I also think Zofi makes a good point." She ignored Zofi's blink of surprise and kept her attention fixed on Andros. "If you'll forgive my saying, Your Majesty—"

"I am your father, Akeylah. You may address me as such."

"Father." Strange. She was used to that word curdling her stomach. Now it made her feel almost...hopeful. Well. Hopeful and guilty. "People turn to evil acts out of desperation." Akeylah thought about Jahen and her half siblings at home. Their hatred. The pain of her mother's death underneath it all. "The Eastern Reach is broken. We were wrecked by the war; now we struggle to feed ourselves, between our lack of laborers and our crop blights. Maybe Kolonya cannot share all of her most valued battle skills with our allies, but surely you can share assistance in times of need. If you help the east rebuild, and reassure Easterners that they are as valued as any Kolonyan, perhaps you can remove their sense of despair, and prevent inspiring more rebellions in the future."

She fell silent. Zofi shot her an approving glance. Even Florencia was nodding.

"We should support our allies," Florencia said. "The ones who behave, anyway."

"It's an opinion we will certainly take under advisement, Akeylah," Andros spoke up. "Thank you for sharing it."

Behind him, Yasmin lifted her hand, spun her closed circle in a fist. Three of the four Talons swept to a halt.

"Ah yes. This next demonstration—" Andros broke off at the sound of a scream.

The fourth Talon hadn't seen Yasmin's signal. She'd been mid-attack when her opponent stopped to stand at attention. The point of her blade sank into the other Talon's bicep, and he shouted in pain as it sliced deep, so deep blood spurted across Yasmin's cheek. Bright red arterial blood.

Akeylah caught a glimpse of bone before the other Talons closed rank around him. She gasped. Beside her, Florencia covered her eyes. Zofi grimaced.

The king, however, seemed unfazed.

Countess Yasmin dropped to a knee beside the injured Talon, who'd already sunk to the grass. She was far enough away that Akeylah couldn't hear what she was saying over the boy's moans, but it sounded angry rather than comforting.

Akeylah's heart pounded. She couldn't tear her gaze from the soldier. Another Talon had removed his helm, revealing a sweating, frightened boy. Younger than Akeylah from the looks of it.

The wounded Talon groaned again. The sound reminded her of the injured soldiers who'd passed through Jahen's house during the war. The way they'd moan and cry aloud at night. Sometimes, when Jahen sent her out to bring the men water, they'd grip her wrist with bloody fists and beg her to end the pain.

"Concentrate!" Yasmin's voice rose loud enough to hear now.

Why was no one helping him? He couldn't tithe. Not after that fight he'd just had. Surely he must have used up all the Arts in his bloodstream. Seas below, Akeylah needed *weeks* to recover after her use of the Vulgar Arts.

And yet, the boy clapped a hand over his wound. She watched, eyes widening, as the blood that pulsed between the boy's fingers trickled slower now. He swayed with the effort, sagged forward onto all fours. But the blood stopped flowing. And a moment later, his skin began to knit itself at the edges.

She didn't realize she was holding her breath until her vision began to spark. She forced herself to breathe out, in again.

A few breaths later, there was only an angry red scar where the boy's bone-deep wound had been before. It wasn't perfect, wasn't a complete healing tithe of the kind Akeylah had seen healthy men manage on injuries they'd only just received. Still, considering how depleted of the Arts his veins must have been, she couldn't believe he'd done this much.

Yasmin shoved back to her feet and said something. Two other Talons swept in, hoisted him to his feet, and slung his arms around their shoulders.

"How did he do that?" Zofi said, her voice low as the Talons began to carry their injured comrade from the field. "How did he tithe again so soon after the last?"

Yasmin turned her attention from the retreating Talons to the single Talon remaining. For a moment, her gaze flicked to her brother. Then it landed on Zofi, and she chuckled. "Did you imagine Travelers were the only people with tricks up their sleeves?" Yasmin called, surprising Akeylah. She didn't realize the countess had been standing close enough to hear that.

Andros cleared his throat. "As I said, our Talons practice prolonged exposure. Much in the way that training a muscle builds its capacity, using the Arts on a regular basis has expanded their abilities. Their tithes last longer and can even be combined, at a price."

"How long will it take him to recover?" Akeylah watched his fellow Talons carry him from the field.

"A week," Andros said. "By then, he should be able to tithe again to heal the wound completely. But we will keep him off the practice field for an extra week after, to be safe."

Closer at hand, Yasmin picked up one of the helms the retreating Talons left behind, along with a sword. She put the helm on herself.

"Is that safe?" Akeylah frowned. "What would have happened just now if he wasn't able to heal that cut?"

"Then we would have bandaged the wound as best we could and waited until he was able to tithe once more."

"But—"

"It is not safe," Andros interrupted gently. "Neither is war. We have to push our Talons, prepare them for strenuous situations. That means some risk along the way, yes."

Yasmin squared off against the single remaining Talon. A Talon who'd already tithed today, who'd just finished a sparring match in which his fellow soldier was nearly grievously hurt.

Akeylah curled her hands around her skirts. Clenched them to keep her fingers from trembling with nerves.

"Normally I would take the field as well," Andros was saying. "But I must reserve my own tithes for healing of late."

Of course. The king must be trying to tithe himself to health. It explained why he appeared a little better today.

Unfortunately, Akeylah knew all too well how little help that would be in the long run. Andros could buy some time, but eventually his blood would reach capacity. Then the curse she planted would win out.

Guilt sat like a lead rock in her gut.

"Now, I expect you are familiar with those rudimentary tithes we just saw—for speed, for strength, for impervious skin."

"Of course," Florencia answered.

Beside her, Zofi snorted. "Who wouldn't? Children can manage them."

Akeylah's face felt hot. "I have tried them a few times...." But it wasn't like Jahen bothered to formally instruct the daughter he never wanted. She'd spied on her brothers' tithes, tried a couple herself, inexpertly, if that counted. But she doubted she could hold a speed tithe for more than a few seconds, or manage a strength tithe that allowed her to pick up an opponent and hurl him halfway across a practice field.

Then again, she *did* know how to curse her own father. For whatever that was worth.

"You needn't understand all the intricacies," Andros replied. "A familiarity with the more unusual tithes, however, will help if you ever need to lead a battalion."

Battalion? Akeylah's stomach churned.

She hadn't thought about that. Hadn't considered the fact that the countess and the king had both fought in past wars. Even the Silver Prince, before his assassination, had ridden to the front lines regularly.

Would she be expected to do the same if the country fell into war again? She prayed their latest peace treaty would hold.

The peace treaty sealed by Rozalind's marriage to her father...

There was that guilt again.

Andros was explaining the next tithe Yasmin and the Talon would demonstrate. "In a situation where you need to launch a stealth attack, such as in the assassination of an enemy commander, this can be of great use."

Her head hurt at the very thought of needing to make a

decision like that. *Launch a stealth attack* to murder someone, even an enemy.

A few paces away, Yasmin raised her hand. A ring glinted on her middle finger. She tapped it with her thumb, and it opened into a slim bloodletter, the likes of which Akeylah had never seen before. An inch-long, razor-thin blade extended from the ring.

The countess swept that razor up the back of her forearm. Akeylah caught one last glint of the ring.

Then the countess vanished.

Across from her, her partner lifted his sword and studied the air, uneasy.

A moment later, he shouted in pain, and a thin cut sprang up on his bicep. He swung wildly, hit only empty air.

Akeylah glanced down and realized that if she watched the grass, she could see faint indents where Yasmin's feet were landing. She traced that up, watched the way the grass and the dirt of the field seemed to bow outward around an invisible form.

She was camouflaging herself with the background. Changing her skin color every step she took to blend into her surroundings.

Akeylah could not imagine how much focus that took.

The Talon and Yasmin continued to parry for a few moments while they watched. "The camouflage tithe takes a great deal of concentration to maintain," Andros was saying. "But it has other uses as well."

Suddenly Yasmin reappeared. She raised her fist, and the other Talon froze at attention.

"For example, we found you can use this tithe to sculpt your features—though you cannot alter your height or basic body shape."

Andros nodded at his sister, and even though her back was turned, Yasmin spun around to face the girls.

She walked toward them as her features began to shift. Her face aged, grew squarer. Her wrinkles wriggled across her cheeks to reposition themselves, a sight that made Akeylah's nausea even worse.

A few paces later, and Yasmin had reached their sides once more. Only now, she'd become an exact replica of King Andros. Both Androses studied the girls, one wearing Yasmin's cruel smirk.

"It helps when you already resemble someone," Yasmin said. "But you can stretch the tithe if you need."

Yasmin shifted to resemble Zofi, wild puff of curls and all. Then Florencia. When she appeared a second later as Akeylah, Akeylah fought the urge to back away. It was unnerving to see Yasmin's sour expression on her own face. Yasmin relaxed back into her normal self, and Akeylah let out a faint sigh of relief.

Andros cleared his throat. "This next tithe, on the other hand—"

"Can I try?" Zofi interrupted.

Akeylah and Florencia exchanged startled looks. Try? *Seas below, don't make me humiliate myself*, Akeylah thought.

"We are only demonstrating the tithes today," Andros replied, "so that you will understand the potential applications in battle."

"What better way to learn than hands-on experience?" Zofi countered. She lifted a brow at Yasmin. "That is, unless you're worried this *drifter* will perform better than your almighty Talons."

Yasmin only smiled. "Very well. I'll call over another contingent of fresh Talons."

If Andros objected, he didn't say so aloud. He darted a single, swift frown in his twin's direction, then considered his daughters one after the other. "Zofi, go with Yasmin. Girls, I'll continue to describe some other tithes for your understanding in the meantime."

Akeylah breathed out a sigh of relief. At her side, so did Florencia. But Zofi? She was grinning like she'd just been given the world's greatest gift.

✣ 12 ✣

Zofi

Zofi sized up the three new Talons who'd marched out onto the field to face her, longknife in her hand. Beside them, Yasmin continued to explain the tithe Zofi wanted to practice.

Camouflage was a new one, after all. But she was realizing now that choosing to use a brand-new tithe in a fight against the most highly trained soldiers in the Reaches might be a tad ambitious.

Oh well. What had Andros said? War wasn't safe. Some risk was necessary when you were preparing for it.

"When it begins, you will need to concentrate *past* yourself," Yasmin said. "Focus on your surroundings and your possessions as well as your body."

Apparently, Yasmin had her outfits specially tailored—each one dyed in a solution mixed with a few droplets of her blood, to allow her to shift its appearance along with her own. Zofi had to make do with slicing the pad of her finger, then dabbing the result along the edges of her tunic and britches.

The cut stung now, and she repositioned her grip on the knife. Across from her, the Talons had drawn their trademark swords, long and curved at the very tip, like a stormwing's talons.

"Melee rules for this session," Yasmin added. "When your blood has been drawn, step out of the circle. Last combatant standing wins."

Zofi tried not to let her surprise show. She figured she'd be paired off to spar. Not be thrown into a three-on-one fight. In a melee, surely the Talons would gang up and take down the outsider before they turned on one another.

Yasmin wants me to fail.

Well, joke was going to be on her. In the inner pocket of Zofi's britches, in several concealed pockets built for this very purpose, Zofi could feel the reassuring weight of the boosts—glass phials filled with her blood, stored in the way only Travelers had mastered. If Yasmin wanted to make this fight harder, Zofi would be more than happy to play along. To win, whatever the cost.

Play their game, she reminded herself. *But more than that. Win it.*

"All of you will use the same tithe," Yasmin instructed. "Camouflage, so Zofi can practice hers." She raised a fist.

The Talons drew thin razors. Not as unique as Yasmin's fancy spring-activated ring, but still more impressive than Zofi's long-knife. One more advantage, since the razors wouldn't draw as much blood from a cut when tithing.

That's all right. She was accustomed to fighting with the odds stacked against her. She tilted her longknife against the outside of her forearm.

She was tired of court frippery. Tired of dressing up, parading around feasts. Tired of pretending she gave a handful of sand about any of these people. They were her enemies, all of them.

The one who painted that message on her headboard most of all.

Blood-Killer. She hadn't been able to drive the words from her mind. Who did it? All night she had stared at her ceiling, sleepless. Could it be one of the Talons? One who had been at the tavern that night, witnessed Elex and Prince Nicolen's fight...

But wouldn't a Talon have reported her to the king? Especially if he knew Elex wasn't the Traveler they should be hunting.

She killed the prince on the border of the Eastern Reach. Plenty of Easterners in that tavern could have witnessed the brawl. Easterners like Akeylah...or any of the other nobles from that region. She'd seen a couple others at the Blood Ceremony, though she didn't catch their names.

Then again, it could be none of those people. It could be a lady's maid, or a random merchant who'd overheard the right conversation at the right time. She and Mother had been careful to speak about that night only in private, usually once they were alone in their tent. But tent walls were thin, and if someone enhanced their hearing and knew where to focus...

She shook her head. This was exactly why she volunteered for this fight. To clear her mind, focus on a game she understood.

"To your marks."

Zofi could feel Yasmin's eyes on her. Sands, she could feel

everyone watching. Andros, the other girls—*my half sisters*, part of her thought, then immediately rejected. And, of course, her opponents. In their helmets, visors down, they looked like the stormwings they'd been named for, a sharp beak shadowing their faces.

She drew a deep breath and straightened her shoulders. *Ignore it all.* Only the fight mattered now.

Yasmin dropped her fist in one swift motion. "Tithe."

That was the last word Zofi heard before she dragged the blade over her skin and closed her eyes. The world melted away. Her veins seemed brighter today, her pulse faster. Even the Arts in the air, the green-flavored, adrenaline-scented sparks, seemed more intense, laser-focused. She drank those into her bloodstream while remembering Yasmin's instructions.

Two heartbeats and the Arts tingled in every inch of her body, itched for release. Only then did she push her concentration out, let the world seep in without leaving the tithe. It felt like staring at a drawing of two images at once—a cat that was also an ocean, a skull that also contained a game of cards. Zofi held both the image of her veins and the world surrounding her in her mind at once.

When she opened her eyes, her skin and the blood-daubed clothing she wore shifted. Her legs went green as grass. When she raised an arm, it shifted to the rose-colored stonewood of the nearest tower, then to blue when she held it over her head.

"Fight," Yasmin said, far too soon, before Zofi had truly adjusted to this new vision.

She stepped back on instinct, tore her attention from her surroundings to her opponents.

The Talons had vanished.

She concentrated, held the dual images in her mind as she sidestepped and danced backward. The air whistled with the sound of a missed strike, and she sidestepped again, zigzagging away as she hunted for an enemy.

There. The grass to her left seemed to be shifting, undulating on itself. She watched until she caught the outline of legs stepping through it, creeping toward the spot where she'd stood a moment ago.

It took every ounce of brainpower to focus both on melding her skin to this world *and* letting her physical gaze unfocus, track her opponent. When she found him, she nearly lost her hold on the tithe lifting her knife arm to strike.

Her arm stuttered on its way into the hit, appeared for a moment as a flash of dark flesh, then vanished again just before her blow landed with a crunch.

Armor.

Zofi spun away just in time to avoid the Talon's responding parry. This game would be harder than she thought.

She heard a distant clang, realized the other two Talons were fighting each other. Thank sands for small favors.

Back to this fighter, then. She circled across the field, let her limbs blend with the changing scenery. The strangest moment came when she passed in front of the spectators and had to meld her skin, so her opponent would see Countess Yasmin standing over King Andros *through* Zofi's body. Their faces, their skin tone, their outfits—it was too many colors to process, too complex an image to hold at once. Their expressions must have gone distorted, because with a rushing sound, the Talon swung.

Zofi raised her blade to parry only just in time. The sword

clanged against the knife, made her tighten her grip as she ducked away.

But now she had an idea.

Zofi circled around the Talon and purposefully let her concentration stutter an instant. A flash of black curls, her dark eyes showing for a moment. The Talon whipped in her direction to charge, putting the spectators behind him now.

Sure enough, it was easy to spot him with Florencia and Akeylah showing through his torso. Their skirts ballooned out and their mouths and eyes looked like a child's approximation of a face. Zofi swung again, this time able to judge better where to land her knife.

A splash of blood dripped to the field. The Talon cursed and, a heartbeat later, reappeared in a flash, grumbling.

Zofi didn't waste time gloating. She followed the sound of sword clashes toward the other two Talons, found them mid-strikes by the blur of motion through the grass. On tiptoe, she approached the nearest, waited for them to lash out, and landed a single dragging hit across their bicep.

That Talon reappeared in an instant. A woman, Zofi noted, as she tore off her helm and stepped away from the field.

Which left only one.

Zofi's skin began to tingle. The tithe would wear off soon. Across, her opponent's skin seemed to flicker—she caught glimpses of deep brown skin against the distant wooden barracks.

But almost as soon as those flickers appeared, they vanished again. Feint? Or had her opponent re-upped their tithe, much like the speeding Talon earlier casting that healing tithe?

It would cost a Talon far more than her. The boy who healed

himself all but fainted afterward. For Zofi, she only needed to crack a new phial.

A compression of air warned her of an incoming strike. Zofi dodged and, her hand reappearing solidly for an instant, reached down to slap her pocket, hard.

Still invisible, Zofi gritted her teeth as the solid glass phial cracked in half. The specially made glass itself was what kept the tithe intact—heated with drops of Zofi's own blood and blown with her own breath, to trick the blood stored inside it into thinking it remained in her body. The phial's outer edges, designed to shatter into pointed shards on hard impact, dug into her thigh, just far enough to let the old coagulated blood inside the phial mingle with the fresh wound.

The new rush of Arts hit her bloodstream hard. She could do whatever she wanted with this—re-up the camouflage tithe or shift to an entirely different one. It felt different than a normal tithe, not quite as sharp, diluted by time. But even that dull influx of Arts was a hit to her senses, starved as her blood was for more.

Her concentration snapped back into focus, the dual images of her own body and the world around her suddenly much easier to hold in her head at once. She zeroed back in on her opponent.

The Talon had vanished, too.

Zofi paced quietly away from the spot where she'd last seen them.

"Decided to stick around after all?" asked a familiar voice, at least ten paces off to her right.

Despite herself, Zofi grinned. "Stooping to fight a Traveler, Vidal?" *Keep talking.* She skipped aside a few steps and scanned the field. No sign of movement. He was better than the other two.

Moved slower, stayed in spots where he only had to camouflage himself against simple backgrounds. Currently, by her best estimate, he had the field and the distant obsidian tower behind him.

"I fight whoever my king asks me to."

She tracked his voice. Let a small smile creep onto her face when she spotted his form, outlined faintly. She'd been wrong. He stood much closer to her, the walnut tower at his back.

Zofi advanced another step.

"I am sorry, Zofi," he was saying, voice lower now. "For the other day, in the street. I was upset; I didn't mean to insult your way of life."

She swung her knife at the spot where he stood. He dodged, just in time to avoid the hit, and the next moment, he slipped out of her line of sight. *Sands.*

"That's all right," she told the empty air. "You aren't the first Kolonyan to insult my people."

"Doesn't make it right. I apologize."

She spotted him again, a few feet away on her left now. His tithe was running thin—as she watched, his skin began to flicker, drift in and out of sight.

She advanced on him. He scanned the grass, eyes wide. "How are you still tithing?" he whispered.

She grinned. Took another step forward, didn't answer.

Vidal's whole body was visible around the edges now.

Her skin itched, a warning sign, and she knew she shouldn't, knew it was ego prompting this, but she reached down and slapped her thigh. Cracked another phial anyway.

Vidal heard the glass shatter and whipped in her direction,

swinging hard. She managed to leap back, the point of his sword grazing her leather tunic. Now he was on the attack, though.

Desperate, Zofi held up the camouflage. But it made her slow, especially using two stored phials of Arts in a row. Her thighs ached where the glass broke her skin, her veins burned with the overuse, and her knife arm was sluggish.

Vidal was completely Arts-less now, just a normal Talon attacking what appeared to be thin air.

Zofi parried his next strike, dodged another, parried again.

"Impressive trick." Vidal narrowed his eyes, searching for her, yet he didn't seem angry. "Someday you'll have to teach me how you do that. Is it your blood that's stronger? Or something about the way you bloodlet?"

She kept circling, silent. Lashed out, but Vidal parried her knife strike at the last instant. Now she had him.

Zofi landed a strike against his chest plate. Another across his blade. Clangs rang across the yard. Not quite finding a way through his armor, not yet, but she would. One last blow…

Something blurred at the corner of her vision.

She faltered. Her instincts kicked in. *Attacker.* She only glimpsed them for a second. Someone using a speed tithe, sprinting past the king and his sister. Nobody else noticed. Nobody saw the runner pause behind Florencia and Akeylah, resolve into the dark shadow of a tall man, hat pulled low over his features.

He only stopped for a second, then kept running, but all Zofi could think about now were those silver letters. *Blood-Killer.*

Crack.

Zofi staggered. Her knife hit the grass. It took a moment for her to register the sting in her arm, the line of red where Vidal's strike had landed.

"Match," Yasmin said, somewhere behind.

With a groan, Zofi let go of the tithe she'd been holding for far too long. Her body flashed into sight, and her limbs went shaky, as drained as though she'd just tried to run a mile after a day without food.

Vidal grinned and offered a hand, palm up. "Good match."

"Best of three next time." She tried to wipe the scowl from her face, didn't quite succeed. She *had him*, damn it. Had him until...

She stole a glance around. The field was empty. Nobody lurking behind the king or the other girls, nobody even visible all the way to the barracks except the two other Talons she'd defeated, backs straight as they awaited their next command.

Great. Now she was imagining things. That blackmail threat had her antsy, dreaming up ghosts.

"Only if you promise to teach me the trick to holding a tithe that long." Vidal searched her face, still smiling.

She smirked. "Why, worried you won't beat me again otherwise?"

"Sun-damned drifters, can't even accept a loss with dignity," the female Talon muttered.

"Don't call her that," Vidal snapped, his voice suddenly sharp as a bloodletter. "She's a Traveler, she's a potential heir to the Sun Throne, and she beat you with more Sun-blessed dignity than you've ever shown in losing, Ishil."

Zofi's eyebrows rose. No Kolonyan had ever defended her before. None of them seemed to even think the word *drifter* was wrong.

For a moment, the field was silent. Then Yasmin gestured to Vidal. "Well fought, Talon."

"And well said," King Andros put in, with a pointed look at the other Talon. She flushed and bowed so low her nose nearly scraped the grass.

But Zofi wouldn't forget the way neither of them spoke up. No one did. Not until Vidal.

Her chest ached a little strangely.

Meanwhile, Vidal was bowing as well. "Thank you, Your Majesty. Countess."

"Thank *you* for your service," Yasmin replied.

King Andros bobbed his head. "We appreciate everything you and your fellow soldiers do to protect our realm."

All three bowed, while Zofi sheathed her knife.

"With me," Yasmin said, jerking her head at the Talons.

"Zofi," the king called. She crossed back to her sisters' sides while Yasmin led the Talons a few paces away to continue the next demonstration. But Zofi couldn't tear her gaze from Vidal, still not quite certain what the ache in her chest meant.

❈ 13 ❈

Florencia

Well, that was quite the display." Ren and Akeylah walked side by side back toward the Keep, Zofi having peeled away toward her tower.

"You don't think..." Akeylah hesitated. "I mean, *we* won't be expected to fight a Talon next time, will we?"

They'd spent the second half of the lesson watching the Talons practice a few other tithes, while Andros explained the battlefield applications of them all. Florencia's head swam with terminology about simulations, tactics, drills... all things she'd never bothered to think much about before.

All things she suddenly would be expected to know if, say, she ever had to command these troops herself.

Her head hurt. She thought about Akeylah's question. "There's a lot more to governing a country than knowing which end of a sword to hold. We need to learn the theory, not the actual practice."

Still, she could not forget Zofi's battle. Or the end, when she remained invisible long after the Talon had reappeared. *How did she do that?* It shouldn't have been possible.

More important, why would the Travelers hoard a capability like that? The ability to continue tithing more could give the soldiers of the Reaches a huge advantage in war. Why keep it secret?

Which got Ren thinking. If Zofi was dangerous enough to harbor secrets like that, what else might she know? Would she be willing to go a step further, sabotage someone?

1,854.

But how could she have learned about Ren's treason? From Danton?

Maybe they were in it together. Maybe Danton penned the note for Zofi; maybe they were both part of the Eastern rebellion. A Traveler assassin killed the Silver Prince, after all. People said he'd been paid off by Genal, but what if he'd earned the coin closer to home? What if the Easterners and the Travelers had formed an alliance?

She grimaced. Until she knew what the blackmailer wanted, she couldn't fathom the possible culprits. There were too many. She'd have to begin with Danton. Find out who he may have told, whether he penned that note. Then go from there.

"Earlier..." Akeylah cleared her throat.

"Yes?" Ren could already tell this half sister's reticence would drive her mad.

"When we were talking about the Eastern Reach. You said you believe we should support our allies who behave. What did you mean, exactly?"

Ren paused to measure her words. "We cannot afford to treat attacks like Burnt Bay lightly."

"But should we withhold assistance from the entire Eastern Reach because some rebels committed a terrible crime?" Akeylah squinted over her shoulder at the practice fields. "Should we punish innocent citizens for that crime?"

"Of course not," Ren replied.

"It's just, I worry…" Akeylah stepped up beside her. "I doubt most Easterners approved of that attack. Seas, I wouldn't be surprised if half the self-declared rebels didn't either. Yet now all Easterners will be branded by it. Have our concerns dismissed and belittled because of one disaster."

Why was Akeylah asking about this? Her heart raced. She saw the numbers again, smelled the lamp oil. *1,854.* "And you're asking my opinion why, exactly?"

Akeylah stopped speaking long enough that Ren dared a glance. The Easterner was blinking in surprise. "I was only curious. You spoke about it earlier, so it seemed you might have some insight into the Kolonyan perspective. My apologies if I was wrong…."

Her hurt seemed genuine. That only put Ren more on edge. "You were," she replied flatly. "Now, if you'll excuse me." Ren hiked her skirt to climb the steps of the ebony tower. The sooner she could get inside and away from this train of conversation, the better. The last thing she needed was more people prying.

"Ah, Lady Florencia."

Sun above, not again.

Ren pursed her mouth as Danton leaned in the doorway, grinning. "This must be your newly discovered sister. Wonderful to see a fellow countrywoman in the Keep."

"Ambassador Danton." Akeylah curtsied.

Ren's pulse skipped. "Do you know each other?"

"Not everyone in the Eastern Reach is acquainted," Danton replied at the same moment Akeylah spoke up.

"Actually, yes." Akeylah flashed a shy smile at him. "You won't remember, but a couple of months ago you stayed at my father's— my stepfather's, that is," she caught herself. "Jahen dam-Senzin."

Thin cover story, if that's what it is.

Could they be working together? Danton and this Easterner?

It would make sense. He'd want someone like him on the throne. Someone sympathetic to his cause. And he must know Ren wouldn't be, not after what he'd done.

"You're Jahen's girl?" Danton tilted his head. "I thought..."

"You'll be thinking of my sister, Polla, Ambassador." Akeylah's smile faded. "I seldom visited our guests, I'm afraid."

Too busy plotting the takeover of a kingdom, perhaps? Akeylah might be quiet, but in court politics as in the jungle, quiet creatures were often the deadliest.

"Well, I look forward to seeing you more often here at court," Danton was saying, though Ren felt his eyes drift to her once more. Clearly he did not stumble across this out-of-the-way hall by accident.

Ren tried her best to look normal. Which was to say, annoyed. "Did you want something, Danton?"

"Yes, though I am afraid it's not on offer at the moment." He raked his gaze up and down her body.

She gritted her teeth. "Why are you following me? I made my position clear."

"Crystal. But I've been hoping occasional exposure to my presence will inoculate you enough to change your mind. At least hear me out, Florencia."

Ren's whole body burned hot. With anger, yes. And, even more infuriating, with something else. Try as she might, she couldn't forget the feel of his mouth on hers, his warm, strong hands, which always knew exactly where to touch to drive her wild.

"Excuse me," Akeylah murmured. "I'm late for an appointment. Sister. Ambassador." She nodded to each in turn, then hurried up the hallway. Ren would have thought a blackmailer would enjoy eavesdropping on this conversation, but perhaps she didn't need to. Not if Danton was here to pressure Ren for her.

Ren watched Akeylah leave, far too aware of the space between her and Danton. The air thrummed with words unspoken.

When the hall was empty once more, Ren grabbed Danton's elbow and steered him toward the nearest servants' corridor.

"Just like old times," he joked as she shoved him through the narrow gap.

"You cannot keep doing that," she snapped.

"Doing what, pursuing you? I thought ladies enjoyed that sort of thing."

"Not this lady." She glared at him. This close, his scent was overwhelming. Maddening. "If you harm my chances at winning this throne, I *will* kill you, Danton."

He smirked. "Is that a threat or a promise?"

"I mean it. You think I'll forgive the way you used me?" She lowered her voice. Even here, they risked being overheard. If a servant wandered past at the wrong moment... "You said there would be no violence. You said nobody needed to die. Well, you were about one thousand, eight hundred and fifty-four bodies off count, Danton."

He winced. "I didn't know that would happen, I swear. I only warned them to give the rebel troops time to escape the city."

"And you had *no idea* they would launch a counterattack instead."

"Of course not." He set his jaw hard. "But King Andros sent those troops to murder people, Florencia. To raze Davenforth to the ground. I saw the deployment order myself."

"How does that make it okay to kill our own soldiers? Men and women we knew. You know how many of the maids lost lovers and siblings on those ships?"

"They knew the risk when they joined the army. If you're going to blame someone for their deaths, blame Andros. He sent them to that bay. He ordered them to ride through Tarik and kill hundreds of people."

Tarik. He'd started calling the Eastern Reach that just before he left the Keep last time. A new tactic by the rebels, reviving a long-dead country's old name, the one that had been forbidden for centuries, to try to make it sound more significant. "Hundreds of *rebels.*"

"What's the difference between a rebel and a Kolonyan soldier when it comes down to it? Both are fighting for a cause they believe in."

"The rebellion wants to divide the Reaches. Weaken us."

"Oh, because we're so united as it is." He gestured at the hall, but she knew what he meant. "These days it's every Reach for Kolonya and Kolonya for herself. You know it. Otherwise you'd have reported me to King Andros the minute those ships sank."

Ren scoffed. "Sure, and damn myself for the trouble."

"That's the only reason you didn't hand me over to the executioner?" Danton's voice softened. For a second, she could have sworn she saw a flash of hurt in his eye.

He didn't get to do that. He wasn't the one being used. "Damn right." *Time for the gamble.* He was a good liar, but if she caught him off-guard... "And now, as if using me to commit treason weren't enough, you want to throw it in my face, too? I saw the letter, Danton."

He frowned. "What are you talking about?"

"Don't pretend." She held his eye. "I'd recognize your handwriting anywhere."

He gazed right back, so intently it seemed almost like genuine concern. "Florencia, I'm sorry. But you must know why I couldn't write to you directly. An ambassador writing to a ladies' maid? How would that look? I had to write to Sarella instead."

That threw her. "What are you talking about?"

"I knew you served her. I thought if I told Sarella I was returning, she might mention it to you, too. It was the only way I could think to let you know I was returning." His voice went sharp, brittle. "I imagined you might be missing me."

She narrowed her eyes. He thought she was talking about his absence. Thought she was reprimanding him for not sending love notes while he'd been away. "And since your grand return, since learning I'm no longer that lowly ladies' maid, you haven't written anything else? Anything more revealing, perhaps?"

Now his brow furrowed. "Florencia, no, I...What do you mean? Did you receive some kind of message?"

She laughed once, sharply. His face fell, and she fought the instinctive guilt that surged inside. *Not my fault he's a traitor,* she reminded herself. "I did indeed. I received the message that you are no longer worth my time." With that, she pushed past him. They were finished here.

Either Danton had become a much better liar in the last six months, or he didn't send that threat.

"I'm worried for you," he called as she walked away. "These people, the king, those other girls...You know the saying. 'Family either strengthens or kills you, nothing in-between.' You don't know how vicious this court can get."

"On the contrary, you did a fine job of teaching me that already." With that, she rounded the corner, out of sight.

It was not proper for her to take these servants' passages, not anymore. She was a lady, meant to travel via the main halls with the rest of the nobility. Right now, though, she was furious, hurt, and she just wanted to get away from here as fast as she could.

Danton called again, his voice echoing. She ignored him and climbed the first staircase she came to. The Keep was a maze of corridors and passages, but Ren hadn't spent years working there for nothing. She knew these paths better than most people knew their own freckles. In no time at all, she slipped through the side entrance to the baths. She'd never used them before. Never been allowed, as a servant.

Now she could bathe whenever she damn well pleased.

The side entrance let out behind a thick curtain. Eucalyptus-scented steam struck her. She breathed in deep, hoped it would calm her enough to think straight.

Now she could cross Danton off the list. Which left her with the real problem. *If he didn't send the letter, who did?*

Akeylah had brought up Burnt Bay twice this morning—once with the king, then again with Ren. Not to mention, she knew Danton. Only in passing, apparently, but she might have learned something when he traveled through her stepfather's house.

Ren made her way to the changing area, stripped off the simple dress she'd selected for the lesson, and wrapped a thick, coal-warmed towel around herself.

The message was crafted for her. Nobody else would have understood it. Just a number painted on a rock. Which meant the blackmailer did not want to reveal the secret, not yet.

They wanted her scared. Cornered. Yet they made no demands. Why?

Perhaps Akeylah wanted to frighten her into leaving the Keep, abandoning her chance for the throne. That would certainly be a coup—a rebel queen on the throne.

Her skin itched. She could not let that happen.

She was so lost in thought that she'd already waded down to her ankles before she noticed the other person in the bath. At the far end, half hidden behind a curtain of mist. The hair caught Ren's attention, a billow of black curls.

For a moment, they simply stared. Danton's warning echoed in her mind. *Family either strengthens or kills you.* A saying from *The History*, about the first known use of the Vulgar Arts. A Kolonyan who cursed her own mother for an inheritance.

Across the room, Zofi reached for her towel. "Don't worry. I was just leaving."

Speaking of family. Here was one more suspect to contend with. She might as well see if she could learn something from this one today, too. Ren forced a pleasant smile. "No, please. Stay."

❊ **14** ❊

Zofi

N o, please. Stay." Florencia waded into the water across from
her. Took a seat on the farthest bench, half a room away.
Everything about her posture screamed exhaustion—slumped
shoulders, hunched chest.

For a moment, Zofi hesitated. Did she want to do this? She
had enough to worry about with the blackmailer. She didn't have
time for her half sister's fake smiles and suspiciously polite invitation to stay.

What does she want?

Then again, if Florencia *was* the blackmailer, this could be an
opportunity to out her.

Besides, Zofi's muscles ached too much from the fight to really
consider leaving this bath yet. She sank back onto the bench and

stretched her screaming legs. Everything hurt—from the exercise as much as the overuse of the Arts.

The maids had sent her here rather than draw her a private bath. *Drifters can use the public baths.* Zofi knew she could have complained to Andros, forced the serving girls to treat her better. Yet truth be told, after the fight this morning, she was too tired to argue.

But Zofi was surprised to see Florencia. She'd taken her half sister for the type who'd enjoy every creature comfort her new-found status offered, private baths included.

Then again, maybe Florencia had other motives.

One way to find out. Zofi swam a few seats closer to her half sister. "I thought I was the one who fought today. You look more tired than me."

Florencia lifted a brow. "Thank you. It's always great to hear you look terrible."

"Not my fault you're easy to read."

"Funny." Florencia groaned and leaned her head back on the sill of the bath. "You're the second person to tell me that this week. I'm starting to think I need to work on my hunter's face."

"What's that involve, more scowling?" Zofi drew her teeth back in an exaggerated grimace.

Florencia snorted. "It's an expression. For when you need to hide what you're actually thinking."

"Sounds like a useful skill for a courtier."

"Why, because this Keep is full of predators?" Florencia smirked, then tilted her head to dip her stick-straight brown hair in the water.

"Predators," Zofi agreed, "and prey. Though I can't really picture you as the latter."

"Should I take that as a compliment?"

"Take it however you like."

Florencia sat up again to wring out her now-dripping hair. "Do you have a problem with me, sister?"

"No more than I have with any other Kolonyan," she lied. Most other Kolonyans, after all, were not nearly so dangerous. Most other Kolonyans weren't family. The next in line to a throne if Zofi abdicated her spot.

Joke was on Florencia. The competition only made Zofi want the throne more. If Florencia won it, it would be the same rules as ever. Kolonya first, everyone else second, if at all.

Zofi could change all that. No wonder Florencia would stoop to threatening her.

"We're not all the same." Florencia ran her hands through her short locks once more, then let her hands drop. "Just as I'm sure not all Travelers are thieves or murderers."

"Aren't we?" Zofi flashed a sarcastic grin.

"You don't have to do that."

"Do what?"

"Act hard." Florencia rested her neck on the edge of the bath. "We all saw you fight today. We know what you're capable of."

"Losing, apparently," Zofi muttered.

To her surprise, Florencia shook her head. "You made your point. Kolonya doesn't know all the military tactics. Travelers have some tricks, too."

"Typical." Zofi huffed out a laugh. "All you saw were the tithes."

"What else should I have noticed? The camouflage was the point of the lesson."

"No, the point was that Talons fight like windup toys. War is an exercise for them, a game."

"You mean you didn't volunteer to fight them just for the fun of showing off?" Florencia replied, and Zofi flattened her mouth in annoyance.

Florencia was partly right, of course. But only partly. "Their style might work in an organized battle, but it won't help if you're fighting to survive."

"Exactly how many battles have you seen, sister?" Florencia's voice went thick with sarcasm.

"Plenty." Because she had. Not in war—she'd avoided the draft, like most Travelers. Why fight for people who treat you like dirt under their boots? But she'd been in enough street brawls, confrontations with local guards or thieves or unruly townspeople looking to teach some drifters a lesson.

Those fights were every bit as life or death as a battlefield.

She thought about Akeylah's words at the feast. *We can change things for our people.* "This court...it's just another battlefield. Only with less practical armor."

Florencia huffed out something between a laugh and a sigh. Then, after a long pause, "I've never heard anyone admit that out loud."

"I imagine it's easier for you. You grew up with these people." She tried not to let her voice go too bitter. "You're one of them."

"Not really." Florencia spread her arms out to float. "I spent years watching from the sidelines, wishing I could enter the fray. I never actually joined the war until now."

And how exactly did you join that war, sister? "Still." Zofi shrugged a shoulder. "You know the rules. You don't stick out like a fish in a wheelbarrow."

"I thought I was a lobster in a dress," Florencia countered, with a ghost of a smile.

Zofi returned it. "Better that than the fish, trust me. At least lobsters have claws."

"Oh, please, you can handle yourself."

"Not against an entire city that hates me simply for who I am," she replied. *And a sister willing to blackmail me for a throne.*

"That's not why people are judging you. It's because of how you dress, how you stomp around like you're better than all of us. Like the rules don't apply to you."

"Why should I obey Kolonyan rules about dressing and bowing and kissing noble's arses?"

"You don't have to." Florencia shrugged one birdlike shoulder. "But don't complain that people treat you differently when you act different in the first place."

"So Kolonyans are only capable of respecting people who act and dress and sound Kolonyan. Is that what you're saying?"

Florencia groaned. "Of course not. But you're not some visiting noble from a culture like the Southern Reach or a peace envoy from Genal."

"Right. I'm just a Traveler, with no homeland and no 'culture.'" Zofi practically snarled that last word. "Tell me again that your people don't hate me just for who I am."

To her credit, Florencia sat with that one in silence awhile.

Before she finally responded, her mouth pursed in consideration. "I suppose we might have a slight bias toward your particular group." She shook her head. "If you'd just *try* to make some effort, Kolonyans wouldn't be nearly so cold."

Zofi narrowed her eyes. "Why, sister, that almost sounds like encouragement."

The Kolonyan snorted. "Don't get used to it. After all, I won't complain if you leave the city. One less sister to worry about."

"Eager to get me out of your way to the throne?" Despite herself, the corners of Zofi's mouth tugged into a smile. She much preferred this. Being open and honest about their rivalry, rather than dancing around the point.

"Only as eager as I imagine you are," Florencia replied. Yet she, too, let a small smile touch her mouth. "I wonder just what that eagerness might drive a person to do."

Zofi cocked her head. "It sounds as though you speak from experience, sister. Have anything to confess?"

"Merely a concern for the character of the successor to our kingdom's throne. We've already had one heir with a less-than-desirable reputation. I'd hate to see the throne fall to someone equally unsuitable now that we've been granted a reprieve from him."

Zofi's eyebrows rose. "You're talking about Prince Nicolen." Was Florencia trying to goad her into admitting something?

But to her surprise, Florencia scowled. "Of course. Surely you've heard the stories."

"He was a skilled warrior. They wrote songs about his bravery on the battlefield."

"That he was. First into the fray and last out of it, every

time." Florencia rolled her head until her neck cracked, a sharp, unpleasant sound in the echoing baths. "But the battlefield wasn't the only place the prince unleashed his temper. He beat his servants on the regular, for 'mistakes' like allowing it to rain on his riding day, or not serving fresh barrafish when it's six months out of season."

She stared at her sister. Studied her reaction as she calculated her response. "Sounds like his murderer did us all a favor."

If Florencia knew something, it didn't show on her face. She just sighed and let her gaze drift past Zofi to the murals on the walls around the bath—King Ilian hunting with his stormwing. The bird's wings took up half the wall. "I don't condone violence," Florencia finally replied. "But I must admit, all of us downstairs felt relieved when news came of his death."

Zofi narrowed her eyes. "And now you're worried his disposition might be genetic, is that it? I hate to break it to you, sister, but whatever blood ran in his veins is in yours as well as mine." *Perhaps you're the one who takes after him, Florencia.* Sending blackmail threats in the dead of night, intimidating her enemies on the way to the throne.

Yet the other girl shook her head. "I don't believe things like that run in the blood. Andros wasn't cruel. He tried to teach Nicolen. Hired the best tutors in every subject. So did the first queen, his mother. That was the problem—they doted on him. Gave Nicolen everything he wanted, whenever he wanted it. It made him believe the whole world belonged to him. That he was the only one whose desires mattered."

"So the only child our father raised himself grew up to become a monster. That bodes well for us." Zofi snorted.

"But don't you see? It wasn't through neglect or anger. It wasn't something inherited or something done on purpose." Florencia's voice went low and soft. "Father just loved his son too much. Nicolen became his weak spot."

"Blaming love for all our idiotic mistakes seems like an easy excuse to me."

Florencia met her gaze and smirked, a little bitterly. "Doesn't mean it's not true."

Thoughts of Elex trickled in. Zofi had killed Nicolen to protect him. She'd done something stupid out of love. And did she regret it? Sands, no. Not even if it got her killed one day. "I suppose."

"Why, sister, did you actually agree with me about something?" Florencia touched her chest in faux surprise.

She almost smiled. "I'm big enough to admit when I'm wrong."

"Well. Perhaps you'll make a worthy contender for this throne yet."

Zofi studied her sister's amused expression. Maybe Florencia wasn't the blackmailer. Maybe she was telling the truth. She didn't seem to be asking any more pointed questions about the prince.

Then again, maybe her sister had a better hunting face than Zofi thought. Maybe she was trying to lure Zofi into a false sense of security—talk about how much she despised Nicolen in the hopes Zofi would relax her defenses.

She stifled a frustrated groan. She hated this. Hated lies and intrigue. She'd rather a direct fight any day. *Play their game.* But direct fights weren't the rule of law in the Keep. Being too obvious wouldn't solve anything. If Florencia *wasn't* her accuser, then

Zofi could stand not to make any more enemies within the Keep just yet.

Zofi extended a hand, palm up, the way she'd seen courtiers do. "May the best candidate win."

Florencia grinned and pushed off the wall. Swam close enough to place her hand palm down over Zofi's. "As long as whichever of us is selected agrees to perform better than the last heir would have."

Her heart skipped a beat. Was that a subtle threat? Florencia hadn't winced once, not the whole time Zofi brought up the prince. And yet, she kept returning to the topic, sounding almost... approving of his loss. "Deal." Zofi squeezed Florencia's wrist.

Florencia did the same. "To change for the better."

"Even if we might not know what that looks like just yet."

Zofi slid a hand under her pillow. Wrapped her fingers around the hilt of the longknife.

It wasn't so much a sound that awoke her as the absence of one. She'd fallen asleep to the swish of curtains, the play of the evening breeze, punctuated by distant calls of animals in the faraway jungle.

Now the room was silent. The curtains lay still, all the fresh air sucked from the chambers. It felt hot, heavy with humidity and something else.

Breath.

Carefully, Zofi cracked one eyelid and peered through her lashes. Shifted her body as though adjusting in her sleep, all the while drawing the knife slowly from beneath the pillow.

There. In the corner. Next to the moonlit curtains and the now-shuttered window, stood a shadow.

She thought about the figure she'd seen on the practice fields that morning. She thought about the headboard. The silver letters. *Blood-Killer.* Whoever this was, they picked a fight with the wrong person.

Zofi threw back the covers and surged to her feet, at the same instant the figure called a single word.

"Zofi."

She froze in her tracks, longknife still pressed instinctively against her forearm, ready to tithe. She never needed to draw blood. The blade fell from her shocked fingertips as she took in the shadow's familiar outline, realized what it meant.

"Thank the sands," she whispered.

·∘[**15**]∘·

Akeylah

*D*amn it all. Akeylah snapped the fourth tome shut and heaved a sigh. A noblewoman at a neighboring table glared.

The library was almost unnaturally quiet, the only sound the occasional rustle of a page turning. Since her first lesson yesterday, Akeylah had spent nearly every waking moment here. The other moments she spent tossing in her bed, unable to sleep, dreaming that every whisper of sound meant the blackmailer's return.

If she couldn't find her blackmailer—and in this court, that seemed like hunting for one particular snake in a nest of a few hundred—then her only option was to erase the hold they had over her. Undo the curse, save the king's life, and free hers in the process.

That or flee home. Back to her stepfather's house—the stepfather who had probably heard by now that she was a bastard, conceived out of wedlock with a king he must hate more than ever. If the man wanted to kill Akeylah when he thought she was his own flesh and blood, what would he do now that he knew she was someone else's child? No longer just a reminder of the wife who died birthing her, but also a symbol of that heretofore-perfect wife's uncovered infidelity?

Akeylah wouldn't last ten minutes.

She had no choice. She needed to stay here. To find a way out from under this threat.

She set aside her current book, *Acolytes of the Arts: A Study of Practitioners from Recognition to the Yrene Epoch.* It listed the exploits of several hundred acolytes, starting with war tithe studies under King Ilian up to injury-healing experiments under Yrene III. Nowhere did it mention the Vulgar Arts.

Akeylah slid that book into the growing discard stack and reached for *Balancing the Arts* instead. A quick browse of the first few chapters revealed only some poorly written ramblings about Arts theory. She frowned.

She didn't need theories about the gods or their blessings. She needed a how-to guide.

Last time, a hint in the town library's ancient *Traveling Festivales and the Arts of the Faires* had led her to the curseworker. Surely somewhere in the Keep's stores, she could find another seed like that. After all, the University—where acolytes of the Sun, the most proficient Arts practitioners in the Reaches, studied the Blood Arts and experimented with new tithes—was right here in the alder tower of the Keep. They used this same library, stored their main source texts here.

The answer was somewhere in this room, she felt sure. And yet...

Akeylah sighed and cast another glance at the stacks. The library was shaped like an upside-down whaling ship, five stories tall and covered floor-to-ceiling in bookshelves, punctuated by ladders and spiral staircases that climbed to dizzying heights.

She could spend a lifetime here and never comb through even a quarter of these books. How in Mother Ocean's name was she going to find what she needed?

"Tough reading?" someone asked.

Akeylah startled and flipped the book shut out of habit. "Oh, I just..." She lost her voice the moment she looked up.

Rozalind leaned a hip against her desk.

"Can I help you, my queen?"

"I was just passing through and noticed you daydreaming." Rozalind bent to study the book cover. Her brown curls brushed Akeylah's bare shoulder, sent a riot of electricity up her arm. "I don't blame you. This looks dreary as a midday stormcloud." Rozalind snatched up the book and opened to a page in the middle, a playful smile on her face.

Akeylah grinned and made a half-hearted grab for the book, but Rozalind pushed off the desk and danced out of reach.

"'The first known instance of the Arts appearing on Reach soil occurred in the year twenty Before Recognition, when the Reaches were still satellite colonies of Genal.'" Rozalind paused to wiggle her eyebrows at Akeylah, though Akeylah sensed that the queen did it to hide her discomfort before she continued.

"'However, it took fifteen years for the Arts to become a unifying force for the Reaches. In the year five BR, the future King Ilian began to experiment with war tithes around the same time that his soon-to-be wife, the Traveler Queen Claera, discovered Genalese-born soldiers could not tap into the Arts.'"

The noblewoman who glared at Akeylah earlier coughed pointedly. The girls exchanged furtive looks, and the mischief in Rozalind's eyes nearly made Akeylah burst into laughter again.

But Rozalind only bent closer, lips inches from Akeylah's cheek, and continued to read in a soft whisper, her rolling Genalese accent more accentuated than ever in this low volume. "'Ilian and Claera presented the Arts as evidence that the gods blessed our land above all others. Clearly the Sun wished to strengthen the Reaches so they could free themselves from their one-time parent....'"

The noblewoman pushed her chair back with a loud enough screech to make Akeylah and Rozalind jump apart. Only then did Akeylah think about how it looked—the queen and her step-daughter bent close together, whispering about Genal and the Reaches.

"We should go," Akeylah murmured.

Rozalind set the book down on the tray. On their way out of the library, she bobbed her head to the noblewoman in apology.

The woman curtsied deeply in response, though not before Akeylah caught a glimpse of the scowl on her face.

It didn't seem the appropriate way for a noble to treat her queen. Then again, she thought about the passage Rozalind had just read. Kolonya had spent the four hundred years After Recognition believing the gods themselves blessed the Reaches with the Arts specifically to defeat Genal. Every war, from the War for Recognition up through the most recent Seventh War, had been fought by soldiers who believed that wholeheartedly.

If Akeylah felt ostracized here as an Easterner, she could only begin to fathom how Rozalind must feel. She was still trying to word a response—*I'm sorry* didn't seem quite adequate, nor did *I wish they didn't treat you this way*—when the mahogany library doors swung shut behind them.

Then Rozalind elbowed her side with a smirk. "You aren't planning to become an acolyte, are you? Because that would be quite a shame."

Acolytes—who taught the menders and the Talons, kept records of every tithe ever discovered, and worked day and night to uncover more—were sworn to celibacy.

"Afraid that life wouldn't suit me." Akeylah caught the queen's eye. In the bright torches of the hall, Rozalind's navy eyes seemed to glow almost as bright as Akeylah's scar. "I'd hate to disappoint all these young noblewomen."

"It's not *their* disappointment I'm concerned with." Rozalind bent closer, and Akeylah felt herself mirroring the motion, drawn like the tide chasing the moons.

She caught herself at the last moment, turned forward just as footsteps rounded the hall. Rozalind didn't even seemed fazed— she just kept strolling along as though nothing had happened.

"So why the sudden interest in the Arts?" Rozalind's tone was lighthearted, conversational.

It set off alarm bells nonetheless. Akeylah could not afford to let people start asking questions like that about her. She had enough problems already.

"King—ah, Father took us to see the Talons practice yesterday," Akeylah said. "And the countess showed us a few tricks. I was curious to learn more."

"I can recommend a few titles if you'd like." Rozalind flashed her another smile, the kind that lit her whole face with sincerity.

"Why, were you debating the acolyte route, too?" Akeylah joked. Then she clamped her mouth shut, remembering. "Oh. Rozalind, I'm sorry, I forgot you can't..."

"It's quite all right." Rozalind looped her arm through Akeylah's. "Most people forget. Even my husband at times. I'm quite the rarity in this part of the world. The only unblessed woman in a sea of warlocks."

"We aren't warlocks." Akeylah laughed.

"That's what we call you in Genal. It's what you'd call yourself, too, if you could see all the magic you can create with the simple flick of a knife."

Akeylah flushed. "The Arts aren't magic. They're a gift from the gods, a practice we have spent centuries studying and perfecting."

"Tell that to your enemies." Rozalind still smiled, though it was hard now, bitter.

"What's it like?" Akeylah asked, before she could help herself. "Not being able to tithe?"

"Normal, for me." The queen shrugged, her arm brushing along Akeylah's. "I never knew anything different. The only thing I knew about the Arts before I came here were the terrible rumors—mostly false, of course. Stories about the warlocks in the west. Descendants of the children who cursed their own parents."

Akeylah's steps faltered. She forgot about that part of the story. Most Kolonyans preferred to, since it bordered on treason.

"That's why I wanted to read more about the Arts," Rozalind was saying, seemingly oblivious to Akeylah's discomfort. "Learn how they came to be, separate the truth from fiction."

Yet Akeylah couldn't stop running over those words. *Children who cursed their own parents.*

Back when the Arts first appeared in the Reaches, there was no distinction between the Blood Arts and the Vulgar Arts. No studies yet into what the gods deemed proper and what would be labeled forbidden cursework.

In the first war, the War for Recognition, some soldiers of the Reaches—first- and second-generation Genalese immigrants, especially—used the Vulgar Arts against their kin. Grandparents and aunts and cousins who had stayed behind and fought for Genal. They were cursed by their own descendants, who pledged their lifeblood to the Reaches.

Kolonya preferred to ignore that piece of history. Now that the inhabitants of the Reaches were so far separated from their Genalese ancestors that no cursework, which was only effective within three or four generations at maximum, could affect them. Now that the Reaches could only curse one another.

"Akeylah?" Rozalind asked.

She shook herself back to the present. *Why did Rozalind bring that story up now?* She couldn't help the unease that settled in her stomach.

"Is something wrong?"

"Of course not." Akeylah forced a too-bright smile.

No. Rozalind could not be her blackmailer. The queen had been nothing but kind—the only person in the Keep to do so without expecting a thing of Akeylah in return.

"I see you haven't learned to lie any better during your time here so far," Rozalind teased.

She swallowed with difficulty. "I'm just not accustomed to being called a warlock, that's all."

With a sigh, the queen tightened her grip on Akeylah's arm. "I fear you'd best get used to that and worse. Take it from me—no one here will let you forget your differences, not for a moment."

What could Rozalind want, anyway? What could she stand to gain from threatening Akeylah, if that's what she was doing, all while playing nice to her face?

The throne. If Andros passed away without an heir, perhaps Rozalind hoped to maintain her hold on the throne. Bring the Reaches back under Genalese control.

"Is that supposed to make me feel better?" Akeylah's voice went soft.

The look Rozalind turned on her then, fierce and protective all at once, made Akeylah's chest ache. Surely that could not be a lie. The desperate, almost painful care in the queen's eyes. "No. It's supposed to keep you alive, Akeylah."

For a long, breathless moment, their gazes held. Akeylah felt her body sway, the way it always did, leaning toward the queen, drawn in by her impossible gravity. "Should I be worried about my safety just now?" Her voice dropped even lower, whisper-soft in this public, albeit empty, hall.

"Always." Rozalind turned, then drew Akeylah back into a slow walk. Akeylah tried to calm her racing pulse. "You're a daughter of the king, a blood relative who could do him as much harm as good. Not to mention you're from an outer Reach, a Reach currently nursing rebellion."

They walked in silence for several paces. "Does it get easier? With time, I mean."

"Not yet." Rozalind shrugged one shoulder. "But it is early days still, even for me. A year is no time at all in the grand scheme of things. Our peace treaty is still fresh. It may hold this time."

"What happens if it doesn't?"

Rozalind laughed without mirth. "Then I doubt I will live long enough to fret about people's poor opinion of me."

A shiver ran along Akeylah's spine. "That's horrible."

"I knew what I was signing up for."

That raised Akeylah's eyebrows. "You had a choice?"

"In coming here? Of course I did." Rozalind smiled again, the dark cloud around her seeming to disperse. Akeylah loved that about her. The seas-damn-it grin she wore while talking about her possible downfall. "Not all Genalese are the big bad wolves you hear about in your bedtime stories."

"I didn't..." She stopped herself. Because of course she'd been thinking about the gruesome stories traders passing through Jahen's house had told. Legends about a bloodthirsty king who killed his own men when they disobeyed, soldiers who flayed enemies alive.

"My father was elected king out of his seven siblings by the nobles' council when he was my age, nineteen. He has five children. He gave us all the chance to run for election if we chose. His heir selection will be next year, just after my youngest brother comes of age."

Election. That sounded more like the old Eastern method of inheritance than the Kolonyan one. Then again, both Kolonya and the Eastern Reach came from Genal. It made sense that different children of the same parent inherited slightly different characteristics—the way she and Florencia had inherited their father's eyes, while Zofi had not.

Akeylah wondered, suddenly, if Genal was where King Andros got the idea to bring all three of his bastard daughters here. Customarily the king named their eldest legitimate child heir—hence Andros's throne, though he was only born minutes before Yasmin. She supposed when it came to selecting a bastard replacement, custom grew more flexible.

"You chose not to run for Genal's throne," Akeylah said.

"My country needed me here. We must end these wars if either of our nations is ever to grow prosperous again."

"Seas know that's true." Akeylah thought about the war-torn docks still visible from her stepfather's cliffside house. "Yet that must have been so hard. Leaving your home, everyone you knew, to come marry a foreign king."

"As I said, I knew what I was volunteering for. This is the first time we have sealed a treaty with a marriage. My father hoped— hopes—it will prove our sincere desire for peace once and for all."

"I hope so, too," she said, even as her heart sank. Rozalind needed to make her marriage work, not just for herself, but to keep peace between nations.

Rozalind seemed to have the same thought, because she untangled her arm. "I believe this is your corridor."

"Yes." Akeylah hesitated.

"I'll see you at dinner." Rozalind searched her gaze until Akeylah's face went hot. "Next time, I promise, we will speak of more pleasant topics."

"Agreed." She managed a small smile. Then she stood to watch the queen depart, her words still ringing in Akeylah's ears. *Children who cursed their own parents.*

It wasn't Rozalind. It *couldn't* be. Yet Akeylah's stomach churned nevertheless. How could she truly know?

At the end of the corridor, Rozalind glanced back at her with an almost-pained expression. Akeylah quickly tore her gaze away. Nothing she could do now. No way to prove the queen's innocence or otherwise. She could only keep her head down and continue her work.

Find a cure for King Andros or die trying.

✳ 16 ✳

Florencia

Every head in the room turned when Ren entered. She dressed impeccably and arrived late, after the majority of the court had been seated. It might just be the usual midweek dinner, but every occasion was an opportunity to advertise her suitability now.

Ren smiled faintly, enough to hint at pleasure without revealing how much she savored this. The jealous whispers of the noblewomen and desirous gazes of the men.

She was born for this moment. And she'd be damned if some underhanded blackmail threat would take it from her.

Ren crossed to her seat near the front of the room, a table laden with the highest ranks of nobility. To her annoyance, the last two remaining seats were across from Sarella and her current partner-in-schemes, the equally insipid Lady Tjuya. She took one of those seats, next to Akeylah. It took her a moment to realize who the other empty seat must be for.

"Our sister is running late," Ren commented.

"Her maid told Father she hasn't been able to get into Zofi's rooms all day. Apparently Zofi locked the door from the inside." Akeylah looked genuinely concerned. "I do hope she's all right."

"It's probably some Traveler thing." Ren waved a hand, dismissive, though her mind churned.

Her conversation with Zofi in the baths yesterday had been intriguing, if nothing else. She couldn't make sense of it yet. All that talk of predators and prey, the prince's assassination, and plots against the kingdom. It almost sounded as though Zofi were suggesting something. Yet she hadn't strayed anywhere near the topic of Burnt Bay. Surely if Zofi were confronting Ren, she would have thrown that accusation at her first.

Unless Zofi was more deceitful than she acted. But having witnessed her half sister's hotheaded, forward approach to their first lesson—volunteering to fight a Talon her first time using a new tithe, for Sun's sake—Ren found it difficult to imagine Zofi maintaining a hunter's face of any kind. Zofi wasn't the type to sit around a baited trap waiting to catch prey. She'd charge headlong into the forest firing arrows blindly until one struck something.

But if Zofi was acting strangely now...

"The Eastern ambassador, you say?"

Ren started from her reverie. Found Lady Tjuya directly across from her, eyes darting between Ren and Lady Sarella.

"That's right," Sarella all but purred. "And he wants to see me again. But I just don't know..."

PRICE

1213

Pickup By:
1/9/2019

Rule

0112423876062

Please take this item to a

self-check station or
staff

member for check out.

Visit us on the web at

lacountylibrary.org

"He's the most handsome noble at court, now that Lord Jaxen is off the market."

"He is rather dashing." Sarella paused to flip her head, short hair skimming her cheekbones as she turned to glance across the hall. Ren followed her gaze to the table where Ambassador Danton dined with Lord Rueno and his daughter, Lexana. "But I worry about his morality."

Ren barely managed to resist snorting into her soup course. *Sarella*, worried over morality?

"Whatever do you mean?" Lady Tjuya fluttered her lashes, her goading about as subtle as a stormwing diving into battle.

Sarella tilted her head toward Ren as she spun her spoon through her bowl. "Apparently the ambassador has a predilection for the . . . lower classes, if you take my meaning."

Ren's ears rang. Worse, she noticed Akeylah tune into the conversation. Akeylah, who witnessed Ren and Danton's interaction in the hallway just yesterday. Akeylah, who knew Danton already, and seemed a much more likely contender for a devious liar than Zofi . . .

Meanwhile, Tjuya pressed a hand to her chest in the most dramatic example of overacting Ren had seen since the last time a circus troop passed through. "Surely no lord would desire a working girl over a lady such as yourself."

"Everyone has a type, Lady Tjuya." Sarella shrugged. "His appears to be serving girls."

Ren tightened her grip on her spoon. *What does Sarella know?*

She danced with him once, after the Blood Ceremony. Perhaps Sarella spotted them. Maybe she was extrapolating.

Or maybe . . .

She thought about drunken Sarella after Lord Rueno's party, grinning like a cat with a macaw in its teeth. *You never enjoyed seeing me with him, did you?*

Maybe Sarella had known all along. Maybe she'd followed Ren in the past, trailed them to the cave, overheard their conversations. Maybe she knew what else Ren and Danton shared, beyond their trysts.

Maybe Sarella was her blackmailer.

Lady Tjuya tutted and fanned herself, as though a lord bedding a maid were the most shocking thing she'd ever heard. "I cannot believe it."

"Don't take my word for it." Sarella caught Ren's eye, widened that grin. "Lady Florencia, you used to work below-stairs."

"Volunteer more than work," she replied, a bland smile on her face. "Father wanted me to know the ins and outs of the Keep. That meant learning how people treat others on both sides of the divide—noble and otherwise."

Let that sink in, you snake. A white lie, claiming she'd known about her birthright all along. Worth it to allay any nobles' concerns about her past, she decided.

Besides, it had been at least one of her parents' plans.

To her credit, Lady Tjuya took Ren's meaning. She ducked over her soup bowl, probably running through all her interactions with the maids in her head, wondering which Ren might be able to use against her.

Plenty, actually. Ren knew Lady Tjuya had a fondness for the bone dice. She had a mental list of people, noble and otherwise, who Tjuya owed debts.

"What a sacrifice." Sarella, on the other hand, was not so easily deterred. "The poor king, pretending his own daughter was a maid, all to help her studies. I should commend him on his dedication." She smirked.

Damn her.

Ren didn't expect Sarella to call the bluff. Would she go so far as asking King Andros outright?

"Indeed, our father was very thorough in his preparations," Akeylah spoke up, startling both Ren and Sarella. "He raised each of us in unique conditions, so that we might bring our diverse expertise with us when it came time for us to join the court."

Ren shot a grateful, if somewhat shocked, glance at her half sister. A ghost of a smile turned the corner of Akeylah's mouth in reply.

Sarella's expression soured. "Well. We must all thank His Majesty for his continued foresight." Her green eyes glittered in the glow cast by the Great Hall chandeliers. "I'm sure he's very proud of your performance, Lady Florencia. You were always the perfect maid. Never untoward. Never inappropriate." Those eyes narrowed. "Never took part in anything that might cause your father concern."

Ren's throat constricted. *What does she know?* Surely she just meant rendezvousing with Danton. Surely Sarella didn't know more than that. Sarella seemed as unlikely a blackmailer as Zofi—both too hotheaded and straightforward. Sarella'd threaten Ren outright, demand payment for her silence. Not send coded messages to unsettle Ren in secret.

Wouldn't she?

Ren was still mulling this over when Josen appeared at her

shoulder. "Excuse me, Lady Florencia. Your father wishes to speak with you."

"Thank you, Josen." A smile lit his face. Aside from Andros, who made it a point to memorize every person who lived under the Keep's roof, most nobles barely remembered the servants' faces, let alone their given names.

"And you as well, Lady Akeylah," he added.

The half sisters rose and approached the head table together. King Andros bent close to Queen Rozalind, his voice a barely audible murmur.

"No, as I said before, they do not believe it to be affected by diet, so this precaution—" Andros broke off. Cut his gaze to Yasmin, then down to where Akeylah and Ren stood at the foot of his table. "Ah, girls."

"Father." Ren and Akeylah curtsied in unison. Ren didn't like the look of the bags under his eyes, or the way his voice sounded. Dry and brittle.

He cleared his throat with difficulty. She thought again of his words, just three days ago, when he turned her life upside down.

I am dying.

The rumors weren't bad. Not yet. *King has a touch of the flu,* people said. She wondered how long they'd believe that. How long before this illness bit too deep to conceal.

"The day after tomorrow," he finally managed, after another louder throat-clearing, "I'd like you to attend to me again. I've sent word to Zofi as well."

"Another lesson, Father?" Ren wondered what it would be this time. More military training? Or perhaps a one-on-one conversation, a chance to talk to the king in private. She hoped for the latter. It would be a chance to learn about her kingdom. To study with the most powerful man in the world.

To get to know her father.

"Yes. Meet me outside the cherry tower in the morning, at seven tolls."

Ren and Akeylah sank into matching curtsies once more. "I look forward to another opportunity to learn from you," Ren replied.

King Andros smiled. "I believe you especially will find this lesson intriguing, Florencia."

"Let us pray to the Sun that you two will absorb more from this lesson than you did from the last one," Yasmin added to Ren and Akeylah. Ren met the countess's hardened gaze with a frown. She wanted to argue. Ask what Yasmin held against her.

But on the other hand, Yasmin had a point. Zofi had managed the camouflage tithe on her first go, then battled three Talons on top of it.

Ren had to do better this time. Prove to the king what she was worth—even if the countess would disparage Ren no matter what she did.

"I endeavor to learn as much as I can from both you and my father, Aunt Yasmin," Ren said. Unless she imagined it, Yasmin's jaw seemed to clench on the word *aunt*.

Beside her, Akeylah curtsied. "I pray for understanding every day, my lady."

The countess barked out a single, bitter laugh. "Glad we agree on one thing."

The king exchanged a look with his sister, though before either of them said anything more, Queen Rozalind rested a hand on Andros's forearm.

"The matter at hand," the queen murmured, and Andros nodded. "Thank you, girls."

Ren knew a dismissal when she heard one. She nudged Akeylah on her way back to her chair, since her half sister seemed stuck in place, staring at the queen. Only when Ren's elbow connected did Akeylah startle out of her reverie and turn to follow.

Ren paced across the Great Hall, heart racing. For someone who'd spent her entire life awaiting this chance, she wasn't handling it very well. She'd all but failed her first lesson, Yasmin made that much clear. And she still had someone threatening her, holding a secret so huge above her head that it made Ren a liability not just to herself but to all the Reaches, should she take the throne.

She reclaimed her seat, Sarella and Tjuya still bent together whispering, a cruel smile on Sarella's mouth. Ren's gaze drifted past her. Toward the maids' corner.

Audrina caught her eye with a sympathetic smile. Ren hadn't spoken to her friend since the Blood Ceremony, but Aud must know who she was now. After the ceremony, announcements went out across the city and throughout the Keep. A pang of regret struck her for a moment—she should have told her friend before she learned from others.

But then an idea began to take hold. Ren dared a tiny smile back, barely more than a flick of her lips. All she'd risk in public. Yet Aud winked and bowed her head, noticing.

The idea took shape.

After all, Ren had one advantage. One thing these nobles couldn't call upon, couldn't use to their advantage. One thing Sarella would never expect.

Ren watched Lady Sarella twirl her fork, halfway through telling Lady Tjuya a story about a now-disgraced nobleman who betrayed his king. She'd find this blackmailer. Even if she had to tick every lord and lady in this court off her list one at a time.

Starting with Sarella. *Let's see which of us is the real expert at subterfuge.*

✳

The knock came just after moons' rise, while Ren was still dressing to attend a concert in the king's private audience chamber later that night. She opened the door to her friend's bewildered expression.

"My lady." Audrina hesitated on the threshold. Ren had sent away her usual maid for the evening, chosen a simple gown she could tie on herself. She didn't want anyone else overhearing this conversation. "Do you need assistance dressing for this evening?"

"Oh, blessed Sun, don't start standing on ceremony with me, Aud." Ren ushered her in and poured Audrina a flute of nectar from her sidebar.

"Sorry, Ren. It's not every day your best friend morphs into a princess, is all." Audrina accepted it and took a swig. "*Sun* that's strong." She peered at the amber liquid.

"Nicer than the cat piss they leave around for us, huh?" Ren flopped onto her bed and patted the space beside her.

Audrina perched on it, still hesitant. Watchful. "How long have you known?" she finally asked.

"Not until the day before the Blood Ceremony." Ren winced. "I'm sorry, Aud. I should have told you myself. I was just so swept up in everything going on—"

"Don't." Aud touched her hand briefly. "You had a lot on your mind. Finding out your whole life was a lie, that your mother concealed this from you and that your father never even bothered to acknowledge you until now...I don't blame you for not being able to talk about it." The anger on Audrina's face when she mentioned the king warmed Ren's heart. Warmed it, and made her feel even worse for only speaking to her friend now, when she needed something.

"Thank you." Ren shook her head. "You always have my back. I don't deserve it."

"Of course you do." Aud grinned. "How many times have you gotten me the assignments I want, or finished my mending...?" She laughed a little. "How many girls can say a princess used to help them darn their charges' socks?"

Ren sighed and tilted her head back to study the ceiling. "Speaking of helping each other out...I hate to do this, Aud, but I need to ask you for a favor."

"If it's within my power, anything."

Guilt tugged at her. Asking this felt like taking advantage of their friendship. In a way, it was. But she'd make it up to Audrina one day.

"It's about Sarella."

"I could've guessed." Aud rolled her eyes and lifted the glass in a sarcastic toast. "She's not too pleased her former maid got promoted above her, I take it."

"Do you know who's been assigned to her in my stead?"

"Yvette, I think. Not sure. I could ask?"

"If you volunteered for the D'Garridas, do you think Oruna would let you swap into Sarella's service instead?"

Audrina's eyes widened.

"I know, she's horrible." Ren lifted her palms. "That's why I'm sorry to ask this of you. Yet you know Yvette would trade with you in a heartbeat to get away from her."

"To what end?" Audrina's frown deepened. "I'll help you any way I can, Ren, you know that, but I cannot afford to jeopardize my position. Not all of us have secret pasts that will elevate our statuses." To her credit, Aud's voice remained steady, didn't dip toward bitterness on that last line. She stated it simply, as a fact. Not something she resented.

Ren wasn't sure whether, in Audrina's shoes, she could have remained so impartial. She loved her friend all the more for it.

"I don't intend sabotage," Ren promised. "Nothing that would put you in danger. I only desire one thing. A tiny thing, really." Ren allowed a smile to creep onto her face. This was one weapon none of these other noblewomen could wield, despite their high births. Because of them, in fact.

After all, how many secrets had she picked up while dressing and undressing those fine women? To the nobility, servants were as invisible as furniture. Sarella wanted to see what D'Andros Florencia was made of? Well, Ren was more than happy to oblige.

"What's that?"

Ren gripped her friend's hand tight. "Information."

❧ 17 ❦

Zofi

Just leave the tray," Zofi called through the door.

"My lady." The maid's voice came through, hard and angry. "The king has sent another message for you. This is not proper."

"I told you, I'll attend the lesson. Day after tomorrow."

"If you are ill, let me send for the menders. It would not do for me to be seen letting my charge suffer."

And there it was. The only reason her maid gave a handful of sand that Zofi had spent the last day holed up in here. "Where was this concern of yours yesterday when I needed a bath drawn?" Zofi called back.

"The public baths are—"

"Perfectly acceptable for drifters. So you said. Now explain why I should give a damn if you get in trouble over me spending dinner in my chambers."

A long silence came from the other side of the door. Zofi waited until she heard the clink of the tray, followed by departing footsteps, before she eased the door open and pulled the tray inside.

"Living here seems like more hassle than it's worth."

"Yes, well." Zofi plopped the tray onto her vanity and shot a glare at the boy sprawled across her bed. "It'd be a lot easier if I wasn't hiding a wanted criminal."

Elex's unruly black curls had grown longer since the last time she saw him. His beard, too, was less scruff and more almost-a-real-beard. It suited him. Aged him, too, which she teased him for.

Teasing was good. It distracted her from the sandstorm in her stomach every time she remembered *he was really here*. Every time she licked her lips, she tasted their last kiss. Every time she blinked she saw the desperate, determined look in his eye when he whispered goodbye.

That was the old Elex. Her best friend, her partner in crime. The boy she grew up with.

This Elex, the one with his boots muddying her comforter and hard-focused black eyes, this was someone else. The man who'd taken his place.

"I told you, I broke in here to save you."

"And I told you, that was an idiotic risk. Plus I don't need saving." Zofi perched on the end of the bed, passing him the dinner plate, which she'd piled high with options.

Elex sat up and took it. Their fingers brushed before he settled back onto the cushions, plate balanced on his stomach, and offered her a bread roll. She accepted it but didn't bite, just rolled it between her fingers.

"Certainly sounds like you do," he said. "You're being blackmailed, for sands' sake."

"It's nothing I can't handle."

"Why risk it? What are you staying here for?" He pointed at the door with an elbow and spilled a few leaves of salad. "So you can be hounded by maids? Have tailors dress you up like some Kolonyan floozy—"

"Not all Kolonyans are so simple," she muttered, thinking about the baths, her conversation with Florencia. Granted, her half sister might *be* said blackmailer. Yet there was something about Florencia's forthrightness, her willingness to call the court what it was—a battlefield—that Zofi couldn't help respecting.

Even if Florencia was currently winning that battle.

"—then paraded around court by a king who's congratulating himself on taming a wild Traveler. Is that it? You like being his show horse?"

"I have a chance to do something important here, Elex."

"Yeah." He rolled his eyes. "Get executed for treason."

Despite the fact that she'd already triple-checked the room for spy holes and hidden passages, not to mention stuffed any cracks in the windowpanes full of spare bedding, Zofi still startled at those words.

"No Traveler has ever been this close to the throne," she replied. They'd been having this argument all day. From the sound of it, they'd continue all night, too. "Think about what it would mean if Andros named me his heir. Think about how things would change for our people."

"You mean *if* this blackmailer doesn't get you killed first? Sure, I can hear the news criers now. 'New record—drifter queen only lasts ten days on the Sun Throne before being executed for crimes against Kolonya.'"

"Be serious, Elex."

"I *am*." He set the plate aside, knelt on the bed. Reached up to cup her face with both hands. His palms felt hot, rough with new callouses. Part of her wanted to ask. Wanted to talk about where he'd spent the last two months, how he'd stayed hidden.

Another part didn't want to know how much he had sacrificed for her.

"You're the one who isn't making sense. Zo, I spoke to your mother. She told me about the Talons taking you. She told me how dangerous it is here."

"For *you*. Which is exactly why she told you not to come."

"Yes, but—"

"Do you know what she told me? She told me to play their game. To act Kolonyan, blend in, make the system work for me. That doesn't mean running home at the first threat."

"She doesn't know about the blackmailer. We can't go back to the band, not while I'm still wanted and you're the daughter of the king, no. But we can go somewhere else. Somewhere nobody knows who we are, far north maybe, or out west."

Zofi shook her head. After hearing Elex's recounting of his brief meeting with Mother, Zofi was more certain than ever about what her mother wanted. And angry as Zofi might be with her for putting her in this situation unawares, she had to agree.

Zofi's family is public knowledge now, Mother had told Elex. *The best thing she can do is wield that family to her advantage.*

"She wants me to stay here. Win this throne."

Elex grimaced. "Your mother hid your past from you. Let the Talons take you without a word of explanation."

"Well, things got a bit complicated when I stabbed my half brother to death," she hissed. Then she paused, rubbed her temple. "I wish she'd told me more, yes."

"Then why are you listening to her advice?"

"Because I agree with it, Elex. No matter where I run now, people will know I'm the king's daughter. They'll try to use me, get me to influence him, maybe even worse. Some enemies of the crown wouldn't bat an eye at torturing me, making me use the Vulgar Arts against my father."

He winced at that word. *Father.* She knew the feeling. Yet she couldn't let him forget who she was now.

She couldn't forget it. "The best thing I can do, now that the world knows I'm Andros's daughter, is own that title. Use it to my advantage—to all our people's advantage."

"How will being executed for treason help anybody?"

"The blackmailer hasn't told anyone yet," she snapped. "Besides, leaving won't change the fact that someone knows what I did. They could tell the king at any time, no matter where I am. At least here I'm in their territory. I stand a chance at finding out who's doing this and why."

"Maybe they're threatening you *because* you're in their territory? Maybe if you leave, the threats will stop. Or maybe not, and we both wind up on the run from Talons for the rest of our lives. If you ask me, that sounds far better than dying in this cage."

"I didn't ask you," she said. Then she bit her lip at the way he flinched. "Look." She caught his hand. "I'm trapped either way,

Elex. Have been since the moment I swung that knife. The only thing I can choose now is my future. And I choose to stay, to at least try to make a difference. If I die doing it, then I die trying to help my people. Trying to stop the hatred, the false accusations, the attacks."

Elex scowled. "We know how to deal with those things. We always have."

"How many of us were attacked without reason the year before last?" It was a low blow, yet one she needed to take. "It was a war year; people were especially riled up. How many of us, Elex?"

Elex turned away.

"Seven," she said when he remained silent. "Seven people out of a band of forty-three. That was almost a fifth of our people attacked, beaten, even killed in one case, and for what?"

He clenched his jaw.

"For fishing at the wrong dock." Leonus and Heine, beaten because a suspicious Easterner thought they were stealing his catch. "For getting married." Karle and Thekla had traveled to Thekla's village in north Kolonya to apply for a wedding license. The locals, who hadn't seen Thekla in years, who had never seen a Traveler with hair as dark and wild as Karle, stopped them at the gate. Accused them of being Genalese spies. When Karle reached for his paperwork, a townie guard panicked. Stuck an arrow into his chest. Only after Thekla showed the guards the papers Karle had been reaching for would they call menders to treat him. By then, it was too late.

Elex pushed off the bed, strode to the window.

Zofi stood, too, stormed after him. "And what about Noemi and Det and Wann?"

"Stop. I get it." Elex shoved the curtain open to glare at the city outside. It looked peaceful in the evening light. Quaint terra-cotta rooftops, sleepy jungle trees beyond.

Appearances were deceptive.

"All the more reason for you not to risk your life surrounded by people who hate us, attack us, kill us just because we aren't like them."

"What if I could stop it?" She rested one hand on his shoulder. Met his gaze in the window, eyes locked over the darkening city. "I'm already a dead woman walking. I killed a prince. One day or another, either when this blackmailer turns me in or if they find some other proof, that secret will get out. Why not spend my last days working toward a better world?"

He reached up and curled his fingers around hers. For a moment—just a moment—she thought she might be winning him over. "There is no better world," he finally murmured. "There's only the one we live in. And if these are your last days, you should spend them at home."

With that, he unlatched the window.

"Elex—"

"I'm not going to sit around and watch you kill yourself. Not after everything I've sacrificed to keep you alive, Zofi."

She flinched. His turn for the low blow. No, she never asked him to shoulder her burden. Didn't change the fact that he had.

"If I make it through this, I'll fix that, too. I'll clear your name, Elex, I swear it."

He laughed once, hard. "Right. As soon as these jackals crown you queen. Save me a seat at the coronation." He stepped onto the windowsill.

186

Zofi grabbed his hand. Used it to pull herself up onto the balcony beside him. "Don't just run. Not this time. At least let me say farewell."

Her lips tingled. Sands, her whole *body* did. It felt like an eternity since she'd last stood like this, inches from him. Two months was a lifetime. So much had changed.

"I can't," he breathed, so low she could barely hear. "I can't say goodbye."

"Then don't." She wove her fingers through his. He clenched so tight her bones ached. She didn't care. "Tell me you'll see me soon. Even if it's a lie."

He smiled. It didn't reach his eyes. "I wish you'd listen. But sands know if anyone can make it out of this stormwing's nest alive, it's you."

She tilted her head to look up at him in the early moons' light. *Stay*, she wanted to say. But she knew he couldn't. He'd risked far too much remaining in the Keep this long. Sooner or later one of these maids would force their way into her chambers and find the most wanted man in the Reaches lying on her bed.

So she cupped his cheek and savored the faint scratch of stubble against her palm. "See you at my coronation," she whispered. "You'll have the seat of honor."

He laughed again, softer now. Genuine. "I hate formal parties, but I'll make an exception. For you."

They stood like that, his cheek cradled in her hand, while the smiles slowly fell from their faces. She didn't need to ask what he was thinking. His thoughts would be mirroring hers right now. And hers were screaming *Don't let him go*. Not again.

A million words lodged in the back of her throat. Everything she couldn't say. *I'll miss you. I don't know how to do this without you. Don't go don't go don't go.*

And one that screamed louder than all the rest. *I love you.*

None of them made it into voice.

Elex kissed her, feather-light. A barely there kiss that only stoked the fire in her veins. It felt like a speeding tithe, like her whole body going electric. She reached for him, for *more*, but he'd already let go. He stepped onto the balcony's edge.

"Wait," she said—or tried to. It tangled up with all the other words lodged in her throat. Came out a shadow, too quiet to hear. He leaped gracefully off her balcony and she flung forward to watch. He'd landed one story down on a neighbor's porch, soundless, on all fours. Before she could even sigh in relief, he dropped to the next balcony.

He never looked up.

If he had, he might have seen the moons catch her eyes too brightly in the corners. Maybe, if he listened hard, he might have heard the sentence that finally forced its way free.

"I love you," she confessed to the humid night air.

Then she latched her windows, pulled the curtains, and, despite the early hour, went hunting for sleep.

Sleep never showed.

An hour later, she was still staring at her ceiling when the alarm sounded. It was a piercing, horrible cry—the sound of a stormwing on the attack.

For a moment, she lay there listening. Heard the cry again. Then her sleep-deprived brain connected the dots. Talons.

Elex.

She flung herself out of bed and to the windows. Tore them open just in time to see a stormwing dive across the night sky, its wings twice as big as any human. A dark, terrifying blot across the stars.

It didn't take long to spot where it and several other storm-wings were headed. In the distance, a whole city block lit up like daylight. The birds dove toward mounted Talons, fists raised to call in their nocturnal hunting partners as they rode toward the lighted street.

Zofi sheathed her longknife and yanked on her boots. Then she sprinted down the tower steps wearing only her nightshirt and silk shorts. She burst out of the tower just as a bevy of mounted Talons reached the road toward the Keep. A stormwing perched on the special bar raised above one Talon's saddle, his warhorse tense with the weight of both the enormous bird and the human rider.

And strung behind him, attached to a long lead, stumbling in the dirt with his hands and feet bound . . .

Zofi ran straight at the Talons. Never mind that they were half a dozen, had stormwings overhead and swords at their waists. Never mind a plan. She reached for her longknife, raced through tithes in her mind.

That's when an arm collided with her waist. It knocked the breath from her lungs. She doubled over, staggered, nearly fell. But the arm held her up. Pulled her back to standing. Two warm hands gripped her shoulders, pinned her in place.

"Zofi. Zofi, relax."

Her vision swam. Narrowed to a pinpoint. It took far too long for her to recognize the familiar face.

"What's going on? Why are you in your..." Vidal's eyes widened in embarrassment when he took in her outfit. His hands dropped.

"I heard the stormwings," Zofi panted. She licked her lips, dared another glance at the Talons. *Snap out of it.* Panic would help no one. "I—I thought...an attack..."

Vidal followed her gaze to the soldiers. To the prisoner stumbling along behind them, face marred by a long scratch from what had to be a stormwing's claw. "It's all right," Vidal said. "There's nothing to fear. This bastard will never harm you or another royal again."

He grinned, though it wasn't happy. It was the bitter triumph that hits your bloodstream after kicking an opponent to the ground. Vidal's eyes caught the torchlights, two frightened Zofis reflected in his wide irises.

"Who is it?" She had to ask. Had to pretend she didn't already know.

Vidal laughed. He actually laughed. "The man who murdered the Silver Prince."

·◦[**18**]◦·

Akeylah

The last place Akeylah expected to end up after dinner was the king's private parlor. But Rozalind stopped Akeylah on her way out of the Great Hall and invited her to hear a new composer perform. When the queen rested a light hand on Akeylah's forearm in passing, Akeylah couldn't say no.

How could she, when all she could think about was the graceful arch of Rozalind's neck, the soft brush of her thumb? The way her dress tonight shone like a silver star, all beads and lace.

The way it made Akeylah's hands itch to touch that fabric. Explore her curves by touch as well as sight...

Now she sat on a narrow bench between Rozalind and Florencia, who had arrived a little while after the performance began. Akeylah tried not to think about the fact that Rozalind's leg was pressed against her own.

Or about the fact that the last time she spoke to Rozalind, the queen conveniently brought up the topic of Kolonyan children cursing their Genalese parents.

Coincidence? Or something more sinister?

"Another round?" Rozalind asked. Her warm breath dusted Akeylah's cheek, startling her back into reality.

"Of course," Florencia replied, at the same moment that Akeylah said, "I'd better not."

Her face went hot. "I mean, if you're both having one more, I suppose…" Her head already hummed from her first two flutes of nectar, one at dinner and the second in this narrow parlor, warm with the body heat of a dozen or so nobles. When Rozalind stood to go for drinks, Akeylah sucked in a deep gulp of air, frantic for some way to clear her head.

It's not the queen. It can't be.

Or, more truthfully, she didn't *want* it to be. If Rozalind was against her, then she truly had no one in this Keep. No friends, no confidants. No one to turn to for help or support or the soft brush of delicate, cool fingertips against hers, setting off sparks throughout her veins…

In the far corner, a violist played a string composition, pleasant background music to the hum of conversation.

"Thank you," Florencia said, after a long, quiet moment. Akeylah thought she must have misheard.

"For what?"

"At dinner. When you backed me up in front of Lady Sarella."

"Oh, it was nothing. She was being quite…" Akeylah pressed her lips together, uncertain how to phrase it.

"Horrible?" Florencia laughed. "She's just angry that I outrank her now, since I used to be her maid. Still, I appreciate the, ah, slight fabrication."

"I'm practicing," Akeylah admitted, before she realized how that sounded.

Florencia's focus sharpened. "Practicing lying?"

"I'm told it's not my forte." Akeylah tracked Rozalind's progress across the room.

"Good to know." Florencia followed Akeylah's gaze. "One tip. It might be advisable not to advertise your weaknesses so openly."

Seas below. Had Florencia noticed her watching the queen?

She resolved not to drink the next glass Rozalind was fetching. She needed her wits intact. "All this must come easy to you."

Florencia raised a brow, though she did smile, too. "Do I seem particularly duplicitous, sister?"

Akeylah almost laughed. "No, I mean...the court. How to behave, what to say, who to flatter or avoid. It must be familiar to you, having grown up here."

"Yes." Florencia shrugged one narrow shoulder. "But the Keep isn't the only place in the world. I imagine there's some advantage in growing up elsewhere, too. Certain things you learn, if you're in the right position to overhear them." Something hard flickered across her face, just for a moment. Then she smiled again, all politeness.

Akeylah thought of Jahen. Growing up, she learned how to appease him. How to be quiet, how to deflect anger. How to take a beating without flinching.

She never thought of how those skills might cross over to life in the Keep.

"I did learn some useful information," she murmured. *Though I doubt it was worth a lifetime of abuse.* "It's strange. You and I share half our blood, yet our lives have been so different. A Kolonyan and an Easterner, raised in separate worlds. Though, I suppose there is some crossover." She tilted her head. "You and the ambassador know each other, too. What a funny coincidence, no?"

Florencia's posture straightened. "The ambassador knows a lot of people."

From her tone, Akeylah sensed she'd misstepped. Asked something too personal. *Damn.* And here she'd finally been having an actual conversation with the girl.

Akeylah was still hunting for the appropriate change of topic when Rozalind set two more flutes on their table. She noticed then that the queen was still working on her first glass, and Akeylah regretted accepting another even more.

"A toast," the queen proposed as she glided back into her seat, closer to Akeylah this time. Her whole side touched Rozalind's, arms brushing as she reached for her glass. "To our newly united family." Rozalind caught Akeylah's eye over the rim of her flute.

"To enlightening conversations," Florencia agreed, lifting her nectar as well.

Akeylah's mouth went dry. "To bad liars," she finally said, which made both Rozalind and Florencia laugh, Rozalind more convincingly than the other girl. They tapped their glasses together, the crystalline sound ringing in the room as the viola music faded.

That's when the doors on the far side of the room crashed open.

Half the parlor leaped to their feet, Florencia included. Akeylah and Rozalind exchanged startled glances.

A uniformed Talon marched across the study to the king. "Your Majesty." He sank into a deep bow. "I bring pressing news."

From the corridor, Akeylah heard more voices, footsteps. Someone shouted. This was followed by a sharp thud, a muffled groan. Then two more Talons rounded the corner, a bound and gagged man suspended between them.

"We apprehended this man fleeing the Keep after an attempted break-in. Prince Nicolen's former valet has identified him as the man who confessed to the prince's murder."

A few nobles gasped. Rozalind snatched Akeylah's hand, pressed it tight. Akeylah squeezed back, reassuring. As for Andros, his expression remained blank, impassive.

"We believe he came to Kolonya City with the intent to harm either you or other members of your family."

Could that mean...?

The Talons marched the man straight to the king and the third gripped his hair, yanked his head up. He was young—younger than Akeylah expected a murderer to be. His hair was a tangled black nest like Zofi's, his features sharp and Northern.

Akeylah wondered if the man—boy, really, he looked barely older than Akeylah herself beneath his scruffy attempt at a beard— had done anything else before being caught in the Keep. Such as, perhaps, sending a threatening message to one of Andros's other children.

Her gaze darted from the boy to her father. She recognized the king's carefully blank expression. She'd worn it often enough in the face of Jahen's rages. She could only imagine how Andros must feel, facing the man who killed his only son.

"Remove his gag," said Andros, voice steady. He rose to his

feet. Any signs of his illness vanished in that moment. He looked every inch the terrifying, legendary king who defeated Genal not once but twice during his long reign.

The rest of the room had fallen dead silent, every eye trained on the king.

"You stand accused of murder," he told the Traveler. "How do you plead?"

"Does it matter?" the boy replied. "You're going to kill me whatever I say. Just get it over with."

"I don't know how your band conducts its affairs, but in Kolonya, we abide by the law. We do not kill on a whim."

The boy laughed. "Tell that to your Talons. Ask how well they behave when they aren't dealing with Kolonyans."

The soldiers bristled. One of the men pinning his arms twisted it hard. The boy's knees buckled, and he growled with pain.

He is so young. The hurt in his eyes was as familiar to Akeylah as the bones in her wrist, the scar on her thigh.

"Stop," King Andros said. The Talon relaxed his grip.

The Traveler panted, still smiling, reckless now. "See?"

"Enough. We have witnesses to your confession after the murder. If you have something to say in your own defense, speak now. Otherwise I must presume your guilt."

In that moment, the boy's gaze drifted across the room and landed on her. For a split second, Akeylah's heart seized. If he *was* her blackmailer, would he try to barter that information? Sell her crime to buy his life?

But his eyes drifted past her to Florencia, then flicked back to the king himself. "I already confessed once. How many times do

I have to tell you? I killed the sands-cursed prince. I'd do it again if I could."

Only the faint pulse of a vein in her father's temple belied his fury.

She recognized that, too. She saw herself in the kitchen, swallowing anger and fear as Jahen shouted, smashed bottles. Maybe she learned more than just how to disguise her own thoughts in that house. Maybe she learned how to see that disguise in others, too.

After a pause, Andros nodded to the Talons. "Take him to the dungeon. In the morning, we'll see whether he has anything more to say for himself."

The lead Talon bowed. "And if he does not, Your Majesty?"

King Andros dropped back into his chair. Only Akeylah seemed to notice how heavily he landed. Andros took a moment to pick up the flute of nectar he'd been swirling all evening, pretending to drink. Now he tilted the glass, considered the amber liquid, and took a long swallow. "Prepare the gallows. If he has no further evidence or information to add to this confession, then he will hang."

✳

"I don't understand why he wouldn't defend himself." Akeylah walked arm in arm beside Rozalind, through the mahogany halls toward her chambers, in a manner that was quickly beginning to feel far too natural.

Could that Traveler be her blackmailer? He'd already killed one member of the royal family. But if so, why wouldn't he speak up and reveal her secret to try to save himself? Was he waiting to tell the king in private?

She supposed she'd find out in the morning. Either he'd be dead by then and the question moot, or she'd be the one in the cell.

And if it's not him? The question nagged at the back of her mind. She hated this. It made her question everyone around her, even people like the queen. The only friend she'd made.

The girl I wish could be more than a friend.

Rozalind shook her head. "Perhaps he simply does not fear death."

Akeylah shivered. "But there must be more to the story. Why did he kill the prince? What happened that night?"

"Some say he was paid to do it. Others say it was a bar fight."

"But he'll die if he doesn't say something. How could a paid assassination or a tavern brawl be worth dying over?"

"Would you die to preserve your honor? Or to stand up for a cause you believe in?"

Akeylah considered the moment Jahen wrapped his fist around her neck. The moment—one of a dozen—when she'd been sure she was about to die. She thought about her reaction. To pray to Mother Ocean, close her eyes, and accept her fate.

"I suppose there are worse things to die for," she finally answered. Like dying for the anger of a drunken old shell of a man.

"Who knows." Rozalind lifted her shoulders. "He might have killed the prince of his own volition. Sun knew the Silver Prince had more than enough enemies. Who doesn't, when you're an heir."

Akeylah grimaced. "Wonderful."

Rozalind took one look at her expression and winced. "I'm sorry, Akeylah. I forget you're new to this life."

This life. Where people expected assassination attempts around every corner. Where handsome young boys who may or may not be paid killers spat at the king and called his soldiers thugs. Where queens tucked your arm in theirs and told you you'd make enemies simply because of who you were.

Then again, Akeylah already knew how dangerous this Keep was. She'd learned that the moment someone scrawled a bloody threat for her to stumble across.

"I didn't ask for this." Akeylah unhooked her arm from Rozalind's. "Any of it. The gowns, the court, the ... the *throne.*"

"You could give it up." Rozalind watched her carefully.

"Yes. I could tell the king 'thank you but no thank you, I'd rather go home.' But to what?" To more beatings? To a life cowering in a corner? "There's nothing there for me. Of course, there's nothing here either—"

"Nothing?" A crease appeared between the queen's brows.

Akeylah winced. "I didn't mean ..."

"I understand." The queen gathered her skirts. "It's a hard place. You can adjust, though, if you find a good enough reason to stay." She caught Akeylah's eye once more, attempted a lighthearted smile. "Selfishly, I hope you do."

Before Akeylah could respond, Rozalind swept up the hall, down the passage to her own chambers. The chambers she shared with Akeylah's father. Akeylah watched her go, continued to stare long after the sound of her footsteps faded.

Finally, she turned toward her rooms. *Let Rozalind go.* It was better this way.

But before Akeylah could take a step, the torches flickered. Once. Twice.

She felt no breeze. Perhaps the oil had run low? She reached for the nearest torch when the whole corridor plunged into darkness.

Her fingers brushed the wall. She held on, waited for her eyes to adjust. Dim moonlight still filtered through the bay windows—only Syxlight at this hour, paler than the other two moons. By its faint beams, she made out a figure at the far end of the hall. Tall, lean. She blinked, and the figure stood one window closer. Ten feet traveled in the span of a second.

"H-hello?" Akeylah shrank against the wall. Bunched her skirts in a fist, in case she needed to run. For the first time in her life, she wished she had a weapon.

She blinked again, and the figure stood another window nearer. Close enough to hear her now.

"Who's there?"

The figure bowed.

"Show yourself," Akeylah demanded. "This isn't funny."

Footsteps sounded from another hall, off at an angle. Akeylah spared a single glance in that direction.

When she looked back, the figure had vanished.

A moment later, the torches flared back to life. The flames licked merrily in their brackets, as though nothing had happened.

"Hello? Is someone there?"

Akeylah peered up the side tunnel to find a servant jogging in her direction.

"My lady, are you all right?"

"Fine." She smoothed her skirts. Glanced back at the spot where the figure had been.

Something lay on the floor. A metal tube, like the scroll the scarlet brought her.

"Can I help you with something? I heard a cry. You sounded distressed."

"No, not at all." A horrible feeling settled in the pit of her stomach. Something told Akeylah she knew what that scroll said.

Who it was from.

"Are you lost? I can help you to your suites." The serving lad bobbed at her side, eager to help.

She waved him off. "I only stumbled. Thank you, but I am fine on my own."

He frowned, though bowed once more anyway.

Akeylah waited until he retreated before she walked over to pick up the scroll. She slid it under her skirts and hurried back to her rooms. Waited until she had the door bolted before she undid the metal clasp with shaking fingers.

Your bloodstained hands will never touch the crown as long as I have a say in it.

Go back where you came from, Easterner.

Or I will show the king exactly what kind of daughter he's sheltering.

The handwriting was beautiful. Each letter curved perfectly across the page, like print in a book.

Her hands shook as she rerolled the note. Part of her wanted to burn it. But she might need it later. Might need it, because...

Akeylah swallowed a deep breath of air. *Because it was a clue.*

A clue as to who was behind this. A way to find the blackmailer, maybe even stop their threats somehow.

She didn't lie to Rozalind. She had no interest in the throne. But she *did* want to stay here. Life in the Keep, dangerous though it may be, was preferable to an undignified death at home, strangled on a kitchen floor. If she died here, so be it. Akeylah had made her peace with death years ago.

At least here, she stood a chance—albeit a small one. Here, she might someday be able to live.

So Akeylah tucked the scroll into her pocket. *Go back where you came from*, it read.

No.

She would find whoever was doing this. Put an end to their threats. And if she couldn't find them fast enough, if they told the king her crime before she reached them? Well, then, she would die on her feet. As strong as that Traveler boy waiting in the dungeons now. As strong as the girl who dug a knife into her thigh to curse the man who abused her all her life.

She might die. First, she would fight back.

✳ 19 ✳

Zofi

Zofi hesitated before the ash-colored stonewood door. This could get her killed.

Doesn't matter.

Elex was worth it. She'd sacrifice anything for him, because he'd already given it all for her. After the Talons hauled him into the Keep, Zofi asked Vidal what would happen to the prisoner. *Trial*, Vidal said. *Unless he pleads guilty.* Then they'd skip the trial. Execute him by morning.

Elex would plead guilty. She knew him. He'd be worried that if he said anything else, if he tried to plead self-defense and invoked witnesses, a full trial, then the truth would come out. Zofi would get tangled up in it, too.

He'd rather die than do that. But she'd rather die than let him.

So, despite the danger, she knocked on the door.

It swung open. "Finally. I was starting to wonder if—oh." Florencia blinked in the Syxlit hallway.

"Sister." Zofi extended her palm faceup. "I've come to propose a deal."

✳

Florencia's chambers looked a lot more organized than Zofi's. She'd taken time to arrange the furniture, add decorations. Zofi squinted at a series of delicate wooden figurines on the mantel. What in sands' name were those for?

Florencia pulled up two chairs, then took a seat. Zofi rested her elbows on the back of the other chair instead.

"Well?" Florencia leaned back. "This must be important for you to come knocking so late."

Her half sister didn't seem like the kind who appreciated small talk. "I need help breaking into the dungeon." The Kolonyan girl was her best bet for finding a side passage, since she knew every back door in the Keep.

Florencia laughed. When Zofi didn't join in, she crossed her arms.

This was a gamble. Florencia might be Zofi's blackmailer, after all. But if so, then she'd at least understand why Zofi needed to free Elex. She'd know the Talons had imprisoned an innocent man.

Elex was worth any bargain. Even a deal with a viper.

"Why in Sun's name should I help you do something so dangerous?"

Interesting. She asked *why*. Not *how*. "You said you wanted to be a better ruler than the prince would have been."

"I fail to see how breaking into a prison makes for good leadership. Especially if you're aiming to visit the man they arrested tonight. The prince's murderer is a Traveler, too, no?"

Sands. Did she just assume they were connected because of their Traveler backgrounds? Or did she know Zofi was the real killer?

"Sparing an innocent man is good leadership," Zofi finally said.

"So you know the murderer?" Florencia pursed her mouth. "When I spoke to you about the prince the other day, you were hiding this the whole time."

Zofi clenched her jaw so hard her teeth creaked. "He's not a murderer. He's innocent." She studied Florencia for a reaction. If the other girl knew the truth, it might show on her face.

The Kolonyan laughed once, without humor. "I saw the Talons bring him in. He confessed."

"He had to," Zofi said, before she could think better of it. Then she winced. Chose her next words with care. "Look, I grew up with Elex. He's a good person."

"Sometimes nice children become terrible adults. Just look at Nicolen. He didn't start out awful; he grew that way." Florencia's eyes narrowed. "Why would he confess if he's an innocent man? Is he an assassin after all? That's what the rumors were saying."

Tread carefully now, Zofi. "It was self-defense."

"Then he should plead that, rather than declaring that he killed the prince and feels no remorse."

"You think anyone would believe him?" Zofi flung her arms wide. "The word of a Talon against a Traveler?"

"There are those in the Keep who know what kind of man Nicolen truly was."

"And are they willing to testify in a trial? Or are they all maids and serving boys, too low in the hierarchy for the nobles to count their testimonials, because they'd never believe their prince capable of such cruelty?"

"Our courts uphold the law, not the nobility's fragile egos."

Zofi snorted. "You might be Kolonyan, but you grew up serving these people. Look me in the eye now, Florencia, and tell me you honestly believe that life here is equally fair to those on the top of the food chain and those at the base. Tell me that if servants testified against King Andros's beloved son—his 'weak spot,' wasn't that what you called the prince?—they'd be believed. They'd keep their jobs and their reputations, with no repercussions."

Florencia met her eye, yet for once, she had no retort.

"Nicolen was a terrible person, you said it yourself. Should my friend die simply for defending himself from a man like that?"

"The punishment for murder is death. My personal opinion doesn't change the law."

"Shouldn't it? That's what leaders do. Decide the rules. After one of us takes the throne, we'll have a chance to be better than Nicolen—better even than Andros. We can give people an honest trial, not the rigged one Elex would be walking into. But right now? We all know how this ends, no matter what Elex says."

"I won't betray my kingdom for a confessed killer."

"I'm not asking you to spring the lock. I just need a way into the dungeons."

"Even if I knew a way—"

"You do, or you'd have asked me *how* in Sun's name you could accomplish such a thing. Not *why*."

Florencia rose to her feet. "Even *if* I did, you still have not given me a compelling reason to help you."

"I'll owe you."

She glanced pointedly around her sumptuous chambers. Florencia already had all the finery anyone could ask for. She was the daughter of a king.

Then again, so was Zofi. "Not money. I'll owe you a favor. Any favor, whenever you need it. No questions asked."

This time, Florencia considered Zofi. Her gaze lingered on Zofi's longknife.

"Please." Zofi's voice dropped to a whisper. "The king won't believe me. The prince was Andros's weak spot, and Elex…" Zofi hesitated. Shut her eyes. "He's mine."

For a long, fraught moment, Florencia studied her. Then she sighed. "*Any* favor?"

"Anything."

Florencia extended her hand. "I'll bring you to the servants' entrance to the dungeons. After that, you're on your own."

Zofi clasped her fingers. "We have a deal, Florencia."

Her half sister's mouth quirked. "I prefer Ren, actually."

"Ren." Zofi grinned. "Let's save a life."

❈

"The cellar is at the end of this tunnel," Ren whispered. "You remember the sequence?"

Zofi nodded.

Ren sighed. "Don't make me regret this."

"It's the right thing to do," Zofi said, not for the first time on the long walk to the dungeons below the alder tower. "More death won't make anything right."

Still, Ren lingered. "Is he worth it?"

"I'd do this for anyone in my family," Zofi replied, thinking of her band. Only when a surprised smile darted across Ren's face did Zofi realize how that sounded.

"Good. Because I might be calling in that favor soon." Ren touched her shoulder, so quick Zofi almost thought she imagined it. "Good luck." Then she vanished, and Zofi carried on alone.

At the end of the tunnel, Zofi rapped on the door in the pattern Ren taught her. With a grunt, it creaked inward. "Food drop was an hour ago," grumbled the guard. "What do you want?"

"Missed a tray," she said in her best Kolonyan accent.

The guard squinted. "Who're you? Where's Merra?"

So much for talking her way in. Zofi threw her full weight against the door. It smacked the guard's eye. He staggered backward while Zofi tumbled into the cellar.

He opened his mouth to shout when the handle of her long-knife collided with his temple. He collapsed, and she set about binding his hands and feet with a coil of rope she found in a stack of maintenance supplies.

Like Ren promised, the root cellar was empty save for some supplies and a row of unappetizing gray mush meals cooling on a sideboard. Five trays, which meant five prisoners. Shouldn't take long to find Elex.

She grabbed the guard's hat and pulled it low on her forehead. Then she rolled him onto his back and considered him for a long moment, memorizing his features. She'd need to get this right the first time. She only had three boosts left, three phials of extra tithes tucked into her pockets. And this would be using up her first tithe straightaway.

Finally, Zofi leaned back on her heels and flicked her blade across her forearm. The world dimmed, blurred, shifted, then returned again.

Zofi—or rather, a much shorter version of the guard she'd just knocked out, still wearing his hat—rose to her feet and picked up a dinner tray. Then she knocked a different sequence on the other door. This entrance, riddled with crossbars, led into the dungeons proper.

A slat in the door slid aside. "What now?"

"Commander called shift change early," Zofi said, voice purposefully deep. "I'm bringing the food in now."

The guard glanced from her face to the food in her arms, even as Zofi reached over—mostly to keep moving and disguise her height—and grabbed a second tray as well.

"About time we got some good news," the guard replied with a yawn as he reached to unbolt the latch. Ren had explained the shifts—this guard will have been on duty since midday yesterday. At this hour, an unannounced replacement would be such a relief he wouldn't view it as suspicious.

He swung the door inward, called "Shift change" over his shoulder.

Behind him, a woman answered, "Thank the Sun."

Then Zofi drove the flat edge of the metal food tray into his windpipe.

The other guard grabbed her sword. "Intruder!"

Zofi was already throwing the other tray in her direction and snatching up her knife instead. At the same time, she shifted her camouflage tithe and vanished into thin air.

Meanwhile, the first guard had scrambled back to his feet. He swung a blade at Zofi's face—or at least, where her face had been an instant before she disappeared. She was already four steps to his right, grabbing a helmet from the table where the guards had been relaxing a moment ago. She hurled it at his temple, then whirled to dodge an attack from the woman.

A line of fresh blood trickled down the female guard's arm—a tithe. That was all Zofi glimpsed before the guard collided with her, moving faster than Zofi could process.

Zofi winced as the woman's blade cut her bicep, but managed to push her off and dance backward into the long tunnel of the jail, still invisible. "Elex?" she hissed, then dodged right away, as the speeding guard dove toward the spot where she'd been.

The woman yelled, though since she was speeding, her voice sounded far too fast, high-pitched and unintelligible.

"Elex!" That earned her another rushed attack, even closer this time. The guard collided with a cell a few steps away from Zofi, and she held her breath while the guard scanned the area, trying to see through her camouflage.

"You sands-damned idiot," Elex finally replied. Two cells back. She parried the speeding guard again and stepped backward.

Another prisoner began to yell.

"Bronze key. Both guards have a copy," Elex was saying.

Zofi dropped to all fours and began to crawl. The woman continued to swing her blade around the hall, spinning this way and that as she hunted for her invisible prey. Thankfully her frantic hunt freed enough space for Zofi to creep past her and untangle the key ring from the unconscious guard.

Unfortunately, the woman noticed that movement.

Zofi barely raised her longknife in time to block the guard's attack. For a moment, Zofi couldn't move, couldn't do anything but parry thrust after thrust. *Just get through this, just stay alive until…*

The woman stumbled. Began to slow.

Zofi felt the pulse of her own tithe wearing thin, too. She deflected another strike and slapped her thigh. The glass phial cracked against her skin, and this time she shifted the tithe, pushed it into speed instead.

Two boosts left.

The guard staggered, weakened from speeding, yet she continued to fight. At least Zofi could keep up now, moving just as fast. She drove the guard back in a flurry of thrusts, tossed the keys through the bars at Elex, then spun to continue the battle.

The woman's speed tithe finally dropped away. "Guards!" the woman screamed, at a normal pitch now.

Footsteps clattered overhead.

Zofi caught the woman's sword on the hilt of her longknife. Twisted the point and wrenched the blade away. The guard's weapon clattered onto the floor. Zofi struck her across the temple with the hilt of her knife.

The guard dropped.

Elex clambered out of his cell. "What in sands' name do you think you're—"

"Run," she hissed, shoving him toward the root cellar. The footsteps on the stairs were deafening now.

Elex leaped through the doorway. As they passed the meal table, he grabbed a jagged, rusty steak knife. One flick, and a line of red appeared along his forearm. He sped up.

Zofi cracked another phial and renewed her speed tithe.

Together, they sprinted through the underbelly of the Keep. A few turns later, Zofi pushed open the exit Ren had showed her earlier. Her tithe faltered. *One phial left.* It would be enough. It had to be.

They burst onto the grassy field between the Keep and stables. Hand in hand, they ran across it, Elex starting to slow now, too. It didn't matter. *We're going to make it.*

Flickering torchlight exploded in front of them. "Stop."

She squinted at the torch. Then the face beneath it, illuminated by the dancing flames.

"Zofi?"

"Vidal?"

The light illuminated just enough for her to make out his bewildered expression. His gaze darted from Elex to Zofi to their clasped hands. Then he bared his teeth. "I should have known."

"Vidal, listen."

"I can't believe it. I defended you to my soldiers—I believed you when you said you were loyal. I didn't even ask questions when you chased down Talons in a nightshirt. Now here you are freeing a murderer."

"This isn't what it looks like. Elex didn't kill anyone."

Somewhere in the distance, a stormwing shrieked. Lights flickered on in the practice field.

"Talk to the king if you have evidence about the crime. I'm not letting you free the man who killed my friend."

"How well did you know your friend the prince?" Zofi shot back. "How well did he treat people he considered *lesser*? Ask the servants."

"Servants gossip—"

"Or ask anyone unfortunate enough to be in his path during deployments. Did you ever ride to the front with him? Did you ever see how he treated his enemies?" She narrowed her eyes. "Or did you see it? See it and justify it—they're only Genalese, they're only Easterners, they're only Travelers.... Did you know what he was deep down, but tell yourself you must be mistaken, because you couldn't possibly befriend a man like him?"

"Enough." Vidal reached for a whistle at his throat.

Zofi drew her knife. Vidal dropped the whistle and unsheathed his sword instead. She felt Elex tense, ready to leap at Vidal, weapon or no.

Then Zofi rested the longknife against her forearm. "I can prove he's innocent. I'll take a blood oath."

Vidal's jaw dropped.

Beside her, Elex grabbed for the knife. "Zofi, no."

She shied away. "It's the only way he'll believe me."

"It's not worth the risk."

"Yes, you are." Zofi spared Elex a single hard glance.

Vidal didn't reach for the whistle again, not yet. She took that as promising.

"If I prove he's not the murderer, will you let him go?" Zofi ignored the shouts in the distance, the clang of armor and the swish of wings overhead. She watched Vidal instead.

His jaw worked. "Why can't you take this to the king?"

"If I could, don't you think I'd have done that already?"

213

"I'd be risking everything, Zofi. My position in the Talons, my life in Kolonya City..."

She glanced around pointedly. There was no one else in sight. Not yet, anyway. "Nobody needs to know you saw us. If another guard catches us, so be it. We won't say a word about you."

"*I'll* know."

"What's more important? The life of an innocent man, or your pride?" She scowled. "I thought you might be different. I thought you saw me as a real person, not just the *drifter* your fellow Talons call me."

She heard another stormwing cry, nearer now. They didn't have much time before another Talon rounded this corner.

"Vidal, please, just let me take the oath."

With a scowl, Vidal spun on his heel. For a heart-stopping second, she thought he was about to shout for help. Then he marched toward the Keep, beckoning over his shoulder. Zofi sucked in a relieved breath and trailed him to a spot between the walnut and mahogany towers, hidden from the stormwings beneath an overhang.

"This is a bad idea," Elex hissed.

"I know him," Zofi replied. "Trust me."

In the alcove, Vidal stopped short. "Swear it."

"Zo..." Elex reached for the knife again. "Let me."

"No. This is my mess." She met Vidal's gaze. "I've tithed already tonight, so this won't last long. I'll talk fast."

A blood oath was one of the easiest Arts to invoke. It barely took any concentration, and little enough of the Arts that Zofi could do it now, even having tithed earlier. Yet it was the least common tithe. Under a blood oath, you could only speak truth. Any lie, no matter how small—even a lie by mistake or omission—would set the oathmaker's veins on fire. Burn them alive from the inside out.

Zofi cut her arm. Her vision went dark, replaced by the map of her veins. Her pulse beat faster than usual as she concentrated on the Arts in the air, on breathing them into her bloodstream. She set their purpose—search out any signs of untruth, any quickening of breath or skipping of her heart.

When she opened her eyes again, her skin smoked in the night air. The oath tithe had begun. It burned, uncomfortably hot, but not enough to do damage. Not yet.

"Elex did not murder Prince Nicolen," she said.

Vidal searched her gaze. When she didn't burst into flames, his brow contracted. "Who did?"

Her veins itched. Burned hotter, brighter, as though sensing her desire to hide this truth. She swallowed her fear. "Me."

To his credit, Vidal's expression didn't even flicker. Only his eyes gave him away. They'd gone hard as stonewood. "Why?"

"He attacked Elex."

"Why would Prince Nicolen attack a random Traveler boy?"

Elex's hand tensed on her arm. Here was the tricky part. A *card game* was the answer she wanted to give. But it made her veins ache and sizzle just to think—because it wasn't right, it wasn't exactly the reason Nicolen attacked Elex.

"Zofi..." Elex warned, his voice low.

"Answer the question," Vidal said.

Her body ached. Burned so hot she could hardly think. "Because he's a Traveler," she said through gritted teeth. With that, the tithe petered out, the night air still hot and humid around Zofi's body as she gasped.

All three stood facing one another, breathing hard. Elex had one arm around Zofi's waist now, propping her upright, though he still looked ready to pounce on Vidal at the first sign of betrayal.

Vidal just stared.

"You heard her." Elex finally broke the quiet. "She'd be dead if that wasn't true. Now it's your call, Talon. Do what's right, or do what your king bids you to."

Lights flashed across the fields. Wingbeats swept overhead. Zofi didn't look away from Vidal. Not until, with visible effort, he lowered his sword.

"Go."

She didn't thank him. She'd do that later. For now, she and Elex simply ran.

The nearest road was only a few hundred yards away. But they slowed as they reached it. Six Talons guarded it. Above, a stormwing circled.

Can we take all six? She only had one boost. Elex had none.

Then a shout echoed across the yard. "Over here!"

Vidal.

The Talons raced toward the sound, calling the stormwing along. Zofi and Elex watched them pass, breaths held. The moment they were out of sight, the Travelers sprinted for the open road.

※

They sat on the bank of the River Leath, across from the enormous trees of the living wall, concealed behind a row of reeds along the water's edge. They'd made it through town without him being recognized, mostly thanks to the cloudy, moonless night and the cloak they'd nicked from a hook outside a tavern near the city gates.

It wasn't dawn, but the clouds were more visible than they'd been a few minutes ago. Pale blue against the darker blue sky.

"I know what you're going to say," Elex finally murmured, "but I have to ask anyway."

She closed her eyes. Breathed in his familiar scent, like thunderstorms in the desert. He smelled like *home*. She longed to relax, to sink into him and forget about anything else—the Keep, the court, the blackmail looming over her head.

It would be so easy to run. To pretend none of this had ever happened. To walk away from Kolonya City and never look back.

Her blackmailer would remain, able to call the king's wrath down on her at any moment. And her people would still be outcasts, abused for sport. Denied basic human dignity.

She might be safe on the run, but at what cost?

"Will you come with me?" Elex whispered, and her heart cracked in two.

If she was lucky—if they both were—she'd never see him again. He'd run to the edge of the world, maybe beyond it. Somewhere the Talons would never find him.

Zofi kissed his cheek, feather-light. "Stay safe, Elex."

He studied her in silence. The sky lightened. The predawn light caught his eyes, too bright at the corners. Her eyes stung. Not tears, not quite. But close.

Finally, he pushed to his feet. She remained sitting, watching.

He glanced at the living wall and its thick canopy of leaves, sway-ing in the early morning breeze.

"Do me one favor?" he asked, back still turned.

She waited until he glanced over to nod. She didn't trust her voice.

He smiled. It looked painful. "Win the throne, Zofi. For us."

"I will," she whispered.

Then he was gone.

❋ 20 ❋

Florencia

The letter arrived with breakfast. Delivered on a gilded silver platter, folded neatly and addressed in prim handwriting. Ren slit the envelope, bored, her head still pounding from the late night. She'd returned to her chambers the minute she left Zofi at the dungeon entrance, yet sleep had proven impossible. Especially once the stormwings began to shriek and the fields around the Keep lit up like daylight. She'd given up on rest and sat on her balcony watching the Talons hunt until dawn lit the sky. By then, she figured her half sister had done it. Helped her criminal boyfriend, whoever he was, out of the city.

Ren ought to feel guilty. She'd gone against the king, against Kolonya. But when she thought about Nicolen, about the black eyes and broken arms she'd seen him inflict on the servants, she could not find it in herself to regret the decision. Whether Zofi had been telling the truth about her friend or not—and self-defense seemed a likely explanation when it came to Nicolen—another death would not make anything right. Nobody deserved a trip to the hangman's noose for ridding the world of a man like that.

Besides, now Ren had one more person to call upon for a favor, should she need one.

She unfolded the note, expecting another invitation. Ever since the king acknowledged her, she'd been receiving invitations to minor nobles' coming-of-age feasts and weddings.

Instead, she found a short handwritten letter.

One count of treason wasn't enough for you, little traitor? You can't skulk around the servants' passages unnoticed forever. Not while I live.
You have until the Feast of the Sun's Glorious Ascendance. Renounce your heritage and leave Kolonya City, or I will see to it that the whole kingdom learns what kind of viper they're dealing with.

Ren reread the note again. Then again. She fought the rise of acid in her throat, the tightness in her chest.

They know. The blackmailer had seen her last night.

She recited the last line under her breath.

Once she'd committed it to memory, she folded the paper once more. Leaned over and dipped it into the candle on her bedside table. She set it back on the gilded mail platter to burn.

The writing disappeared one lick of flame at a time. *Feast. Heritage. Viper.* Finally, the fire ate those, too. She emptied the ashes out the window, watched the wind spin them in delicate spirals past the tower.

Alas, the culprit would not be so easily erased as their threats.

She had until the Sun's Ascendance to figure out who was doing this and whether she could find some way to stop them. She counted the days. She'd lost track this week, with so much happening. It took her a minute to realize. When she did, she sank back onto her bed.

The Feast of the Sun's Glorious Ascendance took place in four days.

A knock made her jump. She waited for her heart to stop pounding and tightened her robe. Her nerves jangled as she crossed the room. She sucked in a deep breath before she opened the door, ready for anything.

"I know you don't want to see me," Danton blurted.

Truth be told, the sight of him filled her with relief. Better a known enemy than a hidden one.

"I just wanted to make sure you're all right, given the news."

Ren frowned, slower than usual with that threat still occupying her attention. "The news?"

He furrowed his brow. "You didn't hear the stormwings last night?"

Oh. "Of course, but..." She lifted one shoulder, casual. "I assumed it was a drill of some sort."

Now Danton outright stared.

She sighed and stepped back to allow him inside. She'd rather not risk half the hallway listening. She bolted the door behind him. "What is it?"

"You've lived in this Keep your whole life—have you ever heard of a *drill* like that?"

"Danton, it was the middle of the night. I was exhausted. What in Sun's name has you so riled up?"

"A prisoner escaped. The one who murdered the Silver Prince."

She rolled her eyes. Luckily her response to Danton was instinctive sarcasm, or she might find it harder to lie. "And what does that have to do with me?"

"He's an enemy of the state. He already went after one royal family member. The family you're part of now." Danton ran a hand through his hair, which currently looked even more mussed than usual. "He had outside help. The guards say someone broke into the dungeons, freed him."

Her eyebrows rose. "Were they able to identify this person?"

"No, but it suggests a coordinated effort. He's likely working for someone outside Kolonya, someone with a grudge against the crown." When she didn't react, Danton's frown deepened. "I was worried about you, all right? You weren't at breakfast."

She nodded at the tray still cooling beside her bed, untouched. "I ordered it in bed. Bit difficult to sleep last night with all the racket."

"You need to start taking these things more seriously. You're a potential future queen, Florencia. A leader. People will be painting a target on your back—the same kind of people who hired that assassin. They killed Prince Nicolen because they want Kolonya heirless. Now there are new heirs—don't you think they'll try and do the same to you?"

"You seem to know a lot about this assassin's motives." She

222

crossed her arms. "Something you want to tell me? Did your Eastern friends have anything to do with it?"

Danton scowled. "We didn't kill the prince."

"*We* now, is it?"

"The rebels. They don't want to bring down Kolonya—"

"Attacking us is a funny way of showing that."

"They just want Tarik's independence. We want to be our own country, not an adjective. Eastern." He scoffed. "As if that's all we've ever been."

"If you're so concerned about the future of *Tarik*, then why are you here making sure a potential heir to Kolonya is safe?"

He groaned in exasperation. "Because I care about you. How many times do I need to explain that?" He took a step closer. She let him. "Florencia, the tides are turning. The Reaches can't survive with Kolonya hoarding all the resources, taxing them hungry and poor. Your father is too set in his ways to see it, but you don't need to be. If you win the throne, you can help us."

"If you think I'll be your puppet on the throne, you've got another think coming."

"I never said that." He caught her shoulders, eyes ablaze. "I want you to win, Florencia. Then I want you to set the east free. Make us a true ally, not a glorified servant."

"Wouldn't an Easterner be a better bet for that goal?" Ren pursed her mouth.

"I don't know Lady Akeylah. I have no idea what she believes. All I know is that you're a good person—you would make an even better queen. But you must be careful. You have enemies everywhere."

She thought of the letter again. *You have until the Feast.* Four days away.

She didn't need Danton's lecture to know she was in danger. She thought about it every second of every day. *1,854.*

At least one person wanted to drive her out of the Keep. But this was her home. The only place she'd ever lived. Ren would be damned if some cowardly blackmailer forced her to run.

Danton was still watching her, those pale eyes wide with worry.

"I know," she finally said. "I'm being careful. I just…" She closed her eyes. Let the fear and worry and frustration she'd been suppressing crash over her. "It's a lot."

Before she could open her eyes again, Danton's arms folded around her. Against her better judgment, she sank into him. Let herself relax, only for a moment, in the familiar embrace.

"You need help," he whispered into her hair. "Loyal allies. I can be that for you again. Like we used to. Tell me what you need—protection, information. I'll get it."

Her throat tightened. It was tempting. Tempting to unburden herself. Tell him everything—the blackmail, the threats. She didn't want to fight this alone. And Danton was the only one who knew what they'd done. She could ask Audrina to help keep an eye on Sarella or anyone else who acted suspicious. But she couldn't exactly go telling her friend *why* she needed a spy. She couldn't admit she'd committed treason.

He betrayed you. He took her information, information that was supposed to *prevent* bloodshed, and gave it to a bunch of bloodthirsty killers.

Ren took a deep breath and twisted out of his arms. "You're

right. I need loyal allies. Which means I cannot trust someone who burned me already. I trust *actions*, Danton, not empty words."

To her surprise, he bowed, deeper than usual, missing his normal pompous flare. "I understand." Without another word, he left. She stared at the doors long after they swung shut.

He was right about one thing. With the fresh blackmail threat came a stark reminder—she could not ignore this. She reached for her bellpull. Time to go on the offensive.

❋

At least Audrina didn't hesitate on the threshold this time. She flung herself onto Ren's bed the moment she opened the door.

"Sun damn her, she's going to be the death of me," Aud groaned.

Ren poured her a larger glass of nectar than last time. "Tell me about it."

Aud rolled over and downed half the flute before she replied. "Sarella is positively inexhaustible. How in Sun's name did you keep up with her for so many years? It's only been one night and I'm already about to collapse. Not to mention the *drinks*. I leave her alone for five minutes and she's downed enough strongwine to knock out an ox."

Ren bit the inside of her cheek to stifle a laugh. That sounded familiar, all right. "She hasn't said anything more about me, though?" Ren prompted.

Aud rolled her eyes. "Oh, plenty. She and Tjuya spent all last night bitching about her uppity maid pulling a fast one on everybody in the Keep. Seems to think you faked your Blood Ceremony somehow. 'The babies were swapped at birth, Ren is just a decoy, not truly the king's daughter,' all kinds of nonsense. But Sarella's always been like that. Eats up any scrap of rumor like it's fact."

"So last night…" Ren's mind raced. Whoever sent this new blackmail letter knew what she and Zofi did last night. They must have seen the two on their way to the dungeons somehow. Or else overheard them plotting in this very room. "I'm guessing she was out late?"

Another groan. "Lord Hane invited Sarella and Tjuya to midnight drinks in the botanical observatory—you know, because they have that fancy new flower meant to smell like a dead body, which for some reason is a noble tourist attraction?" Aud snorted. "Anyway, open bar, so she arrived the moment the party began. Even when all that racket with the Talons started up, she just migrated out onto the balcony with everyone else to watch the hunt and carry on drinking. As if an escaped convict were some sort of entertainment sport, not a serious matter." Audrina scowled and shook her head. "Lord Hane and I only just carried her to bed before I came here. Now I understand the moods you were always in in the mornings, when I used to meet you down in the common rooms…."

Interesting. So Sarella was in no position to have seen her. And, from the sounds of it, not in any shape to pen a threatening message this morning either. But she couldn't rule out the possibility that Sarella might have accomplices. Sarella could have someone spying on Ren just like she was spying on Sarella, delivering notes about Ren's activities during Lord Hane's party. Ren sighed. "Thank you again, Aud. I can't tell you how helpful you're being."

"How much longer do you need me to keep this up, Ren?"

"Just a few more days, I promise."

Aud glanced pointedly at her cup. In response, Ren reached across and refilled it to the brim. "You owe me big-time, you know," Aud replied, though at least she was smiling. "More than just this nectar, delicious as it may be."

"Definitely owe you," Ren agreed. "The free beverages are just a bonus." They leaned back on the bed, nectar in hand, to talk about the other maids, and how Audrina was getting on without Ren. (*Abominably*, she promised.)

All the while, Ren's mind raced. She still needed to find the blackmailer. Clearly she'd need other allies. Someone else to help, someone who had proven trustworthy.

Or, failing that, someone who'd put their trust in her...

※

Ren found Zofi on the practice fields. She shouldn't have been surprised. She leaned on the fence to watch her sister spar with a stuffed target dummy, dull-edged practice sword flashing in the late-morning sun. Ren waited until Zofi paused to catch her breath before she waved.

Zofi jogged across to meet her.

"We need to talk," she said.

Zofi lifted her helm and squinted. "Calling in your favor already?"

Ren brushed her hair from her eyes. "Not exactly."

It took Zofi a few minutes to change out of her armor and back into her everyday clothes—which, in Ren's opinion, looked basically the same. More brown leather, uncomfortable and unfashionable to boot. *To each their own*, Ren supposed. Personally, she'd stick with normal clothing.

They strolled past the practice fields, onto an empty lawn near the walnut tower. Zofi shivered, despite the humidity and the bright sun overhead. Ren ignored it and swung them to a halt in the middle of the grass. Nobody was within earshot, which made for about as much privacy as they could hope for. Ren knew all too well how many hiding holes there were within the walls of the Keep. Outside was safer.

"Well?" Zofi asked.

"Someone saw us last night."

Zofi's fists clenched. "Who?"

"I don't know."

"Then how do you know somebody saw us?"

"Whoever it was sent me a note this morning. A threat."

Her sister sucked in a deep breath. Cast a long glance at the stables, then the faraway practice fields. "Was that the only threat you've gotten?"

Ren hesitated. She trusted Zofi not to tell anyone about last night's adventure, since they'd been in it together. If she reported Ren, she'd go down for the crime, too. But admitting the blackmail was ongoing meant something different. It meant letting on to Zofi that Ren had other sins in her past. Other secrets that could be used against her.

Before she could decide what to say, Zofi cleared her throat. "Because...I've gotten one, too."

Ren's eyebrows rose. "About last night?"

A pause. Then Zofi shook her head. "Something else."

Ren swallowed hard. "Me, too."

"So we've both had someone send us threatening messages." Zofi crossed her arms. "And no idea why or what that person wants."

"I have some idea," Ren replied. "They told me to leave Kolonya City." She sucked in her cheeks. Who would be in a position to find dirt on both her and Zofi? As far as she knew, their father aside, they had next to nothing in common.

Well. Nothing except a third sister.

A sister who, by her own admission, was practicing lying. A sister who knew Danton, who had asked Ren about him pointedly in the same parlor where, minutes later, she watched the Talons imprison Zofi's Traveler boy.

A sister who would win the throne if both Zofi and Ren abdicated their claims.

"Are you thinking what I'm thinking?" Ren's gaze drifted toward the mahogany tower, where she knew Akeylah resided.

Zofi tilted her head. "About who stands to profit if both you and I suddenly decide to leave Kolonya City?"

"If we abandon any chance of taking the throne, yes," Ren said.

A long pause followed. Zofi tugged a strand of hair straight— her hair was far longer than it looked, all up in a poof of curls like that. "My message...it was about something that took place in the Eastern Reach."

"Imagine that." Ren smiled, pointed. "So was mine."

"And if we both give up on the throne," Zofi replied, "there's only one other person the king could choose to name."

"It would certainly make his decision easier if he had only one heir to choose from." Ren squinted. Watched the sun dance on the windows of the tower.

Zofi's fingers drifted toward the knife on her hip. "I think we've figured out our first stop on this hunt...."

⚜ 21 ⚜

Akeylah

Akeylah slept in the library.

Slept was the wrong word. She simply never left, having fled there with the blackmail scroll in her pocket and one goal—find an answer. This time she stacked an entire cart full of tomes from the Blood Arts section, even some without titles or descriptions. She'd read every book in this library if that's what it took to cure her father, and dig herself out of this mess in the process.

At some point, around the time dawn began painting the windows in fiery streaks, she lost track of the words on the page. A few hours later, she woke with a start, ripping said page where it stuck to her cheek.

She squinted through bleary eyes at the daylit library while she tried to paw the remnants of the page from her cheek. Her brain took longer to catch up. Something woke her. What?

"Pleasant nap?"

Oh.

She rubbed sleep from her eyes and reached for the book, reflexive. *Hide it.*

Her sister was faster. Zofi snatched it up and studied the cover. *"The Price of Practice,"* she read. " 'An analysis of the effects of the Arts, both positive and negative.' "

"Reading up on tithes?" Florencia thumbed through the stack at Akeylah's elbow.

"Maybe she's planning to escalate if normal threats don't work." Zofi dragged a finger along her inner arm.

Akeylah flinched at the outright reference to the Vulgar Arts. She peered around the library. It was empty at this hour. Even the grumpy old woman who worked the front desk, muttering under her breath every so often about ungrateful nobles keeping their own damned schedules, had vanished.

"Madam Harknell has taken a much-needed break." Florencia clucked her tongue. "Someone kept her working past her usual hours, I'm afraid. How long have you been here now? More than twelve hours, according to the sign-in sheet up front."

Akeylah pushed her chair back to rise, but Zofi clamped a hand on Akeylah's shoulder, tight enough to hurt. "Sit back. Relax. We just have a few questions."

"What in Mother Ocean's name are you doing?" Akeylah's voice came out softer than she'd like, her throat thick with sleep.

Florencia slammed a book on the table. The crash made Akeylah jump. "Confronting our problems directly. Probably a concept you aren't familiar with. You seem to prefer the coward's approach. Ominous messages, ill-conceived threats..."

Akeylah frowned. "You're going to have to be more specific." Both half sisters looked furious, but it was Zofi she focused on. The fury masked something else, something deeper. Fear?

She'd never seen Zofi afraid.

"You've been blackmailing us," Zofi spat. "We've come to stop it."

Akeylah couldn't help it. She laughed.

"So you find us amusing?" Florencia selected another book, *Blood-Stains: The Price of the Arts.* "I'll bet it has been fun. Tormenting us, trying to make us dance to your tune."

"Too bad we're onto your game." Zofi smirked.

"You've got this all wrong." Akeylah reached for her pocket. Zofi did, too, only her hand closed around a knife handle. Akeylah lifted her hands once more, palms open, before Zofi could draw the blade. "I'm not doing this. Let me prove it."

"What, by letting you cast one of your tithes?" Zofi nudged the stack of books with her hip. "I don't think so."

"Check my pocket. The left one." Akeylah glanced from Zofi to Florencia. "Please. You need to see this."

Florencia held her gaze for a moment before she stepped forward and tugged on Akeylah's skirt. Akeylah tensed as her half sister's fingertips brushed her thigh, the scar more sensitive than ever with someone an inch away. But she'd worn a skirt with thick fabric, like all the dresses she'd commissioned from Rozalind's tailor. The shine didn't show through it, and she doubted Florencia noticed the bumpy ridge of the scar while she rifled through the pocket.

"There's a scroll," Akeylah said. Needlessly, since Florencia drew it out an instant later. "You two aren't the only ones being blackmailed."

Florencia scoffed deep in her throat and unrolled it. "Easily faked."

"Why would I fake something like that?"

Zofi kept her fist clenched around her knife hilt. "To throw us off the trail. You probably guessed we'd figure it out eventually. Come hunting you down. You'd need an excuse when we came calling." Zofi looked to Florencia, whose gaze flicked back and forth along the note. "Well?"

"'Your bloodstained hands will never touch the crown as long as I have a say in it. Go back where you came from, Easterner, or I will show the king exactly what kind of daughter he's sheltering.'" Florencia's gaze flicked to Akeylah. "What does that mean, 'bloodstained hands'?"

"If this person has threatened all three of us, I'm guessing we've all got some stains on our hands," Akeylah replied. "Stains we'd rather not talk about."

Zofi drew her blade. "One of us has more reasons to talk than the other two, though," she pointed out, twirling the knife almost casually.

Akeylah tilted her head back until her whole neck was exposed. "Go on, then. Slit my throat. See if the threats stop." She held Zofi's gaze, unblinking. She was not afraid. She'd made her peace with death long ago.

Zofi's jaw tensed. "Compare it to the sign-in sheet."

"What?" Florencia glanced up from the note, which she'd been rereading.

"Compare Akeylah's handwriting on the library sign-in sheet to that note in her pocket. See if it looks the same."

Florencia disappeared for a moment, then returned with the

guest book in which Akeylah had written her name, the date of her visit to the library, and her purpose. "'Personal research,'" Florencia read with a lifted brow. Then she held the note beside the book. After a pause, she shook her head. "The blackmail letter is much neater than her writing. And this is definitely the same hand my last note was written in."

"Think she could've faked it?" Zofi tilted her head.

"Maybe." Florencia pursed her mouth. "I don't know." Her gaze snagged Akeylah's. "When did you get this note?"

"Yesterday evening. On the way back to my chambers."

"Someone delivered it to you?"

She shook her head. "Not exactly. I—I saw someone, I think. In the halls outside my room. But they were there and gone so fast, I couldn't be sure—the torchlight was flickering, and it was late, and dark...."

Florencia groaned and waved at Zofi. "Drop the blade."

"What if she runs?"

"Then I'm pretty sure you of all people could catch her before she even left the chair. Have you seen the gown she's wearing?"

Zofi glared at Akeylah one last time, then resheathed the knife.

Akeylah straightened in her chair. "Thank you," she told Florencia.

"Don't thank me yet. We're not done here. Was this your first threat?"

"No. There was another."

"A note?"

"Paint."

Zofi perched on the edge of the library table. "Just like mine."

235

She still spoke to Florencia rather than Akeylah, but at least her aggressive posture had shifted to a more relaxed, thoughtful one.

"My first one, too," Florencia mused. "But my second was also a note. Longer, more detailed."

"Your letters both contain the same command—leave this city." Zofi propped her chin on one fist. "At this rate, I imagine the letter ordering me to do the same will arrive soon. So who would want all three of us gone?"

"Someone who wants to destabilize Kolonya," Florencia suggested. "The Eastern rebels, perhaps?"

"Or Genal," Zofi pointed out. "Queen Rozalind is Genalese. If she bears a child, assuming she can conceive before our father gets really ill, that child will inherit. They win the Reaches back by succession, without even needing another war. But only if there aren't other potential heirs in the way."

"I don't think so," Akeylah murmured.

"You're just a little too fond of the queen," Florencia said.

Akeylah shook her head, she hoped convincingly. "Reread the note. *As long as I have a say in it.* It sounds almost...protective. Not like a conqueror. Like someone who already guards the throne, or thinks they do."

Florencia drew up a chair from an adjoining desk and bent over the note. "My last one said something similar. Basically said you can't do this forever, not while I live. But..." She flattened the letter on the desk. "It doesn't make sense. If someone wants to protect the throne, why drive all of us away? Why not pick the successor they prefer?"

"Ren, what would happen if the king didn't name any of us his successor?" Zofi asked.

Ren? Akeylah wondered just what she'd missed between her sisters while she spent her day in fruitless research.

"Kolonya hasn't been without a direct heir since…" Florencia—Ren, apparently—furrowed her brow. "Not since the time of King Gellien. About a hundred years after the War for Recognition. The Third Genalese War killed his heirs. He had to hold a tribunal."

"How does that work?" Akeylah leaned forward.

"He summoned the high nobility from the other Reaches—the families that used to be kings and queens of their individual Reaches, until they swore fealty to Kolonya after the Second War. One contestant came from each outer Reach: a Northerner, a Southerner, a Westerner, and an Easterner. The potentials lived and trained in Kolonya City for a year, until King Gellien officially adopted the heir he selected. With the approval of the regional council, of course."

Akeylah's eyes widened. "Which Reach won?"

Ren rubbed her temple. "I can't recall. Northern, maybe?"

"So our father is descended from Northern stock?" Zofi grinned. "No wonder the Kolonyans don't talk about that much."

"If you go far enough back, we're *all* from the same place," Ren pointed out. "Genal. We're not exactly fond of recognizing our ancestral history." She tapped her fingers on the table. "At any rate, that's what would eventually happen if all three of us turned our backs on the throne. A Reach-wide contest."

"Plenty of motivation for any other Reach to want us gone," Zofi mused. "Especially the Eastern one just now." Her gaze danced toward Akeylah. "Do you think there's some connection between this and the rebellion?"

"Hard to say." Akeylah frowned, thinking about her family.

The man who raised her, Jahen, was descended from the last Eastern ruler to sit the throne. A fact he never let his trader friends forget. But even if Tarik had never sworn fealty to Kolonya, Jahen wouldn't be king now. "Eastern succession doesn't work like Kolonya's. We elect from a group of eligible nobles and merchants— anyone who's proven talented in business. So, if it is Easterners, a tribunal wouldn't be their goal."

Zofi drummed her fingertips on the hilt of her knife, restless. "We need to stop guessing and start acting. We have to find this person and stop them."

"Florencia?" Akeylah reached for her blackmail note. Her sister lifted her hands and let Akeylah slide the note out from beneath her. "This note was delivered to me in an isolated location. I'm guessing your first blackmail threats were as well?" She didn't wait for her sisters' nods. "So it's most likely someone who knows their way around the Keep. At least well enough to deliver this without being seen. Perhaps the Silver Prince's murderer. He must have a pretty good working knowledge of the Keep to have escaped the dungeons...."

Zofi and Ren shook their heads in unison. Then Zofi cleared her throat. "I'm friends with one of the Talons who was tracking him. It was a stupid guard error that let him escape, not any particular knowledge about the Keep."

"Still—" Akeylah started, but Ren cut across her.

"You make a good point. It must be someone who knows the Keep very well, who has years of experience here. Not just some assassin who broke inside the other night and got caught halfway in. Besides, this person had access to our chambers."

"One of the servants, then. Or someone with command of a servant, a noble who grew up in the Keep," Zofi mused.

Ren tilted her head. "My letter came through the mail system. Via the kitchens. The serving boys collect messages and send them up on the breakfast trays, normally."

"So if you asked someone in the kitchens who dropped it off, might they know?" Akeylah asked.

"It's worth a shot."

Akeylah turned to Zofi next. "When did you find your first threat?"

"The night of the Blood Ceremony. It was painted on my headboard."

"That's the same night I found mine," Akeylah murmured.

"I saw mine around dawn," Ren said. "Though I suppose it could have been painted the night before."

"Whoever it was didn't waste any time after our arrival." Akeylah sized up Zofi. "Do you think climbing into your room via the balcony would be easy?"

Zofi hesitated, then bobbed her head. "Shouldn't be too hard. I think."

Something about her tone made Akeylah wonder whether her half sister had already considered that route. Or maybe even tested it herself. "Okay. So someone left my threat in the sky gardens, then climbed into your room. Which tower are you in?"

"Obsidian," Zofi answered. "Near the top floor."

"That's a lot to accomplish in one night. Especially writing my threat in the midst of a crowd."

"Actually, that was probably the perfect time to do it," Ren said. "Any of the staff would have either been preparing food and working the feast, or else sneaking up to the party to try and pilfer extra food or drinks."

"So that doesn't help us much." Akeylah crossed her arms.

"No, but..." Ren's gaze darted to Zofi's. "There's another spot in the corridors where we have reason to believe the perpetrator has been, based on what they witnessed. We could search there. See which passages connect. If we can retrace the person's steps, we may learn something."

Akeylah glanced back and forth. She was *definitely* missing something between her sisters. But she knew better than to pry—not after the way those two barged in here to threaten her. If they wanted to keep secrets, that was their business. Seas knew she had enough of her own to guard.

"What about you?" Zofi rounded on Akeylah. "What are you going to do to help, stay holed up here all cozy and safe in the library?"

Akeylah's eyes drifted past her sisters, toward the stacks at the far end of the room. She hadn't ventured there yet, didn't need to. She'd been too preoccupied by the Blood Arts section. But she'd done a cursory scan of the library when she first arrived. She could see the shelves from here—*Familial Histories & Royal Lineages (Genalese Settlers—King Andros)*. "Yes, actually." She ignored Zofi's scoff. "I'm going to read up on our fellow courtiers. See which branches of the former royal families from other Reaches still exist, and who would be eligible for a tribunal if, say, all three of us happened to renounce our claims at once. Easterners might not work that way, but the three other Reaches do."

Ren actually smiled. "Good. Then we each have our jobs. When shall we meet to discuss what we find?"

"We have our next lesson with Father tomorrow," Akeylah said. "We could talk afterward."

"*If* we find anything worth mentioning," Zofi grumbled.

"We'd better." Ren squinted at the far end of the library, toward the stacks Akeylah indicated. "My last note had a deadline. 'You have until the Feast of the Sun's Glorious Ascendance.'"

Akeylah swallowed hard. "That's..."

"In four days." Ren kept smiling, though, a hard veneer to disguise her worry. "We'd best get moving."

❋ 22 ❋

Florencia

"You may not be familiar with this neighborhood," King Andros said. He sat astride his enormous horse, flanked by Queen Rozalind and Countess Yasmin.

Ren struggled to remain astride her own mount. Did this damned beast have to be so tall?

To either side, Zofi and Akeylah sat on their horses with ease, which only made her grumpier. Akeylah had never ridden a horse before today, either—why did she look so comfortable?

"Relax," Zofi murmured. "It's not like sitting in a chair or a carriage. Loosen up; let your hips move."

Easier said than done.

"These are the skysquats," Andros was saying. "The home of the workforce that keeps Kolonya City running."

Ren lifted her eyes to the strongwall. Rows upon rows of flat wooden platforms enclosed in tarps—"skysquats"—jutted from the stone, supported by thick cables. Rope ladders descended from each platform—six-by-ten-foot tented rooms in which as many as seven or eight people lived, more than twenty rows high. She couldn't even imagine how many people that was. Living like birds nesting along the city's strongwall. Some had to climb down fifty-foot ladders just to walk to work in the mornings.

"Are they safe?" Akeylah asked.

"Completely," King Andros replied. "The skysquats have stood since the time of King Tyman. He built the squats so we wouldn't need to expand outside the walls—in case of attack, external settlements would be hard to defend."

Never mind that it's been four hundred years since the last time Genal reached as far inland as Kolonya City.

"The squats are an economical way to provide our labor force with comfortable housing," Countess Yasmin added.

Ren found it hard to imagine that living on a wooden plank with canvas tarps for walls could be "comfortable."

"Today, we have come here to hold an audience with our people," Andros continued. "We have these in different neighborhoods each month to ensure that everyone in Kolonya City can attend. During these audiences, we listen to our citizens' opinions, answer questions, and allay any concerns they may have."

Their horses rounded the last paved street and walked onto the dirt-packed road bordering the strongwall. Ahead, Ren spotted a wooden stage set up in the middle of the road. And around it...

Sun above.

The street was packed. More people than Ren could count pressed around the stage, and on the far side, a line at least seven blocks long waited. Everyone wore dresses and suits—some threadbare, all clearly the nicest clothes their wearers owned.

A sense of awe stole over her.

These are real Kolonyans. The lifeblood that kept the country's heart beating.

Within the walls of the Keep, it was easy to forget about the world outside. Easy to fall into the trap of thinking that only nobles mattered, only lords and ladies and their opinions. Only Ren's problems, like the blackmailer she ought to be hunting down now, because *three days left until the Sun's Ascendance.*

But these farmhands and laborers were the people real leaders should listen to. Without them, civilization would fall apart.

Ren resolved to put aside her own worries for the day. *Our people must come first.*

The king's procession led directly to the foot of the stage. The platform had been split into three sections, each separated by tapestries to create three makeshift tents. Before each tent, she spotted eager merchants and farmers and laborers. A sea of Kolonyan faces, interspersed with the occasional shaven head of a Westerner or dark hair of a Northerner.

Not many Easterners besides Akeylah, though. And no other Travelers at all—no telltale wild black curls sticking straight up.

That explained why Akeylah and Zofi were already garnering stares.

King Andros dismounted to a roar of applause. The applause continued as Countess Yasmin slid off her horse. When Queen

Rozalind stepped down, however, the applause faltered. Hardly surprising, Ren supposed, given the tentative new peace between their nations.

But when a Talon helped Akeylah from her seat, that unsettling quiet grew deeper. By the time Zofi dismounted, the crowd watched in silent deadpan.

Ren's turn.

She unhooked from the stirrups. A Talon caught her, helped her into a clumsy landing that only made her resent the horse more.

The crowd stared.

She had to admit, that surprised her. Part of her expected to be more popular than her sisters, at least out here, among regular Kolonyans. It stung to receive the same empty response. Whatever these people felt for Andros, their approval didn't extend to his newly recognized daughters.

"As you can see," Andros said to the girls, "there are too many people for me to meet one-on-one. Luckily, we now have more royal family members to go around. We will split into three groups—Akeylah, you and I will meet with the merchants and traders. I believe you have some experience in this area thanks to your stepfather?"

Akeylah curtsied and thanked the king, though Ren noticed she did not quite answer that question. "Zofi." Andros appraised his daughter. "You and Queen Rozalind will take audience with the laborers and masonry guild members. I think you will find their work interesting."

Zofi's brow furrowed at that, but if she wondered what the king meant, she didn't ask. She simply bobbed her head and moved next to the queen.

Ren's stomach sank when she realized what this meant. King Andros turned to Ren. "Florencia, you and Countess Yasmin will listen to the concerns of the farmers. This is a very important task, but I trust you will handle it with care."

The glare Yasmin shot Ren clearly said the countess didn't agree.

Andros led the way onto the stage. The tapestries that made up the tents depicted stormwing insignias and scenes from ancient battles. He took the center tent with Akeylah, while Queen Rozalind led Zofi into the far tent.

Yasmin stopped dead at the nearest chamber, then glowered until a Talon leaped forward to pull the tapestry aside for her. Inside the tent, two uncomfortable-looking chairs stood side by side. Ren perched on one and tried to ignore Yasmin's grumbling.

All right, so she was paired with the least desirable member of the royal family. No matter. She could make the best of this.

This was what she'd been looking forward to, after all. The chance to try her hand at leadership. To hear real people's concerns, help improve their lives.

Then the first farmer entered the audience chamber.

"I was told I'd be able to meet with His Majesty today, my ladies," the man said after he stumbled through his bows.

A beat passed. Ren dared a glance at Yasmin, who watched her expectantly. *Sun.* Was she supposed to answer?

Too late. Yasmin rolled her eyes and leaned forward. "As you can see, we have quite a large turnout this month. We try to meet as many of our citizens as possible—to do that, we must divide and conquer. But I assure you." She smiled. Ren wasn't sure she'd ever seen the countess do that before. It looked painful. "Whatever you say to my niece and me, King Andros will hear. We are his envoys."

"I appreciate that, my lady. It's only, this is an urgent matter, and I think His Majesty will want to learn about it as soon as possible."

Yasmin's smile tightened. "Let us hear it, then, so that we may act swiftly."

The man's gaze darted between them once more, his disappointment ill concealed. Ren resisted a frown. How could she help if people wouldn't share their concerns? They only wanted the king. Didn't even trust his twin sister, let alone Ren.

With a sigh, the farmer relented. "We are experiencing a crop blight, my lady."

A beat passed before Yasmin answered. "His Majesty is aware of this. The agricultural guild reported it two months ago."

"I know, my lady, but this week it took a turn. Yesterday I found half my wheat field dead, the rest infected."

"The guild is developing a cure as we speak."

"With all due respect, by the time the guild finds a treatment, we may have lost the whole harvest. And, speaking for my own family, we haven't the private stores to last until the next."

Yasmin's brow furrowed.

When the countess didn't reply, Ren spoke up. "What does that mean for your family, sir? Will you need to purchase additional food in the meantime?"

He blinked. It seemed to take him a moment to process the query. "It means we will starve, my lady."

Her stomach flipped. *That can't be right.* Kolonyans starving right here in their own city? "We cannot allow that." Her voice rose, vehement. "My father will find a way to feed your family—any family in need—until we cure this blight."

Yasmin shifted in her seat. Concealed behind her skirts, she stomped her foot onto Ren's toe. Ren bit her lip to keep from gasping.

"Thank you so much for bringing this matter to our attention," Yasmin broke in. "I see how urgent the situation has become. I will confer with my brother immediately."

"I appreciate it, Countess." The farmer bowed again. When he straightened, he smiled at Ren. "And, my lady...your promise is generous. Thank you for looking after us. Your father is a wise, kind man. I see it runs in the family."

"I am happy to help my people in any way I can," she replied.

The Talon manning the tent entrance ushered the farmer out. Before he could bring in another, Yasmin lifted a hand to stay him. "What in Sun's name was that?" Yasmin tapped the insignia bloodletter ring she wore against the arm of her chair.

"You heard him." Ren gestured at the tent flap. "His family is starving. He's a Kolonyan citizen. We don't let our people go hungry."

"We cannot afford to promise food to every citizen who begs for it. Not until we know exactly how bad this blight is or how long it will last." Yasmin's voice dropped low, furious. "If we lose the whole harvest, that family won't be the only one going hungry. We can import food from the other Reaches, but half the food we eat in the Keep is grown right here. Prices will skyrocket; we'll barely be able to feed the nobles, let alone the poor."

"And how will we replenish our larders for the next harvest if we allow all our farm workers to die?"

"Farmhands are as plentiful as sunbeams in the sky," Yasmin snapped. "Leaders are not. 'A body cannot function without its heart'—we must protect that at all costs."

Unwise though she knew it was to argue, Ren scoffed. "That quote is about *Kolonya*. Protecting this country above all. Letting Kolonyans starve is the opposite of what *The History* advises."

"*The History* was written by kings. Do you think those men would have survived long enough to pen it if they gave all their own food to their followers?"

This is what Danton means, she realized, *when he talks about the Eastern cause.* This was what Akeylah and Zofi resented, what so many other Reaches felt when they heard *Kolonya first*. The hypocrisy struck her like a sword.

It was never about family. Not for rulers like Yasmin. It was never about taking care of Kolonya, making it the strongest it could be.

It wasn't *Kolonya first*, it was *me first and damn the rest.*

"Bring in the next petitioner," Yasmin told the Talon. Under her breath, she hissed, "And you. Don't speak again unless I ask you to. You've made enough wayward promises as it is."

Ren clenched her hands to disguise her fury.

She'd listen. She'd obey. For now. Because one day, someday soon, this would be her call to make. Her throne to sit on, her people to shepherd. Sun blind her if she'd make the same selfish, shortsighted mistakes as Countess Yasmin.

The girls stood in the fields behind the Keep, having excused themselves after the lesson for a walk. Several hundred yards away, Talons trained fledgling stormwings. The birds flew around their owners on long leather leads. Every now and then, one dove and snagged a sack in its claws.

"Here they are." Akeylah extended two slips of paper, one to Ren and one to Zofi.

Ren squinted at the names. *Lord D'Verre Gavin. Lady D'Rueno Lexana. Lady D'Feraoh Tjuya. Lord Siraaj dam-Senzin.* "What am I looking at?"

Her mind was still on their lesson. All the farmers had told the same story—crops weakening, dying. Families already hungry, with only emptier bellies to look forward to.

Again and again, Yasmin repeated the same platitudes. *The guild is working on it. We will purchase alternate food supplies from the Western Reach. Don't worry.*

Again and again, Ren bit her tongue on the truth. *She's lying.* Oh, they would buy supplies from the Westerners, she was sure. Yet Ren would bet her left leg every single shipment would wind up in the Keep. Even if the larders were full, the nobles would hoard any extra food. *Just in case.*

The farmers would see no relief.

"These are the potential successors," Akeylah said. Ren dragged her mind back to the present.

Right. Blackmailer. Possible candidates.

"I traced the families of each former royal line. West, north, south, and east, in that order. If it comes to a tribunal—"

"Hang on." Ren squinted at the last name. Names worked differently in the Eastern Reach—families stuck with one surname for generations, rather than taking the patronymic forename. "Isn't that your family? Senzin?"

Akeylah grimaced. "My oldest brother, Siraaj. My stepfather's lineage was royalty once upon a time. As I said last time we spoke, Eastern succession didn't used to work like Kolonyan, back when we were a separate country. But since we now operate under Kolonyan laws, he would be the one summoned for the tribunal."

"Well, we can probably rule him out anyway." Zofi laughed. "I mean, he wouldn't threaten his own sister."

"I wouldn't be so sure," Akeylah muttered.

Ren's attention sharpened. "Do you have any reason to believe he could be mixed up in the rebellion?"

Akeylah shook her head. "The rebels wouldn't want him on the throne. If the Eastern Reach ever regained its independence, we would elect a new leader. Besides, my brother might be an arse, but he's not coy enough to pull off a scheme like this."

Ren turned back to the list. "Lexana's family have lived in Kolonya for generations. She's about as Northern as our father. I can't imagine her joining some separatist cause."

"She's still a direct descendant of the last Northern king." Akeylah shrugged. "Our distant cousin, in fact."

Ren pursed her mouth. "Gavin, he's a more recent transplant. His father, Verre, owns most of the farms in the Western Reach. He'll be the one we'll need to buy a few hundred tons of grain from if we can't fix this crop blight." She and her sisters had all heard about that today in their meetings and discussed it briefly before this topic.

"Think the blight could be related to the Burnt Bay attack?" Zofi lifted a brow. "A tactic to starve us out?"

"Seems far-fetched," Ren replied.

"And the blight isn't native to Kolonya," Akeylah pointed out. When they both glanced her way, she shrugged. "I heard about it from the traders before we moved here. It's been going on for months in the Eastern Reach."

"Which leaves Lady Tjuya." Ren paused. At dinner the other night, Sarella and Tjuya seemed thick as thieves. Sarella might not be the blackmailer, but she was easily influenced. Ren knew she fell for every rumor she heard. If Tjuya was smarter than she acted, and knew where to plant rumors...

Though, now that she thought about it, Aud said Tjuya was at Lord Hane's party, too, which took place the same night Ren and Zofi broke into the dungeons. It couldn't be Tjuya either. The blackmailer—or at least someone spying for them—was in the servants' corridors that night.

"We should look into all of them," Zofi was saying. "Don't count anyone out just because you *think* they're loyal. After all, this is the court we're talking about." Her dark eyes went hard as she, too, peered up at the Keep.

Ren almost smiled. "Why, sister. You're starting to sound like a Kolonyan."

Zofi grimaced. "Don't ever call me that."

"Did either of you find anything in your searches?" Akeylah asked.

Ren shook her head. "I checked with the kitchens. Nobody remembers seeing anyone leave a letter for me. But the kitchens are open to the public. It would be nearly impossible to narrow down everyone who visited in one day."

"Same with the place where...the blackmailer saw us," Zofi added after a pause and a glance at Akeylah. "I retraced our steps. There's a passage from almost every tower to that spot—one from the cherry tower, one from the rosewood, one from the obsidian, the ivory, the alder...."

"Anyone who knows the Keep well could have been there, essentially." Ren sighed. "That leaves a long list of suspects, too. Sun above."

"So our first attempt didn't turn over much," Akeylah said. "That's fine. We're still expecting a second letter for Zofi, right? Is there a way we could monitor the mail system as well as her rooms, to try to get the jump on the delivery?"

Ren thought of Audrina. Tailing Sarella hadn't turned up much information, but she could ask Aud for another favor, one that might garner better results. "I can get someone trustworthy to watch the mail stack in the kitchens," she said.

"I can set up some simple traps around my chambers," Zofi added thoughtfully. "Maybe a trip wire inside the door and some warning bells around the window..."

Ren frowned. "Won't your maids set those off all the time?"

Zofi snorted. "As if I have maids."

Well, that explained a few things about Zofi's style of dress.

"Sounds like a plan," Akeylah spoke up. She tried for a smile, but it looked forced. "We still have three days left. This person will make a mistake at some point."

"And when they do..." Zofi drew a finger across her throat.

Akeylah shivered.

Ren just nodded, fists balled. "We'll make them regret standing in our way."

23

Zofi

"I wanted to thank you." Zofi leaned against the stall door and watched Vidal brush down his horse. "For believing me."

He'd kept his back to her so far, but now he cast a look over his shoulder, hazel eyes stonewood-hard in the late-afternoon light. She'd come to the barns right after setting trip wires in her chambers, seeking another outlet for her restless energy. And, admittedly, because she knew she owed Vidal at least this much.

"Nothing to thank me for," he replied after a long pause. "As you said, it was an innocent life. I had no real choice in the matter."

"Still." She couldn't hold his eye. She studied his shirt instead, a thin white undershirt soaked through with sweat from running drills in the midday sun. "You could have chosen duty over truth. You could have let him swing."

Vidal scowled and turned away again. "I'm so glad I risked my honor and my position to spare your already-stained conscience."

"My conscience isn't stained," she replied, automatic.

"Even better. Glad I risked myself for a remorseless killer, then."

"Vidal." She stepped into the stall. He stilled, one hand on the brush, though he didn't look back again. "I told you, it was in defense of my friend. Nicolen was about to murder him. They were fighting over nothing more than a damned *card game*."

Silence stretched for a moment. Then Vidal continued to brush the horse, harder now. "The prince had a temper. Elex must have provoked him somehow."

"And that justifies *killing* someone?" She clenched her fists. "If a man punches you simply for looking the way you do, is that your fault? 'One less Traveler will only better this world.' That's what he said right before he attacked. Does that sound like a good person? Like a prince or a friend worthy of your loyalty?"

When she looked up once more, Vidal had laid the brush aside. He ran his hands through his hair, grabbed fistfuls, tugged a little. Now he was the one who wouldn't meet her gaze.

Finally, he dropped his arms with a groan. "I've heard him say something like that before. On the front, during the war, about Genal. I never thought..."

"Never thought he'd believe that about real people, only war-time enemies?" She lifted a brow.

Vidal shook his head. "It still doesn't make this right, Zofi. You killed a man."

"So turn me in." That made his gaze snap to hers, lock in place.

"And see you hang?" A knot appeared on his forehead. "What good would that do? A death for a death only makes for a bloodier battlefield."

"Then stop beating yourself up. You did the right thing, though I know it must have been hard to go against your orders. Especially to save a drifter."

Vidal winced. "I'm sorry the other Talons called you that. I don't think you're a drifter."

"I am, though." She shrugged. "Kolonyans say that word like it's shameful, but I'm proud of it. I love my band, our lifestyle. It's only when your people say *drifter* like a curse that it becomes wrong."

Vidal studied her for a long, quiet moment.

When he didn't say anything else, she cracked her neck. "Anyway. Whatever you feel about what happened, whatever your reasons for helping, and for keeping quiet about me now...thank you. That's all I wanted to say."

She turned to leave. The barns smelled like home—horses and sweat and hay—and it only made the ache in her chest worse. The hole where Elex should be.

"Zofi," he said.

She looked back. Then the whole world shifted beneath her feet. Her head swam, the edges of the stall went fuzzy and blood-stained, like when you rub your eye too hard with the heel of your hand.

In front of her, where Vidal had stood just a second ago, the Silver Prince leered down at Zofi.

Her skin went cold. She couldn't move, couldn't run, couldn't even make her hand reach for the knife on her hip.

"What's the matter, Zofi?" Prince Nicolen's voice was harsh, guttural, just the way she remembered. It set off a cascade of memories—*blood on her hands, blood in the dirt.* "Aren't you glad to see me?" His mouth gaped wide, a grotesque parody of a smile. The stench of two-month-old graves washed over her.

She wanted to scream, but not even her lungs would obey.

"What a traitor, that Vidal. He told me I was his brother-in-arms. Told me he cared for me. Now here he is forgiving my murderer." The Silver Prince clucked his tongue in disapproval. "Ah well. That's all right. There's still one person out there who will avenge me." He leaned down so his lips grazed her ear. His breath, hot and cold at once, made her knees shake. "You have until the Sun's Ascendance, Zofi. Three days. If you haven't left Kolonya City by then, I'll make sure Vidal isn't the only one who learns your bloody little secret...."

Panic took over. She finally forced her legs to move. Staggered away until her elbow collided with splintery wood.

"Zofi."

She shut her eyes, doubled over. *It's not real, it's not real.* When she looked up again, Vidal stood over her, brow creased. He had one hand raised, about to touch her shoulder, though he hesitated now.

"What just happened?"

She blinked. Rubbed her temple. "I—I'm not sure. Did I faint?"

He shook his head. "You seemed fine one moment. Then the next you were leaping backward into the stall door, looking like you'd just seen a demon."

"I'm sorry. Must be the temperature in here. It's hot, no?" He offered a hand, but she ignored it and levered herself off the wall instead, back onto her feet. "I need some fresh air."

"Are you sure you're all right?" He frowned, peered at her face.

"Of course!" She brushed past him and out of the stall.

"Zofi—"

"I have to go," she called before he could even finish that sentence. Explain whatever he'd been about to say before she left. *Sands.* She quickened her pace, hurried out of the stables as fast as she dared walk.

She needed to talk to her sisters.

✳

Ren and Akeylah met her in the interior courtyard. A calm little plot of grass tucked between the ten towers, decorated with a single trickling fountain in the shape of a stormwing battling a sailfish. The perfect spot to meet undetected. Especially at this hour, just after dinner, with the shadows of the three moons crisscrossing the yard. Only one entrance, no hidden corridors or blind corners. Nowhere for a spy to hide. Plus the trickle of the fountain ensured their voices didn't carry far.

"Well?" Ren swept into a seat beside Zofi on the fountain's edge. "Let's see this next threat."

"I can't show you," Zofi replied.

"We need to trust one another if we want to catch this person," Akeylah said.

Zofi shook her head. "I can't show you because it wasn't a note." She gritted her teeth. She knew how this was going to sound. "It... I *saw* the threat."

Ren's eyes widened. "Who delivered it? What did they look like?"

"No, it's not—" She huffed out a sigh. "I saw a person who couldn't have been here. A dead man. He showed up right in front of me, looking as real as you right now. He told me I had until the Sun's Ascendance to leave or he'd tell everyone my secret."

"We're being blackmailed by a zombie," Ren deadpanned.

"No. It wasn't actually him, obviously. It was a vision. I was with someone else, and they didn't see a thing."

"A mental projection." Akeylah tilted her head.

Ren and Zofi both frowned. "A what?"

"It's a tithe. A pretty rare one—it requires quite a skilled manipulation of the Arts. Not to mention strong concentration skills."

"How could it be a tithe? I didn't do anything."

Akeylah fixed her with a pointed stare. "A tithe someone else performed *on* you, Zofi."

Her brow furrowed. "But that would mean . . ."

"Vulgar Arts," Ren finished. She tapped her lower lip. "You're certain you've heard of this tithe, Akeylah?"

"I just finished reading a book that described it, actually. During the War for Recognition, the Kolonyan granddaughter of a high-ranking Genalese commander used it to convince him that an entire naval fleet was attacking his ships from the east. He ignored his other officers' repeated arguments, turned his whole armada that direction. Then Kolonya routed his ships from behind."

Zofi blinked. "Sands. Handy trick."

"Are you thinking what I'm thinking?" Ren glanced from Akeylah to Zofi and back.

Akeylah nodded. "In order to use the Vulgar Arts against someone..."

The weight that had settled in Zofi's gut ever since the apparition in the stables grew even heavier. Made her stomach rumble, nauseous, as the realization struck. "It must be someone related to me."

·≾ 24 ≿·

Akeylah

Two days left. That was the first thought on Akeylah's mind when the irritable library warden, Madam Harknell, woke her with a summons from the king.

Akeylah, join me in the solarium at once for your next lesson.

She wished she could make some excuse. There wasn't time for lessons, not now.

Two days to find the blackmailer. Two days before she'd either be exposed as a blood traitor or forced to flee Kolonya City to avoid that. Where would she run? Back home to her stepfather?

Either route would kill her. Execution by hanging or execution by barley-liquor bottle. Didn't matter. Death was death.

She had only one possible escape route. Yet time was running thin, and she still had no real leads. She was fast becoming an expert on unusual tithes and the dangers of using the Vulgar Arts, though that didn't help her narrow down suspects. If anything, it only made her more convinced that just about anybody could learn to curse their own family, if they were dedicated and made a long enough study of these tomes.

Which, Akeylah supposed, shouldn't surprise *her*, of all people.

She needed to stay in the library. Keep researching. But she couldn't ignore a direct order from the king either.

"See you tonight, no doubt," Madam Harknell called as she packed her things. If she wasn't mistaken, the woman looked slightly less annoyed than she'd been for the past few days.

Slightly.

"Mother Ocean willing," Akeylah replied on her way out. Harknell groaned, though she waved, too. At this rate, Akeylah would befriend the librarian just in time to invite the woman to her own execution.

Her mind raced.

The facts: Their blackmailer knew the passages in the Keep. They had access to the kitchens and the mail system. They were related to Zofi within at least four generations, and possibly to Akeylah and Ren, as well, though only time would tell. They wanted all three potential heirs gone.

And, as Ren pointed out, they had very pretty handwriting.

Possible yet unproven connections: It could be the Silver Prince's assassin—though Zofi didn't think so, and Ren seemed to agree with her. It could be the same rebel or rebels who orchestrated Burnt Bay—though Ren didn't seem to believe *that* either.

Motivations: Unrest? Wanting to trigger a tribunal and get an heir elected from another Reach, perhaps. Or destabilizing Kolonya in service of some other outside attack.

Akeylah frowned the whole way to the solarium. She entered, lost in thought and still dressed in the casual day gown she wore to the library. She regretted that the moment she looked up and found nine well-dressed nobles watching her.

The solarium, as it transpired, was the strangest place in the Keep she'd seen yet. It sat atop the first tower, its beech walls bone-white. A glass ceiling provided more than ample light in the room—light that reflected off gemstones in every color, set into the walls.

In the middle of the dizzying rainbow stood a sundial, whose shadow fell across a raised, three-dimensional sculpture of the Reaches.

She drew out a seashell-shaped chair across from the map's northeast corner, the last chair remaining.

Besides the usual contingent of King Andros, Countess Yasmin, Queen Rozalind, and Akeylah's half sisters, she counted four others in the room. She recognized Ambassador Danton, though not the other three. Still, it didn't take much effort to work out the significance, based on the pins on each noble's shirt. A Southern great cat, a Northern sand-stepper, a Western heron. And of course, Danton's sailfish.

This must be the regional council.

Rozalind met her eye for the briefest moment, flashed a barely there smile. Akeylah hadn't seen her since they rode side by side to the last lesson, and even then, they'd barely had a chance to speak before Akeylah and the king went to listen to merchants complain about tax prices for hours. She hadn't had a moment alone with Rozalind since the queen left Akeylah standing in the halls outside her chambers, parting words ringing in Akeylah's ears.

If you find a good enough reason to stay…Selfishly, I hope you do.

Much as Akeylah wanted to give her an answer—much as she wanted that answer to be *yes*—she couldn't. Not until she found this blackmailer. Not unless she stopped them from revealing her secret.

Until then, Rozalind was safer unassociated with Akeylah. If Akeylah went down for treason, she refused to muddy the Genalese queen's name on her way out. Rozalind had enough ill opinions to contend with already.

"Thank you all for coming," Andros said. His voice wavered, and he looked visibly tired, the whites of his eyes yellow in the multicolored gemlight. "Forgive me if I sound a bit off—I'm still recovering from a late night."

The ambassadors laughed. Akeylah tore her gaze from her father, focused on the attendees as the king introduced them.

Danton she knew already. Lord D'Morre Perry turned out to be the ambassador of the Southern Reach, Lady D'Vangeline Ghoush the Northern, and Lord D'Ercito Kiril the Western. Ren, seated between Akeylah and Zofi, dug an elbow into her side at Lady Ghoush's forename. Akeylah recognized it, too.

Lord D'Vangeline Rueno was Lexana's father. Lady D'Vangeline Ghoush must be his sister. So not only was Lexana descended from the former kings of the Northern Reach, but her aunt served as ambassador for that region.

Interesting.

"Now, introductions aside." King Andros clapped his hands. "Let's get down to business. Yesterday, my family and I visited the skysquats, where we learned some troubling news about the grain blight. We will need to increase our importation of wheat in the next month, just to be safe. Ambassador Kiril, I hear the Western Reach may have a surplus to sell us?"

Kiril glanced from Danton to the king and back again. "We have sold most of our excess harvest to the Eastern Reach already, Your Majesty, after hearing of a similar blight affecting their crops."

"How much remains?" Andros asked.

"About four thousand tons, Your Majesty."

For a moment, Andros only grimaced. At first, Akeylah thought it was his answer. Then she realized he was battling a bout of pain. Beside him, Yasmin tensed. She toyed with the bloodletter ring on her finger, spinning it around and around. Akeylah wondered if the countess was about to offer it to her brother, to have him tithe for healing in front of all these nobles.

A healing tithe might help the king's pain, though it wouldn't forestall the inevitable, Akeylah knew.

Guilt itched in her veins.

Finally, Andros straightened in his seat. "That will barely tide the city over for a month. Never mind our population in the Kolonyan countryside. We'll need to purchase some of your emergency stocks as well, Kiril."

The Western Ambassador didn't look pleased. "Your Majesty, if the blight moves farther east, into our fields..."

"Our agriculture guild will stop that from happening," Andros said. "Ambassador Danton, how much of the surplus did you purchase for your region? We may need to tap into some of that also."

"With all due respect, Your Majesty, my people are already starving." Akeylah didn't miss the look Danton shot Ren, or the way her sister avoided his eye. "I dug into my own personal coffers to buy that surplus. We cannot afford to sell you any."

"Everyone will need to tighten their belts if we want to get through this season." Somehow, Andros managed to keep his tone calm and lighthearted. "We must share alike. United, the Reaches are strong, but if we let a shortage divide us by hoarding food and supplies selfishly, we will weaken. Leave ourselves open to attack."

Danton leaned forward. "That's all good coming from the most well-fed Reach. But where is that all-for-one attitude when Kolonya needs to tighten her own belt? The outer Reaches starve while you feast."

"We do not feast—"

"What's happening two days from now? The *Feast* of the Sun's Glorious Ascendance?"

Andros paused again. This time, it wasn't pain that tightened his expression, but anger. "The Sun's Ascendance is a religious ritual, a tradition that dates back centuries. It honors the gods, their gifts, and the Reaches' gratitude for those gifts. To let such an event pass uncelebrated would be worse than a defeat in battle—it would be a defeat of our very way of life."

"So you value that *way of life* over actual human lives in the other Reaches?"

"Can we not value both?" Akeylah asked.

The whole room fell silent, her father included. Every eye swiveled her way. She fought the sudden urge to hide under the table.

Because someone needed to say this.

Akeylah straightened in her seat. "We can still hold the event, still honor the Sun's Ascendance and give the gods their due respect. But maybe we can do it in a way that takes into account our present difficulties. 'The gods bless those who care for their people,'" Akeylah quoted *The History*. "We could serve only light refreshments. Save all the food we can."

"Better yet," Ren interrupted, while shooting Akeylah a tiny, grateful smile, "we could send the surplus food to the skysquats. The farmers and workers Countess Yasmin and I met yesterday are hungry and fearful about their futures should this blight worsen. If we ask the kitchens to salt any meat we've purchased, pickle the vegetables, and preserve the grain rather than baking too much bread, we can give those farmers enough food to last several weeks."

Akeylah smiled back at Ren. "Then that's several weeks' less food we'll need to worry about purchasing from other Reaches. It buys us some time, at least."

King Andros frowned, though he didn't answer. Not right away.

"And how do you propose we explain all this to the nobles who attend the Sun's Ascendance expecting a display of Kolonya's strength and power?" Yasmin asked icily. "Not to mention a decent dinner."

"Simple," Zofi said. "Flatter them."

"By asking them to go hungry all evening?" Yasmin tapped her long fingernails on the tabletop.

"No." Akeylah nodded to Zofi, taking her sister's meaning. "Flatter them by talking about how kind and generous they are to share their food in order to strengthen our whole country."

Ambassador Ghoush folded her hands. "Speaking for the

north, my people rely on feasts and festivals to network. To make the trade deals that keep their towns thriving in better seasons."

Ambassador Perry nodded. "We cannot strike profitable deals without sufficient social lubrication."

"Nobody said anything about cutting down on booze," Zofi replied.

Rozalind suddenly clamped her lips tight. Akeylah felt fairly sure the queen was stifling a laugh.

"We won't cancel the festivities," King Andros finally spoke up. He steepled his fingertips under his chin as he considered Akeylah. "We will still hold the Feast of the Sun's Glorious Ascendance, and indeed all the festivities our courtiers have come to expect. These are a necessary function of life in the Keep, as you so astutely point out, Ambassador Ghoush. But we can cut the extent to which we celebrate each event."

Ambassador Perry and Ambassador Ghoush both sucked in breath, about to speak.

Andros ignored them and gestured to a scribe in the far corner of the room. "Send a message to the chefs. Halve the provisions for the Sun's Ascendance. Preserve any ingredients that can be stored, and send a contingent of Talons to distribute those among the skysquats."

The scribe scribbled notes.

"Your Majesty—" Ambassador Ghoush began.

"This seems extreme," Ambassador Perry put in.

"The Sun's Ascendance will be a test," Andros replied. "Afterward, we will meet again to decide whether these measures held up. Now, on our next point of business..."

Akeylah and her sisters traded bright-eyed glances. One small victory, at least.

Around the table, talk shifted to trade prices and the rebuilding of the navy. In between topics, Ambassadors Ghoush and Perry glowered in Akeylah's direction. She ignored it. Stole peeks at Rozalind instead. More than once, she caught the queen looking back and had to hastily shift her gaze, hoping no one else noticed.

"How long do you plan to impose these sanctions?" Danton's voice cut through her distraction.

What did I miss?

"They're only a proposal at this stage." Andros coughed, hard enough to double in his chair.

Danton didn't wait for him to finish, only raised his voice to speak over the coughing fit. "A proposal to make it even harder for Easterners to do business. You want our traders to register with *border patrols* as if we're what, Genalese?" Danton winced and looked to the queen. "Apologies, Your Majesty."

"No offense taken."

Akeylah's heart tripped at the sound of Rozalind's voice.

King Andros cleared his throat. "Only until this rebel nonsense dies down." Then the coughs took him again.

While the king recovered, Danton surveyed the rest of the council. "How long before he starts doing this to your people? How long before you're treated like second-class citizens in your own country? The Reaches call themselves united, but—"

"But we will take steps to protect ourselves when we must," Ren cut in. "If you could maintain a little more control over your people, Ambassador, we would not have needed to raise this issue in the first place."

Ambassadors Perry and Ghoush nodded along with Ren.

"Protection indeed," Yasmin murmured, though Akeylah wasn't sure who else heard. Or what that meant.

Andros's breath wheezed when he sat straight again. Akeylah had heard that sound before. On the docks, when fishing boats reeled in drowning men from the bay. It was the sound of liquid in a lung.

She prayed nobody else at the table recognized it.

"As I said," the king managed, voice tight. "It is only a temporary sanction to prevent further violence."

That word, *violence*, echoed through the solarium.

"We will discuss this in more detail at next month's meeting." Countess Yasmin rested one hand on her brother's shoulder. "In the meantime, I pray to Father Sun that peace will reign in the Reaches."

The ambassadors recognized a dismissal when they heard one. A few murmured agreement with Yasmin, and then the formal farewells began. Akeylah stayed until the last ambassador departed, then rose to follow her sisters out of the room.

The moment she entered the hallway, a familiar, cool touch grazed her arm. She slowed her pace, let Zofi and Ren walk ahead, and grinned at the queen.

Despite the worried crease on her forehead, Rozalind looked as beautiful as ever in a navy silk dress that made Akeylah's face go hot. "You were impressive in there."

Akeylah ducked her head. "I doubt Lord Perry and Lady Ghoush would agree."

"Disagreements are necessary in councils like this. It takes a leader to speak up, to stand their ground when faced with opposition." Rozalind caught her eye. "I told you you belong here."

There it was again. That unspoken question. *Will you stay?* If only Rozalind knew how much she wanted to.

"I may" was all she could answer now. She wouldn't lie, not to Rozalind. She might need to flee the Keep within two days, if she couldn't stop the blackmailer in time.

"That sounds somewhat more promising than the last time we spoke." Those perfect seashell lips of Rozalind's tilted up at the edges. "Last time, you told me there was nothing here for you."

Akeylah's heartbeat quickened. "I lied."

Rozalind stepped forward. Akeylah echoed her.

Footsteps sounded in the solarium. Before Akeylah could react, leap away like she normally would, Rozalind grabbed her hand. Tugged her the other direction, around a blind corner and through what appeared to be a tapestry hanging against a solid wall.

The tapestry, as it transpired, led to a narrow servants' corridor. The tapestry swung into place behind them, and Rozalind pressed a single finger to Akeylah's lips.

That touch alone distracted her into silence.

Outside, King Andros's voice grew audible. "—simply cannot believe it of her."

"Well, you must." Yasmin's voice and footsteps grew louder, too, headed their direction. "Besides, I don't know what is so unbelievable. None of your daughters are suited for leadership."

"What alternative do I have?"

Yasmin huffed. "You already know what I think."

"My echo, I do. And *you* know I find that even more dangerous than the alternative."

"If you would just let me do my job—"

"Your job is to advise me, Yasmin. Not rule in my stead."

Their footsteps crossed in front of the tapestry. Akeylah and Rozalind held their breath, hands still entwined.

But the king and countess didn't seem to notice anything amiss. They continued down the corridor, footsteps receding.

"No," Andros said, though in response to what, Akeylah wasn't sure. Perhaps some unseen gesture. "You're right. If that's the full story."

"Something I've been telling you for Sun knows how long…"

Their voices faded.

"Akeylah, are you all right?" Rozalind whispered.

Something stirred in the back of Akeylah's mind. *Rule in my stead?* What had the king meant? *Perhaps…*

But no. That would be madness. It made no sense. Countess Yasmin was Andros's twin. His trusted sister. His main advisor. Why would she work against him?

Unless she believed she was helping him. If she thought she was protecting the throne from an unsavory successor. Akeylah heard her just now. *None of your daughters are suited for leadership.*

That tone matched the one in Akeylah's last blackmail threat. *Your bloodstained hands will never touch the crown as long as I have a say in it.* Protective, defensive.

Yasmin had grown up in the Keep. She knew every passageway, could order any servant she wanted to run any errand. Errands like delivering letters to chambers or dropping them off in creepy, dimly lit hallways. She didn't believe any of Andros's daughters deserved the throne.

Not to mention, she was a blood relative, Only one generation removed. A close enough relation to tithe a Vulgar Arts curse onto Zofi. Yasmin was skilled in the Arts, had taught them plenty of new tithes during their first lesson. What other tricks might she know? What curses might she have learned in her years of study?

Akeylah reached for the queen's shoulders, gripped them to steady herself. "Rozalind," she said, voice low and desperate. "What do you know about Countess Yasmin?"

❄ 25 ❄

Florencia

"Nice upgrade." Ren eyed Mama's new chambers apprecia-tively. They weren't quite as large as Ren's suite, but close. Located nearby, too, a few floors down from hers in the ash tower. "City view and everything."

"Andros couldn't very well let the mother of his daughter stay in the servants' wing. Not now that said daughter has been acknowl-edged." Mama reclined before her new writing desk, feathered quill in hand.

"You look well, too," Ren said. In truth, Mama looked better than Ren had seen her in years. "Is that a new gown?"

"You like it?" Mama patted her silk skirts. "Just imagine the gowns I'll be able to afford once you're crowned." She laughed. When Ren didn't join in, though, Mama set the quill down. "What is it?"

"Nothing." Ren crossed to the window.

In truth, she'd been thinking about her sisters. About their blackmailer, all the dead ends they'd run up against. Did she really deserve the throne if she couldn't handle tracking down one enemy?

Maybe the blackmailer is right. Maybe she wasn't fit to rule.

"Florencia."

She sighed.

Mama sized her up. "I hope you lie better than this at court."

"You taught me well, Mama, don't fret."

"Tell me what's bothering you." She rose and joined Ren at the window. "Is it the lessons? Your father's illness?"

Ren blinked. "You know about that?"

"Andros told me why he decided to name you when he did, of course."

"Anything else the two of you are still hiding from me?" Ren crossed her arms.

"Nothing he hasn't already spoken to you about by now. He wrote to me when he granted me these chambers. Said he plans to give you and the other girls lessons and see who proves most adept. Which, I might add, is more detail than I've gotten from you this past week."

The other girls. My sisters, you mean. "I've been busy."

"Too busy to visit your mother all week, yes, I noticed." Mama smirked. "And now that you've finally stopped by, you're distracted."

Ren avoided Mama's eye. What could she say? *I committed treason and now someone is using that against me?*

"Ren, whatever's going on, you can always talk to me. I hope you know that."

"I know, Mama." She forced a smile. "I'm just stressed. Between the king's lessons, and getting accustomed to this new life, getting to know my relatives…" She thought about her own adjustment, then about how much more difficult Zofi's and Akeylah's must be. "Not to mention people making comments about those relatives—"

"What comments?"

Ren snapped her mouth shut. She'd been thinking about the stares of the skysquat petitioners, the crowd falling silent when Zofi dismounted. The sideways scowls the ambassadors kept turning on Zofi and Akeylah during the regional council meeting today. Even when Ren agreed with her sisters, Ambassadors Perry and Ghoush reserved their worst death glares for the other two.

Sun above, her own mother just called them *the other girls* like they meant nothing.

Ren used to do that, too. Used to be like Yasmin, dismissing anyone she didn't deem worthy. *Why feed our own farmers when we could hoard all that food for the nobles instead?* And if one day Yasmin needed to choose which nobles should be fed, Ren had no doubt the countess would happily throw half the denizens of the Keep under the carriage wheels.

Exclusion was a dangerous road. It led to—what did Danton say? To treating others like second-class citizens in their own country.

"Just things people say," Ren said. "About the king's new bastard daughters."

"What people?" Mama pursed her mouth, a habit Ren had inherited.

Ren did the same. "Everyone. Farmers, nobles. Sun above, even Yasmin."

To her surprise, Mama scoffed. "Don't put credit in anything Yasmin says. That woman has always been an odd one. If she wasn't Andros's sister, I doubt anyone would put up with her madness."

Ren frowned. "What do you mean?"

Mama waved a dismissive hand. "I served her for a little while, decades ago. Believe me, the things she does…talks to herself, falls into trances and stares at walls for hours. The last year I served her, she wouldn't even let me help her dress. Never lets anyone do it nowadays, I hear. Why do you think she only wears those loose-fitting shift gowns, even though they're terribly out of fashion?"

Ren shook her head. "Well, even if I ignore Yasmin, there's still plenty of other people saying things about us."

"Us?"

"I mean, me and the other potential heirs…"

"Florencia, don't go trusting those girls."

"Mama—"

"A Traveler and an Easterner, could Andros have chosen any worse dalliances? The Eastern Reach is dangerous enough, but having a drifter in the family…"

"*Mama.*" She said it so forcefully her mother stopped mid-sentence, stared. "Those are my half sisters you're talking about."

"I know that, Ren." Mama narrowed her eyes. "I'm just making sure you remember the half that matters."

❋

"Nothing else?" Ren rubbed her temples and gazed into the mirror above her vanity.

277

"Afraid not." Behind her, Audrina sprawled across the bed, a silk scarf in one hand. She wound it absently around her wrist, spun it off, wound it back. "Just the usual boring party invites for you, and nothing at all for either of your sisters. Unpopular pair." Aud leaned back so her head hung over the edge of the bed and peered at Ren upside down. "Want me to keep watching the mail, or got someone new you'd like me to stalk?"

Ren winced at her reflection. "I am sorry for asking all these favors, Aud."

Her friend laughed. "I'm only teasing, Ren. Honestly, it's kind of fun. Keeps me entertained, gives me more to do than just cleaning up after dull noblewomen."

"Still." Ren stood, crossed the room to sit beside her friend. "I promise I'll make it up to you one day."

"Don't worry about it." Aud cracked a smile, though Ren could see the strain around the edges. "What are friends for?"

"Are we still going to remain friends after I asked you to serve under the worst noblewoman in the Keep?" Ren suggested.

Aud snorted. "Depends. Is my assignment over?"

Ren gripped her hand. "You can ask Oruna to swap away from Sarella's service now. And I promise, no more favors."

"For now." Audrina shot her a knowing look. She was smiling, but Ren saw the hardness beneath.

She fought the urge to wince. "Hopefully forever." Though she couldn't help it. Already she was running through suspects. A *relative of Zofi. Someone who knows the Keep.* Which most likely meant someone related on Zofi's Kolonyan side.

The same blood relatives Ren shared.

"Well, if someone does need to be spied on, you know where

to find me." Audrina rolled off the bed and pushed to her feet. "Back to re-beading the skirt Lady Mayuja wrecked the other night." She held the silk scarf out to Ren.

"Oh, no." Ren pushed it back. "Keep it."

A knock sounded at the door.

"Florencia?"

Even through the thick stonewood door, Ren recognized his voice. She tensed.

Audrina did, too. "Speaking of people we ought to be monitoring…" Aud muttered.

"Play nice," Ren scolded as she rose to answer.

Danton was still dressed in the formal coat he wore to the regional council meeting earlier. The sharp cut of the jacket highlighted his even sharper cheekbones, and the dark red matched his hair. She fought her body's instinctive reaction and instead regarded him coolly.

"Yes?"

"I need a moment," he said. He stood at a strange angle to the door, half his body concealed behind the frame. "Alone." Danton eyed Audrina.

Audrina clenched her fists. "My lady," she said, voice carefully measured, "it would be improper for me to leave just now."

Ren lifted her palm, open in peace. "I'll be fine, Aud."

Aud ignored it. She continued to glare at Danton, even as she edged past him and out into the corridor.

Despite a strain evident around Danton's jawline, his mouth quirked into a smile. "I like her," he said as Audrina stormed past, shooting him a death stare. "You can use friends that loyal."

"They're often in short supply, I know." Ren waited until

Audrina left the chambers before she spoke. "What is it, Danton?" she asked once Aud was out of earshot.

He stepped into the room. As he did, he hauled a serving boy inside, the boy's arm twisted behind his back in a vice grip. Ren scrambled to shut the door behind them.

"Tell her what you told me," Danton ordered.

Tears streaked the boy's face. He couldn't be older than thirteen. To judge by his thin arms and even spindlier legs, he didn't have a good position here. Errand boy for the kitchens maybe, or hearth-tender.

"Go on."

The boy swallowed hard and opened one of his pockets. Reached in to produce a tiny blown-glass ornament, dark red in color. "It's not my fault." His voice was so soft Ren leaned closer to hear. "They made me."

"Who made you?" Danton demanded.

The boy hiccuped.

Ren held out a hand.

"Don't—" Danton started, but the boy tipped the object into her palm.

Ren caught it. The glass felt cool, smooth. There was liquid inside, she realized, giving it that dark red color. That glass had been perfectly sealed around it. She couldn't see a cork or a stopper. Just delicate swirls of pale gray glass that enclosed the liquid.

As for the liquid, it was a peculiar yet familiar color. A few shades darker than ruby. The color of...

Her insides stilled.

Blood.

"Told you, I never saw their face. They paid me two hundred kolons. Said they'd pay me double that once I delivered it."

"Delivered it how, exactly?"

"Supposed to put the phial in my lady's shoes, sir. Doesn't matter which one, they said. Near the heel."

Ren frowned. None of this made any sense. What in Sun's name was this phial full of blood for?

"How did they contact you?" Danton demanded. "How were you paid?"

"They met me in the kitchens, my lord. Wore a hood, didn't they, so I couldn't see much of anything under it. They're tall. Kind of deep voice, though it sounded put-on. Dunno the accent."

Danton rubbed his temples in frustration.

"Left me money at my mum's house. She lives just down Masonsgeld Lane, off Battonry, sir, so it's a quick walk from here."

Danton released the boy's arm. The boy cradled his wrist, rubbed it between his thumb and forefinger.

"They told you to deliver it to me specifically?" Ren held the glass phial up to her light. No markings anywhere on it. Just the smooth, almost pretty whorls of blown glass. "Lady Florencia?"

The boy hesitated. Bit his lip. "They said, bring this phial to the chambers of Lady Lady's Maid. Princess..." He bit that lip harder. Waited until Danton elbowed him to continue. "Princess of Traitors and Spies."

"I see." Ren closed her eyes. Counted to three. "And you knew this was me because..."

"Forgive me, my lady. It's just... there's only one lady's maid what's now a princess."

She sighed. "Let him go, Danton."

"Florencia, we need to question him, find out—"

"He's told us what he knows. I won't torture the boy any further." She knelt until she drew to eye level with the child. "Thank you for telling us what you know."

The boy lingered. "Does...does this count?"

Ren frowned. "Count?"

"As bringing the phial here. Only, I don't know if they'll still give me the money, and my mum, she's got the bloody cough, the one what I'll need menders to help with. Her tithes aren't helping...."

Ren held his gaze for a long moment. Then she rose and crossed to her vanity. Set down the phial and picked up a pen. "Bring this note to the menders' guild on Lichtson Street. Tell them to bill any medicine or consultations your mother needs to Lady D'Andros Florencia." Ren tore off the letter and lit a candle to stamp the royal seal onto it. The stormwing image glinted in her chamber light as she handed the note to the boy. "If you have any trouble, come back and tell me. I'll send a messenger directly."

The boy bowed, hesitated, then bowed once more to Danton before he bolted.

As soon as he'd gone, Ren sank onto her bed. "Where in Sun's name did you find that child?"

"Lurking outside your chambers like a lost puppy." Danton hovered next to the bed. "When I stopped to ask him what he was doing, he tried to run. I caught him, got a bit of the story out of him, before you opened the door." He sank onto the mattress beside her. It shifted, rolled her a few inches closer to him until she caught herself with one arm.

"So you've just been lurking outside my chambers as well? Who's the lost puppy now?"

"Touché." He cast her a sideways glance. "You told me you judge people by their actions, not their words. You were right. I'm trying to prove myself, Florencia. I'm trying to do what's right for you, not just make empty promises."

"How did you know to look for a spy?"

"I didn't know what I was looking for. Spy, assassin, or just that Sarella woman poking around. I never expected to find...whatever that is."

They both looked at her vanity. From here, the phial looked innocuous. Just a little red-and-gray glass ornament. If the boy had made it into her chambers and hidden it, Ren doubted she'd have questioned it if she found it.

Assuming she didn't simply put on whatever shoe he hid it inside and break the decoration in the first place.

"Do you think it's a tithe of some kind?"

"No idea. I've never seen anything like it." He frowned, deep in thought. "Perhaps a Traveler device? I've heard rumors they have a way to store tithes, but they're difficult to believe when our own acolytes have been testing storage methods for centuries without success. Besides, the Arts are useless against anyone else anyway, unless—"

"Unless it's the Vulgar Arts," Ren mused. Her thoughts drifted toward the blackmailer, who had already stooped to using that once, against Zofi. Most likely it was someone on Andros's side of the family, someone who could curse Ren as well. Was this her next blackmail threat?

Her forehead ached. She needed to talk to her sisters. If it *was* a Traveler device, perhaps Zofi could provide some insight.

"Let me take it with me," Danton said. "The boy was instructed to plant it in your chambers. I don't like leaving it here without knowing what it is. What it can do."

Ren shook her head. "I'll dispose of it later tonight," she lied. She already knew where she'd take it. Straight to the library, to whatever cubby Akeylah was holed up in tonight, as soon as she tracked down Zofi. If anyone could deduce what this phial meant, it was her sisters—the bookworm and the Traveler.

"You have an idea who sent it?"

She could feel Danton studying her. She met his gaze, put on a defiant expression. Didn't help. The second their eyes met, she felt that old familiar spark, deep in her gut. Her body hadn't forgotten his. Her nerve endings screamed for the release she always found when he pulled her lips to his in a slow, searing kiss.

He was a bad idea. A dangerous one. And yet... *Old habits die hard.*

She forced herself to lean away instead of toward him. "I do."

"And you're not going to share your suspicions." It wasn't a question.

"Danton, there are too many moving pieces in this puzzle already."

"This isn't a game, Florencia."

"So you've said."

"Then stop acting like it's just another court rumor." He caught her shoulders, gently. Rough callouses on his palms, which he definitely didn't have last time he was in the Keep, sparked flames against her skin. "Someone wants to hurt you. You need to be careful. You need friends you can trust."

"Catching one wayward spy does not a trustworthy ally make," she replied. "For all I know, you planted that boy to soften me toward you, and that phial is nonsense." She made a move as though to stand and reach for it.

Danton tightened his grip. "Ren, please."

Ren. Unlike everyone else, he only ever used her nickname when frustrated.

"Or your friends back east sent it." She raised her brows, challenging. "They have a pretty good reason to scare me away from the throne. There's an Easterner they could plant on it now, after all."

He sighed. He was so close she felt the warmth of his breath on her cheeks. "It's not that simple."

"Does the rebellion have operatives in the Keep? Besides you, of course."

Danton scowled. "I'm trying to keep you safe. That's a great deal harder to do if you won't trust me."

"Give me one reason why I should."

He kissed her.

She remembered this. The way he inhaled when he kissed, tilted his head, parted his mouth to entwine their tongues. She did not remember agreeing to the impulse, yet suddenly she was kissing him back. She caught his breath with hers, let him fold an arm around her waist, because she'd already buried her fingers in his hair. He traced her jawline as they kissed—her cheekbones, the corner of her lips. She wrapped her arms around his neck, and when he pulled her backward onto the bed, she let herself fall.

Danton was a bridge. She'd lingered at the top, avoiding the drop for as long as she could. But he was here, warm, real, his body hard against hers, his arms reassuringly familiar. He was here again, he wanted her, and *Sun damn him*, she still wanted him, too.

Danton was a bridge. Now that she'd jumped, she couldn't stop the fall.

·•❧ 26 ❧•·

Akeylah

"I found something."

Akeylah looked up from the nest she'd created of her current reading list. Madam Harknell had completely given up now, and simply left the ladder and the key to the hard-to-reach and restricted-access bookshelves on the cart Akeylah loaded with reading material.

With the librarian out on a three-hour-long lunch break, Akeylah had the whole library to herself.

Well. She did, until Rozalind appeared at her elbow, grinning like she just staged a coup.

Akeylah turned her current read—*Black Guard: Curseworkers During the War for Recognition*—upside down to save her page, and stood. "About the countess?"

Yesterday, Rozalind had admitted she didn't know much

about Yasmin beyond the usual facts. Andros was extremely fond of his twin sister. Yasmin had a hand in most aspects of ruling the Reaches. Both of them had overheard her in the hallway yesterday, saying something about taking over the throne.

But that morning, when Akeylah shared her suspicions with Zofi and Ren over a fraught breakfast, her half sisters had been less than receptive.

"Yasmin can't inherit," Ren had said as she sipped her morning abraca brew. "She's childless, and well past bearing age. That would be a dead end. It's not how Kolonyan succession works."

"Besides, if she knew our secrets, why wouldn't she just tell Andros and oust us already?" Zofi had added through a mouthful of honeyed globe fruit.

Yet despite her sisters' dismissals, Akeylah still thought Yasmin was the best lead they had. The *only* lead, at the moment. Unless you counted pure conjecture, such as Lady Lexana's connection to once-royal Northern stock.

Now here was Rozalind like a gods-send, nodding. "I found someone you need to talk to." She caught Akeylah's hand, and it was a testament to how deep in the books Akeylah was that she didn't even think about the implications of being seen. She just intertwined her fingers with the queen's and let Rozalind pull her through the halls of the alder tower.

Akeylah had never seen the University before.

Its doors resembled the Great Hall entrance, but instead of carvings of various rulers' conquests, it depicted the Arts. She gaped at the panels. One showed the outline of a human body painted over with green and blue and silver. Another depicted a heart, perfectly traced, except where the arteries and veins should be, tree branches sprouted. A third panel was completely abstract, just thick, angry splashes of paint, none of the colors coordinated. And yet, looking at it, that one seemed to come the closest to explaining how the Arts sensed.

"You need to tithe to get in," Rozalind explained.

Only then did Akeylah notice the spindle that protruded from a painting of a rosebush covered in vampyre flies—tiny beetles that lived off human blood. She pressed the pad of her thumb to the spindle, just hard enough for it to nick her skin.

The moment it did, warmth washed over her. It felt like a tithe, and yet different—directed by something outside herself. A single droplet of her blood slid down the spindle's length and collided with the painted roses, which began to glow a faint pink.

With a heavy clank, the door unlatched itself and swung inward.

Akeylah tightened her grip on Rozalind's hand. Rozalind squeezed back.

Together, they stepped through the portal and into the Kolonyan University of the Blood Arts.

A few acolytes stood scattered around an enormous court-yard just inside. The ceiling, five stories overhead, was made of glass, just like in the solarium. It gave this courtyard, with its alder stonewood flagstones and a bubbling fountain nearly buried in flower bushes, the appearance of being outside.

Students sprawled around the courtyard on blankets, noses buried in books. Others sat on the edge of the fountain, feet dangling in the water, and compared notes.

A dozen side doors led off the hall on each level, four on each side of the courtyard, except for the side that housed the main entrance. With five levels in all, that meant sixty rooms. Classrooms, lecture halls, dormitories, maybe a mess hall.

"It's enormous," Akeylah murmured.

"Takes up most of the alder tower," Rozalind said. "Aside from a few lower levels." She tugged Akeylah's hand, led her across the courtyard toward a door in the far corner. A sign declared it the *Elder Acolyte Meditation Sanctuary,* whatever that meant.

One knock and the door swung inward. They slipped into the sanctuary, which felt even darker after the bright sunlight of the courtyard. It took Akeylah's eyes a minute to adjust to the dim.

When they did, she blinked in confusion. The room was empty save for a single candelabra in the center of a round bench. A man in acolyte robes—green and silver, with a bevy of gold medals glinting on his chest, none of which Akeylah could decipher—beckoned them inside.

They took a seat across from him, the candles flickering in the air between.

"Welcome, Your Majesty." The man bobbed his head to Rozalind. At least one person in this Keep showed the queen proper deference, without a hint of judgment as to her origins.

Akeylah studied him.

"Lady Akeylah. Queen Rozalind told me you are interested in learning more about your aunt, Countess Yasmin."

Akeylah stiffened. She wanted information, yes, but she didn't exactly want to go around broadcasting that to strangers.

Yet Rozalind only squeezed her fingers tighter in reassurance. After a moment's hesitation, Akeylah forced her shoulders to relax. She trusted Rozalind enough to ask her for help. The least she could do was hear her out, now that she'd uncovered something.

"I am curious about her life," Akeylah finally said. "I don't know much about the Kolonyan side of my family."

"I see." Candle flames danced in the man's eyes. "Well, I'm afraid this particular story may not paint your aunt in the best light."

"I'd rather suffer the truth now than stumble into it unawares later."

He smiled. "Wise decision." Still, he hesitated a moment before he spoke again. "My lady, I must confess, the story is not one I bore witness to personally."

"Who did?"

"My mentor. D'Perre Casca, the senior acolyte who taught me everything I know. Last year, just after the Seventh War ended, he took ill. The menders in the Keep told him it was a virus, nothing more. But when he did not improve after several weeks, our private University menders examined him and found lethal doses of phantasm venom in his system."

Phantasm venom. The venom the Talons used to poison Kolonya's enemies. A controlled substance, one only Talons had access to.

Well. Talons, and the royals who commanded them.

"It was too late to save him by then," the acolyte continued. "He died two days later. On his deathbed, Casca told me his suspicions about the killer. All this time...I thought the venom had addled his brain, driven him mad. Until you came to me, Your Majesty, asking about the countess. Asking about her experience with tithes and her work at the University..." He glanced at Rozalind once before he continued.

"Casca and Countess Yasmin worked closely together for years, developing new tithes and tools for the Arts. The countess has an insatiable interest in the Blood Arts. But she and Casca were more than just business associates." He leaned forward, anger animating him. "For Sun's sake, she even made him a copy of a bloodletter they designed for his sixtieth birthday, a few months before he died. They were *friends*. For her to turn against him after so many years, I still cannot fathom..." He shut his eyes.

"Did he tell you why he suspected Yasmin had a hand in his poisoning?" Akeylah prompted. Rozalind's thumb smoothed across the back of her hand. In spite of herself, she shifted closer to the queen.

"Seventeen years ago, after Yasmin and Casca had been working closely together for years, Yasmin asked Casca for a favor. He was torn over the request, wrestled with it for days. But Yasmin was the sister of the king, you must understand. A royal, asking for his help. What could he do?"

Akeylah and Rozalind traded glances. Even though she already suspected, Akeylah had to ask. "What did the countess need?"

"She requested Casca's help in working the Vulgar Arts."

For a moment, the only sound in the room was the rustle of Rozalind's gown as she leaned against Akeylah.

The cool press of Rozalind's arm helped Akeylah focus. "What curse? Who did she use it against?"

The acolyte shook his head. "I don't know, my lady."

Akeylah crossed her ankles. "How did your mentor come by knowledge of the Vulgar Arts?"

The acolyte scratched his neck. "I don't know that either. His explanation made no sense. He said it was hidden in the library, in the book kings love best. By then he was delirious—phantasm venom in that dosage causes fever, hallucinations. He kept raving about how he'd been cursed, which made no sense. It wasn't Arts-induced, just ordinary phantasm venom. Probably ingested in his food." He sighed. "At any rate, the countess's cursework left a scar, like all Vulgar Arts do. Casca told me to look to her rib cage for proof."

"And did you?" Rozalind asked.

"Of course not." He half laughed at that, bitter. "What could I do, demand a countess of Kolonya remove her gown and prove her innocence? Besides, I had no evidence beyond the word of a dying man, driven half-mad by the murder weapon."

Something about the story niggled at Akeylah. "If Yasmin meant to poison Casca all along, why wait all those years? It sounds as though he kept her secret for all sixteen years before his death. Why would she suddenly decide to poison him?"

The acolyte shook his head again. "I can only guess. Perhaps something frightened her. Perhaps she thought someone was about to reveal the secret."

I know that feeling. Aloud, Akeylah said, "Thank you for sharing this."

"Of course." The acolyte fidgeted. "And Queen Rozalind, thank you for the, ah...information."

"No trouble at all." Rozalind flashed an easy smile. "Let me know if you require any further proofs of concept."

Akeylah darted a curious glance at the queen, who avoided her eye.

"I'm sure we will. Let me know if there is anything further I can do to help you, as well."

With that, Rozalind rose. Akeylah followed and nodded a farewell. She didn't trust herself to speak again. Not until the main doors of the University clashed shut behind them.

"I wish that acolyte knew more." She chose her words, careful not to use the countess's name. "If she dabbled in cursework, did she have an enemy within her own family? How did she harm them? And what happened a year ago to make her suddenly turn against Casca, if he'd been her friend for so long?" She tapped her fingers against Rozalind's hand without even realizing she was still holding it.

Her mind raced with possibilities. She needed to talk to Zofi and Ren again, soon. Yasmin was more dangerous than they suspected. She'd already used the Vulgar Arts before. If she were their blackmailer, she had the knowledge and the skill set to use them again. Now it would only be a matter of time before she escalated her threats.

They needed some way to stop her. Some collateral.

A spark formed. *Some dangerous secret of Yasmin's own...*

Rozalind stopped dead. Akeylah startled. She hadn't been paying attention, hadn't noticed where they were until she looked up. "Rozalind..." The heavy cherrywood door was impossible to mistake, emblazoned as it was with the stormwing crest.

"Andros is staying overnight with the menders. I have the chambers to myself."

Akeylah glanced behind. "If anyone sees..."

"They won't." Rozalind tugged her inside. Drew Akeylah across the threshold hand-first. "Of all the places in the Keep to be overheard, here is the least likely."

Ignoring the alarm bells ringing in her subconscious, Akeylah stepped inside. "Why is that?"

Rozalind grinned. "Because my husband doesn't plant spies in his own bedroom."

Akeylah laughed softly, torn between worry and overwhelming, maddening, irresistible *desire*.

Rozalind's hands slid up Akeylah's arms to rest on her shoulders. She squeezed gently. "You need to be careful, Akeylah. I don't know why you're looking for information on the countess, but she's already poisoned an acolyte of the Sun to cover her crimes. She's a dangerous person. If I were you, I would stop pursuing this."

"I can't. Believe me, I would if I could." Akeylah reached up to catch Rozalind's fingertips. "But I'll be careful about it."

"Careful isn't good enough." Rozalind tugged her closer. Their noses touched, breaths mingled in the air between. Akeylah rested her forehead against the queen's. "I don't want to lose you."

"You won't," Akeylah whispered.

Rozalind tilted forward, her lips a breath from Akeylah's. *Seas below*, how she yearned to close that gap. Forget everything else. And yet…

She hated to ask this. Hated to suspect anything of Rozalind, especially after her help. But something did not add up. She still heard that last comment echo in her mind. *Let me know if you require any further proofs of concept*, Rozalind had told the acolyte.

"What did you trade?"

She felt Rozalind's brow contract. "Trade?"

"For that acolyte's confession. He thanked you for the information—I can only assume you offered him some in return for that story."

For a long moment, Rozalind's dark blue eyes held hers. The urge to sink into that gaze, to let their lips collide, to forget she'd ever spoken, was overpowering. Yet Akeylah held her ground. Waited until the queen sighed and took a step back.

All at once, she seemed to decide something. Crossed the room in three quick strides and grabbed an item from her desk. "I never showed this to anyone," she said, as she walked back to Akeylah. "Not until I went looking for friends of Countess Yasmin and followed the rumor trail to D'Perre Casca's last living student. Even then, I only shared it to gain his trust. He was terrified of royals—not that I can blame him, after that tale."

For her part, Akeylah only stared at the item in Rozalind's hand, unable to make sense of it.

A bloodletter?

Her confusion grew when Rozalind pressed the razor-thin blade against her arm.

The queen couldn't tithe. She was Genalese. Everyone knew the Arts didn't respond to anyone who wasn't born in the Reaches. That was the whole *point* of the Arts. Gifted by the gods to prove the Reaches' superiority.

Yet, without another word, Rozalind sliced her skin.

And Akeylah watched, eyes widening, as the queen's veins began to glow. The color spread, pulsed across her rich, deep brown skin, slowly turning her to silver. Soon, she shone as bright as any Talon tithing for impervious skin.

As one last proof, Rozalind lifted the thin bloodletter and

stabbed it as hard as she could into her own thigh. The blade shattered on impact.

"How?" was all Akeylah managed to ask.

Rozalind shook her head.

She reached out and touched the queen's arm. Traced her hand all the way up Rozalind's shoulder, her neck, to cup her cheek. Her skin felt cooler than ever now, almost like touching metal. Rozalind stepped closer, cupped Akeylah's face, and when the tithe faded, the silver light receding, they stood a breath apart once more, gazes locked.

"How long have you been able to do that?" Akeylah murmured.

"I first noticed it a few months ago," the queen replied. "I cut my finger on a letter. My vision went dark—I saw *inside* myself, my veins, my heart.... That first time, I was so scared."

Akeylah nodded. She'd always been able to tithe, ever since she could remember, but she could imagine how startling it would be. To discover a sense you'd never experienced before, after a lifetime without it.

"A couple weeks later, after reading a few books on the theory, I tried a tithe." Her mouth tilted up at the corner. "Strength. I broke a stonewood door in my chamber testing it. Had to make up an excuse to the maids..."

"You were born in Genal, you're certain?" Akeylah's voice went soft, pensive. "There's no chance you were born here and brought there at a young age?"

Rozalind let out a ghost of a laugh. "Can you imagine a Genalese queen coming to the Reaches to give birth?"

Akeylah pressed her lips together. *Fair point.* But... "This shouldn't be possible."

The queen half smiled. "Lots of things shouldn't be possible."

"Have you told anyone else? Besides that acolyte and me."

"No one."

"This...It changes everything. Every theory we have about the Arts." Akeylah grimaced. "I wish you hadn't told that acolyte. If he tells the other acolytes, if they decide this knowledge is better off suppressed..."

"I had to tell him." Rozalind's gaze drifted toward Akeylah's mouth. "You needed information on Yasmin, and I only had one secret to bargain."

"Rozalind..." Her voice came out a breath.

"Akeylah, I'd do anything for you. I know I shouldn't, I know this is madness to even think, but—"

Akeylah kissed her.

Rozalind's lips were feather-soft. It felt like landing in the sea after a cliff-dive—impossible, magical, insane.

Alive.

Rozalind sighed. Akeylah buried her hands in the woman's brunette curls. Without warning, Rozalind hooked her waist, spun her around. The room spun. They collided with the bed, tripped onto it. Akeylah landed on top of the queen, her hands roaming along Rozalind's side, down soft curves to sharp hip bones.

She could kiss this girl forever.

Rozalind wrapped both arms around Akeylah's neck and deepened the kiss. Their tongues entwined, and Akeylah was falling, falling...

The queen grinned against Akeylah's mouth. In one quick motion, she rolled on top of Akeylah. Their skirts tangled, and

Rozalind slid a hand up Akeylah's leg, the silk-on-silk sensation driving her wild.

Then Rozalind's fingertips grazed the ridges of her scar, and Akeylah broke the kiss with a gasp.

"Too fast?" Rozalind paused, leaned back, her hair disheveled. "We can slow down." Her concerned expression nearly killed Akeylah. The last thing she wanted to do was stop touching her.

But she couldn't let Rozalind see the scar. Couldn't let *anyone* see it, not ever.

She shouldn't be doing this. *Rozalind is married. To my father. My father, the king. My father, the man I've already cursed.* Akeylah didn't deserve this. Didn't deserve someone like her. She pushed off the bed, straightened her skirts, still breathless.

"Did I do something wrong?"

Akeylah's heart tore in half just meeting Rozalind's eye. "Nothing. I...Rozalind, you're right. This is madness." That didn't help. That only made the pain worse. "I'm sorry."

"Don't apologize," Rozalind began.

"I have to go." Akeylah pushed to her feet, and left the room without a backward glance. If she looked back, she'd never be able to keep walking.

❋ 27 ❋

Zofi

Zofi picked up the round, blood-filled glass. "Your friend intercepted this on its way to your chambers?" she asked.

Ren nodded. "The boy delivering it was told to put it inside one of my shoes." She shrugged. "Whatever good that would do."

Give it the best chance of shattering on impact. Zofi recognized the phial, naturally. She'd probably hand-blown a hundred phials just like it, over the course of her lifetime. But she couldn't exactly admit that right now.

The key to making these phials was the Travelers' most precious secret. If anyone else learned how to do this—how to stopper the Arts and save them for later, craft tithes that would activate on contact with your bloodstream—the Travelers lost any edge they still held over the rest of the Reaches.

"And we're sure that's blood in there?" Akeylah frowned.

Besides, maybe it didn't matter that Zofi was withholding information. After all, she'd never seen a boost like this one. Normally to make a boost, you had to blow the glass yourself. The same person's breath and blood had to go into making the glass. And only that person could activate the tithe it held; only they could use it on themselves. Zofi couldn't make a tithe for anyone else.

Sending a serving boy to deposit a stored tithe in someone else's shoe made no sense.

"It's definitely blood," Zofi said. "And unless you remember bleeding onto a hot glass bowl, Ren, I'll assume it's not yours."

"I think I would recall that."

"Well." She shrugged. "Someone wanted to send you a heartfelt message, I guess."

Ren rolled her eyes.

Akeylah ignored the joke. "There's something else I wanted to meet with you both to discuss. It's about Countess Yasmin."

"I told you yesterday, that theory makes no sense," Ren said. "Why would she turn against her own brother? Everyone knows how close the twins are. And besides, Kolonyan law doesn't uphold the succession of a leader's sibling, especially not a sibling who cannot have any children or carry on the lineage." Ren began to pace through the shelves. They'd sequestered themselves deep in the library, which at this hour—barely the crack of dawn the day of the Feast of the Sun's Glorious Ascendance—was empty. Even Madam Harknell had abandoned her post. She'd taken to leaving the library keys on Akeylah's favorite desk.

Akeylah had taken advantage of that this particular morning and bolted the library door behind them.

"Hear me out."

Both Zofi and Ren fell silent while Akeylah detailed her meeting with the acolyte of the Sun. By the end, Ren had collapsed back onto a chair, and Zofi had drawn her longknife, twirling it between her fingers in a fruitless attempt to calm her nerves.

Today. Today was the Sun's Ascendance, their deadline.

"Why would she wait?" Zofi asked. "If she intended to kill this Acolyte Casca all along, why keep him around for years, then off him suddenly?"

"Something changed, perhaps?" Akeylah suggested. "He was murdered a year ago. After the war ended."

"What changed, then?" Zofi twirled the knife over the back of her hand and caught it with her thumb.

"We signed the Seventh Peace Accords. Andros remarried," Ren said, ticking items off on her fingers. "The Eastern Reach was beginning to grumble about its plight in the war, though the rebellion hadn't really gathered a lot of steam yet. . . ."

Zofi spun the knife back in the other direction. "None of those things explain why the countess would suddenly worry about a sixteen-year-old curse she worked."

"Unless she didn't approve of one of those political decisions," Akeylah mused. "Maybe she'd already gotten it into her head to make a bid for the throne. Maybe *she* was the one behind the Silver Prince's murder, too, and she's been plotting a way onto the throne all this time. First she'd want to tie up any loose ends that might crop up and bite her later."

Zofi exchanged a long glance with Ren, then lifted one shoulder in a shrug. "Or maybe we're overthinking it. Maybe Acolyte

Casca just had a sudden onset of guilty conscience and forced Yasmin's hand."

"Besides, we don't know if his story is true," Ren added. "Acolyte Casca may have gone mad, as his mentee believed."

"True," Akeylah admitted. "But if he wasn't mad, then it means Yasmin has used the Vulgar Arts before. It makes even more sense that she'd use it against Zofi now."

Ren shook her head. "That's conjecture. We need to verify his story."

"What about the ladies' maids?" Zofi interrupted.

"What about them?" Ren asked.

"The acolyte said Yasmin has a scar from working the Vulgar Arts. Surely the maids who help noblewomen bathe and dress and wipe their own bums would have noticed a mark like that."

For a moment, Ren was silent. "Yasmin doesn't use maids."

Zofi snorted. "What do you mean? Every noblewoman uses maids."

"Not her." Ren leaned against a bookshelf. "My mother used to serve her. She told me Yasmin started to act strange. Talking to herself, going into trances. Mama said the last year she worked for Yasmin, the countess wouldn't undress in front of her. After she dismissed Mama from her service, she swore off maids altogether."

Zofi huffed through her teeth and stopped spinning the knife to grip it in one fist. "Funny. That's exactly what I'd do if I were hiding something."

"Perhaps. It's not the only possible explanation." Ren crossed her arms, then cut a glance at Akeylah. "The two of you don't use maids, I hear."

"It's a mutually beneficial arrangement." Zofi sheathed the longknife with a sharp jab. "They don't have to serve a drifter, and I get a small semblance of privacy in my own damned chambers."

"Same," Akeylah said quietly.

"Anyway. One way to find out what our lovely aunt is hiding." Zofi brushed off her britches. "Let me tail her."

"Too risky," Ren said. "I'll ask my friend to do it instead."

Zofi barked out a laugh. "Your friend the ladies' maid? Weren't we just discussing how Yasmin swore those off?"

Ren scowled. "There must be some servants she lets into her chambers. Even just to clean or organize her paperwork."

But Zofi was already dusting herself off and grabbing the library key from atop Akeylah's stack of books. Finally, something proactive. She was sick of all this waiting around. "Let me handle this one. You've called in enough favors, sisters."

❋

Zofi was used to long hunts. She'd gone on more than her fair share, in deep desert crossings when prey came few and far between. She could track burrow lizards, which often took hours to poke their heads out of their lairs, with the best. But this?

Her leg cramped. She eased herself sideways along the balcony to stretch it, one eye still on the thin curtain that separated her from the countess's chambers.

Inside, Yasmin still sat bent over her writing desk. The same position she'd been in for the last hour. If the countess didn't lift an arm to dip her pen in the inkwell every so often, Zofi would have wondered if she'd died in that chair.

Meanwhile, her traitor brain wouldn't stop drifting, the same way it had all night. There was precious little time left until their deadline to defeat the blackmailer, and here she was daydreaming.

Every time she closed her eyes, she saw Elex's troubled expression. The sorrow in his eyes as he left her on the grass outside the city walls.

I should have kissed him one last time.

But Elex's kisses were heavy things. Full of the weight of a lifetime of shared memories, years of hesitant, slow-building tension. The pain that bore down on her chest now, which made it difficult to breathe or think or feel, would only weigh ten times more if she *had* kissed him.

The curtain fluttered. Zofi tensed. But Yasmin was still scribbling away at the veritable tome of a letter she was penning. Zofi relaxed against the stonewood balcony once more.

Someone should really tighten up security around here.

Then again, she supposed lax security happened when your city hadn't been invaded in four hundred years. Kolonya was used to fighting in the far Reaches, not at its doorstep.

Zofi ducked as Yasmin swiveled in her chair. She folded the letter and tucked it into a hidden pocket within her shift dress. Then she rose to her feet. *Finally.*

Come on. Change your gown.

Zofi crouched behind a potted fern. The countess's shadow paced across the room. But a moment later, the distant clatter of the door latch sounded, and the room stood empty.

Zofi stifled a groan. How much longer would she have to sit here trying to catch a glimpse of her aunt dressing? She felt strange enough as it was.

She leaned forward until her head rested against the window-pane. Then she stared through it, across the room at Yasmin's writing desk. Back and forth from that desk to the chamber door.

She was here anyway. And she knew from experience how easy it was to open these windows....

If she couldn't catch a glimpse of Yasmin's scar for herself, perhaps she could find something else of value in these chambers. Other evidence to pin on the woman. It only took half a second to slip her longknife through the cracks and jimmy the window latch's lock.

Sands. If she ever had a say in it, this Keep was getting a security overhaul.

She dropped into the chambers on tiptoe and took in her surroundings.

Gray everywhere. Pale curtains, a light gauze canopy over the bed, white-and-black checkered blankets. Somehow the colors felt out of place, too muted for Kolonyan tastes.

But then, Yasmin had always been a strange one.

Zofi went to the writing desk first. On the desk itself, she found a single gold-embossed pen and an inkwell with a matching plate. *D'Daryn.*

Daryn, Yasmin and Andros's father. Maybe the inkwell was a gift. Zofi traced a finger over the plate, then flipped it over to check for any hidden compartments. Next she went over the desk just as thoroughly. But every drawer matched its dimensions, and the back proved solid wood. No hidden secrets.

The waste bin only contained ashes.

She finished searching the desk and moved on to the wardrobe.

Just one boring dress after another, all in muted colors—grays and whites, mostly, with the occasional black accent.

After the wardrobe, she scoured the walls. No hollow sounds as she tapped along the hideous floral wallpaper. Not even a safe hidden behind an enormous portrait of an overweight man with yellow-green eyes and a familiar tilt to his mouth. He wore his mahogany-brown hair in an old style, long and curled. It almost made him look less Kolonyan. More Northern.

More like Zofi.

King Daryn read a plaque beneath it.

Zofi studied it for a minute. Strange, what people inherited. That smile, she'd gotten that. The eyes, Florencia and Akeylah shared. This man's blood ran in her veins. This king who died three decades before Zofi was born.

"Nice to meet you, Grandpa," she whispered, then continued her search of his daughter's chambers.

On the bedside table, she found a few dog-eared books, tomes with titles like *Kolonya First: An analysis of foreign affairs under King Andros.* She fanned the pages, just in case. No notes or scraps of paper.

Finally, she checked the bed. Felt around the edges of the mattress for any unusual lumps or tears. Nothing in the mattress itself. But under the bed, between two hat boxes (which, sadly, only contained hats), she found a third, square box. Its lid was covered in a thick layer of dust, but it had fingerprints in it. Recently opened.

The simple latch-lock only took a minute to pick. Inside, Zofi found a single curl of dark brown hair. Beside it was a letter. New, to judge by the still-white paper, its edges not yet curled or yellowed with time.

She sat cross-legged on the floor and unfolded the note. It was unaddressed, the letters neatly drawn—almost too neat, as if copied from a textbook.

I heard your concerns. The acolyte knew too much. You were worried after the war, now that peace has finally arrived. Afraid someone would learn what our family truly is. The lengths to which we've gone. All the echoes we've created.

I fixed this for you. I concealed my secret; everything that man did for us. I even used that lovely little joint invention to do it. Wasn't that clever?

Don't you see? I have the skills necessary to lead. I have the brains to intuit what must be done and the daring to follow it through. I should rule. Not my brother. You see it, too, don't you?

The bottom of the note had been torn off. But enough remained to show part of the signature. *Yasm* was visible just above the tear line.

Yasmin.

That's when she heard the clatter at the door.

A key.

Zofi shoved that note into her pocket, slammed the lid of the box closed, and pushed it back under the bed. Then she flung herself across the room onto the balcony, just as the knob turned.

The door opened as Zofi swung the window shut. The latch wasn't redone yet. She couldn't do it now, for fear of making a sound. The curtains fluttered in her wake, partially open, wide enough that she could see clearly through the gap.

Yasmin stepped back inside.

Sands.

Zofi couldn't let go of the window—it would pop open. Instead, she grabbed the longknife at her waist. With her free hand, she drew it and sliced the back of the arm holding the window.

It only took her a second to tithe. Adrenaline made her faster, her mind sharper. An instant later, Zofi vanished into the background. Her lower half blended into the cherry stonewood balcony, and her upper half went blue as the sky above. She held her breath and focused on the clouds in the sky. Shifted so they'd play across her skin, camouflage her evenly.

When she opened her eyes and looked into the room, it took every ounce of willpower she possessed not to startle or scream.

You can't see me.

Yasmin gazed out the window. Straight into Zofi's eyes.

She counted heartbeats. One. Two. Three. Felt her lungs burn with lack of air, and her muscles cramp. Focused on maintaining that illusion—so difficult to spot, unless you knew what to look for. Or unless the camouflaged person moved.

For seconds—or maybe hours—Yasmin held her gaze. Then she turned and strode across her room.

Zofi let out her breath in a soft whoosh.

At the vanity, Yasmin picked up a stormwing broach and fastened it onto her chest. She adjusted the medal, added a second one above it—a golden feather, the seal of the royal crown. Above that, she pinned a golden circle, a symbol of Father Sun, who rules above all things.

She must be dressing for an official meeting, or some state event.

The countess straightened her lapels, gazed into the mirror again. For a moment, Zofi could have sworn her eyes flicked toward the balcony, caught Zofi's again.

Then Yasmin grabbed a shawl from the back of the vanity, draped it over one arm, and marched back out of the room. Zofi didn't let herself breathe properly until the chamber door slammed shut.

Just in time, as her skin itched, began to reappear in spots.

Moving fast as she could, Zofi re-latched the window and leaped off the balcony onto the one below.

That was far too close for comfort.

❋ 28 ❋

Florencia

So you have proof?" Ren turned in the mirror one last time to check the back of the gown she'd selected for the Sun's Ascendance.

Tonight.

No days left. No time to buy. Ren needed to confront Yasmin before the feast began, stop her from revealing the real culprit of Burnt Bay . . . or swing for her crimes.

She dressed for the occasion. The violent purple fabric stood out against her dark skin. Made her look cast in bronze, fierce. Unstoppable. If she was going down, she'd do it in style.

"Sure reads like it to me." Zofi tapped the letter. "'I should rule. Not my brother.' It's even signed by her. And she talks about the acolyte, and about using some joint invention to kill him. . . .

No idea who this was addressed to, or what they were plotting, but still."

For her part, Akeylah had her own most recent blackmail letter open on her lap, comparing the handwriting in Yasmin's letter yet again, even though it was clearly the same penmanship as their blackmailer. "The queen might be able to help us with more proof," Akeylah said. As usual, Florencia noticed her sister's voice go strange and tight when mentioning the queen.. "She has a hunch about the method of poisoning."

Ren paused to study her sister in the mirror. The Easterner was quiet, though resourceful when she needed to be. The past few days had proven that. *Still.* "I don't like that you shared so much detail with Queen Rozalind. How do we know this isn't part of some Genalese plot? Yasmin is clearly working with *some-one.* What if it's Rozalind? Or what if Rozalind set all this up to frame Yasmin?"

"We can trust Rozalind," Akeylah replied without missing a beat. "Besides, of all the suspects in the Keep, she's the one we could cross off. She can't tithe." Something in Akeylah's voice remained off when she said that, a false note that caught Ren's attention.

Then again, Akeylah had always been far too fond of the queen.

"That doesn't mean we can trust her," Ren replied.

"Anyway, why would Countess Yasmin work with the Genalese?" Akeylah shook her head. "She spent most of her life fighting in wars *against* them."

"Why any of this?" Ren huffed out a sharp breath, exasperated. "Why kill her friend if he kept her secret for so long? Why hide a letter that she wrote in her room admitting it? Why black-mail the only three eligible heirs into abdicating the throne?"

"We'll find out tonight." Zofi crossed her arms. "If you ever finish getting ready."

"I'm making sure we have enough proof," Ren said, though she had a feeling the Traveler was talking more about physical preparations than mental.

"Bloody sands. We've got a note in her own writing. We have a witness. What more do we need?"

"Certainty." Ren pursed her mouth. "Otherwise this gamble will never work. Yasmin has to believe we've got enough evidence to throw her into the dungeons unless she listens to us."

Zofi huffed and flung herself backward onto the bed.

Ren resisted the urge to tell her half sister to take her muddy boots off the comforter. Too late to prevent stains now, and it would only worsen Zofi's current mood. Which was just an exaggerated version of her and Akeylah's moods, to be honest.

Apprehensive. Tense. Wishing this night was over with already.

"We have enough." Akeylah met Ren's gaze in the reflection. "Between the letter, the acolyte's testimony, and the extra item Rozalind is bringing…"

"I still don't see why you can't tell us what this item is." Ren fastened a steel-edged collar around her neck. The series of silver plates interlocked across her chest like a shield. Tonight, she had a feeling the court would seem more like a battlefield than ever.

"Because I'm not entirely sure yet myself. The note was vague, in case someone intercepted it. Rozalind knows what she's doing."

"I just hope you're right about her."

Zofi leaped to her feet in a smooth motion. "Well. No time like the present to find out."

"Here's hoping the next time we stand in this room, we're all free from our aunt's treachery." Ren finished the necklace, turned to study her completed outfit in the mirror.

"Here's to cutting the legs out from under our enemies." Zofi grinned cheerily.

"To the future of our kingdom," Akeylah murmured. "May Mother Ocean guide our paths."

For a moment, they paused side by side. Akeylah wore simple white chiffon, her red hair plaited tight against her scalp in the Eastern fashion. Zofi's hair was its usual wild tumbleweed, and she had on boots, leather britches, and a men's nightshirt.

A week ago, Ren would have mocked that choice. Now she understood. If a fight broke out tonight, at least they could count on Zofi to back them up in her supremely practical attire, with a knife tucked into a hidden pocket of those pants. But it was more than just practicality. Something about Zofi's utter disregard for court appearances had become almost... refreshing.

On the surface, you couldn't find three girls who looked less alike.

Yet in the mirror, Ren noticed similarities. The hard press of their mouths. The glint in their eyes. The way they held their shoulders—head high, chin up, muscles braced.

For the first time since they met, they looked like sisters.

"I wouldn't mess with us," Ren said, finally.

"Yasmin won't know what hit her," Zofi agreed.

But Akeylah looped an arm through Ren's. "Whatever happens tonight, I'm glad I have you two on my side."

To her surprise, Ren's throat tightened. "Me too." Then she smirked, shook her head. "Sun above. Remember what we all thought about each other just a week ago?"

"What, you don't think I'm a crazy horse girl anymore?" Zofi raised a brow.

"Oh, I definitely do. But only because you are."

Zofi elbowed her. "Well, I'm pretty sure I was right about you being a spoiled Kolonyan, too."

Akeylah fluttered her lashes, coquettish. "Personally, I knew you would both make trustworthy allies all along. I just so happen to be an excellent judge of character."

Ren snorted, though truth be told, she enjoyed Akeylah's company more now that the girl had begun to come out of her shell a little. "Supremely modest as well, Akeylah."

"More than you," Zofi pointed out. Still bantering, the girls made their way out of the chambers.

Ren hesitated on the threshold, turned to drink in one last look of her suites. One way or another, tonight everything would change. Either they'd clear their names, free themselves of Yasmin's tyranny, or she'd out them, and Ren would never see this chamber again. Or any other bedroom, for that matter, besides a cell in the dungeon.

Akeylah noticed she'd stopped. Rested a hand on her forearm. "You said it yourself, Ren. You wouldn't mess with us tonight." She smiled. A smaller, shier smile than Ren's or Zofi's. Yet somehow more believable for it. "We've got this."

Ren squared her shoulders. "Right. Let's go have a chat with our dear aunt Yasmin."

✳

The central courtyard of the sky gardens had been painted silver, a bright shine that reflected the triple moons overhead. Matching silks draped across the trees, so the entire rooftop seemed to glow. She felt as though she were walking on the surface of Essex, steeped in a wash of moonlight.

It was a reminder of the Silver Prince's legacy. Of the shoes he left behind, shoes one of them would one day step into.

Strange. Ren expected to be nervous. Or afraid. Or excited. Or at least focused on the mission ahead. Instead, all she felt was a pervasive sense of calm.

Maybe it was the girls who stood to either side. Akeylah's sharp intelligence. Zofi's battle-ready stance.

Danton had been right. She needed allies she could trust. She just never expected to find that in two people who, technically, she was competing with for the throne. Even her own mother warned her not to trust her sisters. *Remember the half that matters.* But when push came to shove, against a common enemy, these were the allies Ren wanted by her side.

She caught a glimpse of Yasmin across the courtyard. As usual, the countess hovered around Andros, a hand at his back in case he stumbled or grew tired. Ren's stomach twisted in disgust.

How could Yasmin smile at her twin, act so kind and caring, when she was betraying him? Sabotaging the potential heirs he wanted to teach. Hiding traitorous secrets about those heirs in order to control them. Talking about how she ought to rule in her brother's stead.

Ren thought again about the note Zofi found. *I should rule. Not my brother.*

She'd used the Vulgar Arts against a family member before, decades ago. Was it Andros? Or could his illness now be related? Could she be poisoning him the way she poisoned her lifelong friend Casca? How deep did this betrayal run?

And who was that letter meant for? Why had the countess decided not to send it after all? Did she get cold feet? Change her mind about confessing to whoever it was? But then why save the note, why not destroy the evidence?

No matter. Whatever she was doing, they finally had enough proof to stop her. Especially with the queen's discovery, which she'd relayed to Akeylah as they arrived on the rooftop, who in turn had shared it with the girls. Ren's stomach churned in anticipation of the evidence the queen promised, yet she knew that was what they needed. Something shocking, and concrete enough to show Yasmin they weren't messing about. They knew the truth about her, and they weren't afraid to share it if she made a move against them.

"Where is the queen?" Ren lifted a flute from a passing server and held it to her lips without drinking.

"Lost her after we came onto the rooftop." To judge by the way her gaze darted about, Zofi was tracking the whole court at once.

"Give her one more minute." Akeylah clutched a flute of nectar in a trembling fist.

Zofi shrugged, then stopped a passing server and grabbed rather more hunks of goat meat than Ren thought it a good idea to eat at once. It was a sign of how far they'd come that Ren felt only amusement, rather than mortification.

317

Zofi swallowed audibly, then gestured at the far corner with her remaining fistful of meat. "There's your girl, Akeylah."

"She's not my—" Akeylah broke off in a scowl and slipped away from her sisters. She crossed the dance floor, straight toward a cluster of nobles gathered around the telltale brunette head. Queen Rozalind.

Ren and Zofi traded glances.

"Akeylah wouldn't actually pursue anything there, would she?" Ren asked softly.

Zofi bit off another large hunk of goat meat and chewed for a minute. Then she gestured toward Rozalind and Akeylah, who had just bent their heads together, standing rather closer than most courtiers would for a friendly conversation. "Who knew our quiet sister had a naughty streak after all?"

Ren's lips pursed. "Rozalind is married. To *our father*, no less. If anyone notices, starts asking questions…"

"If raising a few questions means our stepmother keeps helping us this much, can't say I'm complaining," Zofi replied.

"Assuming our *stepmother* isn't someone we need to watch out for in the—"

"Ah, Lady Florencia!"

Ren clamped her mouth shut and forced a smile. She spun to find Lady Lexana behind her, Lord Gavin at her elbow. Lexana had outdone herself tonight. In a tight gold dress, with matching golden clips holding her straight black locks in an elaborate coil, she looked more like a princess than Ren.

"I'd been hoping to run into you tonight. I was going to mail you an invitation to my engagement ball, but then I thought, no, I'll offer it in person." Lexana bounced a little where she stood, the very image of girlish excitement: "A week from tomorrow, in my father's suites. You'll attend?"

Ren felt her smile widening in spite of herself. Lexana had always been one of her favorites. The few times Ren had served her, Lexana had never raised her voice, never demanded late-night errands or requested ridiculous tasks. She thanked her maids by name, remembered their birthdays. "Of course. I would be delighted."

"Grand!" Lexana clutched Gavin's forearm and squeezed.

"Congratulations to you both, by the way." Ren smiled at them. "A little belated, I know, but..."

"Both?" Lexana blinked. "Oh!" She removed her hand from Gavin's arm and laughed again, so high-pitched it strained the ears. "No, Gavin is like a brother to me."

Gavin smiled blandly.

At the same time, Lexana tilted her head, caught sight of someone across the courtyard. "But here's my fiancé now."

Ren followed her gaze and felt every muscle in her body clench. It took effort to breathe through it, to maintain a straight back, an immobile face. *She's mistaken. Or I'm misunderstanding. I must be.*

She watched, stomach sinking in horror, as Danton strode across the dance floor. His gaze swept right past Ren's and landed on the woman at her side.

"Ambassador Danton asked Father for my hand a few days ago." Lexana beamed across the floor at him. "Just before some big council meeting." She sighed happily. "I'm just glad he finally asked. It felt like such a long courtship, months of writing...."

The words all rushed together in her ears.

Months of writing.

A few days ago. Just before some council meeting…

The morning before Ren saw him last. The morning before he came to her chambers with a spy in hand. The morning before he swore she could trust him. Before he kissed her. Kissed her and killed her all at once. She just didn't know it until now.

Vipers anesthetize their victims when they bite. You don't notice the venom until it's already deep in your veins.

"Hello, my dear." Danton reached Lexana's side. Folded his arms around her waist as she leaned up to kiss his cheek.

Ren's body went hot and cold at once. She was on fire; she was frozen solid. She would cut his heart out.

She couldn't. He'd taken hers first.

"I was just inviting Lady Florencia to our ball," Lexana babbled, oblivious.

Danton smiled, the very picture of a loving, attentive fiancé. "That's wonderful." Only then did he lift his gaze to Ren's. Only then did she see past the wall. Realize this was all a show—his affection, his care. He didn't give a damn for Lexana.

Danton only cared about himself. That much was obvious now.

"I would love it if Lady Florencia would attend," he was saying. "It would mean the world for her to bless our union."

She understood. He needed a leg up at court. A way to weasel himself into favor with the king. Courting the king's daughter wouldn't work. Danton wasn't a high enough noble to win a princess's hand.

It's not that simple, he'd said.

Trust me, he'd asked.

She only had herself to blame. The first time he stabbed her

in the back, she couldn't have seen it coming. This time, though...
this time she should have known better.

"Sister."

Zofi's voice dragged her back from the precipice. Jolted her into
the here and now. The gardens awash with laughter and voices.
The king, ambling slowly toward the dais from which he'd give his
speech. Across the room, Akeylah gesturing at them as frantically
as she dared, halfway between Rozalind and the countess, a slim
box tucked under one arm. Bile rose in the back of Ren's throat at
the thought of its contents.

They were out of time. She couldn't afford to waste any more
on the likes of Danton.

"Sun bless you both." Ren nodded at the couple, tore her eyes
from Danton, who was frowning, brows drawn in that puppy-dog
look she always used to fall for.

Never again.

"Let's go," Ren murmured to Zofi. Her sister's glance held a
thousand questions. To her credit, Zofi didn't ask any. She just
gripped Ren's shoulder once, hard. A wordless gesture of support
before they crossed the roof. "You remember what to do?"

Zofi nodded. "Tell Yasmin I need to speak with her urgently
about a plot against the throne. Then bring her to the edge of the
gardens."

Ren flashed a small, pointed smile. "See you on the other side."

❈ 29 ❈

Zofi

Zofi touched the handle of her longknife, just to reassure herself it was still there. Hidden in a concealed pocket, ready to draw at any second.

Judging by the countess's mood, she may need to.

"Well? This had better be worth my time." Yasmin stormed onto the balcony at the edge of the sky gardens, a secluded spot Akeylah had suggested. Rozalind, having handed them one final piece of evidence, had gone to join the king—and make sure he didn't send any messengers to look for his absent sister.

"My brother needs me," Yasmin was saying. "His menders aren't watchful enough—he nearly tripped on the staircase."

"Believe me, Countess," Ren said. "You want to hear us out."

Zofi caught her sister's eye. Ren nodded, and Zofi stepped up behind Yasmin to catch the countess's wrist in one hand, wrenching the woman's arm behind her.

As predicted, Yasmin reacted like a soldier. She stepped forward, twisted to break the hold. But trained though she may be, Yasmin was still an old woman. Zofi caught her other arm during the twist, pinned both at the small of her back.

"What in Sun's name is the meaning of this?" Yasmin shouted.

"You'll want to lower your voice," Ren added. "That is, unless you'd prefer we tell the whole court about your experience in the Vulgar Arts."

The countess stilled.

"That's better." Zofi eased her grip. "Now, promise not to run away until we're done talking, and I'll give your arms back."

Yasmin sucked her teeth for a moment, then nodded once, curt. Zofi let go.

Yasmin rubbed her wrists, one after the other, eyes on Ren. "I don't know what you're talking about. Vulgar Arts. That's preposterous."

"Really?" Zofi stepped around the countess to study her expression. The old bat had, as Ren would put it, a pretty decent hunting face. But there was a defiant sheen to her gaze that Yasmin couldn't quite disguise. "Because you shut up real fast when we threatened to start telling people about it."

"Rumors can be dangerous." Yasmin regarded her coolly. "Even false ones."

"Funny." Ren extended a hand. Zofi drew the letter from her pocket and passed it to her sister. "Because from what I've read here, you have quite the guilty conscience, Countess."

A crease appeared on Yasmin's forehead.

"'The acolyte knew too much,'" Ren began to read. "'I fixed this for you. I concealed my secret.'"

"Saving a letter isn't a crime, last I checked," Yasmin replied. "Breaking into the chambers of a royal family member, on the other hand..."

"'I should rule. Not my brother,'" Ren spoke over her. "'You see it, too, don't you?'"

"Doesn't sound like something a person with a clean conscience writes, if you ask me," Zofi said. "Who were you writing to? Who are your coconspirators?"

"This is ridiculous." Yasmin scoffed.

"Not according to the acolyte we chatted with," Akeylah said. "Does the name D'Perre Casca ring any bells?"

Yasmin sniffed. "He's dead."

Zofi tilted her head. Smirked at Ren. "Sister, what do you think carries a worse punishment? A Vulgar Arts curse, or murdering an acolyte to cover up a Vulgar Arts curse?"

"Mmm, tough call, sister." Ren tapped her chin, pretended to deliberate. "Akeylah, you'll have to provide us with the tiebreaker."

Akeylah withdrew a slim box. "Countess." Akeylah offered the box. Long and thin, shaped like a stiletto knife. "Would you care to do the honors?"

Yasmin stared at the box. Only her eyes gave her away. They widened, fear creeping into the corners.

"No?" Zofi stepped forward. "I'll do it." She grabbed the lid. Withdrew it with a flourish.

Yasmin actually gasped.

To be fair, even prepared for what the box contained, Zofi's stomach rolled. She looked at her aunt instead. "You know the acolytes have a tradition when a senior member passes away?" Zofi tilted the box toward the countess, to afford her a better view.

To her credit, Yasmin didn't flinch. Merely closed her eyes, drew a deep breath.

"They inter the dead in the same clothes in which they died. Still wearing the same accessories, too." Zofi considered the box. "Unfortunately, this particular accessory was difficult to remove from the body, what with the decomposition and all. Afraid we had to take the whole finger."

Nestled in the narrow box was the rotting middle finger of Acolyte D'Perre Casca. And around that finger, dulled from age and from being intombed for a year, was a familiar silver ring. The stormwing crest of the royal house was still visible beneath a year's worth of tarnish, as was the small knob along the edge, the hidden switch that would release the bloodletter within.

They might not be able to pin Yasmin for using the Vulgar Arts. Not definitively. But they *could* prove this.

"Ingenious idea." Ren avoided looking at the container, Zofi noticed. She stared down Yasmin instead. "Acolytes dismantled the kitchens looking for poisoned food, but nobody thought to check for poison here."

"What's the easiest way to get phantasm venom into someone's system?" Zofi asked. She didn't need anyone to tell her this. Remembered it well enough from her introduction to Kolonya City. "Through the blood."

Unlike Ren, Akeylah didn't seem bothered by the severed digit.

She reached into the box and tapped the knob on the side of the ring. The finger jumped in the box as the bloodletter sprang free.

Yasmin clenched her fist around her own matching ring.

"Brilliant, really." Zofi glanced between the rings. "You and Casca designed the ring together, did you not? He must have been thrilled when you gifted him a copy."

Akeylah tilted the box so the razor caught the distant light of the party. Unlike the rest of the ring, which had tarnished with age, the blade still shone, bright and silver.

"Little did he know you'd filled the whole interior of this copy with phantasm venom," Zofi continued. "Every time he closed it, the blade was dipped in a fresh dose. Every time he tithed, a little more entered his bloodstream. And who uses a bloodletter more often than an acolyte of the Sun?"

"What do you think, Countess?" Ren fixed Yasmin with a stare. "If we submit this ring to the acolytes for testing, will they find traces of phantasm venom along the blade?"

"Girls, you don't understand what you're doing." Yasmin finally found her voice. "All I've done is protect our family."

"Oh, it's *our* family now?" Zofi laughed, bright and hard.

"You've a funny way of demonstrating your familial love," Ren interrupted.

"You know, cursing your relatives." Akeylah ticked off her fingers. "Murdering your friends. Trying to steal the throne from your own brother. Blackmailing your nieces into abdicating."

Yasmin's frown deepened. "I don't know what you think you're doing—"

"We compared the letters." Ren held up the letter they'd found under Yasmin's bed. "We aren't idiots. You should have disguised your handwriting better if you were going to pen elaborate threats to us."

Yasmin's eyes darted between the three. "For the family's sake, let this matter drop."

Zofi scoffed.

"That's rich, coming from the woman threatening us." Ren nodded sideways at the box, still not quite looking at its contents. "You started this fight."

Zofi took the hint and shut the lid. Then Akeylah tucked it under her arm once more.

"You gave us no choice," Zofi said. "We just want to do what our father asks. Learn from him; see which of us he chooses for the throne. You're the one who tried to drive us out of the city."

"Tell us," Ren continued. "Who are you working with? Who was that letter intended for? Genal? The rebels? Who's backing you in your pursuit of the throne?"

Something flared in Yasmin's eyes then. A sudden spark of understanding. She uncrossed her arms and drew herself to her tallest. "I've spent my whole life working for this kingdom. Everything I do, I do to protect and strengthen Kolonya, to guard her from enemies, usurpers and pretenders alike. I won't allow the likes of you to destroy it now."

"And yet you're willing to destabilize the throne you care so much about, just because you don't approve of the current potential heirs. Is that it?" Zofi stepped closer.

Yasmin didn't budge. Merely regarded Zofi with a cool stare. "I will pretend you did not accost me in this way, girls, if only for my brother's sake. But attack me like this again and I will not be so magnanimous."

Zofi opened her mouth to retort, but Ren cut in. "Then we have an agreement. You keep our secrets quiet, and we won't reveal the fact that you're a murderer in front of the entire court."

The countess's jaw worked as she debated. Finally, after a long silence, she darted one more peek at the box under Akeylah's arm and nodded, teeth still clenched. "Very well. But I expect no more questions from any of you." With that, Yasmin brushed past, her shoulder colliding with Zofi's.

Zofi reached for her longknife, but Ren caught her wrist. "She didn't answer anything," Zofi protested. "We still need to know how she discovered our secrets."

Ren watched Yasmin go, a faraway look in her eye. "Didn't you hear her? She agreed to our terms. We won. She keeps our secrets and we keep hers."

Zofi blew out a hard breath. "That's not good enough."

"It will have to be." Ren sighed. "At least for now."

"I don't like it," Akeylah murmured. "But I agree." She slid the box and its gruesome contents into a pocket deep within the folds of her skirts. "Now, in the meantime, I believe we have a party to attend."

❄

King Andros's welcome speech went quickly. The moment he finished, half the crowd flooded onto the dance floor. Zofi spent the next few dances watching from the sidelines. She even almost smiled when Akeylah took the floor with Queen Rozalind for a fast-paced two-step.

Several dances later, when a jig she recognized started up—one of the Northern dances she'd been fond of performing with Elex anytime they were traveling through the Glass Desert—Zofi actually debated looking for a partner herself. Then someone touched her shoulder. "Lady Zofi."

At first, she didn't recognize him. Vidal looked older in full uniform, not just because the cut of the suit set off his sharp jaw to perfection. He stood taller, too, shoulders straight, chin high.

"I see you dressed for the occasion as usual." He dared a small smile.

Fair enough. She was wearing trousers and a men's top, for sands' sake. "You mean this isn't in fashion?" She faked a gasp.

"Not quite." His gaze swept over her body, a lingering look that made her rib cage suddenly feel two sizes too small. "Suits you, though."

Last time she saw him, he accused her of murder.

Granted, he'd seemed to be in the process of thinking through the circumstances, of trying to understand her point of view. But still. She regarded him warily, especially when he extended a hand.

"May I have this dance?"

She placed her fingers in his, hesitant. "Sure you can keep up?"

"Of course. Dancing is like fighting. And I can match you in that." Vidal circled his other arm around her waist.

"You wish," she retorted, even as she searched his gaze. She still couldn't make him out. Couldn't understand whether he still blamed her for Prince Nicolen's death, whether this was some ruse, or whether he'd actually had a change of heart.

The music sped up, and Vidal spun her onto the dance floor.

She stepped closer, brought her chest flush against his as they wove between the other dancers, joining the song.

"You know this one," he commented, surprise evident in his tone.

"Just because I don't know Kolonyan customs doesn't mean I was raised without any culture at all." Zofi ducked under his arm, whirled away from him, then back again, their bodies colliding once more.

Vidal was right about dancing and fighting. This style was all about reading your partner, anticipating their next move. Making it up as you went along, two people moving as one. Just like sparring.

As it transpired, Vidal was as skilled at dancing as fighting. The music wove on, and she retreated when he moved in, stepped forward when he went back, both their legs flashing in sync. His fingers tensed at her waist, clued her in to his next move. It felt like a secret conversation, held entirely in gesture.

Before long they flowed across the courtyard, two of the most natural dancers. He was better than most of the boys she danced with up north. Definitely better than Elex, who stepped on Zofi's toes often enough that she'd taken to wearing reinforced leather boots to dance with him.

When the music began to wind down, Vidal steered her toward the edge of the floor. The final strings of music died away just as they ducked beneath the hanging fronds of a veil tree. It, too, had been draped in gauze, and the fabric cast a pale silver shadow over their faces.

It reminded her of the last time she saw Vidal. The hallucination, the Silver Prince stepping into his skin. The memory made it a little easier to keep breathing normally, despite the close heat of his body, the way their chests rose and fell together.

"Zofi." He searched her eyes. "I thought more about what you said."

She tilted her head. Told her legs to step backward, to put some breathing room between them.

Her legs ignored her. "And?"

"I still don't approve of killing if it can be avoided—"

"Lucky I didn't ask for your approval, then," she snapped.

"*But* I understand it. You're a warrior, Zofi, just like me. You saw someone threaten your family, and you reacted. I'd probably have done the same thing in your shoes."

Her throat tightened unexpectedly. "So you believe me."

"Blood oaths don't lie."

"I'm not talking about what I said during the oath. I'm talking about your friend." She lowered her voice to barely a whisper. Vidal leaned closer to hear. "Do you believe me when I tell you what he really was? Can you believe someone else's experience of him, even if you never saw that side of him yourself?"

His face hovered inches from hers. Close enough for her to make out flecks of gold threaded through his hazel eyes. "I have to believe it. I trust you."

His breath dusted her cheeks. He still smelled like the stables. Like horses and hay and *home*. He tilted his head, and she felt herself mirror him, found her eyes drifting lower, toward his mouth.

"Zofi..." Vidal's voice was a whisper, a sigh.

She tried to catch her breath. Tried to tear her gaze back to his, to move away from him. She couldn't do this. Shouldn't. *Think of Elex.*

Elex, who was gone, for good if he was lucky. Elex, who was running to the edge of the world. To a place where no one would ever find him. She'd never feel his arms around her. Never kiss those lips again.

But Vidal...Vidal was here. Reaching for her hand. Curling his fingers through hers, even as his other hand lifted to cup her cheek, his thumb brushing along her cheekbone.

For a moment—one glorious, heated moment—the rest of the rooftop faded into the background. She forgot about Yasmin. About the blackmail, the days of hunting for collateral. She forgot the king and the throne and her sisters and this party. She even forgot about Elex. The abscess he left in her chest.

The world narrowed to this moment. To Vidal, leaning closer, closer, and her body surrendering, her head falling back as she closed her eyes, waited for his lips to find hers.

Then, in the distance, someone screamed.

·⊰ 30 ⊱·

Akeylah

Thank you again."

Rozalind spun her across the dance floor to the final chords of the song. "I told you. I'd do anything for you."

"Most people don't truly mean *anything* when they say things like that. Especially after how I treated you last time." Running away from Rozalind, just when they'd finally, *finally* kissed.

"Don't," Rozalind murmured. "I understand why you left."

Do you? Could the queen understand how *impossibly, terrifyingly, dangerously* happy she made Akeylah feel? Could she understand why Akeylah needed to distance herself?

Of course not. She had no way of knowing about the scar that glowed on Akeylah's thigh. The guilt she bore.

But now...seas below, how could Akeylah push Rozalind away when the queen had *unearthed a body* for her? She lowered her voice. "How in Mother Ocean's name did you convince that acolyte to let you disinter his mentor?"

"He wants justice." Rozalind shrugged one narrow shoulder. "I promised we would see the countess punished for what she did."

Guilt settled in her stomach, thick as syrup. *Justice.* How could they get that for him, when they'd promised Yasmin they would keep her secrets in exchange for their own?

"Well," Rozalind was saying, almost casually, an afterthought. "That, and I did allow him to take another sample of my blood."

The hair on the back of Akeylah's neck prickled. More secrets. "Did he learn anything yet?"

"Nothing. Only that my heritage is pure Genalese, dating as far back as his blood records show—many centuries. I could have told him that myself, but he thought it best to verify for certain." The queen led Akeylah off the dance floor. A server appeared at their elbow, and they both accepted flutes of nectar.

"Has he told other acolytes?"

"He swore he wouldn't. As far as I can tell, he has upheld that promise so far." Rozalind swirled her drink.

So far. Akeylah's mind swam. That was a mystery for another time. She was still reeling from the sensation of finally freeing herself from her blackmailer.

Across the courtyard, the countess was acting as though nothing had happened. Laughing as she followed a lord along a path through the veil-draped trees. How could Yasmin do that? Shrug off this battle as though it were nothing more than a casual encounter at a party?

Akeylah was beginning to suspect she wasn't built for life in the Keep. Already she'd cursed a king, been blackmailed for it, kissed a queen, met two half sisters hiding secrets she could only imagine were nearly as dangerous as her own... all while studying to take the throne of a country at war with itself.

Can I handle this?

Then again, Akeylah had spent her entire life learning how to survive. How to act the part, become whatever she needed to become.

Beside her, Rozalind sighed. "I should go over there soon." Akeylah turned to find her watching the king, surrounded by a group of Kolonyan nobles. Rozalind's expression said she'd rather do anything else.

"Need some moral support?"

The queen shot her a relieved glance. "If you don't mind sitting through about three hours of dull socializing..."

A smile curled the edges of Akeylah's mouth. "Anything for you," she said, voice pitched low. Their eyes locked, and for a moment, Akeylah was back in the queen's chambers, kissing those seashell lips....

"Sister." Ren's voice shattered the memory. "A word?"

"Lady Florencia." Rozalind bobbed her head. "Akeylah, I'll see you in a moment?"

"Of course." Akeylah grinned at the queen. Didn't stop watching her, even when Ren forcibly linked arms with Akeylah and steered her toward the far side of the courtyard.

"Akeylah. Whatever's going on between you and Rozalind needs to stop."

Akeylah shot Ren a startled look. "There's nothing—"

"Don't tell me there's nothing going on; she dug up a grave for you," Ren interrupted in a low whisper. "Look, I'm not judging. But you're attracting attention right now."

Unable to help it, she glanced around the rooftop. Sure enough, more than a few gazes were trained in her direction.

"I didn't realize..."

"Really?" Ren arched a brow. "You have been in the Keep for more than a single day, haven't you? You didn't realize courtiers collect royals' weak spots the way Madam Harknell collects rare manuscripts?"

"Being on good terms with the queen isn't a weak spot." Akeylah's voice dropped. "Look at how much she helped us today. Without her, we'd have been bluffing, hoping that letter alone was enough to convince Yasmin to back off."

"There's being on good terms, and then there's...whatever you're doing." Ren heaved a sigh. "Akeylah, she's from an enemy country; she's married to our *father*, who by the way is the *king*. Not to mention that marriage is supposed to seal a peace treaty. What do you think will happen if it falls apart?"

"It won't—"

"Be smart. Because if *Zofi* noticed you flirting with Rozalind, then other courtiers will, too."

Across the rooftop, Rozalind had embedded herself in the crowd around King Andros. A woman Akeylah didn't recognize said something to the queen, touched her arm. Akeylah could hear Rozalind's laugh all the way from here. Her rib cage contracted.

Ren was right. She shouldn't do this. Part of her—the part that walked out of Rozalind's chambers yesterday—already knew it.

"I'll end it," Akeylah whispered finally.

Ren nodded once, curt. "Thank you."

"No, thank you." Akeylah flashed a weak smile at her sister. "For looking out for me."

Though Ren looked uncomfortable with the praise, she smiled back. "What are sisters for?"

❄

"It surprises me that you haven't heard of Carrowhittaker. As I understood it, it is quite a large supplier of textiles among the Eastern Reach."

"I'm sure it is, Lord Gavin." Akeylah donned her widest, blandest smile. "But I'm afraid I haven't much experience in the textile business myself." She was currently trying to pretend that she didn't remember the strangely pointed remarks Gavin made about the rebellion the last time they spoke, back on the evening of her Blood Ceremony.

That, and wondering whether she could excuse herself to go speak to a potted plant instead. The nearest starlight bush, currently in full bloom, looked like it would make for far more exciting company.

"That surprises me, given it is one of your Reach's major exports."

Everything about the Eastern Reach seems to surprise you, she thought. Aloud, she said, "My stepfather favored the seafood trade himself. Thought it a safer bet than most industries. 'Crops fail and fashions change, but there's always more fish in the sea,' he used to say."

"He sounds like a wise man," Gavin replied.

"He was certainly something." If nothing else, tonight gave Akeylah plenty of opportunities to practice her diplomacy.

That and her willpower. It was taking every ounce of it right now to ignore Rozalind. Ren had replaced the queen at their father's side, chatting with him, while Rozalind slowly extricated herself from his circle. Since then, Rozalind had moved her contingent of admirers closer and closer to Akeylah. She'd spent the last five minutes trying to catch Akeylah's eye, in increasingly less subtle ways.

Akeylah knew she'd need to pull her aside at some point. Tell her they couldn't do this, tell her people would talk.

Had started talking already, in fact.

But that conversation would make it final. Nip whatever this thing was growing between them in the bud.

Selfish though it may be, Akeylah couldn't bring herself to do that. Not quite yet. *After tonight*, she promised herself. Besides, she couldn't easily pull the queen aside for another private conversation here. Not if she wanted to *avoid* more rumors.

"My lady?" Gavin prompted.

Seas below. She zoned back in and desperately rifled through her memory. What did he just say? She was still formulating a polite way to admit that she'd lost the plot, when a series of gasps made her head jerk upright.

A few steps away, King Andros sagged to his knees. He had one arm tangled in Ren's, and she was doing her best to hold him upright. Though, with their father being twice Ren's size, she couldn't make it look convincing.

Two menders darted forward, racing across the rooftop. At that instant, someone screamed.

* 31 *

Florencia

Danton tried to corner her the moment she left Akeylah's side. He managed to get out the syllables "Floren—" before Ren shoved past him.

All she said, over her shoulder, on her way toward her father in the distance, was "No." She was done with his excuses. Done with whatever cheap explanation he'd stumble through this time. Done with him entirely.

Good luck, Lexana, she thought. *Frankly, you deserve better.*

"What do you think, daughter?" King Andros asked when she reached his side. "Did we manage to scale back the festivities sufficiently?"

Ren had almost forgotten the regional council meeting, the conversation around their last lesson. She surveyed the nobles, cast her thoughts back. "I haven't heard anyone complaining about a lack of refreshments," she said. "Though that may be due to the fact that with emptier stomachs, the strongwine is hitting most people a fair sight harder."

Andros chuckled. "Perhaps we should employ this strategy more often."

"Did the cutbacks yield much additional food supplies for our farmhands?" she inquired. The farmer who pleaded with her and Yasmin rose to mind once more.

Yasmin. Speaking of the countess, where was she? Now that Ren thought about it, she hadn't seen her in at least half an hour. She'd tracked her for a little while, just to make sure Yasmin didn't have a change of heart and decide to out her nieces' sins after all. But she'd lost track when Yasmin went wandering through the gardens with Lord Rueno, who was now back in the crowd nearby, talking to Rozalind.

"Enough to tide us over for the next couple of weeks." Andros breathed a deep sigh. "I can only hope that by then, we'll have found some sort of lasting solution to this problem."

Ren forced herself to focus. Yasmin was taken care of. Now she could finally think about something besides the constant, pressing worry about her blackmailer. "Is there any more news from the agricultural guild?"

Andros shook his head. "Just the usual. They're working on a cure; they'll update us soon." He held out an arm. Ren looped hers through it, though she soon found him leaning on her more than the other way around. "You'll find, Florencia, that when one of you sits in my position, people wind up feeding you a lot of useless responses." He said it with a lighthearted voice, a twinkle in his eye.

She recognized the serious tone beneath nonetheless. "How do you convince them to give you honest replies rather than platitudes?"

"Honesty requires trust," he said. "First you need to earn the trust of your subjects. Reassure them that even if they tell you something you don't want to hear, even if the news they must deliver is bad, you will not hold it against them." His smile widened. "Except, of course, in the cases when that bad news is entirely their fault."

Ren smiled, too. "What do you do in those cases?"

"Well..."

She never found out.

At first, Ren thought he paused for drama's sake. When the quiet stretched on, and his weight grew against her arm, her eyes widened.

Andros sank to his knees slowly, as though falling through molasses. Ren gripped his biceps in both hands, tried to haul him upright, or at least hold him halfway long enough for him to catch himself, play this off as a stumble.

Too late.

Nobles were whispering, pointing, staring. Two brown-clad menders darted toward her.

In the distance, a woman screamed.

The menders reached the king's side, took over. Ren staggered when they accepted her father's weight.

Andros looked like he'd been struck. He groped in midair, suspended between the two menders. Ren caught his hand. Squeezed it as the menders guided him toward a chair that someone carried over, running through the nobility at full speed.

Everywhere she turned she found eyes on them, heard shouting, yelling.

A mender elbowed her out of the way as Andros opened his mouth and let out a horrible, wordless cry. It sounded like a Talon's horn, a stormwing's scream. It sounded like pure, agonizing pain.

Then Rozalind was there, crouched beside the king, too, whispering. The mender pried his eyelids back, peered into his eyes. Andros focused on the mender first, then his wife. He seemed lucid, or at least aware of his surroundings. But his eyes kept darting away, to the far edge of the roof.

"No. No..." His lips moved, mouthed words.

Ren cast a frightened glance at the courtyard. By now, she expected to find the whole court watching the show.

Instead, she found most of them drifting away through the trees, toward the parapets. From that direction came a cry for another mender. Then another scream, which it took her a second to recognize as an actual Talon's horn.

A moment later, a real live stormwing came plummeting out of the sky, summoned from its perch at the top of the aerie. It vanished over the edge of the roof, dove toward...something.

What in Sun's name is going on?

She checked Andros again. "Is he all right?"

One of the two menders tending to him nodded curtly. Rozalind crouched by him as well, and a handful of noble lords were asking the queen whether His Majesty needed anything.

Still, Ren hovered, indecisive. She wanted to stay. Help her father. Reassure herself that he was fine, that this wasn't the end yet. That they still had time. Time for him to teach them, to name his heir. To help put this country on the right course.

But the other part of her wanted to know what was going on through those trees.

Then Rozalind met her eye. "Go," she said. "Find your sisters."

That decided it. She lifted her skirts and hurried across the now-abandoned dance floor. It was easy to find the commotion. She just followed the shouts, gasps, sobs. She reached the stone parapets and found almost the entire court gathered. Some were crying openly. Others just looked confused.

But most people, Ren noticed, were peering over the edge.

Her stomach curdled. She took a step closer. Another. The hairs on the back of her neck rose. She wanted to know. She didn't want to know.

What happened?

Someone caught her arm. She jumped, tried to yank herself free. It was only Zofi. "Don't," she warned.

Another hand rested on her other forearm. Akeylah. "You don't want to see it."

"See what?" Ren asked. Her voice sounded hollow.

Ahead, Lady Necia had just reached the parapet. She screamed and swooned. Sarella was right behind her, also gasping, swaying on her feet dramatically until one of the men propped her upright. They all faded into background noise. Sounds and cries that meant nothing. Without thinking, Ren extended her hands, caught both her sisters'. Yet she kept walking forward.

Whatever Akeylah said, part of her knew she had to see this. Knew she wouldn't fully grasp it until she did.

When she reached the edge, Akeylah turned away. Zofi looked with her and tightened her grip on Ren's hand.

Over the edge, hundreds of feet below, the bright light of the triple moons illuminated the figure. Unmistakable even from this height. Nobody else dressed like that, so dark and austere. Broken like a wounded bird, cracked across the cobblestones, legs splayed at an unnatural angle, blood pooled all around.

Countess Yasmin was dead.

⭜ **32** ⭝

Zofi

Three days of lockdown. Three days of pacing her chambers like a caged great cat while Talons searched the Keep from top to bottom. The servants' passages, the main hallways, every last nook and cranny in all ten towers, looking for anything or any*one* out of place.

Andros wasn't going to stop until he found his sister's killer. He insisted she'd been murdered, though he wouldn't explain how he knew this to anybody. As far as Ren had heard, whenever his Talons questioned Andros, the king simply ordered them to keep searching.

That wasn't like him, Ren said. Issuing orders blindly, not explaining his decisions.

Then again, grief could make anybody act different. Irrational, angry, depressed.

Zofi hadn't seen her father since the end of the Feast of the Sun's Glorious Ascendance, when two menders carried King Andros down from the sky gardens on a stretcher. Rumors flew now—what the illness was, how long he'd been hiding it.

Even the kitchen boys who delivered Zofi's meals were talking about it with the Talon now posted permanently outside her chambers—not Vidal, unfortunately, or she might at least have learned more information about the situation. "The menders say he's got a falling sickness," the kitchen boy reported as he drew up outside her door on the third day. "Said it's not fatal, but that's what made him collapse at the Sun's Ascendance."

"Same time his sister dies?" The Talon sighed. "That's some real bad luck."

"Not same time," the kitchen boy said. "Apparently he's had this illness for ages. Though, some people think it's..." His voice dropped.

Zofi pressed her ear to the keyhole.

"—lind. Say she poisoned him, shoved Yasmin. That's why he's holed up in his bedrooms, sick from poison."

The Talon snorted. "Some imagination, kid."

"It's not imagination! She's Genalese; you know what they're like. And you saw her. She was with the king when he collapsed."

"The queen isn't murdering her husband," the Talon said.

Zofi's stomach churned. She owed the queen—all her sisters did. She didn't like hearing this kid talk badly about her.

"Still might've killed the countess, though," the kitchen boy replied, a pout audible in his tone.

"You just said yourself, the queen was with King Andros

when he took ill. The same time Countess Yasmin fell. Now stop spreading rumors and take the tray in."

Zofi leaped back from the door and planted herself at her desk just in time to pretend to be writing a letter when the Talon opened the door and the serving boy carried the tray inside. "Breakfast for my lady."

Funny. *This* was the life she'd expected when she first came to the Keep. A Talon posted outside, meals by delivery only. She just never predicted all the security would be meant to guard her rather than trap her.

Fortunately, Ren had ways of communicating without leaving a room. Her first missive, delivered the morning after the Sun's Ascendance, said, *My friend adds these to your trays individually, not via general post. We can speak somewhat freely.*

Via those notes, Zofi learned about the king's bedridden state. He told his courtiers he collapsed from fatigue on the rooftop. But between that and his rages every night, ordering the Keep to remain on lockdown or fuming at Talons who reported they hadn't found anyone out of place, the rumor mill was starting to churn. Already whispers had begun about his other fits and minor illnesses of late, fainting spells he passed off as related to heat or exhaustion.

It wouldn't be long before the truth came out. Before Andros would need to address his condition with his people, admit the truth of the situation. Zofi only hoped there was enough time for him to name an heir and see her successfully installed before that day came.

What do you think really happened to our aunt? she'd asked Ren in a reply note yesterday morning.

Suicide, came Ren's answer with Zofi's dinner tray. *It's the only thing that makes sense. Maybe she couldn't face the shame of her brother finding out what she really was. That, or she knew she'd be executed for treason anyway, if he learned about her past exploits.*

Zofi noticed Ren didn't mention exactly what those exploits were in the letter. Just in case.

This morning, Zofi found a new letter waiting on her tray. She unfolded it while she bit into a hard-boiled egg.

Funeral today, Ren wrote. *Wear green. Preferably something with a skirt if you can bear it.*

She'd added a postscript, a reply to Zofi's note last night. Zofi had asked whether Ren thought Yasmin might have left anything behind. Posthumous confessions or the like. For some reason, Ren's reply settled her unease.

We'd know by now if she left anything. We're safe.

Zofi didn't need to see her sister's expression to guess how Ren looked when she wrote that. Jaw set, mouth a hard line. Steel in her gaze, which Zofi had come to respect just as much as any warrior's fighting stance.

So Zofi let herself relax as a carriage drove her, Akeylah, and Ren through a muggy late-afternoon downpour.

Andros had taken precautions, still paranoid about the murderer he believed was out there, hunting his family. The carriage was unmarked, escorted by five Talons disguised as merchants. The windows had blackout curtains and thick glass panes. Zofi couldn't even tell which direction they were driving until they drew up outside the Necropolis.

The city within a city, built for the dead.

Having never seen the Necropolis herself, Zofi assumed that

description was a metaphor. But as they climbed down from their carriage onto the stone streets—real stone, not stonewood, since that precious material was reserved for the living—Zofi realized it was literal.

The Necropolis was an exact miniature of Kolonya City. They walked through an imitation strongwall, only twenty feet high and just as thick. Inside, tombs were laid into the strongwall like skysquats—embedded within it, one atop the next, stacked on top of one another all the way up the wall. Each one had a coat of arms on its entrance, rather than names.

Zofi supposed it would get crowded after a few generations, if you carved everyone in the family's forename onto a tomb.

Beyond the strongwall, streets so narrow they had to walk single file led past stone tombs that were miniature versions of the houses their occupants presumably lived in. Some farmers' houses were only one story tall. Others were two or three stories high, with larger-than-life stone animals guarding the rooftops. Macaws and great cats and stormwings peered down from every corner.

Through the "houses'" glass windows, Zofi glimpsed coffins in various stages of decay. She wondered if this was where Rozalind had come to disinter poor Acolyte Casca.

The largest tomb of all stood at the heart of the Necropolis. Near it, Zofi caught strains of flute music.

She stopped in front of the dead's version of Ilian Keep.

Unlike the real Keep, this one was only six stories tall. Each tower was painted like the Keep's stonewood—not only the right colors, but even maintaining the ring patterns of the trees that had been petrified in the bogs out west, then dredged up to build the Keep. Stonewood from those peat bogs was stronger than stone, yet Zofi thought its stone replica here would stand up to a decent barrage.

Each tower had a door of its own. The cherry-red one, however, was open.

It was short and narrow. Zofi would fit easily, but most Kolonyans would have to duck and squeeze. Especially Andros, who was currently kneeling before the door, head bowed, hands resting atop an ebony coffin.

He looked worse than ever. His face was a mask of pain, the whites of his eyes yellow, his hands shaky. As if Yasmin's death had drained the rest of the life from him, too.

Despite her covert attempt to destroy his legacy, Yasmin had been the one propping Andros up. Keeping him going.

Andros spared his daughters a glance, then returned to his task. She watched, brows contracting, as he shoved himself to his feet. Then, to her shock, he bent and started to *lift the coffin*.

She started forward, but Ren caught her wrist.

Tears streaked down Andros's cheeks.

Whatever Yasmin was to her—blackmailer, specter, physical threat of death—she was Andros's support. His sister, his twin, the one person who had been by his side through all his long reign. She thought about her band. She thought about her half sisters standing beside her.

She couldn't imagine how this loss felt to him.

Andros lifted the coffin. Managed to take one step. Dropped the corner, fell forward across it. Sank back to his knees.

"Your Majesty, please." A Talon stepped forward, breaking rank. "Allow me- -"

"No. It has to be a family member," Andros snarled.

Zofi glanced at Ren with a frown. Her sister was distracted, though, watching their father struggle.

Akeylah leaned in close on her other side. "Kolonyan custom," she whispered. "Only family members can inter one another. Some exceptions are made if someone passes away with no living relatives, or if the remaining relations are too infirm, but Kolonyans believe it makes it harder for your relative to enter the Blessed Sunlands unless a blood relation escorts you to the gate."

Ren noticed the whispers and had leaned close enough to catch the tail end. "You sound like a local, sister," she murmured.

Akeylah shrugged. "I taught myself how to read on a Kolonyan book of legends."

The flute music grew louder. Zofi glanced at the players. They wore funeral green, the same way she and her sisters had been instructed to dress. Jungle green, everything from their skirts to their sashes. Zofi had even stooped to wearing a gown, though only because Ren asked nicely.

The green, Ren had explained during the carriage ride, represented the next life. The seed from which Yasmin's soul would grow on in the Blessed Sunlands.

If she's worthy of entrance, Zofi thought at the time.

Now, though, she watched Andros strain to drag her coffin into the tomb. He sank to one knee yet again. Groaned through the pain and surged back to his feet. *She must have been more.* More than just the blackmail threats, the lies. He wouldn't go through all this if she wasn't.

Zofi thought about her mother, her band of Travelers. Elex. They'd done plenty they could be judged for. Stolen, lied, cheated.

Killed, when we had to. Sands knew Zofi had blood on her palms. But she still loved her family, because she knew they were more than the sum of their sins.

Countess Yasmin might have treated them all like they were less than human. She threatened them in private, disparaged them in public, judged them without knowing them. That didn't mean Zofi needed to make the same mistake. To judge a whole person by one piece.

She walked forward and placed a hand on her father's shoulder. He looked up from his crouch, breathing hard.

"I'll do it," she said. "I'm a blood relative."

Andros sat back on his heels. Searched her gaze. "Are you sure? It's more than just carrying this box through a doorway."

She knelt beside him. "What else is it?"

"It's accepting the burden of her soul. You must carry her body to its rightful resting place in the tomb. Only there can her soul find its rightful place in the Blessed Sunlands, among our family. If you fail to inter her body properly, her soul remains trapped here on earth. She'll follow you, remain attached to your spirit until you yourself die, and can carry her in death with you to the afterlife."

Great. So if she failed, she'd face a lifetime of being haunted by her blackmailer.

Zofi must have hesitated for too long, because Andros squeezed her shoulder.

"She didn't hate you, you know. None of you girls."

It took a colossal effort to swallow a snort of laughter. "She had a funny way of showing it."

"Yasmin believed in tough love." A fond smile danced at the

corners of his mouth. "She was always willing to do that. Act the villain. Antagonism builds more character than niceties, she used to say." His gaze went faraway, wistful. "Perhaps if I'd listened to her more with Nicolen, he wouldn't have turned out the way he did."

Nausea crept up the back of her throat. Her father looked so much older, so much more tired than the man she'd met when she first arrived in the Keep, which already felt like a lifetime ago. The wrinkles etched in his face reminded her of the tree rings on the stonewood walls of the Keep.

"I'll take her." Zofi stood and offered him a hand up. "I'll get her where she needs to go."

She'd already put her father's only son in the ground. Now she'd led his only sister into committing suicide—albeit to stop an evil plot against him. Still. Helping him now was the least she could do.

"Thank you, Zofi." He accepted her hand and she helped him to his feet. A Talon stepped forward, helped him back toward a wooden wheeled chair that Zofi hadn't noticed earlier, parked beside the separate carriage Andros must have taken here.

Then Zofi crouched and grabbed the edge of the coffin. But she'd only just begun to lift the heavy box from the ground when another pair of hands caught the lid across from her.

"A soul may be escorted by as many living relatives as they have," Ren said, by way of explanation as she crouched to help Zofi lift the coffin.

A moment later, Akeylah reached their sides and added her strength to support the middle of the coffin. Together, the three carried Yasmin into the tomb.

Inside, a space had been cleared on the lowest shelf, chest

height to Zofi. Other coffins rose above it. On the closest, Zofi read the name *Daryn*. Yasmin's father.

The coffins grew more and more decayed the higher they reached. The farthest, which Zofi could barely see from here, had broken open in spots. She could've sworn she saw a curl of weathered gray hair sticking through the crack.

Below, a metal grate separated them from more coffins. Someone had lit torches today, presumably for the internment. In that flickering light, Zofi spotted more coffins, even older than the ones above, some stone, others wooden and rotten open, the bodies within laid bare.

A skeleton in a decaying green gown seemed to smile up at her. A queen whose name lay somewhere in her ancestry, far enough back that she doubted anyone remembered it except for schoolchildren forced to learn the lineage of Kolonya. There lay her fate. The fate of them all, one day.

Zofi looked the skeleton in the eye and bowed her head.

Someday, death would come for her. Someday, she'd lose this game. Someday the Yasmins of the world would win. Or maybe not, maybe she'd make it to old age and an illness like her father's would fell her instead. Either way, someday she'd be the one in a coffin, reliant on relatives to carry her to rest.

She peered at her sisters. If they were the ones to carry her someday, she thought, she could do worse.

With a grunt of effort, she, Ren, and Akeylah lifted Yasmin onto the shelf. Slid her into position beneath her father.

To her surprise, Akeylah caught her hand, then took Ren's, too. Zofi reached across her and linked her free hand with Ren's, until they stood in a circle.

"Father Sun, grant our aunt's spirit entry into your blessed lands," Ren murmured.

"Mother Ocean, accept her spirit. Bear her to a land where her rest is gentle, her feet dry, and her soul wants for nothing." Akeylah's hand tightened on Zofi's.

Zofi pressed her lips together. The only words she knew were Traveler words. Her people's way of life made them, by necessity, unsentimental about bodies. Once you left your shell, it was nothing—just a husk. They burned the dead on pyres, then drank and ate and sang until only embers remained. Then they scattered those embers to the winds and sang the Traveler prayer.

"May the sands take Yasmin as their own. May her dust join that of our brothers and sisters. May she drift wherever her heart desires, but know always, no matter how far she roams, her heart is always home."

For a moment, the only sound was the flute music outside, drawing to a crescendo.

"It feels like our fault," Akeylah whispered.

"We didn't push her," Ren murmured.

"We may as well have." Zofi sighed.

"What were we supposed to do, let her put us in this tomb instead?" Ren's voice quavered.

Zofi clutched her hand hard. "Of course not. We did what we had to do. But we can't shirk that burden. Yasmin started a war, yes, but we ended it. We fought back. Just because we had to do it doesn't mean we shouldn't feel any guilt." Sands knew she understood that well enough by now.

Ren didn't argue. She just bowed her head again. Akeylah did, too.

Only when the flute music outside died away did they turn by unspoken accord. One by one, they emerged back into the light. Overhead, the thunderstorm had cleared, the late-afternoon clouds parting. The jungle sun beat down hotter than ever. Zofi exited last, and she could already feel the hot muggy air digging into her curls, making them stick up everywhere, tumbleweed wild.

But when Andros lifted his eyebrows in a silent question, *How did it go?* Zofi smiled.

This might be a funeral for Yasmin. For her? It was a rebirth.

·⚜ **33** ⚜·

Akeylah

T hank you for meeting me," Akeylah said as she rose to let Rozalind step into the nook she'd found. She'd stumbled across it this morning, two days after the funeral—the first time in five days she'd been allowed out of her locked chambers. Madam Harknell had grumbled when she showed up, but when Akeylah had asked for recommendations on private reading spots, the librarian had helped her into this hollow behind Naval Warfare.

"Just don't start getting up to any untoward antics in here," Harknell had warned as she stormed off, muttering about "that last girl, little Northern thing, and her latest young lord..."

Akeylah had to admit, she could see the appeal of this as a spot for lovers' trysts. It followed the curve of the tower, making a perfectly circular room, only about four feet in circumference, bordered all around by bookshelves with red settee cushions beneath. The only entrance was a single narrow gap between Naval Warfare and Numerology. Entering felt like crawling into a cocoon of books.

"Please, have a seat." Akeylah gestured at the settee.

Rozalind grinned and curled up on the cushion. "So formal. Did all this time apart make you forget about me?"

I wish. If anything, five days of solitude in her rooms had only made daydreams about Rozalind more intrusive. More painful, given her conversation with Ren on the sky gardens rooftop.

Yasmin was gone, yes. That didn't mean there were no enemies here. They'd defeated their personal threat, but plenty of people still wanted to see the crown fail. There was the Silver Prince's assassin, who yet roamed free. There were the rebels of Burnt Bay, rebels who made Akeylah's life that much harder here, simply for being Eastern.

And there were Rozalind's people. Genal. Who might be mixed up in some or any of those plots, to who knew what degree.

Akeylah perched on the settee beside Rozalind. "We need to talk."

"Nothing good ever followed those four words." Rozalind tried for a smirk. It failed.

"We can't keep doing this, Rozalind."

"Last I checked, we weren't," she pointed out. "We've been locked up for nearly a week."

"You know what I mean. At the Sun's Ascendance, people were talking. Seas know how many rumors have already begun—"

"There will always be rumors, Akeylah." Rozalind caught her hand. Held on tight. "No matter what you do, no matter what I do. When people hate you simply because of your background, your parents, the shape of your face, or the way you wear your hair, it doesn't matter how well you behave. People will believe what they want."

"It's when their beliefs are true that it gets dangerous." Akeylah caught the queen's thin, delicate fingers between her palms. "Rozalind, you're married to *my father.*"

"Your father is a wise man. He knows girls my age don't dream of marrying someone twice their age. And his tastes don't run toward women who could be his daughter. We do what we must for our kingdoms, but in private, we are both free to pursue who we truly desire." Her grip tightened at that word. *Desire.*

Akeylah's face went hot. "Whatever agreement you may have, it doesn't change the public's opinion. If Kolonyans believe the marriage a sham—or worse, think you're cheating on their king—they won't hesitate to turn on you. That could lead to war. And can you imagine if that acolyte talks, if your secret gets out, about your ability to tithe—"

"He won't talk." Rozalind said it with such certainty that it stopped Akeylah in her tracks.

"How can you know that?"

"I haven't spent the last week lazing around my chambers, you know. I spoke to the acolyte, explained that King Andros had no knowledge of Yasmin's treasonous use of the Vulgar Arts. I told him that when Andros confronted his sister, she leaped to her death rather than face his judgment. The hunt for her murderer is to save public face, since the king does not wish to sully his sister's legacy now that she is gone. Naturally, our devoted acolyte understood. He only wanted justice. With Yasmin dead, he has it."

Akeylah pressed her lips together, tight. "But what if—"

"Akeylah. It's taken care of." Rozalind dropped her hand to reach up and cup Akeylah's cheek instead. "As for us, there are ways to conceal ourselves in public."

Akeylah tried for a smile. It made her face ache. "Because being subtle in public has worked so well for us thus far."

Rozalind laughed weakly. "It's difficult to hide the way I feel for you." Then she squared her shoulders. "But I can. I *will*, if it's the only way to be with you. We can meet here, places like this." She gestured at the hidden nook, the most private spot Akeylah could find.

A spot that wasn't even truly private, where Madam Harknell could pop her head in at any moment.

Even Akeylah's own chambers could not be trusted. Ren had shown her more than one hidden listening passage attached to her rooms. The thought of those spy holes gave Akeylah the strength to hold her ground.

"Rozalind..."

"Akeylah, I know you feel this, too." She tilted forward.

Akeylah mirrored the motion until their foreheads touched, the strength she felt a moment ago fading, the way it always did, in the face of this girl. She traced a thumb across Rozalind's cheekbone. "Why can't you make this easy for me?" she whispered.

"Because you make it impossible for me," Rozalind breathed. Then she crushed her lips to Akeylah's.

Just like the first time, the room spun. Akeylah's heart leaped into her throat, her head, out of her body. She kissed back, soft at first, so soft, afraid she'd break this spell. But Rozalind gripped her hair, pulled her tighter, and Akeylah returned that fury. Rozalind bit her lip, and she drew back with a gasp.

Rozalind wasn't Rozalind anymore.

"Still as incompetent as ever, I see." Akeylah's stepfather, Jahen dam-Senzin, sat next to her with a vicious grin on his face.

Her body froze. Her mind, too.

It's not real, part of her shouted. The part that remembered Zofi's story, remembered how her sister described a Vulgar Arts hallucination.

The rest of her was pure panic.

"You always were useless. Could barely handle cleaning a kitchen properly. How in Sun's name did you expect to defeat *me*?" He raised his fist, and Akeylah flinched. That drew a baritone laugh from his throat. "I'm not going to beat you, little girl. Well, not literally, anyway. I've already beaten you in every way that counts." He grabbed something from the bookshelf beside her head. The heavy tome crashed onto the floor between the settees. "Apparently my deadline didn't get this through your thick skull, so here's hoping this will. Understand what I do to my enemies. You're one of them now."

She blinked. His face disappeared. Resolved back into Rozalind's, brows knit in concern, her hands still cupping Akeylah's face.

"Akeylah? What's going on—can you hear me? Breathe, Akeylah."

She didn't realize she hadn't been.

She sucked in a breath. Her lungs seized; her whole body sagged back against the shelf. Now that she'd started breathing, she couldn't stop. She gasped in lungful after lungful of air, all while Rozalind bent Akeylah's head between her knees, rubbed between her shoulder blades, coaxed her through it.

When her head stopped swimming and the black dots at the edges of her vision finally disappeared, Akeylah straightened.

The book was still lying on the floor. She glanced from it to Rozalind and back.

"You bumped it," Rozalind explained. "You were flailing at one point."

Akeylah reached for it. It was a slim, unassuming tome. Red-and-black cover. *Kolonyan Love Songs: romances of kings and queens through the ages.* She turned it over. The back suggested it was a compilation of love poems and ballads, written by, for, or about various kings and queens of Kolonya.

The hair on the back of her neck rose. She thought about the acolyte's story. About his recounting of Casca's last days. About the Vulgar Arts Yasmin had performed. *He said it was hidden in the library, in the book kings love best.*

Maybe that wasn't madness talking after all.

"What is it?" Rozalind was asking, frowning. Akeylah knew she must seem mad. She just appeared to have a fit, and now she was staring at this book like it held the answers to the universe.

But maybe it did.

She opened the cover. Tucked inside was a slip of paper, yellowed with age. One edge was jagged, as if it had been torn from another book, then placed here. Her hands shook as she unfolded it.

Their combined blood must be used to seal the effect, once the union has been drawn together and borne fruit. When both tithe in that manner, the result shall be a binding of the minds, unbreakable, constant, permanent. Whatsoever one thinks or knows or feels, the other shall perceive, as easily as the blood that pumps in their veins.

With this tithe, two become one. Nothing shall be secret between them. All knowledge is shared, all thoughts conjoined.

Take care, for this tithe is both blessing and curse. It leaves an indelible echo, one you can never escape or block or constrain. You should only undertake this effort with someone in whom you place absolute trust.

Recommendation is to remove the fruit of the union once created. Otherwise, if it remains, it will grow into an additional echo, magnified with time and age.

That was the last of the printed words. In the margins, however, someone—presumably Casca—had scribbled notes.

Not considered Vulgar Arts when first discovered (date: 5–15 AR, approx.?)

Added to forbidden Vulgar Arts list under King Gellian (date: 112 AR, see: Treatise on Forbidden Artes Vol. III)

Yasmin & Andros both want to be bound.

Understand they will never have a private thought again. Worth it for communication during war.

Additional: Best performed on relatives but can be done with unrelated pairs as well. Keeping this note for my personal records, to be given to my mentee upon my passing. Recommend this tithe be looked at in future, possibly reinstated as Blood Arts rather than Vulgar Arts curse. Further notes to come as subjects progress with the pairing.

Akeylah reread the page over and over, certain she'd misunderstood. But no. The hallucination she had just proved what she dreaded—the blackmailer was still out there. This letter only sealed the proof. Yasmin couldn't have been the one hunting them.

"Echo," Rozalind said. Akeylah had almost forgotten she was

there. "That's what Andros used to call Yasmin. His echo. I thought he meant twin, but…"

Suddenly, all the little moments Akeylah had glimpsed between them fell into place. The way they'd tilt their heads in time together. The way they finished each other's sentences aloud.

Andros screaming when Yasmin was pushed, long before anyone else knew. He could feel it. He felt everything she did, saw, heard. Which meant Yasmin couldn't have known about their secrets. Otherwise Andros would have known, too.

Rozalind was frowning. "So they were what, telepathically linked? Can the Arts do that?"

"Vulgar Arts can, apparently." Akeylah shoved out of her seat and stuffed the paper into her pocket.

"Where are you going?"

"I have to find my sisters."

Whoever their blackmailer was, they were still out there.

* 34 *

Florencia

R en leaned her head against the tile of the baths. *Thank the Sun*. At last, some space to clear her head and process the past few days.

The funeral two days ago finally made this all feel real. Yasmin was truly gone. And however guilty she may feel for having a hand in the countess's death, it meant her and her sisters were free.

Free to look ahead. Free to take the next step in their paths. Free to focus on their lessons, their studies with the king. Free to make the most of his time while it lasted, learn everything they could.

Free to find out what decision he'd eventually make. Which one of them he wanted to name heir. Which girl would wear the crown after he passed.

Funny. Ren went into this thinking it would be her, hands

down. Her mother's daughter through and through, she'd planned to defeat her sisters in pursuit of that crown. To do whatever it took to win. Though she'd also assumed it would be easy—a Traveler and an Easterner stood no chance against a Kolonyan, she thought.

Now?

Now she wasn't even sure whether she would make the best choice. And if her father did by some chance choose Ren to follow him, she wasn't sure she could sit on a throne without her sisters on either side.

Maybe that was what Yasmin had been to Andros. His support, his aid, his most trusted partner in all this. Ren could understand why her death broke him, even though it relieved her.

At the end of the day, maybe they'd never learn why Yasmin jumped. Why she preferred death to facing her demons. Maybe she was sick of all the lies. Maybe she didn't want to see the expression on her twin's face when he learned what she'd hidden from him. She'd lied about so much. Kept secrets—his daughters' secrets as well as her own. The murder she committed, the Vulgar Arts she used, whatever it was she used them for...

Ren pulled her knees up to her chest and hugged them. Too many mysteries to worry about now.

The scents of mint and juniper hung in the steamy air this afternoon. It relaxed her, made her eyelids heavy. Soon, her body grew heavy, too. She sank a little lower, let the water reach her neck, her chin.

She thought about the cutbacks from the Sun's Ascendance. They seemed to work. Nobody complained overmuch, and the leftover food would keep people like the farmer she met fed for weeks. Hopefully that would buy them enough time to face the next problem—how to cure the crop blight.

If they could overcome a problem like that, well, then maybe fixing things in the Eastern Reach wouldn't be as impossible as it sounded either. Akeylah had some good points about the rebellion—about what might be driving them. If she could implement other changes, changes like cutting back in Kolonya on the whole, to help the Eastern Reach more, maybe she could stop another Burnt Bay from happening.

Her belly clenched. 1,854. She hadn't thought about that number in days. Hadn't felt that guilt, because she'd been too distracted by the rest. All the other concerns, fears, fights.

She'd been so focused on defeating Yasmin. But wasn't she just as bad as the countess, if not worse? Yasmin had killed one man. Ren had murdered hundreds.

She sank a little farther toward the surface of the water.

Her body felt so heavy...so weak. Tired.

Her vision swam. She blinked, and for a moment, it seemed as though the water was no longer bath-colored but a deep navy blue. The color of the ocean, or so she'd heard. She'd never seen it in person.

She tried to move her limbs. Instead, she found herself sliding lower. The water came up to her chin. Now her lips. Now over her mouth.

She blinked. The water stayed navy blue. On its surface bobbed tiny Kolonyan ships. She'd never seen a naval fleet, never seen a boat bigger than a paddleboat on the River Leath. But she'd seen paintings, drawings of the legendary Kolonyan fleet, which used to dock at the mouth of the River Leath, down at Great Cat's Cove in the Southern Reach.

The ships in the bath seemed to grow. The walls of the room melted away. The ships got larger, the huge wooden hulls hewn from trees in the jungle right here around Kolonya, then sailed south on barges to the port, where the River Leath spat into the Cradle Sea. Where the water was deep enough to build vast ships, each loaded with dozens of men and cannons.

One of those enormous ships seemed to swallow her up.

She appeared to stand in the belly of the ship. It rocked gently. All around her, Talons half-dressed in uniforms, or some completely naked, snored in hammocks that swayed gently with the motion of the ship.

It was a quiet night. No fighting.

Because that wasn't how these men died.

In the far corner, the few Talons still awake were gambling. They toasted beers, cracked a joke. Their whispered laughter carried across the dark cabin.

These were the soldiers of Burnt Bay on the eve of a revolution.

Tomorrow, she knew, they planned to make landfall in Davenforth. It was a sleepy little port town of no consequence. Just another Eastern city, and a small one at that. Except this city had elected to harbor rebellion leaders. Or at least, the city didn't kick the rebels out when they asked for help hiding from the Talons who marched across the Eastern Reach hunting them.

Tomorrow, these ships planned to launch cannons at the mayor's castle, perched on the windy cliff at the edge of the city. Tomorrow, these soldiers expected to pour out of their sleepy cabin berths onto the beaches and storm through the town.

They were here to kill traitors. They'd settle for anyone they could find.

Ren stretched out a hand to touch the nearest Talon, still sleeping. She found she couldn't move.

She could still see, though. Still smell gunpowder in the air, and hear a deafening bang.

It was so dark....

"Fire! Fire on the starboard bow!"

People scrambled around her. Ren tried to stagger after them, toward the stairs, but she couldn't move as the ship around her exploded. Fragments of wood went flying. Bodies went flying, too—parts of them, anyway. She felt hot liquid against her cheeks. Not bath water. It stank of sulfur and copper.

The crack of the ship was deafening. She felt it in her bones— a sudden rent in the world. The boards beneath her feet split, and then she was out in it, in open air, breathing fire and staring across a sea of misery.

The ship had broken in two. One half sank across from her, men screaming and leaping from the masts, red men jumping into redder waves.

Flames licked across what wood remained above water. Her half of the boat sank slower. Slow enough to give her time to look around. To watch the other ships in the distance meeting the same fate.

When the freezing-cold water of Davenforth Bay finally swirled around her ankles, her knees, her thighs, someone grabbed her hand.

Ren looked down. Found a soldier holding on to her like a lifeline.

"You did this," he spat, teeth red with blood. He'd been shot. She noticed the trail of blood drifting away from his torso, through waves that licked ever higher around their bodies.

The water reached her stomach. Her chest.

"I...I don't..." She yanked on her hand. Tried to wrench it free. *This isn't real. I'm home in the baths. I'm safe.*

"You did this, Florencia. You killed us all." He spat as he talked. His blood flecked her cheeks. Joined his comrades' blood in staining her face, her body, her hands. So much blood...

She opened her mouth to reply. To argue. But the water was at her neck now, her chin. She clamped her mouth shut as she was pulled under. For a moment she still saw the shipwreck. The sinking black water of the bay, lit by flames above.

Then the baths returned. White marble tile, bright sunny lights set into the walls.

Thank the Sun.

Ren reached up.

She still couldn't move.

Her arms were lead. Her legs were stone. Her whole body felt weighted, made of lead. She opened her mouth to scream, then realized her mistake. Water poured past her lips, down her throat, into her lungs. It ran up her nostrils, invaded every inch it found.

She heard a voice again. A laughing voice. Not the man who clung to her in the sinking ship. A different one this time. Quieter. Gentler.

"This is how you made them feel," the voice crooned. She couldn't make sense of it. Male or female, old or young. It was in-between, a nothing sound.

Because it's in my head.

"I told you to leave. I warned you. You had until the Sun's Ascendance, didn't I explain?" A sigh.

Ren reached for the lights again. Her arms were so heavy. So impossible to lift...

"I should let you drown like those poor soldiers and sailors. It's a terrible way to die. Slow. Painful."

She managed to cross her arms on her stomach. She dug her nail into the soft skin under her wrist. Tried to break the skin, to tithe. Instead, her nail bent backward, softened by the water, too weak to cut.

"The kind of death an impostor like you deserves."

Her foot glanced off something. Tile. The bottom of the baths. She focused all her energy into that muscle. Into standing up.

No use.

The lights began to flicker. Darken.

"It's time for me to take your place."

Despite the heat of the baths, Ren's whole body felt cold. Cold, and heavy, and so damned useless. What was the point? They were right. She deserved this. Deserved to die like the men she killed.

"It's time for the true heir to rise."

The darkness caved in.

ACKNOWLEDGMENTS

Ten years, 230 (and counting) rejection letters, and seven shelved novels have left me with a lot of people I need to thank now that my firstborn is finally out in the world, so please bear with me.

Mom, thank you for being my first fan and my first critic. I'm sorry for that time when I was six years old and I told you I wanted to write fiction because journalism didn't count as real writing. I'm so glad I inherited your love of words.

Dad, thank you for passing on your wild imagination. Your bedtime stories might have given me a pathological lifelong phobia of werewolves, but they also inspired me to start spinning my own weird tales.

To my agent, Bridget Smith, who believed in me years ago when I was still writing about dystopian flooded NYC—thank you for championing my every harebrained idea, for cheering me on through every rejection and publishing house closure, and especially for always cheering on the queermances most.

To the Alloy team—Annie Stone, Joelle Hobeika, Joshua Bank, Eliza Swift, Hayley Wagreich, Sara Shandler, and Viana Siniscalchi. Thank you for the endless sea of notes, for sticking with *Rule* through its many iterations, and most important, thank you for choosing me to help craft this world.

To Little, Brown—Pam Gruber, who molded the lump of ugly

clay this book started out as into a readable novel, to Hannah Milton, Annie McDonnell, Allie Singer, Erika Schwartz, and Marcie Lawrence (how did you know my inner teen goth would love this cover?), and everybody who helped get *Rule* out into the world, I am forever grateful for your belief in this book.

To my writing professors—Rachel Simon, who taught me how to Rewrite (with a capital *R*); Donna Jo Napoli, who encouraged me to write a YA novel for my linguistics thesis (most fun thesis work ever, by the way); and Elizabeth Mosier and Catherine Gilbert Murdoch. Thank you for being role models when I needed them most.

To everyone who ever rejected me—honestly, thank you. The feedback, the encouragement, and even the rejections from agents or publishers who just weren't feeling my style, those all inspired me to push harder, write better, keep trying.

To my many critique partners over the years—Corrie Wang, Lindsay Smith, Elliot Wake, Kyla Buckingham, Molyneaux Matthews, Ghenet Myrthil, Lindsay Neff, Justine Champine, Allison Goldstein, Jodi Harawitz, Ora Colb, Clara Moskowitz, Heather Walters, and everyone who has ever read one of my books and given me constructive feedback, which is at least half the people I know on the planet... thank you all. Every little bit helped more than I can possibly express.

To Natasha Sanders, my comic partner in crime, thank you for having the same taste in creepy stories that I do, for teaching me how to collaborate across artistic disciplines, and for all your illustrations (both the beautiful and the disgusting).

Rebecca Friedman, thank you for keeping me gainfully employed while I gallivanted around the world writing this thing.

To so many people in the NYC publishing world, including Ellen Wright, Zoraida Córdova, Susan Graham, Brigid Black, Heidi Heilig, Ashley Woodfolk, Jordan Hamessley, Enrica Jang, Dahlia Adler, Erin Schneider, Rebecca Yeager, Rachael Ballard—thank you for writing with me, working with me, venting over whiskey, or just letting me awkwardly hide behind you at networking events. Extra props to my first boss, Al Cascio, for pretending not to notice me very obviously drafting novels during office hours.

Kristin Romanias, Eva Bastianon, Shunan Teng, my fellow Mawrtyrs, my Wiley cohort (especially Julie Sturgeon, Amy Molnar, and Jean-Karl Martin), my internet weirdos—all my friends who put up with me on the regular, you're gems of humanity, and I love you so much.

Kevin, Emily, Andrew, John—I can only curse one of you with the Vulgar Arts, but you're all my siblings. Thank you for the backyard adventures and the late-night murder mysteries, but most of all for being the roots I can always go back to, no matter how far I wander. (And Emily, thank you for taking custody of the demons while I do said wandering.)

To D'dary and Hive, thank you for the lulz, for pony, and for being the (many) other halves of my scattered brain. (Cia, thank you for lending me your name.)

Meraki, thank you for being this book's first cheerleaders and my support system whenever I got so deep in revisions that I forgot to eat/go outside. I could not have written this (or survived last year) without you. (Extra love to Neha Rathore for the epic author photo.)

Finally, thank *you*. Every single person reading this. Whether you love it or hate it or use it as toilet paper (hey, I get it, desperate times...), thank you for coming with me on this journey. It's been a lifelong dream to share my stories with the world, and you, reader, are the one who made that dream come true.